"And what abou[...] you got to celebr[...]

"Ah. . ." Julien stared down at his ingredients without seeing them. Nothing. He was revisiting the grief from losing his sister. He had a major problem in what to do about the show that was due to start filming within days. He probably had to face a court case over custody of his nephew that highly likely to get very nasty.

No. Nothing to celebrate there.

He looked up, ready to admit defeat and agree that champagne might not be the most appropriate thing to drink.

And then he got caught by those eyes again. What it that he could see?

Hope?

Optimism?

belief in fairy tales, even?

Something shifted in his chest and he found himself saying something he hadn't thought of til now.

got to hold my sister's baby for the first time lay." The words came out as little more than a n[...] at is abs[...]

I2674374

THE BABY WHO SAVED CHRISTMAS

BY
ALISON ROBERTS

All rights reserved including the right of reproduction in whole or in part in any form. This edition is published by arrangement with Harlequin Books S.A.

This is a work of fiction. Names, characters, places, locations and incidents are purely fictional and bear no relationship to any real life individuals, living or dead, or to any actual places, business establishments, locations, events or incidents. Any resemblance is entirely coincidental.

This book is sold subject to the condition that it shall not, by way of trade or otherwise, be lent, resold, hired out or otherwise circulated without the prior consent of the publisher in any form of binding or cover other than that in which it is published and without a similar condition including this condition being imposed on the subsequent purchaser.

® and ™ are trademarks owned and used by the trademark owner and/or its licensee. Trademarks marked with ® are registered with the United Kingdom Patent Office and/or the Office for Harmonisation in the Internal Market and in other countries.

Published in Great Britain 2015
by Mills & Boon, an imprint of Harlequin (UK) Limited,
Eton House, 18-24 Paradise Road, Richmond, Surrey, TW9 1SR

© 2015 Alison Roberts

ISBN: 978-0-263-25174-6

23-1015

Harlequin (UK) Limited's policy is to use papers that are natural, renewable and recyclable products and made from wood grown in sustainable forests. The logging and manufacturing processes conform to the legal environmental regulations of the country of origin.

Printed and bound in Spain
by CPI, Barcelona

Alison Roberts is a New Zealander, currently lucky enough to live near a beautiful beach in Auckland. She is also lucky enough to write for both the Mills & Boon® Cherish™ and Mills & Boon® Medical Romance™ lines. A primary schoolteacher in a former life, she is also a qualified paramedic. She loves to travel and dance, drink champagne and spend time with her daughter and her friends.

For Liz

With fond memories of our visit to
St-Jean-Cap-Ferrat

With love

CHAPTER ONE

SOMETHING WAS GOING very wrong for Alice McMillan.

She was not supposed to be enjoying herself right now.

'I'm sorry...'

Silent, one-sided communication had become a habit even though the feeling of connection had faded over the months of this year. Now it only served to increase the prickle of guilt.

'But it *is* gorgeous... You must have loved it, too.'

All those years ago. Twenty-nine, to be exact. A period of time that had included Alice's conception.

Having stepped off the bus from Nice in the heart of the small town of Villefranche-sur-Mer, Alice crossed the road to start walking downhill, skirting around a man on a ladder who was part of the team installing a huge pattern of tinsel that would hang over the centre of the main street like a giant tiara. She'd printed off a map before leaving Edinburgh and the route looked easy enough. All she had to do was find the beach and follow it. At the other end was the start of the peninsula that was St Jean Cap Ferrat and the address she was heading for looked like it was within easy walking distance.

There was a small market happening on a grassed

area opposite the bus stop. Stalls were selling things like cheese and preserves, hand-made soaps and Christmas decorations. There was music coming from somewhere and the smell of hot food made her mouth water. When had she last eaten? That bag of cheese and onion crisps and a bottle of water on the last leg of her long train journey didn't really count.

She had to edge her way through a group of people who seemed to be there to socialise rather than shop but they made way for her politely and the smile of the man at the stall was welcoming.

'Bonjour, mademoiselle. Qu'est-ce qu'il vous fait aujourd'hui?'

This might be her first day ever in France but Alice had been surrounded by the sound of this language since her arrival in Paris early this morning. She'd already learned that the best response was a smile and an apology that she didn't speak French.

The apology was genuine. Most people learned at the very least to say 'please' or 'thank you' in the language of a country they chose to visit and Alice could do that in Spanish or Italian. Even Greek. But not French.

Never French…

'One of those, please.' Alice pointed to a baguette that had been split and filled with a thick slice of ham and some cheese.

'Of course.' The man switched languages effortlessly. 'You are English?'

'Scottish.'

'Ah… Welcome to Villefranche.' The sandwich was being wrapped in paper. 'You are here on holiday?'

A holiday? A place you chose to go to relax and enjoy yourself? No. This journey was definitely no holiday.

But Alice smiled and nodded as she handed over some money because the truth was far too personal to tell a stranger and too complex to explain anyway. She wasn't even sure she understood herself why she had made the impetuous decision to come here and now that she *was* here she felt like she was on an emotional roller-coaster.

It was a relief to get away from all the people. The buzz of conversation and laughter faded and the group of people she passed near the tourist attraction of the old citadel were clearly English tourists.

There was a marina below the citadel and Alice found a bench where she could sit and eat her sandwich in the afternoon sunshine. There was a man working on a boat nearby. Joggers went past and people walking their dogs or pushing prams but nobody seemed to notice Alice and she gave herself a few minutes to bask in the sunshine, enjoy the delicious fresh bread with its perfect filling and get her bearings.

She could see the curve of the beach not far away—past a line of restaurants and cafés and she could see the tongue of land that had to be St Jean Cap Ferrat. She knew the main village was out of sight, on the other side of the peninsula, but there were lots of houses on this side and one of them was the address she was heading for. Right on the coastline, in fact. If she knew where to look, she would probably be able to see it from here.

But what, exactly, did she think was going to happen when she knocked on the door? That she would only have to come face to face with this famous racing-car driver called André Laurent and he would somehow recognise her as his daughter? Or that she would show him the faded photograph she'd found hidden in her mother's most private belongings to remind him of their relationship and then disbelief would morph into amazement and finally joy?

That she would, again, have at least one person that she could think of as family?

Nerves kicked in. This had been a stupid idea. She wouldn't be welcome. It was quite likely she would have to turn around immediately and retrace her footsteps and then what would she do? With the knowledge that the big city of Nice was so close and there was bound to be plenty of hotels, she hadn't even tried to book a room for the night or find out what time the buses stopped running.

Maybe she should just turn around now.

Alice closed her eyes and waited and, yes...there it was. That feeling that this was the right thing to do. That flicker of hope that it might even be the best thing she had ever decided to do. Okay, it was a huge gamble and it was quite possible that it would turn out to be her worst decision ever but there was only one way to find out.

And there was *something* important here.

She could feel it. A sense of...belonging?

Well, that wasn't so crazy, was it? She was half-French. She might have been brought up to dismiss this heritage as something to be ashamed of but there could be no denying that the lilt of the language around her and the feel of these streets and houses was touching a part of her she didn't recognise. A part that held whispers of contentment. Of being *home*...

Hence the silent apology to her mother.

Jeanette McMillan would have been so horrified by her making this journey it was no wonder that the very idea would have been unthinkable while she was alive. Even now, Alice could hear an echo of the words that had stopped any queries about her genetic history.

'Your father was *French*…' The biggest insult ever. 'And he tried to get rid of you…'

Curiosity about even the country had to be firmly squashed because she'd loved her mother and any intermittent yearning to find out who her father might be had been something that had needed to be kept even more private, especially in recent years when her mother had already been coping with more than anyone should have to bear.

How sad was it that she would never know if her mother had loved this place as much as Alice knew she might be capable of loving it herself?

She opened her eyes again and scanned the buildings she could see more closely. Maybe the bar where her mother had been working when she'd only been eighteen was nearby. Had it had a view of this sparkling blue bay of the Mediterranean dotted with yachts or had it been tucked away amongst the ancient stone buildings on the steep, cobbled streets of the old town?

That flicker of hope ignited into tendrils of excitement. Had her mother felt this sense of freedom as she'd embarked on her first adult adventure? Alice had left it far too long to stretch her wings but how could things have been any different with first her grandmother and then her mother having to suffer through such unbearably slow and debilitating terminal illnesses?

But she was here now and everything felt new and wonderful. This hadn't been a stupid idea at all. This was magic—as if she was taking the first steps into a real-life fairy-tale. It was a shame she didn't have time to explore this historic part of the small town right now but time was marching on and it was winter. Daylight wouldn't last past about five p.m., and she didn't want to be trying to find her destination in the dark.

Her breath came out in an incredulous huff at the reminder of the season. This bright warmth was another wave of the magic wand—like the feeling of the scenery and the sound of the language was proving to be. Had it only been two days ago that Alice had been wrapped up against the bone-chilling temperatures of a Scottish winter? She'd shed her coat hours ago but still felt overdressed in her long-sleeved jumper and skinny jeans that were tucked into short boots.

The coat felt heavy over her arm as she followed the signposted walkway to the beach. It was a good thing that the few items she'd deemed necessary for a trip that might only last a day or two had fitted into a small backpack so she didn't have anything else to carry in her hands.

The beach was almost deserted, wavelets lapping at the golden sand. Even now, the sea looked inviting and Alice knew that the water temperature would probably be warmer than any beach in Scotland in midsummer. No doubt it got horribly crowded here in the high season, though, given that it was such a popular playground for the rich and famous. Didn't people like Madonna come here for holidays?

And Monaco was only a short drive down the coast. The place where her father had apparently become so famous and another Mecca for the kind of people that had always seemed like an alien race to Alice McMillan. She wasn't just visiting another country right now—it felt like she was heading for a different planet.

The path seemed to end in a car park, which was momentarily confusing, but then Alice spotted the stairs tucked against the steep bank. There was a path that followed a railway line at the top of the stairs and moments later she saw a street with a sign that gave her a name she recognised. Pulling a now crumpled map from her back pocket, Alice kept walking and it was less than ten minutes later that she came to another road that clearly led down towards the coastline again. The view back over the bay to Villefranche was spectacular but there seemed to be a downside to living on this street. There was certainly no room for anyone to park. There were vans and trucks parked nose to tail, and further down the hill she could see a large group of people milling about.

As she got closer, she could see that a lot of them were holding cameras.

Paparazzi? Was Madonna taking a winter break, perhaps? In the same street her father lived in? It wouldn't surprise her. When she'd found the street on the internet, it had looked like every house could be an exclusive resort—the dwellings massive, with huge gardens and swimming pools of Olympic size. The gates advertised just how prestigious this real estate was. Ornate black iron with gold gilding that were at least twice Alice's height, decorated with security features like cameras and intercoms. There were even security guards standing in front of the most ornate she'd seen so far. This property was also the one attracting the attention of the media. There was more than one television crew set up amongst a bank of cameras.

Disconcertingly, as Alice skirted the back of the small crowd she discovered that this was the end of the road. There were no more houses. With her heart thumping, she checked the map again. Okay, she'd known her father was famous. But *this* famous...?

The voice so close to her ear made her jump. She crumpled the map in her hand but it was too late. The man had seen the red circle and her notes and he was asking her something in a tone that was unmistakeably extremely interested.

Alice didn't bother to apologise this time. She shook her head and stepped back.

'I don't understand. I don't speak any French. Not even a single word of it.'

The man only spoke louder. And faster. He even took hold of Alice's arm and started pushing her towards the crowd.

Alice tried to pull her arm free. She had no idea what was going on but she knew she'd made a mistake now and the sooner she got away from here the better. The fairy-tale was taking an ominous twist and she needed to think about this. About taking a different approach to reach her goal, maybe.

This was frightening. Her unwelcome companion was now talking to someone else. About *her*. Her hand tightened around the ball of the map. This was nobody else's business.

How awful would it be if the media discovered that André Laurent had an illegitimate child before he did?

'It's okay,' the second man said. 'You're not in trouble. My friend is just wanting to know why you look for the house of Monsieur Laurent?'

'I... I need to talk to him, that's all. About something...important.'

'*Talk* to him?' The reporter, if that's what he was,

couldn't have looked more astonished. '*Mon Dieu...*
Don't you *know*?'

'Know what?'

But the two men were talking to each other again.
In low voices, as if they didn't want to be overheard.
They were still attracting attention, though.

'Come with me.'

'No... I think it might be better if I come back another time...'

But Alice was being firmly ushered forward. Towards the gate and the uniformed guard. Another rapid
conversation followed, with the second reporter providing translation.

'He wants to know who you are.'

'My name is Alice McMillan. I'm...' Suddenly,
this was terrifying. She was in a strange country and
couldn't understand a word of what was being said
around her. Something was going on and there was a
grim note in the atmosphere. How was it that she hadn't
noticed the presence of the police on the outskirts of
this group? What if she found herself in trouble simply by having arrived in the wrong place at precisely
the wrong time?

She seemed to have unwittingly walked into a nightmare situation and maybe the only way through it was
to be honest.

She swallowed hard. And then she stood on tiptoe
and spoke quietly enough that only the security guard
could hear what she said.

'André Laurent is my father.'

The phone would not stop ringing.

You would have thought that after this morning

things would have settled, but there had been no sign of things calming down the last time he'd checked.

Without altering the stride of his pacing, Julien Dubois flicked a sideways glance at the floor-to-ceiling windows of the grand salon. Not that he could see more than a glimpse of the driveway between the trees edging such a private garden but he knew it led to the massive gates that locked the property away from the rest of the world. And he knew what was waiting on the other side of those gates.

What were the vultures outside the gate waiting for, exactly? A clip of a celebrity looking grief-stricken? Or better yet, *not* looking grief-stricken, which would give them permission to go digging into a background that was dripping with juicy topics.

How old was he when the mother died?

How long is it now since the tragic death of his sister?

What had caused such a family rift?

What reason could he have to hate a national icon like André Laurent so much?

Who are the people in the house with him?

What's going on?

On the other side of a room big enough to easily host a ball was a corner of the house that had a view of not only the main garden and the pool complex but a glimpse of the private beach with the background of the bay and Villefranche beyond.

Of course the owner of this house would have chosen this jewel as his man cave. The rich red of the Persian carpets was as sombre as the dark glow of the enormous mahogany desk. An entire wall was a gallery of trophies and photographs with a gilt-framed monstrosity of the man himself behind a dense spray of champagne as he celebrated one of his early wins in the Monaco race.

Julien's jaw tightened as he deliberately ignored the real reason he loathed the image but really...it was a shameful waste of a magnum of Mumm Champagne.

The muscles of the rest of his body were as tense as his jaw by the time he'd taken two steps into the room. He didn't want to be in here at all but he'd discovered it was a place that contained some particularly useful technology. Not the huge screen that had an endless loop of overpriced cars racing through the streets of Monaco. No...it was the smaller screen that provided a live feed to every security camera the property boasted. He knew which corners of the screen came from the cameras on the gateposts because checking them was becoming a half-hourly ritual.

He only needed the crowd to thin out enough and he would be able to escape a property he'd never intended setting foot inside in the first place. It wasn't as if he was getting anywhere on the mission that had brought him through the gates. It was clearly a stalemate.

The media interest didn't seem to have died down at all yet, unfortunately. And what on earth was going on right in front of the gate?

A girl looked, for all the world, as if she was *kissing* one of the security guards. No wonder he looked so shocked, stepping back and staring at her as if she was completely crazy.

Julien found himself leaning closer to the screen, as if that would help him see the image more clearly. The woman was nothing like any journalist he'd ever seen. Was it because she wasn't holding a camera or microphone? Maybe it was the odd accessory of what

looked like a child's schoolbag on her back. Then she
turned enough for him to see her face and he realised
that his impression probably had more to do with body
language than anything else. The confidence was missing. The pushiness...

Yes. She looked like a fish out of water. Bewildered
even, as the guard moved further away from her, reaching for his phone.

Frightened?

The urge to offer protection was instinctive. Well
honed. And quite enough to trigger a wave of a grief
that he'd believed he'd come to terms with by now.

He'd tried, so hard, to keep Colette safe...

And he was failing her again, even now...

If only the tears of grief would come, they might
wash away some of the anger building today but it
wasn't going to happen here in this room of all places.

And it wasn't going to happen now. Not with a phone
ringing yet again. And this was his personal mobile, not
a house landline, which meant that it was a caller he
needed to take notice of. His solicitor, probably. He'd
walked out on the argument still going on in the small
drawing room on the other side of the foyer but decisions had to be made about which legal documents had
precedence. Was he going to win the battle he'd come
here today to fight?

But this call was not a summons back to the tense
meeting. It was coming from outside the gates, from a
member of his own entourage.

A glance at the screen gave him the odd feeling of a
breath of wind that targeted only the hairs on the back
of his neck. As he answered the call, his gaze went
straight back to the security images. He could see his

caller. The bodyguard his solicitor had deemed necessary for this potentially volatile visit.

'Sorry to disturb you, Monsieur Dubois.'

'What is it?'

'There's a girl here…an English girl…'

His gaze shifted fractionally. Yes, he could still see her. Just standing there, looking lost. He wasn't the only one looking her way either. In the boring hours of waiting for something newsworthy, any distraction for the reporters was probably welcome.

'And?'

'And…' The security guard muttered something incomprehensible.

'Pardon? You'll have to speak up.'

'I'm not sure that's a good idea.' On the screen, Julien could see the guard turn his back on his audience and step even further away. He spoke in a hoarse whisper that hissed over the line.

'She's saying that Monsieur Laurent is her father.'

Julien's breath came out in a derisive snort. 'Of course she is. She won't be the first to turn up with a convenient claim like that now. Send her packing.'

'But…she wants to talk to him…'

'What?'

'I know. It's bizarre but she really doesn't seem to have any idea what's going on. I thought it might be better to deal with it away from prying eyes and ears.'

Julien closed his eyes and cradled his forehead in one hand, applying pressure to both temples.

Could this day get any more complicated?

After a long silence he forced his eyes open again and let his breath out in a defeated sigh.

'Fine. Send her up to the house.'

* * *

Alice McMillan wasn't used to being the centre of attention.

It was unnerving the way she could actually feel the intense interest of the crowd of people behind her as the massive gates were opened just far enough to let her squeeze through in the company of the security guard she had whispered her secret to. She could imagine the crowd pressing closer as they shouted questions at her.

She should feel safer shut away from the pack but, if anything, Alice felt like she was falling further into a rabbit hole, like the Alice she'd been named for. Tumbling into an alien world that she was not at all sure she wanted to visit. She lifted her chin. No…this was a fairy-tale, she reminded herself. She was Cinderella and she was being escorted to the palace where the ball was about to begin.

The guard escorting her to the house was completely silent and it was a long walk. Plenty of time to look around. At a perfectly manicured garden with enough palm trees to make it look like a tropical island and citrus trees with lemons bright jewels against a glossy green background. The blue of the infinity pool was an almost perfect match for the sea it blended into, and the house…

The house looked like the kind of mansion people paid good money for the privilege of being allowed to enter. Not quite a palace but an ancient, stately villa with pillared terraces and enormous windows that probably did have a ballroom tucked away, along with a whole wing for staff quarters. It loomed ever larger as Alice walked towards it and by the time they reached the stone paving leading to the biggest front door she had ever seen, she could feel the shadow of the house settling onto her like a dark cloud that was menacing enough to suggest an imminent storm. The heavy chopping beat of a hovering helicopter overhead added to the unreality and made her feel as if she'd stepped into a movie. A modern twist on an old fairy-tale. Some kind of psychological thriller perhaps.

The guard stopped and jerked his head towards the door.

'*Allez. Il vous attend.*'

The message was crystal clear. Somebody was expecting her arrival.

Her *father*?

Oh, Lord…this was all far more dramatic than she'd ever imagined it could be. Maybe she should have paid more heed to the advice her gran had given her so many years ago.

'*Don't ever go looking for your father. You're better off not knowing…*'

Too late now. She was here and…and the door was opening, possibly by the very man she had come here to meet. Despite the hammering of her heart, Alice took a deep, steadying breath and walked on. She even summoned a smile as if that would somehow make her more welcome.

Disappointment that the wrong person had opened the door was remarkably crushing and her smile died instantly. Who was this young man who'd been sent to greet her? An employee? Yes, that seemed most likely. A personal assistant maybe. Or a press secretary.

Someone who'd been given clear instructions to get rid of her as quickly as possible judging by the look on his face. The glare from those dark eyes, along with the fact that he was dressed from head to toe in black, made it all more sinister. A glance upwards and he then seemed to melt into the shadow of the house as he stepped back.

'Come inside, please,' he said. 'There will be photographers in that helicopter and they have very sophisticated lenses.'

His English was perfect but his accent more than strong enough to reveal his nationality. He looked French, too. Following him across an ornate foyer and through a room with a parquet floor that was easily big enough to entertain a couple of hundred people in, Alice had plenty of time to notice those superbly tailored clothes and that smoothly combed hair that was long enough to have been drawn back into a small ponytail.

She could almost hear her grandmother clicking her tongue and muttering darkly about foreigners and their incomprehensible habits but a wayward thought sneaked in that if there was any casting going on for this real-life fairy-tale, this man might have blown any competition out of the water as far as the role of the handsome prince went.

A room like a conservatory could be seen leading from the end of this ridiculously large room. Behind glass doors was a forest of indoor plants and cane furniture and beyond that Alice could see the mirror-like surface of a swimming pool. She was led towards the other side of the house, however. Into a room that was overwhelming full of...stuff. Pictures and trophies and even a wide-screen television that had a movie playing silently.

And then she saw the enormous portrait in its elaborately gilded frame and her mouth went completely dry.

This was her father's office. These were his trophies. He was probably the driver in that speeding car in the movie.

Wow... He was larger than life in every sense in here. Supremely successful, charismatic...incredibly wealthy. Would it matter to him that she wasn't any of those things? Would he accept her for simply being his child? *Love* her even...?

The hope was so much stronger now. A happy ending was beckoning. She couldn't wait to meet him. Okay, she was nervous and knew she might be shy to start with but this meant *so* much to her. Surely he would sense that and give them a chance to explore their connection?

Her guide shut the door behind them. He walked past Alice and then turned. For a long, long moment he simply stared at her. Then he gestured towards an overstuffed chair that was probably a priceless antique.

'Take a seat.'

It was more like a command than an invitation and it ignited that rebellious streak that Alice thought she'd left behind with her schooldays. She stayed exactly where she was.

'As you wish.' The shrug was subtle. The way he shifted a large paperweight and perched one hip on the corner of the desk was less so. This was his space, the action suggested. Alice was the intruder.

Another piercing stare and then a blunt question. 'Who are you?'

'My name is Alice McMillan.' It was the first time she had spoken in his presence and her voice came out more softly than she would have liked. A little hoarsely even. She cleared her throat. 'And you are...?'

The faint quirk of an eyebrow revealed that his bad manners had only just occurred to him.

'My name is Julien Dubois. Who I am doesn't matter.'

Except it did, didn't it? He was a gatekeeper of some kind and he might have the power to decide whether her quest had any chance of success.

'Where are you from, Miss McMillan?'

'Call me Alice, please. Nobody calls me Miss—even the children in my class.'

'You are a teacher?'

'Yes. Pre-school. A nursery.'

'In England?'

'Scotland. Edinburgh at the moment but I was brought up in a small village you won't have heard of. Where it is doesn't matter.'

Good grief...where was this urge to rebel coming from? The feeling that she'd done something wrong and had been summoned to the headmaster's office perhaps? It was no excuse to be rude enough to fling his own dismissive words back at him in exactly the tone he'd used.

That eyebrow flickered again and he held her gaze as another silence fell. Despite feeling vaguely ashamed of herself, Alice didn't want to admit defeat by looking away first. His eyes weren't as dark as they'd appeared in the shadows of the entranceway, she realised. Much lighter than her own dark brown, they were more hazel. A sort of toffee colour. He had a striking face that would stand out in any crowd, with a strong nose and lips that looked capable of being as expressive as that eyebrow, but right now they were set in a grim line, surrounded by a jaw that looked like it could do with a shave.

'And you claim that André Laurent is your father?'

The disparaging snap of his voice brought her drifting gaze sharply back to his eyes.

'He is.'

'And you have proof of this?'

'Yes.'

'Show me.'

Alice slipped the straps of her backpack from her shoulders. She sat on the edge of the uncomfortable chair to make it easier to open the side pocket and remove an envelope. From that, she extracted a photograph. It was faded now but the colour was still good enough to remind her of the bright flame shade of Jeannette McMillan's hair and that smile that could light up a room. A wave of grief threatened to bring tears and she blinked hard, focusing instead on the man in the picture. She raised her gaze to stare at the oversized portrait again.

With a nod, she handed the photograph to Julien.

'My mother,' she said quietly. 'I wouldn't have known who she was with except that she kept these magazine clippings about him.' She glanced down at the folded glossy pages still in the envelope. 'Well hidden. I only found them recently after she…she died.'

If she was expecting any sympathy for her loss it was not forthcoming. Julien merely handed the photograph back.

'This proves nothing other than that your mother was one of André's groupies. It's ancient history.'

'I'm twenty-eight,' Alice snapped. 'Hardly ancient,

thanks. And my mother was not a "groupie". I imagine she was completely in love…'

'Pfff…' The sound was dismissive. And then Julien shook his head. 'Why now?' he demanded. 'Why *today*?'

'I… I don't understand.'

'Where have you been for the last week?'

'Ah… I went home to my village for a few days. And then I've been travelling.'

'You don't watch television? Or read newspapers?' He raised his hands in a sweeping gesture that her grandmother would have labelled foreign and therefore ridiculously dramatic. 'How could you not *know*?'

'Know what?'

'That André Laurent crashed his car three days ago and killed himself. That his funeral was *today*.'

'Oh, my God…' Alice's head jerked as her gaze involuntarily flicked back to the huge portrait. 'Oh… *no*…'

From the corner of her eye, she could see that Julien was following her gaze. For a long second he joined her in staring at the image of a man that was so filled with life it seemed impossible to believe that he was gone.

But then, with the speed of a big cat launching itself at its prey, Julien snatched up the paperweight from the desk and hurled it towards the portrait, creating an explosion of shattering glass, leaving behind a horrified silence that only served to magnify his chilling words.

'I wish he'd done it years ago… If he had, my sister wouldn't have married him. She would still be *alive*…'

CHAPTER TWO

THE SHOCK WAS mind-numbing.

The pain this stranger was feeling was so powerful that Alice could feel it seeping into her own body to mix with the fear of knowing that she was alone with an angry man who was capable of violence. Compassion was winning over fear, however. His sister had been married to André Laurent. Presumably she'd been in the car with him in that fatal crash. She wanted to reach out and offer comfort in some way to Julien. To touch him…?

No. That would be the last thing he would accept. She could see the agonised way he was standing with every muscle clenched so that male pride could quell the need to express emotion. With a hand shading his eyes to hide from the world.

And self-pity edged its way into the overwhelming mix.

Alice had lost something here, too.

Hope.

She'd tried to keep it under control. Ever since she'd finally found the courage to return to the cottage that had been the only real home she'd ever known because it had been time she faced the memories. Time to accept that she'd lost her only family and that she had to find a way to move forward properly from her grief. To embrace life and every wonderful thing it had to offer and to dream of a happy future.

It had been time to sort through her mother's things and keep only those that would be precious mementos.

She'd grown up in that tiny house with two women. Her mother and her grandmother. Strong women who'd protected her from the disapproval of an entire village. Women who had loved her enough to make her believe that the shameful circumstances of her birth didn't matter. That she was a gift to the world simply because she existed.

Maybe it had been a bad choice to make the visit so close to Christmastime, when the huge tree was lit up in the village square and the shops had long since decorated their windows with fairy-lights and sparkling tinsel. The sadness that this would be her first Christmas with no family to share it with had been the undercurrent threatening to wash away the new direction she was searching for, and finding that envelope that had provided the information about who her father was had given that undercurrent the strength of an ocean rip.

Had given her that hope that had exploded into something huge the moment she'd walked into this room and seen that portrait. She had been ready to love this man—her unknown father.

She'd still had a family member. Someone who'd been denied any connection with the women who had raised her but with a connection to herself that had to mean something. She was a part of this stranger.

His daughter.

It felt quite possible she had loved him already. And

now she had lost him before she'd even had the chance to meet him. She would never know if there were parts of her personality she might have inherited from that side of her gene pool. Like that rebellious streak maybe. Or the unusual gurgle of her laughter that always turned heads. Her brown eyes?

Yes. Even behind the shards of broken glass clinging to the frame of that portrait and the mist of the champagne spray, Alice could see that her father's eyes were as dark as her own.

He looked so happy. Confident and victorious. And there was no denying how good looking André Laurent had been. Despite the disparaging reaction of the silent man beside her, Alice just knew that her mother had been in love and had had her heart broken. Why else had she never tried to find another relationship?

She would never even discover whether André remembered her mother. If she had, at least, been conceived in love on both sides.

Yes. That hope of finding something that could grow into a new but precious version of family was gone. It was dead and had to be buried. Like her father had been only this morning.

Her breath hitched and—to her horror—Alice felt the trickle of tears escaping.

And then she heard a heavy sigh.

'*Je suis désolé*. I'm sorry.' Julien's voice had a very different timbre than she had heard so far. Softer. Genuine? Whatever it was, it made his accent even more appealing. 'I should not have done that.'

Alice swallowed the lump in her throat. The fear had gone. This man wasn't violent by nature. He had just been pushed beyond the limits of what anyone could bear. She knew what moments of despair like that could feel like.

'It's okay,' she said, in barely more than a whisper. 'I understand. I'm very sorry for your loss.'

The response was a grunt that signalled it was not a subject that he intended to discuss any further.

Alice was still holding the photograph of her parents. It was time to put it back in the envelope, along with the clippings that had supplied the name missing from her birth certificate. She slipped the envelope into the side pocket of her backpack and zipped it up. Then she picked up the straps to put it back on.

'Where are you going?'

Alice shrugged. 'I'll find somewhere. It doesn't matter.'

Julien moved so that he was between her and the door. 'You can't go out there. You can't talk to those reporters. They would have a—what do you call it? A... paddock day with a story like this.'

There was a faint quirk of amusement to be found in the near miss of translation. 'A field day.' She shook her head. 'I won't talk to anyone.'

'They'll find out.' Julien's headshake was far sharper than her own had been. 'They'll discover who you are and start asking questions. Who else knows about this... claim of yours?'

Alice was silent. What did it matter if he didn't believe her? Nobody else knew anything more than what had been impossible to hide. That her mother had gone to work for a summer in the south of France. That she had come home alone and pregnant.

'Do you have any idea what the Laurent estate is worth?' Julien's gaze flicked over her from head to foot, taking in her simple, forest-green jumper, her high-street jeans and the well-worn ankle boots. The backpack that dangled from her hands. 'No... I don't suppose you do.'

He was rubbing his forehead with his hand. Pressing his temples with long, artistic fingers that made Alice wonder what he did for a living, which was preferable to feeling put down by her appearance. Was he a surgeon, perhaps, or a musician? The black clothes and the long hair fitted more with a career in music. She could almost see him holding an electric guitar—rocking it out in front of a crowd of adoring fans...

'I need to get advice.' Julien sounded decisive now. 'Luckily, I have my solicitor here in the house with me. And I expect a DNA test will soon sort this out.'

'There's no point now.'

'Pardon?'

'I came here to meet my father. If he'd needed that kind of proof I wouldn't hesitate but it's...too late now. It doesn't matter because I'm never going to meet him, am I?'

'But don't you want to know?'

Did she? Maybe it would be better to find out that André Laurent *wasn't* her father, however remote that possibility was, because then she could walk away knowing that she hadn't lost something that had been real and so close to being within her grasp.

And if he was, she wouldn't be haunted by knowing that her father was still out there in the world somewhere but impossible to find. She knew in her heart that she was right but there was something to be said for having written confirmation of some things, wasn't there?

So Alice shrugged. 'I guess so.'

'Come with me.' Julien opened the door. 'I do not want to be in this room a second longer.'

With what was probably going to be her last glance at her father's portrait, Alice followed him out of the office. She expected to traverse the length of the enormous room again but, instead, Julien stayed at this end of the house and threw open the glass doors to the conservatory. He waited for her to enter, his face expressionless. Perhaps the effort of keeping that anger under control left no room for anything else.

Even a hint of a smile would do.

The memory of that soft tone in his voice when he'd apologised was fading. Oddly, Alice wanted to hear it again. Or to see something that would suggest it had been genuine. That she was correct in thinking that she'd caught a glimpse of the real person buried under this grim exterior. A person she had, for an instant of time, felt a connection with.

But his tone was just as empty as his face. All that was left was the accent that still tickled her ears and made her feel as if there was a secret smile hovering just over her lips, like a butterfly waiting to alight.

'Have a seat,' he said. 'Are you hungry? I can ask the housekeeper to provide something for you.'

'No. Thank you. I had lunch not long ago.'

'As you wish. I shouldn't be too long. Please, wait here.'

She didn't really have a choice, did she? She could walk out of the house but those security guards wouldn't open the gates without getting permission and even if it was given, she would then face the media pack and… and she'd always been hopeless at lying.

Probably thanks to her father's genes, Alice had failed to receive more than the blue eyes that every member of the McMillan clad had had. She had been quietly thankful that she had escaped the flaming red hair that ran through generations of her mother's family. It hadn't been banished entirely, but her version was a rich auburn instead of orange. It was a shame she'd missed the olive skin that had been evident in that portrait of her father, though. She had pale, Scottish skin—inclined to freckle with any sunshine and turn a bright red when she blushed.

Which was what she always did if she tried to tell a lie.

Walking between the cool green fronds of huge, exotic ferns in tall terracotta urns, Alice headed for a cane couch with soft-looking, cream upholstery. Unbidden, a memory surfaced that provoked a poignant smile.

She had been about four years old and she'd done something bad. What had it been? Oh, yes… She'd been rebellious even then and she had gone to play somewhere she hadn't been allowed to go alone—behind the hen house and down by the creek. Knowing that the mud on her shoes would reveal her sin, she had taken them off and hidden them under a bush. When the query had come about their whereabouts, tiny Alice had given innocence her best shot and she'd said she didn't know where her shoes were. The fairies must have taken them.

Her mother and her grandmother had simply looked at each other.

'She's blushing, Jeannie. She's no' telling the truth.'

'Aye…'

And then the two women who'd ruled her universe had turned their gazes on Alice. She'd never forgotten what that silence felt like as they'd waited for her to confess. The guilt and the shame of it. They'd never had to wait that long again.

Not that she had any intention of confessing to any reporters but Julien was probably right. They already knew her name because they'd been right there when she'd introduced herself to the security guard. It wouldn't take long for them to chase down a story and if she was confronted by leading questions, her skin would betray her.

She could feel a prickle of heat in her neck, just *thinking* about having to lie.

At least she was safe here. The world outside those gates could be as far away as her home as she sat here in this quiet space amongst the greenery, looking out over the reflection of palm trees on the swimming pool. Her gaze was automatically drawn further—to where the water fell over the end and made it look as if the cruise ship in the distance was sharing the same patch of ocean.

And then Alice felt a shiver dance down her spine. The atmosphere had changed as noticeably as if a cool breeze had blown through the room. She didn't have to turn her head to know that Julien had returned.

Maybe she didn't feel so safe in here after all.

She was sitting on one of the couches, looking out at the view.

Julien could only see her profile but it made him realise he hadn't really looked at her until now. Or rather he'd looked at her as simply another issue that had to be dealt with on one of the darkest days of his life.

Now he could see her as media fodder and wouldn't

they have a feast? This Alice McMillan was tiny. A few inches over five feet perhaps and slim enough to wear children's clothing. That bag she was carrying looked like an accessory to a school uniform.

And there was no denying how pretty she was. That tumble of richly coloured, wavy hair… Given how unpretentious the rest of her clothing was and the fact that her nails weren't even painted, it was highly likely the colour was natural and it all added up to a brand of woman that Julien had no idea how to handle due to an almost complete lack of experience. Even his own sister had morphed into one of the polished beauties that every man wanted to be seen with. Did other men always have that nagging doubt about how genuine they really were?

The memory of tears slipping from chocolate-brown eyes that had reminded him of a fawn made him groan inwardly. Imagine how that would go down in a television interview. She would have the whole world on her side.

André Laurent and—by association—his sister and then he himself would be branded as heartless rich people who were uncaring of an impoverished relative. If, of course, her claim was true. And why wouldn't it be? Given the endless stream of women in that man's life, the probability of a legacy like this was certainly believable and, according to the legal expert he'd just been speaking to, the implications were enormous. He kept his tone light enough not to reveal the can of worms that was potentially about to be opened, however.

'The news is good,' he said. 'We have made some enquiries and apparently there have been great advances in DNA testing and a result can be found within a matter of a few days. All we need is a simple mouth swab from you. Someone is coming to the house soon, to do what is needed.'

She nodded slowly and then bent her head, a thick curl of her hair falling across her cheek. She pushed it back as she looked up again.

'But they would have to match it, wouldn't they? It's too late to get a sample from my…from André. Monsieur Laurent,' she added quickly, as though she didn't have the right to be so familiar.

'M'sieur.' Without thinking, Julien corrected her pronunciation to make the 'n' silent. She really didn't know a word of French, did she? Then he shrugged. 'It seems that there are many items that may suffice. Like his toothbrush. Someone is coming who is an expert. He works with the police.'

'The *police*?' A look of fear made her eyes look huge against that pale skin.

It was like that moment after he'd hurled the paperweight at the image of the man he'd despised so much and he realised he'd scared her enough to make her cry. A shameful thing. He didn't treat women like that. He didn't treat *anyone* like that. This whole disaster was turning him into a person he really didn't like and this woman was making it that bit harder to sort out the issue that was so personally—and urgently—important. This made her someone he needed to remove from his company at the earliest opportunity so it shouldn't matter at all how she was feeling.

But it did.

It made him want to reassure her. Comfort her even.

He turned away so he didn't get trapped in those eyes. He shrugged off the unwelcome sensation that something very private was being accessed. Like his heart? How long had it been since he'd felt the urge to protect a woman? Maybe he'd given up on trying to care after Colette had made it so clear he'd been wasting his time. That he didn't understand. All those years and, in the end, they had counted for nothing.

'A coincidence,' he said, the words coming out more sharply than he might have chosen. 'This man also runs a private paternity testing company.' A sigh escaped that had a whisper of defeat about it. The need to reassure was too powerful. 'You are not being accused of anything.'

Yet, he added silently. But then he made the mistake of looking at her again. No. She wasn't here to chase five minutes of fame or a share in a vast fortune. There was no mistaking her sincerity. Or her vulnerability. She not only believed that André was her father, it held a huge significance for her. It had to be simply another coincidence that she had arrived with such unfortunate timing.

It could be an hour or more before the DNA expert arrived from Nice with his testing kit and it would be extremely impolite to leave her waiting here alone and it would be imprudent to antagonise her. For everybody's sake, this matter had to be kept as private as possible.

'So...' Julien lowered himself onto a couch facing Alice. 'You are a teacher?'

'Yes.'

'You like children, then?'

'Of course.'

'Do you have any of your own?'

That startled her.

'No... I'm not...um...married.'

'Neither was your mother.'

Maybe she wasn't quite as vulnerable as he'd thought. A flash of something like anger crossed her face and her chin lifted.

'She suffered for that. There are communities where it's still considered shameful to produce an illegitimate child.'

Julien blinked. If the mother had suffered, it was logical to assume that the child had as well.

'Why did she go back, then?'

The stare he was receiving made him feel like he'd asked a very stupid question. There was something even more disturbing in that look, however. Pity? Was he missing something fundamental?

'Brannockburn was her home. She was very young and her heart was broken. She needed her mother.'

A broken heart? Well, she probably hadn't been the only woman who'd believed that she might be the one to tame André Laurent. He could hardly brand her as a complete fool when his own sister had fallen under the same spell decades later.

'I'm sorry...' Her apology was unexpected.

'What for?'

Alice was twisting a lock of hair in her fingers as she shifted her gaze to the doors that led back into the house. 'You've lost your sister. You must have family here. Your mother perhaps? I'm intruding on a very personal time. I'm sorry. Obviously, I wouldn't have come if I'd had any idea of what had happened.'

'My only family was my sister,' Julien said quietly. 'And I lost her three months ago. She died in childbirth.'

* * *

A heavy silence fell but Alice didn't dare look back at him.

Had the baby died as well? Had they both recently lost their only living relatives? Not that there was any real comparison. He'd known his sister and she'd only lost the potential of knowing her father. But she knew what it was like to lose the person who was the emotional touchstone in one's life. Her mother had seemed far too young to be taken but how old had Julien's sister been? Probably only in her thirties, as he looked to be himself.

This was a tragedy in anybody's terms and Julien clearly blamed her father and hated him for it. She had come here claiming a close relationship to André so it was no wonder she wasn't welcome. Had André been as reckless on public roads as he'd been on a racing circuit? That would give credence to the idea that the crash had been his fault but Julien had said his sister had died in childbirth months ago. How could André be blamed for that?

A cold chill ran down Alice's spine. Had it been an abortion that had gone horribly wrong? That was part of her own history, in a way. The only reason she existed had been because her mother had refused to go along with what had been deemed compulsory.

The silence grew heavier. And more awkward.

And then it was broken by something totally unexpected.

The wail of a baby.

CHAPTER THREE

ALICE FOUND HERSELF staring at the doors as the sound grew louder. Julien had gone pale. He got to his feet and walked past her without a word. Without thinking, Alice stood up and followed him.

There seemed to be two groups of people at the other end of the huge room. Two men wearing dark suits, facing each other and talking loudly. Behind the second man were two women. One was older and wore an apron. A younger woman was carrying the baby, who couldn't be more than about three months old. The age of the youngest of the children who attended the pre-school educational centre she worked for.

The age Julien's nephew or niece would have been by now?

Julien was walking swiftly, as though he intended to stop them coming any further. Alice was a few steps behind by the time they all stopped.

They spoke French, of course, so she couldn't understand a word but she could pick up a sense of what was going on. There was a problem of some kind and Julien wanted nothing to do with it. She couldn't be sure that he'd even looked at the baby, having positioned himself alongside one of the men so that he was only facing the other man and the older woman. Their voices rose over the sound of the baby crying and the younger girl was looking ready to cry herself.

Alice might teach the older pupils at the Kindercare Nursery School but she had had enough experience with the youngest children to know that this baby wasn't well. The crying was punctuated by coughing. He had a runny nose and kept rubbing at his eyes with a small fist. His mother, if that's who she was, jiggled the bundle she held with what looked like a desperate attempt to comfort him. When she looked away from the heated discussion happening between the others, she met Alice's gaze and there was a plea in that look that Alice could not ignore.

She moved closer, her arms outstretched in an invitation to give the mother a break from a stressful situation. Astonishment gave way to relief as Alice took the baby, unnoticed by anyone else. She walked away, back towards the conservatory, with the thought that she could at least give them a chance to talk without having to shout over the wailing, which was probably becoming a vicious cycle as the loud voices distressed the baby further.

'It's okay, sweetheart,' she told the baby. 'You're just miserable, aren't you? Look, it's cooler in here. Let's get that blanket off you and let you cool down, shall we?'

The tone was one she used with any unhappy child and her movements were calm and confident as she unwrapped the covering that would be far too hot for a baby who was probably running a temperature.

'You've got a cold, haven't you?' Spikes of damp, dark hair covered the baby's forehead and Alice smoothed them back. 'They're rotten things, colds, but you know what?'

The exaggeration of her question seemed to have finally caught the baby's attention. He hiccupped loudly and opened his eyes to look up at Alice.

Dark eyes that had that baby milkiness that made it hard to decide whether they were blue or brown.

'Colds go away.' Alice smiled. 'In a day or two you're going to feel ever so much better.'

She unsnapped the top fastenings of the sleep suit to allow a bit more fresh air to cool the baby's skin. Miraculously, he'd stopped crying now, so Alice rocked him gently and started singing softly. It was amazing how comforting it was to hold this tiny person. For the first time Alice felt as if she was welcome in this house.

Needed even.

The baby's eyes drifted shut and only moments later there she was sitting in the conservatory again but this time holding a sleeping infant.

A quiet one.

For a few seconds Alice watched the baby's face as it twitched and settled deeper into sleep. Who was he? Julien's child perhaps? Was that young woman his wife? Or his girlfriend perhaps, given the speed with which he'd suggested it wasn't necessary to be married to have a child. If either scenario was correct, her opinion of him was dropping rapidly. He should have been trying to help, not making things worse.

Not that she could hear the sound of any arguments any more.

In fact, it was so quiet she glanced up with the worrying thought that they might have all gone somewhere else and left her with the baby.

To her horror, she found that there were five people watching her from the doorway.

Julien looked angry again. His words were cold.

'What, exactly,' he bit out, 'do you think you are *doing*?'

Wasn't it obvious? Alice said nothing. The younger woman was standing with her head down as if she knew she had done something wrong. Julien said something and she started to move towards Alice but then the older woman halted her with a touch on her arm and spoke. Another discussion started amongst the group with rapid, urgent-sounding words.

At the end of their conversation the two women and the men turned and walked away. Alice knew her face would be a question mark as Julien turned back but he didn't meet her gaze.

'It seems that this is the first time the baby has slept in many hours. It would be to his benefit not to disturb him for a little while.'

'He's not well. I think he's running a temperature.'

'A doctor has been summoned.'

Julien stopped his pacing amongst the greenery with his back towards Alice.

Alice broke the silence. 'What's his name?'

'Jacques.'

'Is he your son?'

Julien turned very slowly and his expression was… shocked. Appalled even—as if the very idea of having a child was the worst fate he could imagine.

'Of course not.'

Alice frowned. 'Then why is he here? Whose baby is he?'

Julien closed his eyes. 'My sister's.'

It was Alice's turn to be shocked. That made him Julien's nephew. An orphan who had only just lost his father and was in desperate need of any remaining family. But Julien didn't seem to want anything to do with little Jacques. Because he was also André's son?

Oh… Another shock wave rocked Alice. If André *was* her father, then that made this baby her half-brother.

Part of her own family…

She loved children anyway and would do anything to help one who was in distress but her compassion towards this infant had just morphed into something much bigger. Something totally unexpected and potentially hugely significant.

She stared at the sleeping infant's face, the dark fan of eyelashes over cheeks that were too red. A patchy kind of red, like a rash of tiny spots. Even asleep, his tiny hands were in fists and he still felt too hot. The patch of skin she had exposed by unbuttoning the sleep suit was also red. Spotty, even.

The mind-blowing implications of a genetic relationship were pushed aside. Alice pulled open the suit a little further. Yes…the rash was everywhere. Faint but unmistakeable.

'Oh, no…'

'What?'

She looked up to find Julien had stepped closer. It was the first time she'd seen him look directly at the baby and it was a fleeting glance, almost as if he was afraid of what he might see. Perhaps he had good cause to feel afraid…

'I thought he only had a cold,' Alice said. 'But…but this looks like it might be measles.'

'How do you know?'

'I've seen a lot of pictures. There was an outbreak in Edinburgh last year and we had a lot of our children absent because of the quarantine necessary. One of them had an older sister at school who got very sick.'

'Quarantine?'

'Measles is a notifiable disease in most countries. It's highly contagious and it can be dangerous. The girl I was talking about got one of the worst complications—encephalitis—and she...she died.' Alice paused to draw in a breath. 'Even one case and anybody who's been within possible contact has to be quarantined for about two weeks. Unless they've been immunised or have had measles themselves.'

'Have you had measles?'

'Yes. When I was a child. Have you?'

'How am I supposed to know something like that?'

'From health records perhaps. An immunisation card that your mother would have kept.'

He shook his head. 'I don't know of anything like that.' He had taken a step back, as if that was enough to protect himself, and that bothered Alice. She cuddled Jacques a little closer.

'You've been in the same house,' she said, rubbing in the unwelcome information. 'The same room. Contacts can spread measles before they start feeling sick themselves. There was a case in the States last year where everybody was placed in isolation because they'd been sitting in a doctor's waiting room where there'd been a case of measles earlier that day.'

Julien shook his head again, more slowly this time. 'That is not going to happen here. It cannot. The situation is difficult enough as it is.' He took another step back. 'It's not as if I've touched the child.'

Alice felt a stirring of real anger. Why *not*? This baby had never known his mother and his father had died days ago. Had there only been hired help to offer comfort? He wasn't even looking at Jacques again now. As if he could make the problem disappear by ignoring it. And then he spoke again, on the end of a sigh.

'I have been forbidden to see Jacques,' he said. 'Ever since my sister died. But she made me his guardian and that is why I'm here today. To collect him.'

It still made no sense. 'But you still haven't *touched* him? Seen him even?'

'The Laurent family have another court order. His grandmother is arriving later today also with the intention of taking guardianship of Jacques. That is why the solicitors are here. It is a very delicate situation. My solicitor advised me not to make things worse and… for me…'

He *was* looking at Jacques now. With an expression that broke Alice's heart.

'For me, I knew it would only make things so much harder if I saw him and then…he was taken away.'

So he really *did* care.

Any anger Alice was feeling towards Julien evaporated. She had no idea why he'd been refused contact with his nephew after his sister had died but, whatever the reason, it had to be unfair. Cruel, in fact. If there were sides to be taken in this dispute, she had just put herself firmly on Julien's side.

The impression lasted only for a heartbeat. Julien's almost desperate expression vanished as his attention was caught by something he heard. He turned his head towards the windows.

'Someone is arriving,' he announced. 'Let's hope

it is the doctor, who can sort this out. Let's hope that you are wrong.'

Or was it the DNA expert who had been summoned to sort out the other problem that was pending? Was he hoping she was also wrong about who she thought her father was?

To Alice's relief, the doctor looked like a kindly man. Grey-haired and a little overweight, with deep smile lines around his eyes—a quintessential family GP. He came into the conservatory accompanied by the two women.

The older woman went to take the baby from her arms and he whimpered the moment as she touched him. Alice rocked him again. She didn't want to let him go.

'Shh,' she whispered. 'It's okay, little one. We all want to help you.'

He cried out more loudly when the woman touched him for the second time and the doctor cleared his throat and then spoke in excellent English.

'Perhaps it's better if the baby stays with you while I examine him, *mademoiselle*. He seems to like you.'

Alice nodded. Was it too far-fetched to imagine that the baby was aware of a connection between them? Or maybe it was because she knew how unwelcome *she* was in this house as far as Julien and probably any other members of the household were concerned. This baby had no idea of the trouble she was causing and now he was causing trouble himself, poor little thing, so there *was* a connection to be found quite apart from any yet-to-be discovered genetic one. They were both problems. He needed protection, this little one, and she was just the person to provide it.

She held the baby while the doctor took his temperature and listened to his heart and lungs. She helped him undress the baby down to his nappy so that he could see his skin. Jacques whimpered miserably at the disturbance.

'He needs paracetamol, doesn't he?' Alice asked the doctor. 'And sponging with lukewarm water?'

'Indeed. You are familiar with nursing children?'

'I'm a pre-school teacher. We often have to deal with sick children and I've done some training. I've never dealt with a case of measles, though. Is that what it is?'

'It would seem very likely. He has all the symptoms, including Koplik's spots inside his cheeks. Are you immune?'

'Yes. I had measles as a child.'

'Do you have documentation to prove your immunity?'

'No...' Alice closed her eyes on a sigh. The need for such documentation would never have occurred to her as she'd embarked on this impulsive journey.

'Are you aware of how serious this is?'

She nodded. 'I've kept up with news of outbreaks since we had a scare in Edinburgh.'

'Then you'll know that a case has to be reported and that there are very strict isolation and quarantine procedures that must be followed. I need to offer immunisation and prophylactic treatment to everybody who cannot prove their immunity.'

Julien had been standing within earshot. 'Quarantine is completely out of the question for me. I am due in Paris for filming in the next day or two. It's a Christmas show that's been planned for many months and cannot be postponed.'

The doctor sighed. 'I know who you are, Monsieur Dubois—of course I do. My wife is one of your biggest admirers but...' he raised his hands in a helpless gesture '...rules cannot be broken, I'm afraid. Not when it could put the health of so many others at risk.'

Alice blinked. The doctor looked to be in his sixties and his wife was one of Julien's biggest fans? If he wasn't in an edgy rock band, what sort of music did he produce? Romantic French ballads perhaps, with the accompaniment of an acoustic guitar? Was he doing a collection of Christmas carols for a seasonal show? No. Somehow it didn't fit—especially right now, with that angry body language.

With a sound of pure frustration Julien pulled a mobile phone from his pocket and walked away as he held it to his ear. The doctor turned to the two women and began speaking in French again.

Concerned expressions became horrified as he kept talking. The younger woman burst into tears. Voices rose as panicked questions were asked. Behind her, Alice could hear Julien also raising his voice on his telephone call. Everybody was sounding upset and all Alice could do was to sit there and hold the baby. It was the doctor who finally noticed that Alice was being completely left out of the conversation.

'Marthe—the housekeeper here—has grandchildren at home and she's worried,' he explained. 'Nicole—Jacques's nanny—has much younger siblings that she visited only yesterday. They are both very scared and want to take their quarantine periods in their own homes. This is possible, as their contacts will also have to be isolated. I will be visiting their households as soon as I leave here.'

Alice looked down at the baby she was still holding. And then she looked up at the doctor and nodded her head. 'I can look after Jacques.'

'I can see if there is a nurse available who is prepared to come into the house for the quarantine period but I doubt that any arrangements could be made until tomorrow. It would be very good if you could care for him until then.'

Julien snapped his phone shut. 'No,' he said. 'Mademoiselle McMillan cannot stay in this house. She will have to find a hotel.'

'That would be the very worst thing she could do. This is a very serious matter, Monsieur Dubois. I can take a blood sample from her but it may take a few days to prove immunity and even then she may be discouraged from leaving the house.'

'You don't understand. There's another matter that is pressing.'

'Oh?'

Julien turned his gaze to Marthe and Nicole, who were whispering together near the doorway, looking desperate to escape and get back to their own families. A few words from Julien and they both disappeared.

Julien continued speaking in French to the doctor, who blinked in astonishment as his gaze settled on Alice. She could feel the prickle of a blush starting. Any moment now and the colour of her cheeks would rival that of Jacques's.

There was sympathy in the doctor's smile when Julien had stopped speaking.

'You are having quite a day, my dear, are you not?'

'Mmm…' The kind tone almost undid her but Alice was not going to cry in front of Julien again.

'The reason you came here is not important right now. What matters is that you *are* here and we are lucky that you have experience with young children. Or maybe it's more than lucky.' There was compassion in this kindly doctor's eyes. This was a man who'd spent a lifetime caring for people who were sick and vulnerable. Who had a wealth of understanding of the intricacies of human relationships. 'It could be that you are this little one's big sister, yes?'

Alice nodded slowly, her throat suddenly too tight to swallow. The tears were harder to hold back now. She would have stepped up to care for this baby no matter who he was, but the idea that she had a member of her own family who desperately needed her help was overwhelming.

She had come to this place to try and find the only living relative she might have.

This might be a bizarre twist to her fairy-tale but it seemed like she might have actually achieved her goal. And it came with an entirely new world of hope.

And, for one night at least, she could hang onto that hope.

The doctor patted her shoulder. 'Tomorrow will be a new day. In the meantime, I will leave you all the medications you might need. Here, let's give him his first dose of paracetamol and then I will take the blood samples I need from you and Monsieur Dubois.'

It was Julien's turn first. And then it was Alice's turn and she couldn't free an arm while she was still holding Jacques.

She looked at Julien.

The doctor looked at Julien.

It was crystal clear what the logical solution was

but Julien seemed frozen. Alice could sense his fear.
He'd never touched this baby. Was he afraid that he
would drop him or was his reluctance due to something
deeper? An even harder barrier to overcome?

She could hear the echo of those heart-breaking
words.

*'...it would only make things so much harder if I saw
him and then...he was taken away.'*

Touch was a far more powerful sense than sight,
wasn't it?

But he cared. And, like herself, Jacques was his relative. Was he feeling the same kind of overwhelming
connection that she was?

He had more right than she did to feel like that. More
right than she did to know the joy of cuddling this small
person.

Slowly, she walked towards Julien. She held his gaze,
trying to offer both reassurance and encouragement.
When she was so close that the baby was touching them
both, his arms came up. So slowly. And then she felt the
weight being transferred and Julien's gaze dragged itself away from hers and dropped to the face of his tiny
nephew. He turned away then, as though he wanted to
keep this moment private.

Mon Dieu...

How shocking was this?

The first time he had touched his sister's child.

He'd had no choice but to back away from any desire to see his nephew while André had still been alive.
Even today, in the hours he'd known he was in the same
house, it had been easier to comply with the legal advice

to keep his distance. Maybe he'd known what he would feel in this moment. This emotional connection. The vulnerability of a tiny being that would suck him into offering not only his protection but his love. A breeding ground for feelings of guilt and worry and love that might eventually be thrown back at him as not having been good enough, but nothing could prevent him from providing any of it. He already loved this nephew despite trying to hide from that knowledge. He'd never intended being in this position again. He didn't know if he was strong enough.

But, once again, it seemed that he had no choice and he'd come here to do what his sister had asked him to do—to take guardianship of his child if anything happened to her. And now that he was holding him, how could he ever let him go? If he lost the legal battle with Madame Laurent, it was going to haunt him for the rest of his life.

The baby's eyes were wide open. Perhaps he was as shocked as Julien was at this unexpected physical contact. Could babies sense what people were thinking? Did he know he presented a threat out of all proportion to his size?

Maybe he did. Maybe he wanted to be back in the embrace of Alice's arms. How strange was it that she had been the only person able to comfort him in his misery? Did he sense the likely connection between them? A half-sister was a closer relation than an uncle.

Dark eyes stared up at him, making Julien wonder again how much was being understood. Too much, it seemed. The tiny face began to crumple. The small body squirmed like a fish that had been landed and needed to get back to the water to survive. And then that dreadful, unhappy wailing began again.

He paced back and forth as he waited for Alice to swap the ball of cotton wool she was pressing to her elbow for a plaster. He watched the doctor pack his things back into his bag and heard him say that he would deal with all the precautions needed for everybody who would be leaving the house to enter quarantine in their own homes—including the solicitors. He saw him leave and knew that in a very short space of time he would be alone in this house with Alice McMillan.

And still the baby was crying. More quietly, though. An exhausted sound of misery.

And there was a terrible smell. It was the odour that was really the final straw. Julien's sense of smell and taste were finely honed. They had to be to be as good at his work as he was and this…this was making him feel decidedly ill.

He needed help.

The doctor had been right. It really was very lucky that Alice was not to be allowed to leave the house.

Julien did his best to summon a smile as he moved closer. Preferably one that was apologetic. She hadn't bargained on any of this when she'd come to this house, had she? He'd not only been rude to her, he'd been violent in front of her and now she was as much of a prisoner here as he was, at least until the results of those blood tests came back. She had every right to be angry with him. To refuse to help even.

The smile came out a bit broken and he knew he was frowning fiercely so he had to say something.

'Alice…' The tone of her name came out as a plea

that made him wince inwardly but this was a moment when he simply had to swallow his pride. 'I think that I…need your help. *Please*…'

CHAPTER FOUR

IT WAS SOMEWHAT startling to discover that she really liked this man.

Maybe it was the way he said her name, with an inflection and accent that made it sound so much more exotic. More like *Elise* than Alice.

Maybe it was the desperate edge to the word 'please'.

Or maybe it was the expression in his eyes. This was not someone who was used to feeling out of control of any situation and he was hating every second of this but he was too emotionally exhausted to fight any longer. Of course he was. He'd been dealing with who knew how much grief and hatred and mistrust, maybe even fear, all in the space of the short time Alice had been there?

It wasn't that she felt obliged to help. She would have gladly cared for Jacques without anybody even asking. He was her brother, for heaven's sake.

But now her heart went out to Julien in spite of everything. She wanted to help *him* just as much.

Silently she held out her arms and took the baby. She couldn't help screwing up her nose.

'Phew... He needs a clean nappy.'

Julien nodded. He was taking a step back, the

way he had when he'd heard about the possibility of measles.

'Where's the nursery?'

'I have no idea.'

Alice kicked herself inwardly as she remembered that he'd never been allowed to see his nephew so, of course, he hadn't visited this house. There was a lot more going on here than she had any knowledge of. Undercurrents that were powerful and dark.

Through the glass walls of the conservatory she could see cars leaving. The doctor's car with the housekeeper and the nanny. Then two other cars that presumably held the men in suits. The idea that the three of them were now alone in this vast house should have been alarming but this was simply another twist in the strangest day of her life and Alice felt curiously calm.

Thankfully, Jacques was settling in her arms, with just an occasional hiccup to let them know he still wasn't happy. She took a slow, inward breath as she shifted his weight to hold him more comfortably.

'Let's go and find it, then, shall we?' She offered a tentative smile with the suggestion. She might be the one who knew what to do but she didn't want to be left to do it entirely by herself. It felt as if she was doing something wrong, taking over the house of complete strangers, let alone taking over the care of their child. 'I expect it will be upstairs somewhere?'

Alice could sense Julien's hesitation so she held eye contact. Her message was silent but firm.

There's only the possibility that this baby is my brother. He's definitely your nephew. I know you think it might make things harder for you but you know what the right thing to do is...

His nod was so subtle she wouldn't have picked up on it if she hadn't been deliberately attempting a bit of telepathy.

And maybe there was a silent message coming back in her direction.

I know. I'll try...

Nothing was said aloud and, with Jacques now drowsy, it was in complete silence that they both left the huge room. The foyer was much bigger than Alice had noticed when she'd first come in. Had she not even looked up to see the gallery of the second floor that ran around three sides of this incredibly high, square space? No. She'd been focused on the fact that the man who'd greeted her was far too young to be her father. On his dark clothing and the ponytail that would have made her grandmother shake her head disapprovingly.

It didn't bother Alice. In fact, she quite liked it. There was no doubt that Julien was a very good-looking man and the smoothness with which his hair was combed back made it look as elegant as his clothing, but the short tail had a curl to it. Did he wear it loose when he was performing? Did it frame and soften his face and brush his shoulders in soft waves?

She'd quite like to see that...

The brief distraction of her train of thought vanished as she let her gaze roam the towering space. It was too much like a museum to feel like a home. The floor was marble and there were pillars supporting scalloped archways that were echoed on a smaller scale all around the second floor. A life-sized sculpture was in one of the archway recesses, illuminated by small floodlights. It wouldn't have surprised her to see a tour group appear in the wake of a guide, except that she could feel the emptiness of the vast house almost echoing around them.

Julien didn't say anything until they reached the top of the stairs. Behind them they now had a birds'-eye view of the impressive foyer. Directly in front of them was a massive painting in an ornate gilt frame that looked as if it was by some famous artist. A scene of overdressed people with heavy-looking wigs and miserable expressions and cherubic children with cheeks as pink as Jacques's. On either side they were faced with the wide balcony and its choice of countless doors.

'*Incroyable...*'

'Pardon?'

He swept his hand in a gesture that took in everything around them. 'I don't understand,' he said. 'This is not a home. It's a...a...'

'Museum?'

'*Exactement.* A gallery to display wealth. How could anyone want to *live* here?'

His sister had wanted to. Was that what he couldn't understand?

'I expect Jacques's grandmother is just as wealthy?'

'It's not the money,' Julien said. 'It's the way of thinking. The...first thoughts?'

'Priorities?'

'*Oui.*'

Walking briskly, Julien was throwing open doors. Alice caught glimpses of over-furnished bedrooms with four-poster beds and heavy velvet drapes. An overly masculine one and then a very feminine one beside it. Had his sister not shared a room with her husband?

Interior doors stood open to give a glimpse of bathrooms with marble floors and golden tapware. There was a huge sitting room with luxurious cream leather seating and a television screen big enough to make it a private movie theatre.

'I just thought of something.'

'What?'

'The grandmother. She won't be allowed to come to the house, will she?'

'No…' Julien turned his head as they walked further down the gallery that ran parallel with the front of the house.

'Or to take Jack away. Not for…for ages. A couple of weeks perhaps. Will that give you enough time?'

'I don't know if time will be enough.'

'It couldn't hurt, though, could it? Showing that you can care for him?'

Julien was silent. He had opened another door and here it was. A room that looked like an interior designer had used to fill a brief for the perfect nursery.

The ceiling was a pale blue with fluffy white clouds and a golden sun with a smiley face. The blue blended into the top of the walls but then gave way to green canopies of trees that sheltered every farm animal you could think of. The grass they stood on was sprinkled with a rainbow of flowers. Piles of toys that Jacques was far too young to appreciate—like model racing cars that were miniature Ferraris and Maseratis—filled the corners of the room but the important things were there as well. A comfortable chair for someone who needed to feed a baby. A cot with a colourful mobile hanging above it and a row of teddy bears at the foot end. On the wall behind the cot huge wooden letters in primary colours spelled out the name 'JACQUES'.

Each letter was intricately adorned with tiny pictures of animals and toys.

Alice went straight towards a change table that had shelves stuffed with disposable nappies and wipes and creams and gently put Jacques down on the soft, washable surface. She stroked his hair back and smiled as he opened his eyes.

'You were loved, little one, weren't you? What a beautiful room they made for you.'

Julien said nothing. He was still opening doors.

'There's a small kitchen,' he reported. 'And a bathroom. And a bedroom that must be for the nanny.'

'Are there bottles and things in the kitchen? Tins of milk formula?'

'There's a lot of things.' Julien's voice faded as he moved back. 'Yes…bottles and cleaning things. A microwave oven.' She could hear a cupboard door closing. 'Many tins. It looks like the baby section of a supermarket.'

A rubbish bin with a tightly fitting lid was available for the soiled nappy and wipes, and by the time Julien had finished exploring and arranging items that might be useful on the bench Alice had given Jacques a quick sponge bath and fastened a clean nappy in place. Now he was sucking on his fist and grizzling.

'I think he's hungry. I'll make up some formula.'

'Do you know how?'

'I've seen it done. I don't work with the very young children at our nursery school very often but our staff kitchen is shared by everyone. There'll be instructions on the tin if I forget.'

'In French,' Julien reminded her.

'Oh...of course. Could you translate for me?'

'Of course.'

'Could you hold him? I'll need two hands.'

'Why don't you hold him and tell me what to do? I'm used to being in kitchens. I can follow a recipe.' He took off his black jacket and rolled up the sleeves of his black shirt.

He was avoiding contact again but Alice let it go. Something had changed since they'd entered the nursery. The cold, empty feeling of this vast house had been left behind in favour of these bright colours and attention to detail—the evidence that this little person had been wanted and loved. Some of the weirdness and tension had gone.

Julien actually looked a lot happier in this small kitchen as he found the measuring spoons and distilled water and made up the bottle of formula. Clearly, he could have easily done it by himself by following the instructions but Alice found herself enjoying watching. He had clever hands and his movements were deft and confident. He only frowned when he took the bottle from the microwave.

'I haven't found a thermometer. How can we check the temperature?'

'Sprinkle a few drops on the inside of your wrist. It shouldn't feel hot.'

Jacques's whimpers became a demanding cry as he spotted the bottle and Alice hurried towards the chair near the cot. She could see Julien wiping down the bench in the kitchenette as she settled back to feed the baby and it struck her as odd that a rock god could be so domesticated.

Nice odd, though.

* * *

The bench was as spotless as possible and all the kitchen items were back in place. There was no reason for him to stay here any longer.

Except...he didn't want to leave.

As he turned away from the bench he could see Alice sitting in the chair, feeding the baby. The light in the room was fading rapidly and she'd turned on the nearby lamp.

His sister had never had the chance to sit like that—her head bent and one hand supporting the end of the bottle. Had she dreamed of what it might be like to have a baby staring back at you like that, with a tiny hand that also seemed to be holding the bottle?

Memories raced even further back as he leaned a shoulder against the kitchen door. Had Colette felt the kind of love for this infant before he was born that their mother had given the two of them once, so long ago? The kind of love that had made him protect his little sister against so many odds? Had those dreams and that love stirred these poignant feelings of loss and regret but also shone a light of hope into a dark space?

The hope that came from a fresh beginning. A chance to start again and make things right this time.

He could feel that hope himself and it was like nothing he'd ever felt. But, then, he'd never been so emotionally exhausted. So beset with problems that were coming at him from so many directions. This was a brief moment when he could actually avoid thinking about any of those problems.

Or maybe not. The buzz of the phone in his pocket came a split second before the ringtone.

He moved to the windows as he answered the call.

It was dark outside now but he could see the glow of light from the street beyond the gates. A car that was waiting for permission to enter.

He raised a hand in an apologetic gesture towards Alice as he headed for the door and she smiled her understanding as she nodded.

A dreamy kind of smile, he noticed only after he'd left the room. Did holding babies automatically have that kind of effect on women? Maybe it had something to do with the soft glow of light bathing the chair and making Alice's hair glow like the last embers of a fire. Or how dark her eyes were in that pale face. Or simply how tender that smile had been.

Whatever it was, it had changed Julien's perspective. She didn't need to enhance or bleach her hair colour or have some stylish cut. She had no need of the layers of make-up he thought any attractive woman relied on. Alice McMillan wasn't simply pretty, as he'd first thought.

She was stunning.

The realisation came on top of that strange feeling he'd got watching her with the baby. It was still sucking him back in time as he hurried downstairs. Sending him over ground so old it felt new again.

How much of all this was his own fault?

If he only spent more time with Colette, she wouldn't have been able to hang out with her friends so much, using movies and trashy magazines to sculpt her view of a perfect life where only money was needed to put the world right and give her everything she could possibly want. He'd fed that belief himself, in fact, by working so hard and being so careful of every euro he earned.

If he'd been more of a father figure, perhaps she

wouldn't have fallen for a man who'd been thirty years older than her.

The regret was so intense it was painful but somehow, in the back of his mind, he could still sense that smile Alice had given him. Could still feel the softness of that moment of hope.

Crazy, considering everything that had happened today. Was it any wonder his thoughts were so scrambled? He was heading out to the gates to meet the DNA expert—a bizarre twist to this dreadful day that he could never have imagined. The quarantine on top of that was like a bad joke.

But Julien wasn't laughing.

What was that saying? You had to laugh or you would cry?

He couldn't do that either.

He seemed to have forgotten how.

Minutes ticked by in the quiet nursery.

Jacques had finished his bottle of milk and Alice lifted him to her shoulder and began to rub his back. He nestled against her and she could feel his breath on her neck. The misery of his day had caught up with him and now that he was clean and fed, she could feel the heaviness of an infant slipping into deep slumber.

His body didn't feel unnaturally hot now but that was probably because of the paracetamol the doctor had administered. He would need some more during the night. His warmth was comforting and Alice loved the tiny snuffling sounds he was making. She had probably been sitting here cuddling him for too long, though. He needed his own bed and a good sleep to help him on his journey to recovery.

He made no protest as Alice laid him gently into his cot. She pulled the blanket back and tucked him in with only a sheet for cover. She would check again soon to make sure he was neither too warm nor cold. There was a lump down the side of the cot and when she pulled it out, Alice found it was an old toy. A faded rabbit that looked as if it had been knitted out of brown fabric.

A very different toy from all the bright new offerings in the room so it had to be special in some way. She tucked it in beside Jacques, with just the head and ears above the sheet.

She needed to find somewhere to sleep herself before too long—in the nanny's room perhaps. Not that sleep would come easily if she didn't get something to eat. Lunch seemed a very long time ago now and her stomach was rumbling.

And where was Julien? It had to be more than half an hour ago that he'd received that phone call and vanished but she couldn't go looking for him. The house was far too big to hear a baby crying. She certainly couldn't hear any sounds coming from downstairs. It was too quiet, in fact. Reaching up, Alice wound the handle on the mobile above the cot. The carousel of bright toys began turning slowly to the soft notes of 'Brahms's Lullaby'.

It was then that she noticed the baby monitor handset on the shelf beside the cot, tucked in between a soft toy unicorn and a dragon. She turned it on and suddenly an image of Jacques appeared on the screen above a speaker grill. Startled, Alice looked around and finally spotted the camera mounted on the wall at the end of the cot.

She'd heard parents discussing baby cams but had

never seen one in action. This was perfect. She could go in search of something to eat and not only hear if Jacques woke up, she'd be able to see him. A quick visit to the nursery bathroom to freshen up and Alice was ready. Eager even.

It was only because she was alone in a strange house, she told herself. Any adult company would do. It wasn't that she wanted to see Julien again.

So why did her heart do a funny double beat thing when she tiptoed out onto the gallery and saw the tall, dark figure coming towards *her*?

Julien was carrying something.

'I have the testing kit,' he told her. 'We couldn't allow the DNA expert to come into the house but he's given me very detailed instructions on how to take the test. He's waiting outside the gate to collect it when we finish. I've already found the items that might be sufficient from... André.'

The hesitation was tiny but spoke volumes. How much did you have to hate a person to make it difficult to even say his name?

And the reminder of why she had come here in the first place had wiped out that warm glow that cuddling a sleepy baby had given Alice. It had certainly eliminated any inexplicable excitement that seeing Julien had provoked. This was business. A necessary step that might give him permission to send her packing. How could she have forgotten how unwelcome her arrival had been? That she might only have a single night to clasp that hope of family to her heart?

'Fine.' Her voice was tight. 'Tell me what to do.'

'No. I have to do it. I'm the one who has been briefed.'

Julien's tone was brisk. 'Come with me. We need a place with good light.'

He took her to one of the bedrooms that they had opened a door on during their first exploration of this second floor. The feminine one. They went through the bedroom into the en suite bathroom, which was clinically bright once all the lights had been snapped on.

Alice put the monitor handset on the marble top of the vanity unit.

'What's that?'

'A monitor. So I can hear when Jack wakes up. See?' Alice touched the screen and the image of Jacques's face appeared. Like all babies, he looked like an angel with that cupid's bow of a mouth relaxed in sleep. The sweet sound of the lullaby still playing made the picture all the more adorable.

'Jacques.' Julien corrected her pronunciation, emphasising the soft 'J' as he busied himself pulling items from the bag he was carrying.

'We do two tests. One is a back-up in case there isn't enough DNA in the first sample.' He placed two small, plastic vials on the vanity top. Then he took a long packet and peeled open the end to reveal a stick that he took hold of carefully.

'I must not touch the swab or I might contaminate it.' He stepped closer to Alice. 'Open your mouth, please.'

Suddenly, this was excruciatingly embarrassing. She had a strange, *extremely* good-looking man standing close enough to kiss her and he'd asked her to open her mouth. Alice had to close her eyes as she complied. She could feel the prickle of heat rising rapidly from in front of her neck to her face. Please, let this be over quickly, she begged silently.

'I have to scrape the inside of your cheek for forty-five to sixty seconds,' Julien told her. 'The pressure will be firm. I have to collect cheek cells, not your saliva.'

Oh… God… How long could sixty seconds feel like?

For ever, that was how long. The swab on the end of the stick was like a toothbrush made of firm cotton balls. She could feel it moving up and down on the inside of her cheek. She could feel Julien's hand so close to her face she was sure that her lips were registering the warmth of his skin.

It was doing something very odd to parts of her body that had nothing to do with this test. Quite apart from the blush, her heart was hammering and there were butterflies dancing deep down in her belly.

'Bien…' The swab was finally removed from her mouth and then Julien concentrated on opening the plastic vial and inserting the swab into the liquid it contained. Then he pressed a spike on the end of the stick that released the swab and allowed him to screw back the lid of the vial. She watched his face in the mirror as he focused on his task. His hair wasn't as smooth as it had been. A thin tress had escaped the ponytail and flopped forward.

The butterflies, which had almost stopped dancing when the procedure had finished, started beating a new tattoo as Alice failed to head off a totally ridiculous desire to reach out and smooth that wayward tress back into place.

It was unfortunate that Julien chose that moment to raise his gaze and caught her looking at him in the mirror. For a heartbeat, time stopped as they stared at each other in the mirror. The bright lighting made it so easy to see the way his eyes darkened. Had he guessed that

Alice was thinking about touching him? Had the urge suddenly become contagious?

Hurriedly, she dropped her gaze and Julien cleared his throat at exactly the same moment.

'One more,' he said. 'And then we're done.'

This time, Alice stood like a statue while her other cheek was scraped and she didn't risk any glance towards the mirror as he dealt with the swab and then sealed both vials into a plastic specimen bag.

There was a moment's silence when he'd finished and Alice almost wished to hear a baby's cry from the monitor, which would give her an excuse to flee. Was Julien looking into the mirror again? Looking at *her* as she avoided looking at *him*?

It was still heavy in the air—that moment when they hadn't been able to look away from each other's reflections. Something had happened. Some nameless, unexpected, *unwanted*…thing.

'You need to sign this consent form. Here—I have a pen.'

He handed her the pen and as he did so his hand brushed hers.

No more than a whisper of a touch but it felt like her skin had been burned.

Alice's signature had never been quite this shaky before. She folded the paper and handed it back and this time she looked up at Julien.

There was no getting away from it. Now that it had happened, this thing couldn't be taken back. Even if she didn't look, she had been sure it was still there.

And looking had just confirmed it.

CHAPTER FIVE

WHAT, IN GOD'S NAME, had just happened there?

The last few days—ever since he'd heard about André's accident—had made Julien feel as if his world was tipping on its axis, and the events of today had already made the angle a lot steeper. At the precise moment he'd met Alice's gaze in the mirror for the second time, it had felt like he'd just fallen off the edge of it.

Those *eyes*...

Who was this woman? This flame-haired Scottish pixie who'd not only crossed his path so unexpectedly, she was now an integral part of his life being brought to a crashing halt.

And...it felt...*good*?

Who knew where that moment could have gone if her stomach hadn't suddenly rumbled too loudly to be ignored—a sound that made Alice blush scarlet.

'Oh...pardon *me*.'

The way the colour flooded her face was fascinating but Julien wasn't going to make things any more weird by staring. And how was it that he'd only just noticed how intimate a space a bathroom was?

'You're hungry.' He turned on his heel as he made the redundant announcement. 'Come... I will get these delivered to the gate and then we'll find out what the kitchen has to offer.'

He kept a step or two ahead of Alice as he led the way downstairs but he was acutely aware that she was following. Was she still blushing? He'd never met a woman who blushed. Or whose stomach rumbled like a train, for that matter. Julien's lips twitched at the thought of either of those occurrences happening with any of the sophisticated, perfectly groomed women who'd always been available and more than willing to share his companionship and his bed.

This foreign pixie was certainly very different.

Nice different. It made him think of times with Colette before she'd learned to be sophisticated.

Not that it was unusual to remember things from the past—especially in the last few months when the grief had had to be endured, but this was the first time it could bring even an inward smile. When something poignant but sweet was stronger than any associated pain.

He sent the samples out with the security guard and remembered to issue instructions that no one else was to come through the gates, no matter how certain they were about their rights. Madame Laurent could be referred to his solicitor for more information. Or her own, for that matter. Both those men were now probably confined to their own homes and less than happy about it but what could they do?

What could any of them do about it?

At least he could do the thing that was guaranteed to relieve stress.

He could cook.

'Oh, my goodness...' Alice stopped in the doorway to the kitchen. 'This looks like a commercial kitchen.

You could cook enough to feed an army in here. Or run a restaurant.'

And it was clean, Julien noted with satisfaction, eyeing the expanse of stainless-steel benches.

'There's no fridge!' Alice exclaimed. 'How strange...'

'There'll be a cold room, I expect. And a pantry. You're right...this has been set up as a commercial kitchen. Look...' Julien walked past the hobs and ovens and through an arched doorway into a scullery. Sure enough, there was a pantry and if he'd thought the cupboard in the nursery had looked like a section of a supermarket, it was nothing on what was stocked in here. The cold room was just as well stocked.

'Oh...' Alice's eyes were round with surprise. 'Look at all that *cheese*...' She grinned at Julien. 'I *love* cheese...'

It was the first time he'd seen her really smile and he got that strange falling sensation all over again. He found himself smiling back because he couldn't help it.

'Take some out,' he told her. 'See if you can find some bread and olives. There'll be a wine cellar somewhere but we'll make do with what's cold. Here...take this one. I'll see what I can find to cook with.'

'But it's champagne... *French* champagne.'

Julien's lips twitched again. 'I wasn't aware there was any other kind.'

'But...'

'Mmm?' Julien was gathering some ingredients. Minced beef and garlic and chilli. Greens and parmesan cheese. He needed something quick and easy. Pasta and salad should be perfect. Reaching for a bottle of balsamic vinegar, he became aware of the silence behind him. He turned to find Alice looking bewildered. He raised his eyebrows.

'Champagne is for celebrating something,' she said quietly.

Julien stopped thinking about food. 'Maybe we can find something to celebrate, then.'

Her eyes widened. 'Like what?'

Oh, no… How insensitive was it to suggest that she should be celebrating something when she'd just found out that her probable father was deceased? He had to think fast as he moved past her to drop his armload on a bench.

'You may have discovered a brother,' he suggested. 'And…and have you ever been to France before?'

'No…never…'

'*Donc…* There you go. That is definitely worth celebrating.'

'And what about you? What have you got to celebrate?'

'Ah…' Julien stared down at his ingredients without seeing them. Nothing. He was revisiting the grief from losing his sister. He had a major problem in what to do about the show that filming was due to start on within days. He probably had to face a court case over custody of his nephew that was highly likely to get very nasty.

No. Nothing to celebrate there.

He looked up, ready to admit defeat and agree that champagne might not be the most appropriate thing to drink.

And then he got caught by those eyes again.

What was it that he could see?

Hope?

Optimism?

A belief in fairy-tales, even?

Something shifted in his chest and he found himself saying something he hadn't thought of until now.

'I got to hold my sister's baby for the first time today.' The words came out as little more than a whisper and he was embarrassed that he was showing so much emotion in front of a stranger. He cleared his throat. 'And I have a reprieve from having to deal with Madame Laurent.' He offered a crooked smile. 'That is absolutely worth celebrating, *n'est-ce pas?*'

She'd made him smile.

Sort of. One of those oddly endearing lopsided ones like he'd given her when he had asked for her help with Jacques, but it felt like a victory because there was something very sombre about Julien's face—especially his eyes—and she got the impression that he didn't smile, let alone laugh, very often.

She sat at the big central table in this enormous kitchen, with the baby monitor in one hand and a glass of champagne in the other, and watched Julien cook.

The champagne was astonishingly delicious and Julien…well, he was just as astonishing. The way he chopped vegetables with a speed that made her blink and then scooped them up to drop them into a food processor as if it was the easiest thing in the world to do without making a mess. He got two frying pans going on gas flames on the hobs and in one of them he was adding things to minced beef like mustard and balsamic vinegar and a huge handful of herbs that had also been chopped with lightning efficiency. The smell was starting to make Alice feel very, very hungry and the champagne on her empty stomach was making her head spin a little. She watched as Julien tossed the contents of the pan, which mixed the contents more efficiently than a wooden spoon, which would have been her choice of implement.

'You really know your way around a kitchen, don't you?'

A snort that could have been laughter came from Julien. 'I should hope so. I've been working in them for twenty years now.'

'Twenty years? You don't look old enough to have been working that long.'

'I'm thirty-five.'

'You started working when you were fifteen? After school?'

'No.' Julien carelessly sprinkled a handful of sea salt flakes into a pot of boiling water and then tipped a packet of pasta in. 'I had to drop out of school.'

'Why?' Alice wouldn't normally ask such personal questions of someone she had only just met but the champagne was making her reckless.

'My mother died. I had to get my sister away from our stepfather and I had to support her. The only job I could get was washing dishes in a restaurant. Sometimes I was given other jobs to help the chefs and…and I was good at it.' He lifted his glass in a toast. 'And so I learned to cook.'

He'd taken off his tie and unbuttoned the top of his shirt before he'd started work in the kitchen and his sleeves were pushed up as far as they could go. The escaping tress of his hair had been joined by a couple more and his cheeks were pink from the heat of the stove. He looked dishevelled. And…as delicious as the smell of whatever he was cooking. Alice could only begin to imagine how many fans he must have.

'And you're a musician as well...'

'*Pardon? Je ne comprends pas...*'

The puzzlement on his face made the meaning of his words clear.

'The show you were talking about? The film crews? I thought...you must be a singer. In a band.'

He was looking at her as if she'd lost her mind. 'It's a show for television. Food television.'

Alice's jaw dropped. 'Food television? You're a... *chef*?' Images of a rock star were being blown apart. No wonder the doctor's wife was such a fan. Maybe the media waiting outside the gates had nothing to do with how famous her father had been.

'*Exactement*. The Christmas show I was talking about? It is for a morning television show on Christmas Eve. I am demonstrating a traditional English Christmas dinner to compare with another chef who is doing the French one.' Julien drained his glass of champagne and came over to the table to refill both their glasses. 'The actual cooking will be pre-recorded but I will be a guest on the live show to talk about it on the day. If my test doesn't confirm my immunity so that I can leave this house, it will be a mess that will be very difficult to deal with. A lot of people will be extremely annoyed.'

As if in sympathy with the statement, a whimper came through the monitor. It was a startling reminder of the responsibility they both had to Jacques and for a long moment they both stared at the screen of the handset but, with another tired-sounding cry, the baby settled back into sleep.

Julien sank into the chair opposite Alice, his gaze

still focused on the screen, his brow furrowed. 'What is that?'

'What?'

'In the bed with him? That…'

'Oh…it's a toy. A rabbit. I thought it must be special because it looks very old.'

The way Julien's throat moved suggested that he was having trouble swallowing.

'It's *le lapin brun*… It was Colette's special toy when she was tiny. I…didn't know she had kept it.' His voice cracked. 'She must have put it in the nursery before he was born because… I don't think she ever saw him after he was born…'

Tears sprang to Alice's eyes. 'That's so sad…' Then she shook her head slowly, in disbelief. 'Such a tragedy… Was…was she very sick?'

'*Non*. She had come to see me only the week before. The first time I had seen her in over a year and she had never looked so well. She was so excited about the baby. It made her want to reconnect with her own family, she said. It made her remember…'

He had closed his eyes and that gave Alice permission to let her gaze linger on his face as he seemingly became lost in his own thoughts.

Dear Lord, even when you couldn't see those astonishing eyes, he was a beautiful man with those strong features and such a sensitive-looking mouth. Eyelashes that caught your attention because they were a little longer than you'd expect on a man—like his hair.

This was no time to ask what had caused such a rift between these siblings. Whatever it had been, it sounded like they'd been ready to forgive and forget. 'What did she remember?' Alice asked softly to break the silence.

'That her first memories were of how I'd looked after her. How important I'd been in her life for ever. That she didn't want to lose that and that, maybe, this baby could help bring us back together. And I thought she was right. She texted me when she went into the hospital and so I went to visit and…and I saw her die…'

'Oh, my God… *No*…' It was instinctive to reach out to touch him. To cover his hand with her own.

His eyes were open again and the shock of his words cut even deeper as she saw unshed tears making them glisten.

'They said it was an *embolie*. I don't know the word for it in English…'

'An embolism?'

'*Probablement*.' Julien shook off the translation as unimportant. 'Something to do with the water around the baby and it gave her an attack of the heart and… *Il ne pouvait rien faire*… They tried. I *saw* how hard they try…'

That his English was fractured only made this more heart-breaking. Alice could feel Julien's distress so deeply that, unlike him, she couldn't stop tears escaping, but he didn't need her reaction to make the memories worse. He needed something very different.

Comfort.

With a huge effort Alice banished her tears and steadied her voice. She squeezed Julien's hand as she spoke.

'I love it that Jacques has the rabbit,' she said softly, paying careful attention to pronouncing the name correctly. 'One day you'll be able to tell him how special it is. And how much his mother must have loved him to give it to him.'

The glance she received was almost bewildered. And then Julien gave his head a tiny shake as if he was sending those memories back where they belonged. In the past. He stood up, sliding his hand from beneath Alice's with no acknowledgment that she had touched him, and her fingers curled as she pulled her hand back.

She could only see his back now.

'Let's eat. My penne ragout will be ready.'

He was too tired to feel particularly hungry.

Or perhaps his brain was too occupied with other things to notice he was only picking at his food.

The words Alice had spoken were turning slowly, a new ingredient that was going to simmer in his head, along with everything else that had happened today, like a kind of emotional ragout.

Memories associated with the brown rabbit were strong enough to throw the mix off balance. The sight of it shocking enough to make him talk to someone about that terrible day for the first time.

Maybe it was easier to be open with a stranger?

Except that it hadn't felt like he'd been with a stranger. Alice was different. She was real. And she cared. That human touch of comfort had almost left a brand on his skin that he could still feel.

He hadn't seen that toy for so many years he had forgotten how important *le lapin brun* had been. Colette would not go to sleep without it. And if he'd taken her to hide—under a bed perhaps—to escape one of their stepfather's drunken rages, then brown bunny made it so much more bearable. Little Colette would cuddle the toy. And he would cuddle Colette.

And now Jacques was sleeping with it and Alice

had found something good about that. Something to celebrate…

But that was confusing the flavour he'd been so sure was the right one for whatever recipe his head and heart were inventing—the cocktail of grief and resentment and even hatred. He could imagine Colette putting the toy into the bed she had prepared for her baby and gifting him the thing that had brought her such comfort, but for him to have it suggested that André had known of the toy's significance and he'd wanted his son to have something precious that had belonged to his mother…

Because he'd cared?

Because he'd loved Colette that much?

If that was true, then he himself had been wrong in trying to stop the marriage by persuading Colette what a terrible mistake she was making. It would make those strained months of him not being welcome in his sister's home—after the wedding he'd refused to attend—a stupid, wasted opportunity. And the sworn hatred between the two men wouldn't have overridden almost everything else at Colette's funeral.

He knew he had failed her but maybe it was in a different way than he'd thought.

'This is amazing…' Alice's words broke the increasingly negative spiral of his thoughts. 'It's the best pasta I have ever eaten. It's…it's *magnifique*…'

Her passable attempt at a French word made Julien tilt his head in acknowledgement of both her effort and the compliment. It made him look up and catch her gaze and it seemed like every time that happened it became more familiar and the hit of whatever it was that the eye contact gave him became more powerful.

He couldn't identify what it was but there was no

getting away from the knowledge that it warmed something deep inside his chest. It was something as real as the comforting touch she had given him. Maybe he hadn't known how precious little of anything that real there was in his life.

'*Merci beaucoup.* I am delighted that you like it.'

Suddenly Julien felt hungry himself. Really hungry. He loaded up forkful of the pasta coated in the spicy sauce and could taste it properly now. Yes, that balsamic vinegar had added a perfect, balancing note to the sweetness of the tomatoes and the bite of chilli.

A small thing in the grand scheme of things but it was often the small things that could be unexpectedly important, wasn't it?

Like an old, battered toy...

By the time Alice had finished eating her delicious meal it was obvious that she could barely keep her eyes open.

'Dessert?' Julien offered. 'Some coffee, perhaps?'

'No, thank you. I... I should go and check on Jacques and then I think I need some sleep myself. I thought I would use the nanny's bed, if that's all right? That way I'll be close when he wakes. He may need a night feed and I'm sure he'll need some more paracetamol before morning.'

Morning. The start of a new day and who knew what new problems might present themselves? Julien rubbed his temples. He had more than enough to deal with now. Too much. Top of that list would be to call a teleconference and try to organise a way to manage the fallout if he couldn't film the Christmas show. He had tried to contact the head of his production team as soon as the doctor had dropped the quarantine bombshell but he hadn't got through. And then he'd been completely distracted, hadn't he—at first by the appalling thought of Alice having to stay in the house and then by the emotional roller-coaster that had started the moment he'd held his sister's child in his arms for the first time ever.

It was all too much. He needed some time out and maybe it wasn't too late to try and make the first of those calls tonight. He pulled his phone from his pocket and was already scrolling his contacts list as he spoke.

'I'll use one of the rooms near the nursery,' he told Alice. 'You can call if you need help with anything.'

'Don't worry... I'm sure I can cope.' There was a moment's silence and he knew Alice was looking at him, waiting for him to look up, but he resisted the urge. Enough was enough. If that peculiar sensation he got when he met her eyes kept happening, he might have to try and identify it so that he would know how to deal with it. And he had the funny feeling that giving it a name might only open a whole new can of worms.

He knew she had gone by more than the sound of her boots on the flagged floor of the kitchen.

Her departure also left the room feeling disturbingly empty.

CHAPTER SIX

THE MESSAGE HAD been crystal clear.

It felt like they'd been so close in those moments when Alice had been holding Julien's hand as he'd told her about the tragedy of his sister's death but he hadn't even looked at her when she'd excused herself to check on Jacques, and whatever barrier he'd put up around himself, having pushed her away, was still firmly in place the next morning.

He barely came near the nursery for the whole morning, other than to bring her a tray of coffee and some amazingly melt-in-the-mouth croissants, still warm from the oven, at seven a.m. At nine a.m., with a phone in his hand, he came briefly to the door to ask if Jacques was any worse and if she needed the doctor to visit today. He vanished as soon as she shook her head.

Being abandoned upstairs with an unwell baby should have felt lonely. Scary even, but the time was passing quickly and, for such a huge house with only one other adult in it, it felt surprisingly busy.

Phones were ringing at frequent intervals and delivery vans began arriving from mid-morning. From the nursery windows Alice could see them coming up the driveway, and if she was near the door to this suite of rooms she could hear Julien talking downstairs or faint clattering sounds from the direction of the kitchens.

Would he deliver another tray for her lunch? And then dinner after a whole afternoon alone with Jacques? By one p.m. Alice felt like she'd been sent to Coventry—as punishment perhaps for engaging in a conversation that had become too personal. She didn't even try and ignore her rebellious streak this time. As soon as Jacques was down for a sleep after a lunchtime feed, she took the baby cam monitor and marched downstairs.

Her determined stride faltered at the bottom of the stairs. There were boxes littering the foyer. A suitcase. And…

'Good *grief*…'

Julien appeared from the kitchen, wiping his hands on a dish towel.

'*C'est horrible, n'est pas?*'

'*Horrible.*' Alice tried to repeat the word. 'It's a…a *monster.*'

A monster bright blue teddy bear that was in the corner beside the door.

'It is a gift from Madame Laurent. It has a tag that says, "For my beloved grandson"'

Alice let out an incredulous huff. 'It's five times the size of her grandson. It would probably terrify him.'

'That is why I have left it down here.'

'And the suitcase?'

'Some clothing and other things I needed. I can arrange for some to be brought for you?'

'I'll manage. I have a spare shirt and…' a blush threatened as she stopped herself mentioning underwear '…things. I'm fine. I just came down for…' *Some company.* 'For something to eat.'

'Come.' Julien's hand wave encompassed the boxes. 'I have had many things delivered, including some work that needed extra food.'

Alice followed him into the kitchen. There were pots simmering on the stove and the table was covered with sheets of paper, most of which had glossy photographs along with the text.

'Is that a recipe book?'

'They are the—how do you say it—proofing pages?' Julien began scooping them into a heap. 'There is a deadline and I want to check some of the recipes by cooking them again. What would you like for your lunch? A mushroom risotto perhaps? Or chicken Dijon?'

Alice chose the risotto. He presented it to her on a tray but Alice didn't want to leave the room, even if he was busy working. She sat at the table and watched him. She hadn't intended interrupting him any further but she only took a few mouthfuls before her good intentions evaporated.

'How do I say "I love it" in French?'

The smile was the kind of lopsided one he'd given her more than once now. Maybe that was the only way Julien smiled. It meant something, though, because he stopped what he was doing and came to sit opposite her.

'*Je l'aime.*'

Alice repeated the phrase. 'And if I want to say "I *don't* like it"?'

'*Je ne l'aime pas.*' Julien frowned. 'You *don't* like the risotto?'

She grinned. 'No. *Je l'aime*. A lot.'

'*Beaucoup.*' He listened to her repetition. 'You have a good accent,' he told her.

The praise was unexpected and Alice felt suddenly

shy. 'I think I'd like to learn French,' she admitted. 'I was never allowed to take it at school and I haven't really listened to it properly before but…it's beautiful. Like music.'

'It is a beautiful language.' Julien gave her a curious look. 'Why were you not allowed to learn at school?'

Alice had to look away. 'Because of who my father was, I imagine. My mother never talked about it but my grandmother hated anything French.'

Julien let her eat in silence for a minute. 'Perhaps your mother hated André Laurent, too, after the way he treated her.'

'I don't think so. If she had, she might have found someone else she could fall in love with and she never did. I don't think she even tried.'

'Perhaps your village was too small.'

'It was small but Mum trained to be a nurse after I was born and she met a lot of people through her work.'

'And she had you to care for.'

'Yes.' Alice glanced at the monitor as she ate another mouthful of the delicious risotto. 'I can imagine loving my child so much that I would be wary of anything that might change my life.' Then she laid down her fork and sighed 'Or maybe her heart had just been broken too badly. I know a lot of people think it's nonsense but—for some—I think there really is only "the one".'

Julien was giving her another one of those odd, unreadable looks. 'And you? Are you one of the "some"?'

Again, Alice had to look away. How silly was it that her heart had started thumping so loudly she was afraid he might hear it? But she nodded slowly.

'Yes. I think I'm one of those people.'

Julien's chair scraped as he pushed it back abruptly. 'I hope you find this "one", then, Alice.'

She took her plate over to the sink beside which he was working again. 'Sometimes that's not enough,' she told him. 'He will have to find me, too.'

It was the sound of the baby crying early the next morning that woke Julien.

It was still crying as he pulled on his jeans. A sharp cry that was suddenly alarming.

Still too sleepy to think clearly, he threw open his door and ran to the nursery. Jacques was in his cot. Alice was nowhere to be seen.

'Alice?'

There was no answer. The kitchenette was deserted and there was no sound of running water from the bathroom.

The noise level was still increasing. Julien walked to the cot and stood looking down at his nephew. He had no idea what he should do. Surely Alice would come through the door and rescue him?

Jacques was sobbing. His little fists were waving in the air and his face was bright red.

'Shh...' Julien said. *Alice vient bientôt. Tout est okay...*

Except it wasn't okay. Jacques let out a piercing shriek and he couldn't stand there and do nothing. Reaching into the cot, he picked up the baby and then held it against his chest. A still-bare chest, he realised belatedly that now had a warm little head resting on it as he rocked the baby and tried to make soothing noises into the miniature ear.

Miraculously, it seemed to be working. The shrieking lessened to a wail and then to a series of hiccupping sobs. And then Jacques started rubbing his nose on Julien's chest and the movement got slower and slower and then stopped. Julien noticed two things. That Jacques seemed to have gone back to sleep and that one tiny fist was locked around his thumb.

No. Make that three things. He had picked up this distressed baby and had been able to comfort him. He felt proud of himself. And then he felt…something much deeper. This tiny person was trusting him enough to fall asleep in his arms. To protect him from any evil that might be present in the unknown world around them. Such absolute trust from a being so completely vulnerable was doing something peculiar to his heart because it felt so full it could burst.

He should go and find Alice and hand over the care of the baby because this was precisely what he had been afraid of. Feeling the kind of bond that would inevitably lead to heartache, no matter how this situation got resolved.

He had known it would only make it harder to hold his sister's baby and Alice couldn't be far away so he could escape.

He just didn't want to move quite yet.

Alice had been running up the stairs as she'd heard that alarming shriek over the monitor.

She'd gone down to the kitchen to find something for her breakfast because Julien wasn't awake yet and she'd stupidly left the monitor there to go and find a downstairs bathroom. How long had he been crying like that?

She wasn't even halfway up the stairs when the increased force of the baby's cries made her check the screen of her monitor and that was when she saw that Jacques wasn't alone.

Julien was standing beside the cot. Half-dressed. Good grief, he hadn't even fastened the button of his jeans and she could see the white fabric of his underwear exposed. As for the rest of him…oh, my… A torso and arms with sculpted muscle that begged to be traced with gentle hands. A face that was so twisted with indecision that a sympathetic smile tugged at Alice's lips and she wanted to hug even more than stroke this man.

She should keep going and rescue him because he clearly had no idea what to do about Jacques but Alice's steps involuntarily came to a halt. She was holding her breath when she saw Julien reach into the cot and then she had to swallow past a huge lump in her throat as she saw him cradle the baby against his bare chest and start rocking him.

It was an image that would have melted any woman's heart but it was bigger than that for Alice because it got added to her memory of whatever had happened between them that had been reflected in the bathroom mirror and had since been banished.

He was an extraordinary man, wasn't he?

Completely out of her league, of course. A television star, for heaven's sake. Probably extremely wealthy and able to take his pick of a vast array of eager women.

What would she have to offer that could possibly interest someone like Julien Dubois?

Obviously nothing, which was why he had backed off so quickly. Alice started walking again. She took a deep breath and tried to shove her thoughts somewhere that wouldn't show on her face by the time she got to the nursery. If there had been a 'thing' and it hadn't been simply her imagination, then Julien had banished it and she needed to follow suit unless she wanted to totally humiliate herself.

The 'thing'—along with that heart-stealing sight of him holding Jacques—had to be jammed into a mental jar like the ones that Julien brought out from the pantry when he was cooking. Big, square glass jars with metal lids that held things like caster sugar or salt. The thing needed to be trapped and the lid tightly screwed into place. The jar couldn't be opened and the thing couldn't be allowed to grow because that might shatter the glass and possibly be as catastrophic as the way the glass on her father's portrait had shattered when Julien had hurled the paperweight at it.

So Alice wasn't even going to *think* about the muscles on that bare chest and arms. Or those unfastened jeans...

She would keep her gaze firmly on the baby when she entered the room. She would keep out of Julien's way as much as possible and when they were together she would stick to something completely safe—like the basic French lessons he had started giving her over dinner last night.

It should work.

It *had* to work.

CHAPTER SEVEN

THE PHONE RANG at exactly nine o'clock in the morning.

The way it had for three mornings now.

'Tell him that the rash is fading on his face,' Alice called in response to Julien's query. 'It certainly hasn't spread any further down his body and his temperature is normal quite a lot of the time.'

'Do you want the doctor to visit today?'

Alice shook her head, adjusting the weight of the freshly changed and fed baby in her arms from her position on the gallery, looking down to the foyer that Julien was crossing as he headed for one of the landlines in the house. 'We might need some more paracetamol syrup, that's all.'

There would be no problem having it delivered, along with any other supplies Julien deemed necessary. Vans were still being admitted through the gates every day. More gifts had arrived from Madame Laurent. Nothing as awful as the giant teddy bear but none of them had got as far as the nursery—they were piling up around the blue monstrosity in the foyer, which Alice could see from the corner of her eye as she walked with Jacques around the gallery instead of going straight back to the nursery.

Maybe she wanted to hear the sound of Julien's voice as he carried on his conversation with the doctor. No sooner had it stopped than the phone rang again. A shorter conversation this time and then a much longer silence. So long that Alice decided it was time to return to the nursery, so the sound of her name being called again startled her.

'Alice?'

Elise. It still gave her a tiny flutter of butterflies in her stomach, the way Julien pronounced her name. She turned to peer down into the foyer again.

'I'm here.'

'Could you come downstairs, please?'

Alice's heart skipped a beat. Something had changed. She was used to the level of tension in this house and how serious and almost aloof Julien was but there was a note in his voice that she had never heard before and it made her feel as if she was being summoned to the headmaster's office because she had done something wrong and she was in trouble. Her heart was in her mouth by the time she got to the bottom of the stairs.

Had the blood-test results come back to prove her immunity to measles? Was she about to be sent away and the care of Jacques assigned to someone else? Or was Julien also safe and he could escape to meet the deadline of filming his Christmas show in Paris? Alice wasn't sure which scenario would be worse. She didn't want anything to change, she realised. Not just yet.

'What is it?'

'Come…' Julien led her across the foyer, not towards the grand salon, as she might have expected for a formal discussion, but into the kitchen. This was the only room that she'd spent much time in other than the nursery.

It felt like home. Despite the size and how professional this area of the house was, it didn't have the kind of museum feel the rest of the house did, with the opulent architecture and priceless antiques so carefully positioned. Julien probably felt more at home here as well, which was why he'd chosen to use it as an office as well as a test kitchen.

Not that there were any papers strewn over the table yet this morning.

'Sit down.' The invitation was terse enough to make it sound like a command but, for once, any rebellious streak on Alice's part was dormant. She sank into a chair beside the table and shifted Jacques so that he was sitting on her lap, cradled in one arm. She rested her other hand on the tabletop, ready to provide extra support quickly if it was needed. Jacques looked up at Alice and then reached out a chubby hand to grab a fistful of her hair. He was only holding it, not tugging, so Alice let it be and shifted her gaze to Julien, who had sat down at the end of the table right beside her.

This was different, too. If they ate together, he sat opposite her. This felt more intimate. More serious. Alice swallowed hard. Something bad must have happened and the news was going to be broken gently. But she was an orphan already and had no other family so what did she have to lose?

'Oh…' Alice whispered. 'The DNA results have come back, haven't they?'

'*Oui*. The call came just after I spoke with the doctor.'

The sinking feeling was so horrible that Alice had to close her eyes. 'I was wrong, wasn't I? I'm not André's daughter. Jacques is not…not my brother…'

'Au contraire...' The touch of Julien's hand covering hers as it rested on the table made Alice's eyes snap open. 'That is exactly the truth. You are, without doubt, the child of André Laurent. And you are Jacquot's sister.'

Alice gasped. The flood of emotion revealed how much she had had resting on this news. There was grief there. For the father she would never know. For her mother who had lost the man she loved and then lost her life far too soon. But there was joy, too. Immeasurable joy and hope for a future she had never imagined.

She tried to smile but imminent tears made it impossible. She tried to fight them. Tried not to be so acutely aware of how her skin felt where Julien's hand was covering hers. It felt like support. Protection. And something much more visceral. Attraction mixed with both grief and hope felt remarkably like being in love, didn't it?

She couldn't go there... Couldn't even let the thought rest long enough to take a recognisable shape.

'Jacquot?' she queried, her voice choked.

Julien shrugged. 'It is a... How do say it? A pet name? Like Jamie instead of James.' He smiled at the baby, reaching out to touch his cheek gently. 'It seems you have a big sister, little Jacquot.'

Alice lost the battle with the tears. The skin on her hand was still tingling where he'd been touching it and she knew exactly what the stroke of that finger on the baby's cheek would feel like. Tender. Caring...

The tears rolled down her cheeks in big, fat droplets.

Julien glanced up and then stared at her, his brow furrowed. 'This news has made you unhappy?'

Alice shook her head. What had Julien said? *'Au*

contraire,' she managed on a stifled sob. 'I... I couldn't be happier.'

A sudden tug on her hair made her look down and, as if he knew how momentous this news had been, Jacquot stared back up at the two adults.

And then it happened. His little face crinkled and then split into a grin—the first real smile Alice had seen him make.

The alchemy of her emotional turbulence found a new direction. The one it should have had all along. This was the moment that she fell completely in love with this baby.

Her *brother*...

It was a crooked little grin. Rather like the only way she'd seen his uncle smile. Alice lifted her gaze and that might have been a mistake because it hit her again. It was so huge, this love that she had for Jacquot. Her heart could burst with the enormity but it wouldn't because some of that love was spilling out and Julien was somehow caught up in the fallout. Words formed and came out in a whisper.

'He looks like you.'

Julien met her gaze. His eyes looked bright—with unshed tears perhaps? 'I was just thinking how much he looks like Colette.'

The poignant undertone of his words made Alice want to gather him close and cuddle him the way she was cuddling Jacquot. The corners of her own mouth were still curling, as they had done in an instant response to the baby's smile, but now she could feel them wobble. She could see exactly the same struggle between happiness and sorrow hovering over the edges of Julien's lips and when she was brave enough to catch his gaze again, there it was.

The thing…

And this time it was powerful enough to feel like a punch in her gut, maybe because she recognised it for what it was. How could she not, when she'd just fallen utterly in love with her little brother?

Julien Dubois wasn't just caught up in the fallout of what she was feeling for her little brother. He was a part of what was causing this tsunami of emotion. She had somehow slipped past the warning signs that she might be in danger of falling in love with him.

For some reason she couldn't identify, there was a sense of connection in that particular look they had shared more than once now that was sucking her in and making her imagine things that couldn't possibly be true. How ridiculous was it to get a flash of thought that this man could be the person she had been searching for ever since she'd been a naïve teenager and had begun dreaming of a fairy-tale happy ending in her search for love?

They didn't even speak the same language, for heaven's sake.

They had absolutely nothing in common, other than a genetic connection to a small, orphaned child.

No wonder she hadn't been able to dismiss the memory of how that eye contact had made her feel. Or how it had been magnified by the sight of Julien standing half-naked with Jacquot in his arms. With the skin of her hand still buzzing with the memory of his touch even though it had been removed now, the air around her felt volatile. As if something could very well explode.

That imaginary glass jar perhaps?

Alice dragged her gaze free of Julien's so fast he didn't have a chance of being the first to break that contact.

They both seemed to feel the need to change the subject and they both spoke at exactly the same time.

'The doctor said…'

'I think I'd better…' Alice stopped and blinked. 'What did the doctor say?'

'That the nanny, Nicole, is showing signs of having caught measles. She has the spots inside her cheeks. I've forgotten what he called them.'

'Koplik's spots. Oh, no… That makes this a more serious outbreak, doesn't it?'

'It would appear so. But he said that Jacques will not be contagious within another day or two and he's found a children's nurse who can come into the house and care for him. Marthe—the housekeeper—could also return as her tests have shown her to be immune.'

'*No*…' Alice surprised herself with the vehemence of her response so it was no wonder that Julien's eyebrows shot up. 'I want to look after him,' she added. 'He's…' A smile curved around her soft words. 'He's my brother.'

Julien frowned. 'It may take some time before your relationship to Jacques can be legally acknowledged. The French system of law is complicated and offices will close down for some time over the Christmas period.' His frown deepened. 'There have been repeated calls from Madame Laurent—his grandmother. She is impatient to have the child collected and taken to her home in Geneva at the earliest opportunity.'

'Have him *collected*?' Alice was shocked. 'This is her *grand*son. How could she be prepared to let total strangers come and take him away from his home? How frightening would that be? It's hard enough that he has people he doesn't know looking after him when he's sick but at least he's in a familiar place.'

'She buried her only son a few days ago. I imagine it's a taxing time for an elderly woman.'

'How old is she?'

'Given that her son was in his early sixties, I expect she's well over eighty.'

Far too old to be taking on the task of raising a baby, then. But then another thought struck Alice and it made her catch her breath.

'Good grief...do you realise that Madame Laurent is also *my* grandmother?'

Julien's chair scraped as he pushed it back. 'Of course. I hadn't thought of that.'

And it was clearly an unpleasant thought. Alice was closely related to a man he loathed. He was disappearing behind the barriers again and Alice didn't want him to go. It wasn't fair to dismiss her because of who her father or grandmother was.

'Did the doctor say anything about the blood tests? Do we know if we're cleared for immunity for measles now?'

Julien shook his head as he got to his feet. 'No. Those results are not back and although he expects it won't be any later than tomorrow, they will be too late to help. A decision about my travelling has to be made today. This morning. So the show will have to be cancelled. There is no way around it and it is a disaster.'

'You would have been allowed to travel if you had proof of immunity?'

'Yes. And I expected it would have come well before

this or I would have taken the offer of being immunised again but it is too late now.'

'But other people who are immune are allowed to come into the house, aren't they? Like the nurse that we don't need?'

'It would seem so.' But Julien wasn't really listening. He had his mobile phone in his hand and was staring at the screen as he moved towards the door.

He was moving further away with every heartbeat and Alice could feel the distance growing. She should just let him go. If she couldn't see him, maybe she could clear her head—and her heart—of the nonsense that had taken root.

But her mouth opened before she could stop it.

'Why can't you film the show here?'

'Quoi?' Julien stopped in his tracks and turned to face Alice. 'What did you say?'

'It's just an idea…' And probably a stupid one judging by the look on Julien's face. 'This is a huge kitchen. It could be in a restaurant somewhere. How many people do you need to film a show?'

Julien shrugged. 'A skeleton crew might be only a cameraman and a sound person and someone to do the set-up and lighting. My producer perhaps.'

'What if you could find people that had proof they were immune to measles? Or if they had no chance of catching it? The kitchen has a back door, doesn't it? They wouldn't need to go into the house and I could keep Jacquot out of the way…'

The look of concentration on Julien's face was as fierce as he'd looked when he'd been cooking in the last couple of days.

'I don't know… There would be a lot of questions

that need to be asked. An impossible amount of orga-
nisation to do if it was possible...but...'

But there it was.

A glimmer of hope in what had been an insurmount-
able problem that Julien had been putting off making a
decision about because the repercussions were so huge.

Nobody in his management team would have thought
of this possibility because they had no idea what the
kitchens were like in the Laurent mansion but why
hadn't it occurred to him?

Yet again, the little Scottish pixie had waved a magic
wand.

Perhaps.

There were a dozen or more phone calls that needed
to be made and Julien didn't want to waste a single
minute.

An hour of calls being made and received stretched
into two hours and then three. Strings were pulled. Con-
cessions made. Permission granted. Plans put into action.

Julien took the stairs two at a time. He burst into the
nursery and Alice whirled around from where she had
been bent over the cot, tucking the baby in for a sleep.

The curtains had been pulled to dim the room but
a shaft of sunlight had found the gap between them
and Alice turned into it, her hair glowing like a halo
around her head.

Julien took a stride towards her. And then another.
He caught her shoulders in her hands and bent his head
to kiss her on one cheek and then the other. A perfectly
ordinary greeting between French friends.

'You are an angel,' he told Alice. 'You have solved

the problem of the show. *Merci, chérie. Merci beau-coup.*'

Maybe it was the way his heart had been captured by a baby smile that had made him remember his little sister with such a burst of love. Maybe it was the way Alice's eyes were shining with such joy at his exuber-ant appreciation of having the wheels of a solution al-ready turning. Or maybe this had just been something that had become inevitable ever since that first moment of being caught by those extraordinary eyes.

Instead of leaving the kissing within those polite parameters, Julien bestowed a third kiss. Directly on Alice's lips.

A brief kiss—but not nearly brief enough because now he knew what it was he'd been trying to avoid de-fining. That peculiar sensation he got when he looked into her eyes was nothing compared to the electric shock that came from touching her skin. Touching her hand had been manageable. Kissing her cheeks even. But the touch of his own lips on hers?

It was so powerful. This sense of…recognition.

Of finding something you hadn't had any idea you were even looking for.

It couldn't be real. It had started when he'd been in an emotionally exhausted state and right now he was high on the relief of a massive problem being on the way to resolution.

Julien needed to remember that this woman was the daughter of the man who'd been his enemy. Who had put the knife in and twisted it in those first awful mo-ments of trying to come to terms with his sister's death.

'*You'll never see her son. My son—unless it's over my dead body…*'

And she was the granddaughter of Madame Laurent—the matriarch of the family he despised who was just as determined to take his nephew out of his reach.

He was already on his way out of the room as the shock waves of his impulsive action faded into ever smaller ripples.

Julien needed to make sure he didn't touch Alice McMillan again, that was all. And that should be easy with the chaos that was about to descend on this house.

The kitchen was out of bounds for Alice as soon as the first of the convoy of trucks and vans began arriving later that day. The sound of voices and furniture scraping and even loud hammering could be heard coming from the kitchens as she wandered around upstairs with Jacquot in her arms, keeping him amused while he was awake.

Julien brought her a mug of coffee and a fresh baguette filled with ham and cheese as a late lunch.

'Filming will start very soon. There will be more than enough food for dinner later but it may be quite late. Will you be okay to wait?'

'I'll be fine. Good luck—I hope it goes well.'

Alice filled in the time easily to begin with. Jacquot was clearly feeling much better today and the smiles came more often. He even giggled when she squeaked one of his toys in his bath and Alice ignored how wet she was getting from the splashing as she leaned over to kiss him.

'You are adorable, Jacquot. I love you so much…'

It was a joy to feed him after his bath and to sing softly to him as he fell asleep and it was in the quiet moment before she put him into his cot for the night that the idea first occurred to Alice.

She could raise her little brother. She could give him a home and love him to bits, and if Julien could be persuaded that it was a good idea they could both be all the family this little boy could need. Surely the grandmother would agree that it was best? She was an old woman and it wasn't as if it was someone outside the family taking on Jacquot's care. She was his sister but she could be a mother as well.

The idea grew wings as she tucked Jacquot into his cot. Maybe Madame Laurent—and possibly Julien—would insist that Jacquot be brought up in France but Alice could manage that. She would learn this beautiful language. Julien could keep teaching her.

She could keep seeing her tiny brother's uncle. Become part of his life and maybe he would kiss her again...

Alice found she was touching her lips with her fingers as she stood there looking down at the sleeping baby. It took very little imagination to pretend that this feather-light touch was how it had felt when Julien's lips had touched her own.

Suddenly the time that needed to be filled became interminable. There was nothing Alice needed to do unless Jacquot woke again and, with the baby cam handset, she was free to wander anywhere in the house.

Downstairs...where Julien was...

She fought the desire for a while but it got the better of her and eventually Alice crept downstairs with the intention of maybe peeping through the kitchen door. As she got closer, the alluring aroma of roasting meat made her stomach growl so loudly she had to stop and press her hand against her belly, willing it to be silent.

Another few steps and she could hear Julien's voice. He was speaking in French and the tone was confident. Light. As if he was smiling as he spoke?

She had to see. The kitchen door wasn't completely shut and the space inside was brightly lit. Surely nobody would notice if she pushed it open a fraction more and watched for a few minutes?

No heads turned as she pushed the door open further and then Alice forgot to worry about interrupting what was going on. She barely recognised the space. It wasn't so much the professional lights and microphones on the end of long poles that looked as much out of place as the man with a huge camera balanced on his shoulder. It was more that the kitchen had been turned into a Christmas wonderland.

Long ropes of greenery threaded with fairy-lights hung in loops on the walls a little below ceiling height. A tall tree stood in the corner, with tiny lights sparkling amongst red and silver themed decorations, and a wreath of mistletoe hung from a central light fitting. The huge kitchen table had been pushed to one side of the room and decorated as if a family was about to sit down for Christmas dinner.

Fine white china, gleaming silverware and crystal glasses marked each place setting. Christmas crackers with red and silver paper lay beside each plate. There were places for platters of food to rest on wrought-iron trivets and any remaining space on the table was covered with candles in glass holders with wreaths of greenery studded with red berries. The flickering flames of the candles glinted on the silver cutlery and champagne flutes.

There was Christmas music playing softly in the background. Carols that were instantly familiar and beloved to Alice because they were being sung in English. Memories of Christmas dinners shared with her mother and grandmother brought a lump to her throat and Alice had to look away from the table.

To where Julien was standing behind the island bench, smiling into a camera as he spoke. His hair was neatly tied back in the usual ponytail but his face looked different. Had make-up emphasised those thick, dark eyebrows and lashes, the shadowing of his jaw and the beautiful olive tone of his skin or was it the white chef's tunic he was wearing, underneath a striped apron, with the neck unbuttoned and the sleeves rolled up? Maybe the difference was simply that he was smiling in a way Alice hadn't seen. A non-crooked way.

He looked happy. More than that—this was a man who was sharing something he was totally passionate about. The superb knife skills as he diced an onion and celery sticks and the way he could toss a frying pan full of tiny pieces without spilling a thing might be showmanship but they were as natural as breathing to Julien.

Such a contrast to how she'd seen him standing—bewildered—staring down at his howling nephew when he'd had no idea of what to do.

The sight of him now made her catch her breath but the memory of him holding Jacquot had caught her heart completely.

She might think she'd stayed in control but, in retrospect, that had probably been the moment she'd gone past the point of no return when it came to falling in love with Julien Dubois.

Or had that moment been when she'd caught his gaze when they'd both been under the spell of Jacquot's first smile?

Or maybe when he'd brushed that kiss on her lips this morning?

Trying to identify when it had happened was pointless. It was probably the combination that had filled that jar past bursting point. Alice could almost feel the pieces shattering and the emotions the jar had contained rushing out to fill every cell of her body.

It was creating a heat like nothing she had ever experienced.

Desire that was so much more than purely physical.

She'd never wanted the touch of any man the way she wanted Julien Dubois.

As if he felt the force of that desire, Julien suddenly glanced up from what he was doing and his words stopped in mid-sentence. His hands froze in mid-air just as he was about to add another handful of ingredients to the frying pan and for an insanely long moment it felt as if the world had stopped turning.

He knew exactly what she was thinking and…for that moment Alice could swear he had caught that desire like a match to a fuse and it was about to explode.

The moment was shattered by a bark of incredulous sound that came from a man holding a clipboard and the cameraman sounded like he'd uttered a succinct oath as he lowered his camera to turn and stare at Alice. Filming had clearly been interrupted and it was only then that Alice realised she wasn't peering around the edge of the door any more. When had she stepped right into the kitchen without noticing herself moving? In that delicious stretch of time when her bones had been melting and she'd been unable to think of anything but her longing to be with Julien?

What on earth had she done? Was it possible to pick up filming at the place they had stopped or would they have to film that whole demonstration of preparing whatever it was in the frying pan again? A peek in Julien's direction revealed that he was as angry as everybody else in this space. A girl holding the microphone and somebody else beneath a light stand had moved so they could join in the incredulous staring.

She didn't need to understand a word of French to know that more than one person was telling her to go away and not come back but it was Julien who made sure she understood by translating.

'Go away, Alice. Do not come near here again.'

It sounded more like *Do not come near me again*.

Mortified, Alice could feel the worst blush ever flood up from her neck into her face. Even her ears felt like they were burning.

'I'm sorry,' she said. 'I'm terribly sorry...'

She closed the kitchen door behind her as she fled.

CHAPTER EIGHT

HEADLONG FLIGHT DIDN'T leave any room for rational thought.

Instead of running upstairs to the safety of the nursery suite, Alice found she had gone in the direction of the first place she'd felt safe in this house.

The conservatory.

The room was dark but there were muted floodlights in the garden that illuminated the swimming pool and filtered in through glass walls to provide a hint of green on the dark shapes of the indoor trees and made the white furniture easy to find. It was the same couch she'd sat on when she had held Jacquot for the first time that Alice chose to curl up on to wait out the shame of the trouble she'd caused.

And the pain of the way Julien had dismissed her.

She'd been remembering her family the last time she'd come in here alone. The way her mother and grandmother had always been able to know if she wasn't telling the truth. Would they be able to see what felt stupidly like a broken heart right now?

He's French, her grandmother might have sniffed. *What did you expect?*

But her mother? Might she have given her comfort

because she would understand? Had André sent her away looking like he'd never wanted to see her again when she had already gifted her heart to him? When she had been carrying his baby in her belly?

She had no idea how long she sat there, failing to win a battle with tears of self-pity, but Alice finally pulled herself together.

It was ridiculous to feel like she had a broken heart. This wasn't a fairy-tale, this house was not a palace and Julien wasn't any kind of fantasy prince. He'd been forced to live in the same house as her with the rest of the world shut away and, yes, there had been moments where she could convince herself that something amazing was happening between them but he was back in his real life now and she had absolutely no part in it. It had been the promise of being able to do that that had led to him kissing her in the first place.

The worst part of it all was that he'd seen the desire that must have been glowing from her face like a neon sign. He'd been so shocked he hadn't been able to look away. It wasn't that he felt the same way at all. He'd been...appalled.

There was no point wallowing in it. It might be as soon as tomorrow that the results of those blood tests came through and that Jacquot would be deemed to be no danger to others. This quarantine would end. Jacquot would be taken into the care of his grandmother and she herself would have to go home and she would never set foot in this house again. The opportunity to find out anything about her father that she couldn't find printed in a magazine or revealed in a television interview would be lost for ever.

Her heart thumping, Alice got to her feet and went

to the room that Julien had taken her to when she had first arrived. Flickering screens from the security system showed her where she could turn on a desk lamp rather than the main lights of the room. Even in the soft light the shards of glass still clinging to the oversized portrait of her father was a shocking reminder of that violent action of Julien's and the pent-up grief and hatred it had revealed, but Alice pushed any thoughts of him away. She was here in the hope of finding something that might let her believe her father hadn't been a man worthy of that kind of hatred. Maybe something she could keep to give Jacquot in years to come.

There were stacks of magazines with pictures of André Laurent on their covers. Silver trophies and framed photographs of André with people that Alice could recognise as being famous. Film stars and someone she thought had been a French president. Moving behind the desk, she found a smaller photograph in a heart-shaped silver frame. A much older-looking André with his arms around the waist of a very beautiful, young, dark-haired woman who had to be Julien's sister.

Alice picked up the image and studied it. They were looking at each other rather than the camera and it was impossible not to catch the impression that they were very much in love. It was a picture of a private moment and it made Alice catch her breath, wishing that the photo of *her* parents had been this revealing.

It was a double frame that could be closed and in the other side was a photo of a baby with tufts of dark hair. Jacquot. Had it been taken on the day he'd been born? When André had lost the mother of the only child he'd known he had? It didn't matter. What did matter was that it showed how important his brand-new family had been to André and it was something that Jacquot would treasure when he was old enough to understand. Alice set the frame carefully to one side of the desk.

She would come and get it when she was leaving the house and then somehow, some time she would find a way to give it to her little brother.

She sat there for a long moment and then idly began opening desk drawers. Maybe she was hoping she might find cards that had been kept with messages of love in them but there seemed to be only stationery items like embossed paper and pens. A lower drawer had a business diary and appointment cards. Plane tickets to Geneva had been booked for Christmas Eve and there were passports with the tickets…two of them. One had a shiny, unmarked cover and had been issued only last week—a baby's first official document.

Alice closed the drawer slowly. Had André been planning a family Christmas to help him get through the grief of this first celebration without his wife? Would Madame Laurent be struggling with her own sadness and that was why she was so eager to collect Jacquot? It could be that she might welcome her as well.

Movement from the screens caught her eye and she watched as the headlights of cars and vans lit up the driveway and went out the gates. The road outside looked empty. Had the media finally given up on getting a story or pictures? It was another clue that normal life would be resumed in the near future but it felt curiously as if something important was slipping through her fingers.

The baby cam monitor showed Jacquot to be sleeping peacefully and maybe it was time for Alice to follow his example. The delicious smell of the Christmas feast that had been prepared in the kitchens should have been just as enticing when Alice reached the foyer but, despite her earlier hunger, her appetite was nothing like it had been when she had come downstairs earlier.

And when she saw who was emerging from the interior kitchen door, it vanished completely.

Julien had shed the striped apron. He'd unbuttoned the white tunic completely so that it hung open and most of his chest was bare. He was wearing faded denim jeans that had been hidden by the apron and maybe he'd kicked his shoes off because his feet were also bare.

And he'd taken the fastening off his ponytail. This was the first time Alice had seen him with his hair loose and she'd been right about how it framed and softened his face and brushed his shoulders in soft waves. It took away that professionally polished look and gave him an almost disreputable edge. A muted but irresistible hint of 'bad boy'.

And then she noticed how tired he looked.

And how his face changed when he saw her.

Her mouth went very dry. 'I'm so sorry, Julien,' she said quietly. 'I hope I didn't disrupt the filming too much.'

He flicked his hand. 'It was of no matter. We redid that part when I could concentrate again. It is finished now and only needs editing.' He was giving her an intense look that Alice couldn't interpret.

'I have never lost my focus like that,' he said, walking slowly towards her. 'What is it about you that can do that to me, Alice McMillan?'

'I... I...' *Have absolutely no idea*, she wanted to say. *Maybe it's the same thing that you do to me...*

Her words had evaporated and she didn't need them anyway because Julien hadn't stopped moving and now he was standing right in front of her. As close as he'd been standing that first night when he'd taken the sample from the inside of her cheek.

Once again, she was aware that she had an impossibly gorgeous man standing close enough to kiss her but this time it wasn't embarrassing. This time it was the most amazing moment of her life because she knew that that was exactly what *was* going to happen.

And it wasn't going to be an afterthought to a friendly kiss on both cheeks. Oh, no... The way Julien's hand slid behind her neck and cradled the back of her head meant that this was going to be a *real* kiss...

Except it wasn't. It was so far away from anything Alice had ever experienced that it was a fairy-tale kiss from a handsome prince. A prince who sensed that her bones were melting and scooped her into his arms and held her against his bare chest as he carried her upstairs and into a room well away from the nursery. It must have been the one he'd chosen on the first night here because it had the black clothes he'd been wearing carelessly thrown over the back of a chair.

The huge four-poster bed fitted right into this fantasy and, if Alice had had any qualms about whether she should let this go any further with a man she'd only met days ago, they vanished the moment Julien laid her on that bed and his lips covered hers again. Had he sensed a heartbeat of indecision? The gentle touch of lips suggested exactly that and the moment Alice knew she was completely lost to this overwhelming desire was the moment that gentleness got edged out by an increasingly fierce passion.

The buttons on her shirt popped open and then his lips were on the swell of her breasts and Julien was telling her how beautiful she was. How irresistible. That he was saying it in French didn't matter. In fact, there could be no other language that could make words like this so compelling. So believable...

How on earth had he been able to focus enough to finish filming that show when all he'd wanted to do had been this from the moment he'd seen her standing in the doorway, looking at him the way she had?

And he wasn't disappointed. *Au contraire*, he might have had a great deal of experience in lovemaking but it had never been this good. Because he'd never touched or been touched by a Scottish pixie with magic in her eyes. And in her hands. And in the soft sounds she made as she responded to every move he made. The cry she couldn't stifle when he took them both over the edge and into paradise...

She stayed in his arms as he waited for his heart rate and breathing to get back to within normal parameters, her head snuggled in the dip between his shoulder and his heart as if the space had been created for just that purpose.

The silence could have been awkward—as these moments usually were—but it was far from that. It was good. Too good because he felt like he'd like to stay like this for ever, and that meant the moment had to be broken before he had time to think about it any longer.

'*C'etait bien*?' he asked softly. 'It was good?'

'Oh...*oui*...' He could feel the curve of her lips against his chest. '*Je l'aime.*'

It felt like the chuckle came from a place he'd forgotten existed. Amusement that was a mix of pride and a deep fondness and possibly a twinge of sadness as well. The only person in his life who had ever made him feel something like that had been Colette—when she'd been young and trying to do something grown up but could only manage cute. Another silence fell, which made him wonder if Alice was trying to think of something else she could say in his language. Instead, the silence was broken by the loud growl of her stomach, which made him smile again.

'You are hungry, *chérie*. I happen to know where there is a Christmas dinner that will still be warm. *Est-ce que tu voudrais diner avec moi?*'

Some of the food had been left in one of the massive ovens to stay warm.

Apparently more than one version of things had been cooked because the filming had needed different stages of the cooking process within a short time period. Most of it was stored in the cold room now and Julien warned Alice that she might be eating Christmas dinner more than once.

Alice sat at the end of the table with a flute of champagne in her hand and watched as Julien placed platter after platter of amazing-looking food in the spaces between the dozens of flickering candles.

A turkey and a jug of aromatic gravy with a curl of steam above it. Wedges of roasted pumpkin and crispy, browned potatoes. Sweet glazed carrots and Brussels sprouts. Bread sauce.

'Oh…you did pigs in blankets. My absolute favourite.' Alice picked up one of the tiny sausages wrapped in bacon and baked until crisp. 'Oh, yum. How do you say "yum" in French?'

Julien had a carving knife in one hand and a sharpening steel in the other. '*Miam-miam*,' he told her.

He'd just put his faded jeans and his black shirt on before they'd left his bedroom and the shirt was only buttoned halfway up but it didn't matter that he wasn't wearing his white tunic or even that he hadn't tied back his hair again once he began sharpening that knife. He was every inch the professional chef and this had to be the sexiest thing Alice had ever seen a man doing.

Her pig in its blanket remained barely tasted and her champagne was forgotten. The pleasure Alice was getting from simply watching Julien was as much as she could cope with because it took far more than just her eyes. Her whole body was watching and remembering every touch he had given her. Every stroke and every kiss and—if she never experienced it again—she would never forget this blissful afterglow if she lived to be a hundred and two.

With the succulent meat carved and served, Julien piled their plates with a sample of everything else he had cooked for his traditional British Christmas dinner.

Alice wondered what the other chef had done for his French version but she didn't want the conversation to turn professional. She wanted to bask in this delicious glow for a little longer. To talk about things that mattered only to themselves.

But she didn't want to say too much either. Whatever was happening here was new and fragile and there was a danger of breaking it with the pressure of words that were too heavy or smothering it with a layer of too much emotion. Maybe talking about food was safer.

'This is the best Christmas dinner I've ever tasted,' she told him. 'As much as I adored my mum and my gran, they could never cook like this. The turkey was always dry.'

'Putting butter under the skin makes a difference. This is how I do it in my restaurant.'

'Are you open on Christmas Day?'

'No. But we serve Christmas meals for two or even three weeks of December. By the time Christmas Day comes, the last thing I want to eat is a goose. Or a turkey.'

'So what do you cook to celebrate Christmas Day?'

Julien shrugged. 'It's not something I celebrate. It means nothing to me other than a day to be alone and rest.'

Alice stopped eating. So there was no significant other in his life who he would spend a special day with? It should be a relief to know that but, instead, it was almost frightening. Was Julien a lone wolf? Was he alone by a choice that was unlikely to change? She stared at her half-eaten meal but, however delicious it was, she had no inclination to eat anything more.

'What about when you were a child?'

Julien followed her example and put down his fork, picking up his glass instead. 'Celebrations were something to be feared when I was a child.'

There was nothing Alice could find to say in response. She could only look at Julien's face in the soft light of the candles and hold her breath until the ache in her chest eased a little.

Julien drained his glass of champagne and reached for one of the bottles of wine on the table. The ruby-red liquid filled the crystal glass and he offered it to Alice but she shook her head, remaining silent as he closed his eyes and took a long sip of his wine. And then another. And then he opened his eyes again but kept his gaze on the glass in his hand as he began talking quietly.

'My father walked out on us when I was five years old. He'd married my mother because she was pregnant but he told us many times that he'd never wanted a child. When it became apparent that another child was on the way, it was too much and he left.'

'Oh, *Julien*…'

Alice's heart ached for that little boy who'd known he hadn't been wanted. Who had probably believed that it was his fault that his father had abandoned them.

'My mother couldn't cope alone so she married again as soon as she could. She chose an angry man who could use words as well as his fists as weapons and the worst times were always when he drank too much. Celebrations like birthdays and especially Christmas were the days he always drank too much.'

As if the reminder disgusted him, Julien put his glass down and pushed it away. 'It's too easy to hurt a child,' he murmured. 'That's why I will never have one of my own.'

The ache around Alice's heart took on a hollow edge as if it was surrounded by a bottomless pit. 'But you have Jacquot now. You are his guardian…'

'Which means I have to ensure that he is safe and cared for. I can't bring up a child. I work long hours in my restaurant. I have to travel a lot for my television work and my recipe books. Other time is taken up with production and editing. It would be impossible to live with a baby.'

'But he has to be *loved*,' Alice whispered. 'That's just

as important as being safe and cared for. Maybe *more* important.' She'd seen how much it had meant to him that Colette's precious rabbit toy had been bequeathed to her baby. And the way Julien had looked when Jacquot had smiled at them both. 'You said he looks like Colette and…and I know you loved your sister…'

He must have loved her very much to have dropped out of school to protect her from their stepfather.

'How old were you when your mother died?' Alice asked, when Julien said nothing.

'Fifteen.'

'And Colette was…?'

'Ten. A child.'

He hadn't been much more than a child himself. 'And you were allowed to be Colette's guardian when you were so young?'

'I would have lied about my age if anyone had asked but it turned out there was nobody who cared enough to find out.'

'That must have been *so* hard…'

Julien picked up one of the pigs in blankets from his plate with his fingers and bit into it, tilting his head to shrug off her comment.

'I worked,' he said a moment later. 'First one job and then two. Even three at one time. I had found a cheap apartment for us. Colette went to school and she looked after herself after school. She knew it was the only way we could stay together. We were the only family we each had. We had to help one another.' He looked at the food in his hand and then put it down, as though his appetite had vanished.

'It only worked because she was old enough to do

that,' he added. 'I couldn't have cared for a baby then. I couldn't now.'

'You *could*…' Alice whispered. 'If you wanted to.' *If I helped you…*

But her offer remained unspoken because Julien had raised his hand as if warning her off.

'I *don't* want to. I've been down that path before. Tried to protect someone and keep them safe and…and I did not do it well enough… *C'est tout.*'

Alice could hear the pain in his words. He had loved his sister so much. She didn't understand why he was taking so much blame for her death but maybe it was because it was still so recent. Grief was not helpful to rational thinking, was it?

She spoke quietly into the silence.

'She knew how amazing it was—what you did for her. That's why she made you the guardian of her child.'

Julien gave that half-shrug. This wasn't something he really wanted to analyse. 'So she said. I think I told you that she came to see me just before her baby was due to be born. She wanted to give me the legal document about the guardianship. It was the first time I'd seen her in more than a year. Since she'd married André. A marriage that I'd tried to stop.'

'Why?'

'Because he was far too old for her. And he was well known for his excesses. Fast cars. Beautiful women. Too much alcohol…'

So this was why he blamed himself? Because he hadn't protected her from a relationship that had led to a baby's birth that had proved fatal? It wasn't logical. It wasn't even acceptable. 'But they loved each other.'

'Pfff…' The sound was as dismissive as when Julien had made it in response to her suggesting that her mother had been in love with André.

Julien had been both a brother and a parent to his sister and he knew about that kind of protective love, but had anyone ever protected *him*? Did he even realise it could be safe, given that his parents had failed him and even his beloved sister had walked away from his life when he'd thought he was still protecting her? Had he ever allowed himself to be *in* love? Or *felt* truly loved by someone?

It would seem not.

What on earth made her think she had any chance of breaking through a barrier like that?

It would need a miracle.

But miracles did happen sometimes, didn't they? And what better time of year to find one than at Christmas?

There was a clock ticking, though, and it wasn't just counting down the hours until Christmas Day.

And miracles needed to be planted to have any hope of growing.

Alice took a deep breath.

'If you're Jacquot's guardian, you will get to choose who can raise him, won't you?'

'That's my hope. And if it's away from the Laurent family I will still be able to visit him. To watch over him as he grows up and help when or if I'm needed.'

'He needs to be with someone who loves him,' Alice said again. 'I love him. He's my brother. Choose me, Julien.'

He met her gaze and Alice's heart skipped a beat.

But then, after a long moment, he looked away.

'*Non. C'est impossible.*'

CHAPTER NINE

THOSE EYES...

He would never forget how they looked in this moment. He had crushed something beautiful. Naïve perhaps but something so genuine that it felt like he was hurting a child by not protecting it from the harshness of reality.

'*Je suis vraiment désolé, chérie...* I am truly sorry...'

He touched her face as he spoke and the way she tilted her head to press her cheek against his fingers was heart-breaking.

He had to take his hand away before he gave in to the urge to hold her in his arms and start kissing her. Promising her things that it would be foolish to even consider. He used his hand to massage his own temples as he let his breath out in a sigh.

'You are single, yes? You don't have a boyfriend or fiancé?'

The blush was a display of intense emotion he was getting used to from Alice. That flash of pain that could also be anger made him realise how stupid the question was. She had just given him more in bed than any woman ever had. And this was Alice. She did not have a deceitful bone in her body. She would never cheat on any man.

'You work as a teacher. You love your work?'

'Yes, but—'

'But you would sacrifice your lifestyle in order to care for a child?'

'Isn't that what you did for your sister?'

Julien shook off what sounded like admiration. He had only done what he'd had to do. And he hadn't done it well enough, anyway.

'You would not be viewed as a suitable guardian to raise a baby,' he said. 'And you would want to take him out of the country.'

'Not necessarily.'

'You have a house in Scotland, yes?'

'Yes…'

'Jacquot is French. The last member of what has been a very powerful family in France. His father has always been adored as a national icon.'

'But didn't you say that Madame Laurent lives in Geneva?'

'The border between France and Geneva is merely a formality for many French people. Besides, it is only one of her houses. I understand she has a luxury apartment in Cannes and she may choose to live here in *this* house, which I believe was the family home when André was a child himself.'

A house they both knew was a mausoleum totally unsuited to raising a child.

'I could live in France.' There was determination in those liquid brown eyes now. Passion even. 'I'm half-French.'

'That would be difficult. You don't speak our language.'

Her chin lifted. 'I'm learning.'

She was. The shy echo of her words when he'd asked whether their lovemaking had been good—*Je l'aime*—gave him an odd tightness in his chest that made it hard to draw in a new breath.

'Yvonne Laurent is a powerful woman who is used to getting her own way. I don't even know if I can win what I want to get from her. It may be up to the courts to decide whether the relationship of an uncle is more important than that of a grandmother.'

'I'm his sister...'

'A half-sister. And that would probably have to be endorsed by a court as well. The French legal system can be very slow. Especially if someone has the money to delay proceedings. Cases can drag on for months. Years even, and that would not be a good thing for a child. Small children can understand more than you might think...'

Like he had when he'd started protecting Colette from the moment she'd been born? So she would never know that it was also her fault that their father had gone?

He could see the empathy in her eyes now. He shouldn't have told her so much about his childhood. She could read between lines, couldn't she? She knew how bad it had been and she wanted to make it better somehow.

To make him feel loved?

The pull was so powerful it was painful but he couldn't give in to it. There was no room in his life for someone to be that close. No room in a heart that was too scarred to love and lose again.

'But you are going to fight,' Alice said softly. 'To get what you want. Custody of Jacquot?'

'No.' Julien shook his head. That would mean he would become a parent again. He would have the kind of responsibility he had already proved with his sister that he could not honour well enough. 'I simply want regular access. For the boy to know I am his mother's brother and that I will help him in whatever way he needs as he grows up.'

'Maybe I could have access, too?'

He had to admire her optimism. The hope she could find in every dark corner. Like the way she had seen something good in an ancient toy that was waiting patiently to be of importance one day.

'Maybe fighting isn't the way to win,' Alice said slowly. 'This woman doesn't know that she is my grandmother. If Jacquot is so important to her, it could be that she might listen to her other grandchild. If I don't threaten her, maybe I can persuade her.'

'*Peut-être.*' Alice McMillan could probably persuade anybody if she looked at them like that. He was in danger of being persuaded that he could gift his heart to someone again and he knew that wasn't true. He had found the safe place to be years ago. Away from someone who would see him as a husband and father.

He needed to break the spell that was being woven around him here, in the light of all these romantic candles. In a kitchen that was a room that would always feel like home, no matter where he was. In a Christmas setting that was always redolent with the idea of family...

'Have you had enough to eat? There is a plum pudding with brandy sauce. And custard. Would you like to taste it?'

'*Peut-être*,' Alice enunciated again, carefully. And then she smiled at him. 'Actually, yes, please. I would love to.'

It was good to move. To take the plates of their unfinished first course away and make a clear space to start again. To move on.

A little showmanship with the pudding came as naturally as breathing these days and it was comforting, too, because it was a demonstration of who he was. What his life was about.

He put the pudding on its platter in front of Alice and moved a candle closer. He held a silver ladle full of brandy over the flame of the candle to warm it and then tipped it just enough to catch the flame and ignite. He never got tired of the magic of that blue flame and the way it flowed so dramatically over the curve of the pudding as he slowly poured it.

'*Oh…*' Alice's gasp of appreciation was another echo of their time in his bed and Julien couldn't dampen a hunger that had nothing to do with food.

He stayed quiet as he served their dessert but Alice had something to say.

'It won't be long, will it? Until…until our quarantine is over.'

'No. I'm hoping the test results will come through tomorrow. I hope also that they are good because I have to go to Paris the next day. It's Christmas Eve and I need to be present on the live broadcast of the show if possible. To appear by a remote connection would not be good enough.'

'Hmm…' Alice paused, a spoonful of pudding halfway to her lips. 'We only have a short time together, then...'

'This is true.' He couldn't tell her that her words gave him a sinking feeling, as if a huge stone had lodged in his gut. To imagine there could be any time together after this was as impossible as the notion of her becoming the guardian for her little brother.

Alice's head was bent, her gaze on her spoon. And then she peeped up through a thick tangle of dark lashes with a look that would have rendered any red-blooded male completely helpless. 'We should make the most of it, then...'

Julien took the spoon gently from her fingers. He cupped her chin and raised it so that he could kiss her with equal gentleness.

'Je suis d'accord. Absolument.'

It couldn't do any real harm, could it? To enjoy the company of such an intriguing woman? At least, this time, he wouldn't have to make the decision to walk away—the way he always did when a woman was getting too close. It was going to happen naturally so why not make the most of every moment they had left? It might only be a matter of hours.

Starting with what was left of this already remarkable night. With luck, Jacquot was well enough to sleep in his own bed right through until morning as long as he was fed and clean and, thanks to the baby monitor, there was no need for Alice to return to *her* own bed.

He was more than happy to share his.

It was the first time little Jacquot Laurent had slept through the night.

It was also the first time he had woken and not immediately cried for attention. Instead, the sounds that came through the monitor handset were soft chirrups and coos, as if the baby was experimenting with talking to himself.

Alice awoke to the sounds with a smile already curving her lips. And then she realised she was still snuggled against Julien's bare chest with his arm around her and his fingers carelessly draped across her breast and the smile seemed to turn inwards.

She had never felt contentment like this. A weariness that felt blissful because of what had been experienced instead of sleep. Alice tilted her head so that she could see Julien's face. Relaxed in slumber, he had lost the solemn air and intensity she had grown accustomed to. A tress of that surprisingly soft hair had caught on his lashes and lay across his cheek and lips. Alice reached up and gently brushed it back into place. Maybe her grandmother would have disapproved of Julien's hairstyle but Alice was never going to forget the thrilling tickle of that hair on her skin when Julien had been kissing and tasting her body. Her neck…her breasts… her belly…and, *oh*…

A pair of gorgeous hazel eyes were on her face and Alice knew she was going to blush so she ducked her head.

'Jacquot is awake. Listen…'

Julien also smiled. 'He sounds happy.'

'He must be hungry. I need to go to him.'

'Of course. And I should go and do something with that disaster of a kitchen. Shall I bring you some coffee before breakfast?'

'Please…' Alice rolled away but Julien's arm tightened around her and pulled her back.

'You have forgotten something, *chérie*.'

'Oh? What?'

'This…' Julien kissed her. A brief caress and then a more thorough one. 'It is a French custom, the morning kiss…'

'Mmm…' If it hadn't been for a more demanding cry coming from the monitor, the morning kiss would no doubt have become much more than that.

Was it too much to hope that they could have one more night together? Alice wondered as she hastily pulled on her clothes and made her way to the nursery. This felt like the start of something new. Something wonderful. Something that was too good to be true?

She heard the phone ringing as she had Jacquot in his bath, squeaking the rubber duck to make him smile and kick his feet. Was it nine a.m. already? The doctor was as reliable as an alarm clock. She had her little brother dressed and ready for his new day by the time Julien came to the nursery, carrying a steaming mug of delicious-smelling coffee. A wide grin appeared on the baby's face.

'He knows you,' Alice said. 'Here…he needs a cuddle from his uncle.' She took the mug of coffee from his hand and eased the bundle of baby into Julien's arms. Neither of them made any protest about the contact and Alice beamed at them both before taking her first sip of coffee.

This was progress. If Julien could bond with Jacquot as much as she had, they could join forces to make sure this baby had what he needed so badly—people to love him to bits.

'Was it the doctor who rang? Did you tell him how happy Jacquot sounded this morning?'

'It was and I did. He said that there doesn't need to be any further restriction to keeping him in the house if he's well enough to go out.'

'Oh…' That meant that he could be taken out, didn't it? Taken away…

'He also said that the results of our blood tests are finally back. We are both immune to measles. There are no further restrictions on either of us either. I have already booked an early flight to Paris tomorrow morning. And…'

Alice held her breath. Julien was looking down at the baby in his arms, who must have been enjoying the sound of his voice as much as she was because he smiled again, so energetically it made his whole little body wiggle. And Julien was smiling back but then he looked up at Alice and his smile faded.

'And Madame Laurent is driving down from Geneva this afternoon to make arrangements. She intends to take Jacquot back to her home tonight.'

The lump in Alice's throat was too big to swallow. 'What time is she due to arrive?'

'I'm not sure. Early this evening, I expect.' Julien's face was as sombre as the first time she'd met him but there was a depth of softness there that was very new. 'I'm sorry, *chérie*…there seems to be nothing I can do to stop this. Nothing I can do to help you.'

Alice looked away as she blinked back tears but all she could think about was the man standing there, holding the small baby. They were both the people she now cared about more than anyone else in her world.

And she had less than a day to be with them both. She pulled in a shaky breath.

'There is one thing you could do.'

'What is that? I have a few urgent matters I must attend to first, like discussing how to handle this with my solicitor, but I will have time this afternoon. If I can do this thing for you, I promise you I will.'

Alice turned back. 'I will have to leave France tomorrow and I feel like I haven't seen nearly enough. Could you take me somewhere that I will remember? Maybe somewhere...' her voice became quieter, hopeful '...that is special to you?'

She saw a flicker of doubt in his eyes. Was he reluctant to let her any further into his life?

'We would have to take the little one with us.'

Alice nodded. 'I know where things are. Like the nappy bag and a pram. Or there's a front pack. I can make up a bottle of formula that any café could warm for us.' She bit her lip. 'Have those journalists gone? You don't get harassed in public for being famous, do you?'

'I know how to deal with that.' His expression changed. A decision had been made and there was a hint of a smile on his lips. 'And I think I know where I can take you. Somewhere special enough for your last day in France. I will attend to what I must do and you get yourself and Jacquot ready.'

Alice took the baby from his arms and smiled up at him. 'Will I like it?'

'You will love it.' He turned to leave the nursery.

'You have forgotten something, Julien.'

'Oh...?'

Alice stood on tiptoe, leaning over the baby to kiss him. 'It's a Scottish custom,' she said softly. 'The goodbye kiss...'

It was even better than the kiss, she decided moments later—the way she'd made him smile.

* * *

Some time out to clear his head was the best thing he could do for this afternoon. After a string of telephone conversations between himself, his solicitor and Madame Laurent's solicitor, it had been agreed that a brief family meeting might be the best first step. Nothing official, such as taking Jacquot away from the house, would happen before tomorrow.

This was the opportunity Julien had requested for the key players to discuss the situation without outside input and legal arguments to inflame tempers. Alice's words had stayed in his mind—that perhaps persuasion might be more effective than threats. He had called for a temporary truce and, amazingly, Madame Laurent had agreed. The only thing she didn't know was that there were now three key players rather than two. And that the third one was a granddaughter she didn't know existed.

Alice could either be an ace up his sleeve or be seen as a threat that could close doors for ever. It was impossible to know which way the dice might roll but Julien was trying to channel some of Alice's optimism. It might help all of them.

Being recognised was not usually a problem and the media contingent outside the gates had given up and gone elsewhere days ago but Julien did need to be careful this time. He was breaching the court order that the Laurent family solicitors had arrived with on the day of the funeral to prevent him taking his nephew anywhere, and there was still the problem of Alice's connection to the family becoming public before Yvonne Laurent had time to accept the bombshell. It might have been easier to stay discreetly in the house for one more day but he'd made a promise and he was not about to dishonour that.

So he wore a black fisherman-style pullover under a coat with its collar turned up and hid his hair beneath a black woollen beanie that he wore low on his forehead because the day was too overcast to warrant sunglasses. Fortunately the chances of being recognised were low anyway, because the last thing anybody would expect would be to see him out with a woman who had a baby in a front pack, well bundled up for any winter chill with tiny arms and legs poking out of the contraption like a miniature snowman.

It hadn't been hard to think of an appropriate place to take Alice to give her a taste of France at Christmastime. He and Colette had been taken there once, as children, and it was probably the happiest memory of his entire childhood.

It was a bonus that the clouds were thick and dark enough to make it seem much later in the day than early afternoon because it made the Christmas lights of Nice's *marché de Noël* almost as bright as they would be at night. The enormous pine trees along the Promenade du Paillon were thickly dusted with artificial snow as they walked through the park to the Place Massena, and as they got closer they could see that the ice-skating rink was full of families out with their children and the giant Ferris wheel was turning. The massive Christmas trees were sparkling and there were crowds of shoppers at the stalls selling hand-crafted gifts and food and mulled wine.

And Alice looked as excited by it all as Colette had been when she'd still been a small child of about seven or eight. Those brown eyes that had captured him from the moment he'd seen them produce tears in André's office that first day were shining with joy now and Julien felt his chest expand with his own pleasure in having chosen this experience as his gift for her last day here.

That she was here with her baby brother in her arms made it even more special.

'Stand here, so that the Ferris wheel and the Christmas trees are behind you. I will take a photo for you.'

He would keep a copy of that photograph himself. If the sadness from the past tried to suck him back, he would be able to look at that smile and remember his Scottish pixie, who could always find something to celebrate.

He was missing Alice already. How stupid was that?

Would she miss him? Would she remember this time with him? Maybe a memento would help. A gift from one of the stalls perhaps?

Alice had turned to watch the Ferris wheel. Or was she watching the people on the skating rink? It was a colourful scene. There were coloured lights around the edges of the rink and overhead. Many people were dressed in Christmas shades of bright red and green and most of them were wearing Santa hats or reindeer horns. The people closest to them right now were a man and a woman who were holding the mittened hands of a small boy as he wobbled on his skates between them. A family, enjoying a Christmas outing. If she could have what she was wishing for, Julien thought, that could be Alice in a few years' time, with the father figure she chose to share her life with as she raised her baby brother.

The thought sat uneasily. He didn't want to imagine Alice with another man but it was inevitable, wasn't it? What man could resist those eyes? That spirit of optimism or that generosity as a lover? And it was no more than she deserved—to find that man and have babies of her own to cherish. He had no right to feel the way he did. Resentful almost?

Julien shook off the unwelcome train of his thoughts. He was here to give Alice a happy memory of France. He went to take her hand so that he could lead her towards the stalls and find a gift but her hands were busy, adjusting the straps of the front pack.

'Is it heavy? Would you like me to take him for a while?'

There was surprise in her eyes. And then something he couldn't identify but it looked curiously like satisfaction.

'Yes, please,' she said. '*Merci beaucoup*, Julien.'

It felt completely natural to take Julien's hand, once the front pack was securely in place and his hands were free. There was so much to look at as they wove their way slowly through the crowds, admiring the goods on offer at the stalls, but Alice kept looking sideways.

Was there anything more appealing than the sight of a tall, broad-shouldered man with a tiny baby on his chest?

And when you loved them both, was there anything that could make you feel more like your heart was so full it might simply break from joy?

She needed to find something else to look at before that joy escaped as tears.

'Oh, look…those hats have sparkles. Aren't they pretty?'

They were only woollen hats but they had large diamantes glued all over them and soft, furry pompoms on the top.

'Would you like one?' There was a furrow just visible under Julien's hat. 'I hadn't noticed that you didn't have a hat. Are your ears cold?'

'No, but I would love a hat anyway.' As much as she loved the concern in his voice and the idea that he cared if her ears were cold or not. 'The sparkle would always remind me of where it came from and when.'

'What colour would you like?'

'Black.' There was no hesitation on Alice's part. It would match Julien's hat but with a bonus. 'It makes the sparkles stand out more.'

Julien spoke to the woman running the stall and money changed hands. Instead of having the hat put into a bag, he put it on Alice's head, tucking her hair back from her face. Then he touched her nose with his finger.

'*Très mignon*,' he pronounced. 'Very cute. *Tout comme tu.*'

The stall owner said something then and Alice saw the warmth in his eyes vanish.

She nudged Julien. 'What did she say?'

He shook his head, turning away. Confused, Alice glanced back at the woman. Her confusion was being reflected back at her and the woman raised her hands in a puzzled gesture.

'I say only that he has a beautiful wife and the most beautiful baby in the world.'

Oh... That would have been a shock to a man who was a lone wolf and had decided long ago that he would never have a child of his own. No wonder the pleasure of this outing began to fade. When Jacquot finally woke a short time later and let them know he was hungry and needed changing, it was obvious that Julien was relieved to hand the baby back to Alice.

And the spell was broken. Even the lights and music

and the crowd of happy people couldn't fix what had been broken and it was Alice's turn to feel relieved when Julien suggested it was time to go back to the house.

They drove back in Julien's car in silence and he used a remote to open those extraordinarily ornate gates that had been Alice's first glimpse of this property.

It was only the second time she had passed through these gates into her father's estate. The first had been nearly a week ago but it felt like for ever because of how it had changed her life.

It felt like yesterday, too, because that time was etched into her memory for ever. She'd been so hopeful on her arrival but nervous as well. There'd been the media crowd to get through, helicopters hovering overhead and a grim man who'd met her at the door.

How different things were now. The media had given up and gone. There were no helicopters and she'd seen through the grimness that Julien had been wearing like a cloak to cover the vulnerability of a man who was capable of loving greatly but only felt safe to pour that passion into his work.

A man she had utterly fallen in love with.

But she felt far more nervous than she had that first time she'd been escorted up this driveway because there was a car parked on the curve of the driveway where it looped past the front doors to the mansion. A huge, gleaming black car. The kind that a very wealthy woman might be chauffeured to her desired destination in. The chauffeur was still sitting in the car but the back seat was empty.

Madame Laurent had clearly arrived and must have had a key to her son's house. She was waiting for them inside.

The nerves were there because Alice knew that this perfect day was almost over. That—very soon—she might have to say goodbye to both the man and baby she loved so much.

But the woman waiting for them was also the grandmother she had never met.

There was still a glimmer of hope.

CHAPTER TEN

YVONNE LAURENT WAS a perfect example of aristocratic elegance.

A tall, slim woman with beautifully coiffed silver hair and expertly applied make-up, she was wearing a twin set and pearls beneath the jacket and skirt of a tailored suit.

Alice was still wearing her forest-green jumper over one of the two shirts she'd been washing out every day and the jeans that were probably overdue for a wash were tucked into boots that had been getting a little more scuffed every day. And she had a silly hat with a pompom and sparkles on her head.

The visitor awaiting their arrival in the foyer barely gave her—or Jacquot—a second glance.

'*Bonjour*, Julien.' Her voice was as measured and controlled as her appearance but Alice understood nothing more than the greeting as a rapid conversation followed the polite kissing on each cheek. Julien ushered the older woman into the drawing room opposite the entrance to the grand salon and then turned back to Alice.

'She thinks you're a nanny,' he said in a low voice. 'I will explain why you are really here but it may be best if you take the little one up to the nursery in the meantime.'

Her nod of acquiescence was stiff. She could excuse the lack of interest in someone thought to be no more than hired help but she had this woman's grandchild cuddled against her chest and Madame Laurent had made no effort to try and see the baby's face. And this was supposed to be her precious grandchild that she was determined to care for?

The hope that she might welcome an adult grand-daughter was evaporating. It was a relief to go upstairs. To change Jacquot and hold him in her arms while she fed him his bottle. To sing to him softly as she tucked him into his cot for what was possibly going to be the last time.

To wait. It felt like her future was lying in the hands of others but there was nothing she could do but wait.

And hope...

'Madame Laurent... I'm sorry that it has taken circum-stances like this to meet you.'

She'd been at Colette's funeral, of course, but she'd been by André's side and Julien had kept his distance. He hadn't been welcome. At his own *sister's* funeral...

He couldn't afford to let any bitterness loose right now, however. And they were both dealing with the grief of losing a loved one. Surely that gave them a connection that would allow persuasion rather than threats—as Alice had suggested?

'I realise that this is a difficult time for you,' he said quietly. 'I am truly sorry for your loss, *madame.*'

The pale blue eyes he was looking into filled with tears. Yvonne Laurent lowered herself onto the over-

stuffed cushion of a small couch and opened her handbag to extract an embroidered handkerchief that she
pressed to a corner of one eye and then the other. Finally, she spoke.

'My grandson is the only family I have left in the
world.'

'Indeed.' Julien sat on the edge of another couch,
facing her. This certainly wasn't the time to tell her that
she was wrong. That she actually had another grandchild.

'It is the same for me, *madame*. Which is why I
hope we can find agreement to keep him safe. Cared
for. Loved…' The last word brought another echo of
Alice's voice to the back of his mind. It felt like she was
here in the room with him and it made it all the more
important to make this work.

Even Madame Laurent's sniff was elegant. This time
she pressed the handkerchief to her nose.

'That is exactly what I will do for Jacques. I am the
one who can care for an infant. You…you have important work that must keep you extremely busy. You
would not have the time for such a young child.'

Julien stiffened. He could *make* time, if he had to.

'You are a national icon, Julien.' Yvonne looked up
to meet his gaze and her smile was poignant. 'My son
was also. I understand the kind of pressure that goes
with such a status.' When she blinked, her eyes glis-
tened with tears again. 'I adored my son. I will give the
same love and attention to my beloved grandson. I will
provide the best nannies. Find the best schools.'

Julien dipped his head in acknowledgment. He could
well believe that no money would be spared in providing for Jacquot but that wasn't the point.

'He's my nephew. My sister's child. I want to be part of his life.'

'Of course…' There was empathy in her tone now. 'I understand how important that is. I know there were… ah…difficulties in your relationship with my son but that is of little consequence now. This is about what is best for Jacques, is it not?'

'Yes.' Julien hadn't expected Madame Laurent to be so accommodating. He found himself smiling at her.

'I am not a young woman,' she said. 'While I can, of course I wish to provide a home for my grandson but I know there will come a time when he needs more than a safe nursery. A time when he needs a father figure. A time…' her indrawn breath was shaky '…when I will not be here to help him.'

'I want him to know who I am. I want to be part of his life.'

Madame Laurent tilted her head. 'You may visit whenever your schedule makes it possible. You will be made welcome at my estate.'

'And if anything happens to make it impossible for you to care for him?'

'I hope that will not be for a long time but, in that event, your guardianship will take priority.' Yvonne Laurent tucked her handkerchief back into her handbag. She got to her feet. 'If you're happy, I will have all of this documented by my solicitors and will bring the papers with me tomorrow when I come to collect my grandson.'

Happy? He should be. Madame Laurent had just agreed to everything he'd been trying to win when he'd come here in the first place. More, even. To be assigned indisputable guardianship of Jacquot if it became necessary in the future was an insurance policy that made this better than he could have hoped. But something was stopping any personal celebration and he knew what that something was.

Alice.

'Before you go, *madame*, there is something I should tell you about.'

'Oh...?'

'You have more than your grandson here in this house.' Julien took a deep breath. 'You also have a granddaughter.'

Madame Laurent stared at him. '*Non...c'est impossible...*'

Alice felt like she'd been waiting for ever.

Had Julien told Madame Laurent that she now had two grandchildren? Should she go downstairs? Brushing her hair, Alice wished she had packed some more clothes other than a spare shirt and clean underwear for this trip. Not that she owned anything like a power suit herself but why hadn't she thought to include a dress? Because she hadn't thought to present anything other than who she really was when she'd come in search of her father and that how the package was wrapped was of no importance?

Julien had seen through her lack of designer wear and sophistication. Or had he? If she had simply been a diversion from the boredom of being confined, it wouldn't have mattered what she looked like. Considering her an acceptable companion in the kind of world he normally inhabited might be a very different matter, especially if the people in that world were anything like

Madame Laurent. And if they were, a tiny voice whispered, would she even want to be there?

It needed every ounce of her courage to make the decision to go downstairs. Alice retrieved the photograph of her parents from her backpack, pushing aside the memory of how Julien had initially dismissed this evidence of her mother's relationship with André. The DNA test had been done and there could be no dismissal now. She hesitated a few moments more, however, checking—as she always did—that the baby cam was on and working before leaving the nursery.

But she didn't even get as far as the door because it was blocked by someone coming in.

Madame Laurent.

'Miss McMillan, it appears that you have a very unexpected connection with the Laurent family.'

Her English was so perfect it had virtually no accent and it made Alice realise how much she loved the way Julien spoke her language and could make it sound so much softer and almost as musical and inviting as his native tongue. How much she loved the way he said her name. It made the way this woman spoke seem so much harsher. Controlled and clipped. Cold...

She looked past Madame Laurent's shoulder in the hope that Julien had come upstairs as well but the doorway and the gallery beyond were empty.

She was alone. With her grandmother.

'I... I'm very happy to meet you,' she said quietly. 'I'm so very sorry for your loss. It's been devastating for me to have come here too late to be able to meet my father.'

Yvonne was staring at her but there was no more

warmth in either her expression or her body language than there had been in her voice. Then her gaze ran down the length of Alice's body, pausing as it reversed its journey.

'What is that?'

'Oh… It's a photograph. The only one I have of my parents together. It's what made me come here…' It was a wonder Alice's hand wasn't shaking as she held it out. 'Would you like to see?'

The focus of this woman's stare was unnerving.

'Her name was Jeannette McMillan. She came to work here in a gap year when she was eighteen. It was where she met your son, André.' Alice knew she was speaking too fast. Saying too much, but she needed desperately to break through what seemed an impenetrable barrier. 'Where she fell in love…'

Yvonne Laurent's breath was expelled in a dismissive snort. An echo of Julien's reaction. Was it a cultural thing to discount an extreme emotional connection? Surely not. Everybody knew that Paris was the city of love.

'I remember her.' The words dripped ice. The glance Alice received then sent a chill down her spine.

'I fail to understand what went wrong. The arrangements had been made. I had paid their exorbitant fees myself so that the unfortunate pregnancy could be dealt with discreetly.'

The mix of emotion that hit Alice was peculiar. There was anger that someone had been prepared to pay a lot of money to make sure she didn't exist. But there was a flash of something close to joy there as well. So it hadn't been her father who'd been the driving force in trying to get rid of her? It had been *this* woman. Her grandmother.

'*I* was that pregnancy,' she said slowly. 'And I was loved. By my mother. And by my *other* grandmother.'

Any rebuke her words held fell on deaf ears.

The huge diamonds in her rings flashed in the soft light of the nursery as Madame Laurent smoothed her perfectly groomed hair.

'I should sue that clinic,' she said. 'They told me the procedure had been completed. That the girl had been sent out of the country and would no longer be a problem.'

'Maybe they took pity on my mother when they saw how frightened she was. Or how much she wanted the baby of the man she loved.' Alice's voice was low. She was talking aloud to herself rather than trying to make conversation with someone she now knew she could never connect with.

Another derisive sound from Yvonne Laurent made her lift her chin and stare back at her, probably with the same kind of disgusted look she had been subjected to herself. This was unexpectedly devastating and a part of her needed to hit back.

'Perhaps it was André who made different arrangements,' she said. 'Perhaps he paid the clinic an even more exorbitant fee so that he could keep my mother safe. From *you*…'

'No. My son would not have done that. His racing career was everything to him. He was young. He could not have kept doing it if I hadn't provided the funding and he knew that was going to stop if he had anything more to do with a—a *waitress* who'd been stupid enough to try and catch him by producing an unwanted brat. She wasn't the only one. He was pursued by a great many like her. *Les salopes*… Trash…'

Alice stepped back as if she could get out of range of such venom. Her steps took her closer to the cot where Jacquot lay sleeping. It was then that fear stepped in. Not for herself—it didn't matter what this woman thought of her—but she was suddenly and dreadfully afraid for this innocent baby who was in danger of being brought up by a woman who was giving every impression that she was incapable of compassion, let alone love.

'And Jacquot?' she heard herself whisper. 'Is *he* an unwanted "brat" as well?'

'Of course not,' Yvonne Laurent snapped. 'He is a legitimate child and the heir to the Laurent name and fortune.' Her eyes narrowed. 'If you think you'll be getting any money from me, *mademoiselle*, think again. Maybe I wasn't careful enough the first time I tried to deal with you but I will not be making *that* mistake again.'

'Are you *threatening* me?'

'I am giving you some advice. Go back to the village you came from and do not ever come here again.'

Alice's inward breath was a gasp of horror. 'Jacquot is my *brother*...'

'No.' The word was final. 'Jacques Laurent is my grandchild. My *only* grandchild. You...' The rings on her hand flashed again in a gesture that could have been used to brush dust from a polished surface. 'You are *rien. Nothing.*'

'You don't care a jot about him,' Alice hissed. 'You haven't even *looked* at him since you came into this house.'

Madame Laurent's eyebrows rose just a little. Enough to suggest a refined astonishment.

'The child will have the best care that money can provide. And I will raise him to be as much of a credit to the Laurent name as his father was.'

Alice let out a long breath. 'I wish I'd met my father,' she said slowly. 'I wish I could have thanked him for making sure I didn't grow up here—with you as my grandmother. I was genuinely loved and that...that is of far more value than anything money can buy.'

The moment's silence was brief.

'Have my grandson ready to travel by tomorrow afternoon. And be ready to leave yourself. I do not wish to see you again.'

And with that, Madame Laurent turned and left the nursery, having not taken a step closer to Alice. Or any nearer the cot that contained her *only* grandchild.

Alice was shaking from head to toe as she did something that would probably be frowned on by any baby-care guides. She lifted a soundly sleeping infant so that she could hold him in her arms and press her cheek gently against his downy head.

'I won't let it happen,' she whispered. 'I love you. Your uncle Julien loves you too, I know he does...and... and I love *him*...and I wouldn't have fallen in love with anyone who could let this happen so I know that you will be safe...'

Alice came downstairs as Madame Laurent's car was on its way to the front gates.

She looked pale. Shocked even.

Yvonne Laurent had looked a little pale herself when she'd come down a few minutes ago but that was understandable. To be presented with a relationship to an adult was a very different thing from meeting a vulnerable child and they would both need time.

And it wasn't really his business, was it? Nothing had changed. On leaving, Madame Laurent had only confirmed that she would be here tomorrow afternoon with their agreement legally documented.

So he smiled at Alice.

'All is well that ends well—is that how you say it?'

'Sorry?'

'A good result. I did not expect Yvonne Laurent to be so understanding. To agree to more than I had requested, in fact.'

'I... I don't understand...'

Alice had stopped moving. She sank down and sat very still, staring at him.

'There will be no need to go to court. She has agreed that I will be a part of Jaquot's life. That I will see him regularly and that, in the future, when she is no longer able to devote her life to her grandson, I will become his guardian.'

'Devote her life to him?' Alice looked horrified. 'Are you *kidding*? She doesn't care a jot for him, Julien. I don't think she even loved her own son. She wouldn't even *look* at Jacquot and she certainly isn't going to acknowledge me as his sister. She's an evil woman, can't you *see* that? She said the most horrible things about my mother. About *me*...'

The anguish in Alice's eyes was unbearable and it was too much like the kind of pain Julien had seen in other eyes, so long ago. It wasn't something he could fix and it might make things worse if he tried. To get too involved would only bring pain and hadn't he caused enough of that already? He was still too raw to cope with fresh wounds. He hadn't been able to protect Colette so what made him think he could help Alice?

At least he had protected Jacquot to the best of his ability.

And he could protect himself. He could feel himself turning inwards already, in search of that safe place.

'I expect that communication was difficult. Perhaps she wasn't able to express herself very well in your language.'

'Her English was perfect,' Alice said. 'Better than yours.'

If anything, her gaze was more intense now. 'You love Jacquot. You can't let this happen to him.'

She was looking at him the way she had when he'd told her so much about his childhood. As if she wanted to wave her magic wand and make him feel better.

Make him feel loved...

He couldn't go there. He didn't want to feel loved because that's how it all started. The need to give back. To love in return and to give everything you had. Then all you could do was wait for the inevitable pain when it got ripped away from you.

Just a few more steps and he could be in that safe place again. Couldn't Alice understand?

'You make everything about love,' he said. 'But that gets in the way of thinking with your head and not your heart and that's a dangerous path where too many people get hurt. Yes, my heart knows I love Jacquot but my head knows that what has been arranged is best. For everyone.'

Alice's eyes were huge in her pale face. 'You're afraid to take that path but you know that's what really matters. For everybody. *Especially* Jacquot...'

* * *

Her heart was breaking. She could feel it happening and the pain was unbearable.

The barriers were there again and more solid than ever.

The doubts she'd had during that awful time of waiting in the nursery surfaced again and this time they had vicious claws.

Julien had never said he loved her. He'd never even hinted that their time together would continue. He'd given her this special day because he'd known it was going to be their last and…and he'd been relieved when it was over. Look at the way the pleasure had been sucked out of the day when the woman at the hat stall had suggested they were a real family.

The spell had been broken then and now it was no more than a little sparkly dust. It would take no more than a heartfelt sigh to send that dust into oblivion.

He'd told her all along that it wasn't real. That it wasn't simply his work that stopped him from being able to raise a child. That he didn't *want* to…

Was there any point in trying to tell him that Jacquot's grandmother was an evil monster? What could she do? He'd been offered the perfect solution in which he could stay in that safe place he'd invented. The place where he didn't have to take the risk of truly loving.

Or being loved.

It was so obvious that Alice had reached the end of the road. That she was defeated.

'It makes no difference that I'm his sister, does it? That I can love him with all my heart and soul?'

That I could love you like that, too…

But she couldn't tell Julien that she loved him because he didn't *want* to be loved. Being rejected by Madame Laurent was one thing. To invite rejection from Julien was another thing entirely. Why make this even worse for herself?

And he wasn't going to tell her that he loved *her* because…because he didn't. It was that simple. He didn't know how to. She'd been right. She'd been no more than a distraction during a difficult time.

'I know you love Jacquot.' Julien's tone softened. 'And I…'

Something flashed in his eyes. It was a fleeting glimpse through the barriers. An echo of the 'thing'—that extraordinary connection they had found with each other. Oh, God…had she been wrong? Was he going to say that he loved *her*? That would change everything. They could fight this together. And *win*…

'And I must thank you for everything that you've done for him.'

The disappointment was crushing. Why did she keep buying into that fairy-tale when she should know better by now? Alice dropped her gaze so that Julien wouldn't see her pain.

'Maybe, one day, I can arrange for you to see him again but, for now, things must be as they are. *Je suis désolé.*'

Alice stared at her hands. It was really over.

'I'm sorry, too,' she whispered. 'More than you'll ever know.'

Julien was moving away. Towards the grand salon. Towards her father's office perhaps?

'I have to speak to my solicitor. Madame Laurent is returning tomorrow and it might be easier for you if you are not in the house. I will arrange for someone to come and care for Jacques until I get back from Paris. Marthe perhaps. And I will see if a flight can be arranged to take you home. Would you prefer to fly into Glasgow or Edinburgh?'

Alice pushed herself to her feet and turned her back as she prepared to head back upstairs. Her response felt strangled. Like her heart.

'Edinburgh.'

It was so late by the time he had all the arrangements in place there was no time for anything more than another strong cup of coffee, a shower and a change of clothes before his taxi would arrive to get him to his early flight to Paris.

Julien left the printout of the plane ticket to Edinburgh he had finally managed to secure on the kitchen table where Alice would find it when she came down for breakfast. He had also printed out the voucher for the taxi that would come and collect her. Marthe would be here by then and he would be getting on his return flight from Paris. By the time he was landing in Nice, her plane would have just taken off. They would both be in the sky at the same time, but flying in very different directions.

He would never see her again.

Along with the ticket and taxi voucher, Julien left the colour image he had used the technology in André's office to print. The photograph of Alice, with Jacquot in her arms, at the Christmas market in Nice.

He owed her at least a small memento.

No. He owed her much more than that but if he began to count then it would only make everything more difficult. More painful.

The picture said it all. That this time had been pretence. No more than a Christmas time fairy-tale and real life wasn't like that.

Could he leave without saying goodbye?

No. Of course he couldn't. The force that was still pulling him towards this extraordinary young woman was too overwhelming to even begin resisting and surely he could cope. He just needed to peep through the window of his safe place—he didn't have to step outside it.

There was no sound coming from the nursery but the door was ajar and there was the soft glow of a nightlight to be seen. Julien pushed the door open a little further but then he stopped, his planned speech of farewell and thanks evaporating.

He'd heard Jacquot crying when he'd been downstairs and again when he was getting out of his shower but now the baby was a silent bundle in the cot and Alice was curled up in the chair asleep with her head in the crook of her arm. Her hair was a tangle of curls and her face looked as if tears had dried to leave streaks.

If he woke her, would she cry again?

And, if she did, would he be able to stop himself taking her into his arms and holding her close to his heart?

Buying into that dream again for just a few moments longer? Making those promises he knew he had no hope of keeping? Making things worse for them both in the long run?

It was the hardest thing he'd ever done, turning to walk silently away from that room, but it was best that he did.

Best that he focused on what he had to do in a matter of only a few hours, which was to present to the world the face of a man whose absolute passion was his career. A career that might once have seemed as much of a fairy-tale as a happy family but was reality.

And he had to hang onto that for all it was worth.

Because, when all was said and done, it was all he really had to count on.

CHAPTER ELEVEN

JULIEN HAD GONE.

Alice knew that she and Jacquot were alone in the house from the moment she awoke.

Because it felt like a part of herself was missing.

The part she had given to Julien...

Jacquot was still asleep after a fretful night, probably due to the distress he must have sensed in her, so she moved slowly and quietly around the nursery, her feet feeling as heavy as her heart. After a brief shower she packed her few items into the backpack she had arrived with. The photo of her parents—now more precious than ever—was tucked carefully back into the side pocket. The action reminded her of the photograph she'd found in André's office of Jacquot's parents and her vow to find some way to give it to him one day. She needed to remember to go and fetch it.

It was still dark well after the baby stirred and Alice gave him his breakfast bottle and then bathed and dressed him. She gave him extra kisses and cuddles this morning and talked to him.

'I'll find you one day, sweetheart. I expect you'll learn to speak English and I'm going to take French lessons, so by the time I see you again we'll be able to talk to each other.'

She thought of all the baby milestones Jacquot would have in the next few years, like saying his first words and taking his first wobbly steps. The pain of knowing she wouldn't be able to witness or celebrate those milestones was astonishingly painful.

She'd found what she'd come to France in the hope of finding. Someone that was family to her. Jacquot had accepted her from the moment they'd met. Even now, the memory of how she'd been the only one able to comfort him when he'd been sick and miserable brought a smile to her lips. One that twisted in what felt like grief as she acknowledged that this gift of family was going to be wrenched from her in a matter of just a few hours.

And Julien hadn't even said goodbye.

The tears would come, nothing was surer, but Alice wasn't going to let it happen in the scant time she had left with her little brother. So she pasted a smile on her face.

'Shall we go downstairs, darling? So that Alice can have a cup of coffee?'

There would be no warm, buttery croissants ready for her this morning but it didn't matter. She couldn't have eaten anything anyway. Her stomach already felt like a stone and that stone became a painful boulder when she walked into the kitchen to find what had been left on the table for her.

The note was written in elegant handwriting. She could actually see Julien's hand holding the pen as she picked it up. Those long, clever fingers that were capable of magic in the kitchen. And in the bedroom…

Marthe would be arriving at ten-thirty a.m., the note

informed her. Half an hour before her taxi was due to arrive to take her to the airport.

'*Merci, chérie,*' the brief note ended. '*Au revoir.*'

Au revoir. One of the language lessons over a meal had been about saying goodbye. And this really meant goodbye. If you intended seeing someone again, you said something like '*à demain*'. Until tomorrow. Or '*à bientôt*'. Soon.

The endearment was probably automatic. Like a London cab driver calling you 'love'.

It meant nothing.

Except that wasn't true, was it? She'd seen a part of Julien Dubois that instinct told her very few other people saw.

That 'thing'. That connection they'd found when they'd looked at each other in the bathroom mirror that first night had been an attraction that went very much deeper than anything physical. She knew, beyond a shadow of a doubt, that Julien had felt it too. He was choosing to deny it. To run away.

And she understood. She might hate it but she had thought about nothing else in the sleepless hours before she'd finally succumbed to exhaustion last night.

She had told him that he was too afraid to take the path of love and it was true. He was protecting his heart but who could blame him when he'd lost everybody he'd given his heart to? His father had abandoned him at an impressionable age. He'd said himself that small children understood more than you would think and that was why he wanted to spare Jacquot the insecurity of having people fighting over his custody.

His mother had died at another impressionable age, when he'd been in that awkward transition period between child and adult, but he'd been mature enough to take responsibility for his young sister and devote his life to supporting and protecting her. Alice wasn't sure what had happened in recent years but the rift when he'd tried to protect Colette from marrying someone he hadn't trusted had to have been devastating. And just when it had looked like they were about to reconnect, he had lost his sister under tragic circumstances that were still raw.

No wonder he couldn't offer anyone else a part of his heart to keep for ever. There weren't that many parts left. And yet he'd tried, with Jacquot. He had been fighting to at least be a meaningful part of his nephew's life the day she had arrived here. There'd been an enforced disruption to the negotiations thanks to the quarantine but now he had exactly what he'd intended fighting for.

He had no idea what Madame Laurent was really like and, in trying to tell him, she had only made the distance between them greater. Maybe he hadn't been able to hear what she'd had to say because, if he believed her, it would destroy the victory he thought he'd won. Maybe that was why he hadn't risked waking her to say goodbye?

Had he felt the connection with her that he'd been unable to deny when he'd printed out this photograph of her at the Christmas markets?

Or had he remembered, instead, the shock of that stallholder assuming they were the parents of the small baby in their company? A happy little family. That he had a child of his own when he'd vowed that he would never let that happen.

As if he knew his part in the fantasy, Jacquot reached

up and caught the corner of the photograph in his small fist, crumpling it with surprising strength.

'Oops…' Alice gently extracted the glossy image. However painful it was in this moment, she was going to keep this. It didn't matter that it was now crumpled because she'd remember the tiny hand that had caused the damage and that made it even more precious.

She barely glanced at the plane ticket and taxi voucher because her intention of putting this photograph into her backpack beside the one of her parents had reminded her of the other photograph she was planning to take with her. The one in the heart-shaped, silver frame.

'Come on.' She smiled down at Jacquot, who now had a handful of her hair. 'Let's go to Daddy's office.'

She hadn't been in here since the night she'd interrupted the filming of the Christmas show that was probably being aired on television right now, with the hosts of the breakfast show chatting to Julien between clips. Was he wearing his white chef's tunic and that blue and white striped apron? Had it only been the night before last that he had emerged from the kitchen to kiss her senseless and give her the most memorable night of her life?

Such a contrast to the first memorable moment he'd given her, when he'd hurled that paperweight at her father's massive portrait. She stood in front of it for a long moment, ignoring the shards of glass and even the reason for the photograph. Instead, she looked into her father's eyes. Dark eyes, so like her own, that gleamed with such confidence and joy.

A man capable of great passion. Like Julien. But her father hadn't been afraid to love more than his career. He'd loved Colette, she was sure of that. Picking up the photograph in the silver frame only convinced her more. She clicked it shut. She was going to believe that André Laurent had loved *her* mother, too. He had been a victim of his upbringing perhaps. Overindulged and dependent financially on a woman who had no heart.

It was more of a stretch to believe that he'd helped Jeanette to escape the planned termination of her pregnancy but maybe her mother had severed contact so completely he'd known there was no point in trying to find her. The birth of his son at such a late age must have been a miracle. How sad that it had come at such a price, though. Had he been distraught? Had that contributed to his reckless driving that had taken his life?

He hadn't intended to die. Sinking into the desk chair, Alice used her free hand to open the drawer she'd opened the last time she had been in here. Yes. There were the tickets and passports ready to take Jacquot to his grandmother's house for his first Christmas.

Alice actually shuddered at the thought of being in that woman's company for anything, let alone a celebration like Christmas.

It was just as well she wasn't going to be here this afternoon to see Jacquot handed over to a woman who had no love in her soul. The family name was all Madame Laurent cared about, not the person who was carrying that name.

A flash of anger cut through weariness that went bone-deep.

How could Julien even think of allowing that to happen?

Maybe he wasn't the person she thought he was. Maybe she'd invented a prince for her fairy-tale and then she'd been stupid enough to fall in love with him.

No. In her heart of hearts she knew that wasn't true. Julien didn't know the truth or he would not let this happen. Nobody would.

Her arms tightened around Jacquot as she ducked her head to plant a kiss on his head. She'd promised this tiny person that she wouldn't let it happen. That his Uncle Julien wouldn't let it happen. But…but…

Alice blinked tears away as she raised her head, her glance grazing the drawer and its contents again as she did so.

Unbidden, her hand went out to pick up one of the items.

Jacquot's passport.

The idea was ludicrous. An act of rebellion that would get her into far more trouble than any of her childhood pranks.

But it wasn't impossible, was it?

Marthe wasn't coming here for another few hours. She had a voucher for the taxi company that included a phone number. If they spoke English—as most people seemed to here—she could change the time of her pick-up.

She had a plane ticket. A three-month-old baby didn't need a plane ticket because it got held in its mother's arms.

And who was going to check whether she actually was his mother? It was Christmas Eve and bound to be bedlam at any international airport.

She could keep Jacquot safe even if it was only for a short time before she was caught. She could keep him safe for his first-ever Christmas. Make him feel wanted and loved for no more than who he was. Her brother.

The idea was growing wings. The mix of nervousness and excitement felt rather like when she'd first arrived here. It would take courage to do it because she knew how wrong it was.

But then she looked down at a tiny face and Jacquot looked back and her and grinned his crooked little grin.

No. It wasn't wrong. It wasn't exactly the right thing to do either.

It was the *only* thing to do.

The airport was so chaotic Julien didn't remember to turn his phone back on until he'd finally managed to flag down a taxi and was stuck in the crazy Christmas traffic as he headed back to St Jean Cap Ferrat.

Ten missed calls from Marthe?

He knew his heart actually stopped for a moment because he felt the painful thump of it restarting.

Something had happened to Jacquot.

Or Alice.

His fingers shook as he tapped the screen to return the call. A moment later the housekeeper's voice was a distressed garble.

'I don't understand. Of course Alice has gone. Her plane will have taken off by now.'

He'd seen a British Airways plane taking off as he'd hurried through the crowds to escape the airport and he'd wondered if that was Alice disappearing from his life for ever. It had only made it more urgent to escape. To do what had to be done and then retreat into the only life he knew he could depend on. His own.

He was only half listening to Marthe's next words.

'How could she have taken Jacquot with her? You were there when the taxi came.'

He closed his eyes as he listened to the explanation. The taxi company had been and gone by the time Marthe had arrived at the house. Alice had left a note to say not to worry but the plan had been changed. That Julien would know why. So she'd been trying to ring him. Again and again.

But his phone had been turned off. Of course it had. He couldn't afford to have it ring when he was on a live television show and he hadn't bothered turning it back on when he had been about to fly.

If Alice had been on that plane he'd seen taking off, she hadn't been alone. She was taking her little brother back to Edinburgh and from there to whatever isolated little village she came from. What was its name? She had told him once. It would come to him.

Right now, the enormity of what had happened was sinking in as his taxi cleared the worst of the traffic and picked up speed. There was only an hour or two at most before Yvonne Laurent arrived to collect Jacquot and when she found out what had happened all hell would break loose. Would she think that he'd had a part in this himself? Would it send them all back to square one in a battle for Jacquot's custody?

How long did it take to fly to Edinburgh? No more than three hours, he suspected. Time enough for the full force of the law to be unleashed. Alice would be arrested the moment she arrived. Prosecution by the Laurent solicitors would be relentless and unforgiving. Jacquot would be taken away from her and brought back to France by strangers. He would be frightened and that was enough to make Julien angry. Very, very angry.

How could she do that?

What had she been *thinking*?

There was no reason for Marthe to stay in the house. Julien sent her home to her family. He screwed up the note Alice had left and hurled it to the floor of the kitchen. And then he began pacing, still unable to believe what she had done. He went in the direction of the nursery, as though he had to see for himself that it was uninhabited.

Which, of course, it was.

There was no sign that Alice had even been here but the absence of the baby whose name was proclaimed in those bright wooden letters on the wall was horrific.

The cot had been neatly made and propped against the soft bumper pad at the head end was a toy.

Le lapin brun.

Somehow that was even more shocking than Jacquot's absence. Alice had known how precious this toy was. She had said herself that she was happy it was there for him. That, one day, Julien would be able to tell him how special it was. How much he must have been loved.

He had to pick it up and, as he did so he remembered the last time he'd reached into this cot. When he'd been half-asleep and half-dressed and had gone into the nursery in response to that alarming cry from Jacquot.

And he remembered how he'd felt, holding that tiny baby against his bare chest. The pride in being able to comfort him. The absolute trust he was being endowed with to protect this baby from any evil in the world.

He could hear a whisper that sounded like Alice's voice.

She doesn't care a jot for him... I don't think she

even loved her own son... She's an evil woman, can't you see that?

Alice had felt that same level of trust from Jacquot, hadn't she? And she'd been brave enough to do something about it, however ill advised that had been. Anger was fading now, being replaced with something that felt more like respect. Admiration even.

But now Julien had the battered old bunny in his hand and he remembered the feel of it as if it was only yesterday that he had been handing it to his little sister to comfort her. How she would take it and clutch it to her chest and then wriggle into his arms to be held and comforted some more.

And finally...having not cried since his father had walked out when he'd been only five years old—even when his stepfather had beaten him or when his mother had died, leaving a scared youth to try and fight back against an unfair world—Julien was able to cry for his sister.

Racking sobs that felt like they were tearing his heart apart as he sank into the chair he'd seen Alice asleep in only this morning. Tears that soaked the toy he had pressed against his cheek. But curiously the pain didn't seem to be destroying what was left of his heart. When he was finally spent, there was an odd calmness to be found.

The beginning of peace perhaps?

It was only then that Julien became aware of something in the chair he'd been sitting in. Something with uncomfortably sharp edges. He reached underneath his legs and pulled out the handset to the baby monitor. Its red light was glowing but there was no point in keeping it on when there was no baby to watch over, was there?

Julien pushed a button but the light stayed on. He pushed another one and, unexpectedly, an image filled the screen. Did this state-of-the-art baby monitoring equipment actually make a video recording when it was switched on?

Apparently it did.

And the last time it had been switched on had been last evening. When Yvonne Laurent had gone up to the nursery after receiving the shocking news that there were *two* grandchildren of hers in the room.

He watched—and listened—in growing horror. Was this really the same woman whose words and tears had convinced him that they shared the same dream for Jacquot's future?

'The arrangements had been made. I had paid their exorbitant fees myself so that the unfortunate pregnancy could be dealt with discreetly.'

'...a waitress—who'd been stupid enough to try and catch him by producing an unwanted brat...'

'Jacques Laurent is my grandchild. My only grandchild... You... You are rien. *Nothing.'*

How hurtful must that have been? Words could hurt just as much as fists and he knew only too well what it was like to feel so unwanted. Rejected.

His little Scottish pixie had come here wanting nothing more than to find family in time for Christmas.

She'd found that her father had died only days before.

She'd found a tiny brother she could love and she'd been desperate to be allowed to raise him herself.

And she'd ended up being dismissed as *nothing*.

The anger was there again now but it wasn't directed at Alice. When the vicious old woman that his nephew was unfortunate enough to have as a grandmother arrived he was going to tell her exactly how wrong she was about Alice McMillan. Nothing? She was *everything* that Yvonne Laurent could clearly never be. Warm. Loving. Vibrant. Able to make life something to be celebrated, no matter what.

And…

Julien caught his breath as he focused on the small screen again. What was that? He studied the buttons on the handset properly this time so he could rewind and play that part again that he'd barely noticed during his outraged thoughts.

'I love you. Your uncle Julien loves you too, I know he does…and…and I love him…and I wouldn't have fallen in love with anyone who could let this happen…'

Mon Dieu…

The cascade of emotion was enough to bring tears to his eyes again but these were not tears of grief.

They felt more like joy.

And then Julien heard the doorbell ring. It was probably his solicitor, who was due to arrive before Madame Laurent in order to check that the legal paperwork was irrefutable. Paperwork that would now need to be ripped into shreds.

He got to his feet, the brown bunny in one hand and the handset of the monitor in the other.

Alice had left him one final gift, hadn't she?

The weapon he needed to win this battle, once and for all.

No. Make that two.

Unintentionally, she had also given him words of love.

Would they still hold true when he'd dismissed what she'd told him about that encounter with her grandmother? When he'd done what must have seemed so unforgiveable in her eyes? When he'd turned away from her so deliberately in order to protect himself?

There was only one way to find out.

But there were other matters to attend to first.

It was dark by the time the plane landed at Edinburgh airport even though it was only three p.m. Leaden skies held the weight of a snowstorm that everyone was hoping would hold off for at least twenty-four hours to give families time to gather for Christmas.

In rural Scotland, well to the north, it was already snowing. Tiny flakes sparkled in the headlights of her rented car as Alice finally parked in front of the cottage that had been her home since the day she was born.

The home she had celebrated every single Christmas in, with the decorations her mother had loved strung from every available anchoring point, a tree with flashing fairy-lights and gifts underneath, a fire burning brightly in the grate, Christmas carols coming from the CD player and the smell of a feast being prepared in the kitchen.

Home...

Jacquot was asleep in the car seat she had also rented. She carried him into the small stone house.

A very cold and dark stone house.

Aside from her brief visit back here last week, nobody had been living here for many months and there was no power on. No fire in the grate. Probably very little food in the pantry even. The shops would be shut and she didn't even have a close neighbour she could call on. There was no Christmas tree, no decorations and no music.

It was so quiet she could hear her own heart beating.

Until Jacquot woke and started to cry.

Alice undid the safety harness and scooped him into her arms. She wanted to cry herself.

What had she done?

What had she been *thinking*?

CHAPTER TWELVE

CHRISTMAS MORNING.

Somehow they'd survived the night.

Leaving Jacquot cocooned in blankets, tucked into the car seat that doubled as a carrier, Alice had used the light of her phone to find candles and then she'd built a fire in the ancient Aga stove in the kitchen that her grandmother had insisted on keeping because she'd been cooking on it ever since she'd come here as a young bride. At the same time she started a fire going in the open grate of the only living area in the house.

Feeding Jacquot was no problem now that she had a means of heating water because she had packed plenty of formula into the nappy bag, along with everything else she might need for a baby for a few days. She must have looked a sight at Nice airport yesterday, with her backpack on, a baby strapped to her chest and a well-stuffed carrier bag in each hand, but she'd been right in guessing that officials had been too busy to ask awkward questions. Instead, she'd found people eager to help a struggling young mother who'd had too many burdens to juggle. She'd got priority boarding and had been allowed to take all her bags onto the plane instead of checking any in, which had made for a much faster getaway when they'd arrived in Edinburgh.

That had been the worse time. The flight had been long enough for Alice to convince herself that Julien had arrived back in St Jean Cap Ferrat and would have been as furious as Madame Laurent to discover what she'd done. That the police would have been called. She had fully expected them to be waiting for her at Edinburgh airport.

But they hadn't been there.

And now she was several hours' drive away and, as if fate was lending her a helping hand, snow had fallen heavily all night. With any luck, it would take at least until tomorrow for roads to be clear enough to access Brannockburn easily.

She might not have the luxury of a few days' grace but it felt like she could count on having today.

Christmas Day.

And that was what mattered, wasn't it? This was Jacquot's first Christmas and she wanted it to be filled with all the love it was possible for a family to share. All the magic of Christmas.

Except there was nothing that said 'Christmas' about this house, except for the candles that she'd lit again once she was up for the day.

It was warm now, thank goodness. Rather than using the bedrooms upstairs, Alice had slept on the couch all night, getting up to look after Jacquot, who had slept in his nest of blankets, and stoking the fires each time.

But there was no tree. No decorations and no music. And certainly no smell of anything delicious being prepared in the kitchen—only the faint reminder of the can of baked beans Alice had heated for her breakfast.

They needed a tree.

'When I was little,' she told Jacquot, 'we all used to put our wellies on and go out to the big old pine tree beside the henhouse. I was allowed to choose the branch and Mum would saw it off. We had a red bucket full of sand that we kept on the back porch beside the firewood pile and we stood the branch up in that.'

The red bucket was still there. She'd seen it last night when she'd hurried in and out with armloads of small logs to fill the indoor basket.

She tickled Jacquot's tummy as he lay on the cushion of folded blankets, kicking his legs, and he grinned up at her.

With Julien's grin…

No…she couldn't go there… She wasn't going to cry today. Not on Christmas Day. She needed a distraction. Fast.

'What do you think, sweetheart? Shall we do it? If we were very quick, and chose a branch close to the ground, it wouldn't take long enough for us to get *too* cold because it's not snowing at the moment. And I know where the decorations are—in the boxes under Gran's bed. We won't be able to have the fairy-lights and I'm sorry I don't have any gifts for you but…but we could still make it *feel* right and I can take photos so that, one day, you'll know how special your sister wanted to make your first Christmas.'

There was another bonus to her plan. It would take most of the day to do everything she was suddenly desperate to do and it would stop her sitting around, thinking about Julien. The hardest moment came when she realised she needed a hat before she went tramping around in the snow and the only hat she had was the one Julien had bought for her at the markets in Nice. She pulled it over her head anyway.

'It's Christmas,' she told Jacquot, as she slipped her arms into the straps of the front pack. 'We need all the sparkles we can find.'

The daylight hours had come and gone in a flash. Here it was, four p.m., and it felt like night-time. Alice pulled the curtains over the windows to keep the warmth inside and she could see the starry shapes of fresh snowflakes sticking to the dark glass and piling up on the windowsills.

She was cutting them off from the outside world but it felt good. This was a private celebration and, as she turned and caught the full effect of the living room, it was perfect enough to make her catch her breath.

Okay, the hastily harvested tree branch was lopsided but it didn't matter because it was staying upright in the red bucket. And it didn't matter that it didn't have sparkling lights because it was plastered with every bauble Alice had found in the old boxes and with so many candles on the old sideboard and the mantelpiece, as well as the firelight, the glossy decorations were twinkling anyway.

Garlands of fake spruce and ivy, generously sprinkled with bunches of red berries, were looped above the doorways and from the heavy beams in the ceiling.

The beautiful stockings that her grandmother had lovingly embroidered were hanging above the fire and Alice had put tiny tea-light candles in glass tumblers on the hearth. The huge wickerwork reindeer her mother had loved stood guard on either side of the fireplace, proudly wearing their red collars and golden bells.

It didn't matter that there were no gifts under the tree either. Jacquot was too young to know the difference and Alice had the best gift she could possibly have already.

Family.

'We need a photo,' she told her tiny brother. 'I've never done a selfie before but here goes.'

She was wearing a Santa hat she'd found amongst the decorations and she'd dressed Jacquot in a little red sleep suit she'd packed with his things. Standing in front of the tree, with the baby tucked into the crook of one arm, Alice used her other hand to try and hold her phone far enough away to capture both their faces and some of the background.

It wasn't working. If she tilted the phone enough to put Jacquot's face in the picture, it cut off the top half of her own head and the tree was nowhere to be seen. 'I give up,' she sighed finally. 'I'll just take a picture of you and then we'll use my phone to have some Christmas music.'

The battery was not going to last much longer so Alice had to choose a favourite carol to listen to while she prepared Jacquot's Christmas dinner of a bottle of milk.

With the much-loved sound of 'The Little Drummer Boy' playing, she cuddled Jacquot for a minute longer, singing softly along with the song.

And then she froze.

No…it couldn't be…

But then she heard it again.

An insistent rapping on the front door of her house. Her time with Jacquot was about to end.

She'd been caught. It was time to face music that would have none of the joy of any Christmas carols.

She kept her head down as she opened her door, expecting to see the polished boots of more than one police officer.

She did see boots but they were old and soft looking, like a favourite pair a cowboy might wear. And they were beneath a pair of faded denim jeans. Alice's head jerked up.

'*Julien*…'

She had been hunted down by the person she was most ashamed to see and she could feel her face flood with burning colour as she thought of how much trouble she must have caused him.

But he was smiling. '*Bonjour, Alice. Joyeux Noël. May I come inside?*'

Speechless as she absorbed the sound of his voice again, Alice could only nod as she stood back. He was carrying a suitcase in one hand. No…it wasn't a case, she realised as he came into the light of the living room. It looked like…like a *picnic* hamper?

And he was holding something in his other hand as well.

Brown bunny.

Julien saw the direction of her gaze and held up the toy.

'I think you forgot something,' he said softly, holding it out to her. 'Something important.'

Her hand was trembling as she took the toy and she still couldn't think of a single word to say. This was the last thing she'd expected. Why wasn't he furious? Berating her for the crime she had committed in kidnapping Jacquot? Snatching him from her arms and disappearing back into the gloomy chill of the dark, snowy afternoon?

Finally, she found her voice, already sounding rusty. 'How did you find me? How did you *get* here?'

'I remembered the name of your village. Getting here was a little more problematic, especially when my car got stuck in the snow, but a very nice man with a tractor rescued me and, even better, he knew where your house was. I have walked the last mile or so. My feet are very cold.'

'Oh...come over near the fire.'

'Soon.' Julien put the hamper down and took off his coat. Then he pulled the hat off his head and the hair that had been tucked out of sight fell softly to touch his shoulders.

He stepped closer. 'You have forgotten something else. Or maybe you didn't know about it.' He bent to kiss Jacquot's head and then touched Alice's cheek with equal gentleness as he met her gaze.

She couldn't look away. The 'thing' was still there but it had changed. Grown. In fact, it was so huge it seemed to be sucking all the oxygen out of this room. Not that it mattered because she was too stunned to think about taking a breath anyway.

His hand traced her cheek, brushed her ear and then slid beneath her hair to cup the back of her head. Alice's lips were already slightly parted as she looked up, her heart so full of love it felt painfully stretched, and Julien matched his own lips with hers so perfectly it was like a dance as much as a kiss as they moved together.

'It is a French custom,' he whispered. 'The Christmas kiss.'

Vision blurred by tears made Alice blink. She couldn't believe any of this. It was a dream. A fairy-tale. Real life wasn't like this.

Except, right now, it appeared that it was.

Julien was stepping back. He picked up the hamper. 'There was so much food still in the cold room,' he said, 'I thought I would bring you Christmas dinner.'

Alice had thought that the traditional meal was the one thing she had needed to complete this Christmas celebration for Jacquot. But, in the wave of a magic wand, it had now appeared and she knew she'd been wrong.

What she had really needed to complete this perfect little Christmas was to be with both the people she now thought of as family.

Jacquot *and* Julien.

A single tear escaped and trickled down her cheek.

Miracles really did happen at Christmastime, didn't they?

'I have champagne, too,' Julien added. 'Because we have something to celebrate.'

'We do?'

'*Oui*. But first I must apologise. I had no idea about the terrible things Madame Laurent said to you. I had no idea what sort of person she really was because, I think, her acting skills are excellent. I should have listened. I will always listen in future, *mon amour. Je suis vraiment désolé.*'

That French was being spoken in this house, of all places, should have felt like a betrayal to her grand-mother and mother but instead it felt like the two halves of who she was had finally been fitted together like a jigsaw puzzle. Or maybe she was feeling whole because Julien was here with her. Whatever the reason, the picture that the neatly fitting pieces were making was beautiful.

Jacquot's whimper reminded her that it was time for him to be fed but Alice hesitated. The shock of seeing Julien was wearing off and questions were filling her head. Serious questions.

'How do you know what she said? Did she *tell* you? Why? And where is she now? What's going to happen to me?'

Julien smiled. 'One question at a time, *mon amour*. Here, give Jacquot to me or would you like me to prepare his bottle?'

In answer, Alice transferred the bundle of baby from her arms to his and Jacquot, bless him, looked up at his uncle and forgot he was hungry. He practised his best smile instead. Julien followed Alice to the kitchen and watched as she reheated the pot of boiled water on the hotplate over the oven.

'Did you know that the baby cam could record things?'

'No.' Alice spooned formula into the bottle. If she had, she might have gone back to watch a particular scene more than once. The one where Julien had picked up his tiny nephew and held him against his bare chest. A scene that had captured her heart so decisively.

'It was lucky that you'd turned it on before Madame Laurent came into the nursery. It recorded everything she said.'

Alice's eyes widened. 'That's right... I'd turned it on because I'd been about to come downstairs and find you...'

'It gave me the evidence I needed to confront her.

My solicitor reminded her that what she had done had been ill advised and illegal if your mother had been more than twelve weeks pregnant. That, in any case, if this recording became public, her reputation would be ruined and if she contested the issue of guardianship any further, then that was exactly what would happen.'

Alice gasped. 'She must have been *so* angry.'

Julien nodded, a sombre expression on his face. 'So angry the doctors said later that it must have raised her blood pressure to a terrible level and that is why she had the… I don't know the word…*un accident vasculaire cerebral*…'

'A stroke?' Alice guessed, shocked. 'Oh, my God… Is she…is she still alive?'

Julien nodded again. 'But she is badly affected. I rang the hospital this morning before I left to check on her progress and it is thought she will need specialist care for a long time.'

Alice absorbed this information slowly as she shook the bottle and then tested the temperature of the formula on her wrist.

'So she can't take Jacquot even if she wanted to fight for custody?'

'No. My guardianship will be uncontested. Ironically, that was part of our agreement that she had already signed. That if anything happened to her, this is what would happen. From now on, he will be in my care.'

Alice nodded slowly, trying to take it all in. So that was why Julien had come instead of the police. He was here to take Jacquot back to France with him.

'Would…?' She had to clear her throat so her voice didn't wobble. 'Would you like to feed him?'

'You give Jacquot his dinner.' Julien gently transferred the baby back to her arms. 'I would like to give you *your* dinner and I need to make it hot.' He was smiling now. 'Do you remember the last Christmas dinner we ate together?'

How could she forget, when it had happened after he had taken her to his bed for the first time? By the look in his eyes right now he was remembering exactly the same thing.

'And do you remember I said you might be eating Christmas dinner more than once?'

Alice's knees felt a little weak. Was Julien referring to a repetition of more than eating a traditional meal? She needed to sit down while she fed Jacquot, who fell asleep before he had even finished his milk.

And then Julien brought her a glass of champagne and sat beside her on the old couch as they drank it. Silently, they sat together, soaking in the warmth and light of this Christmas scene Alice had created today.

'You really are a pixie,' Julien told her finally. 'You make the world a special place wherever you are.'

He took her empty glass and put it on the coffee table with his and then he put his arm around her and Alice snuggled against him, tilting her face up to receive one kiss and then another. They couldn't go upstairs to a bedroom and leave a baby in a room with a fire and a dozen candles but, unexpectedly, this felt better than sex. Deeper.

More like real life instead of a fairy-tale?

'Why did you leave *le lapin brun* behind?' Julien asked softly. 'Did you know I would find it?'

Alice nodded, loving the feel of Julien's chest beneath her cheek. She could hear his heart beating.

'I hoped so,' she said. 'I knew how much it meant to you. That it was the one thing Colette had given her baby that had been hers from her childhood. It was the link…the *love*…and I hoped that one day you would be able to give it to Jacquot so that the chain of that love wouldn't be broken.'

'Colette used to hold it when she was frightened.' Julien's voice cracked as he spoke. 'And I used to hold her. Like this…' His arm tightened around Alice and she snuggled closer.

'I'm not afraid to take the path of love,' he whispered, his lips very close to her ear. 'Not any more. I will love Jacquot for every day that I live and I will protect him in every way that I can.'

Alice pressed her lips together to stop them trembling. 'You will take him back to France?'

'I have to, *cherié*. You know that, yes?'

Alice nodded.

'But there is something I am also hoping…'

Alice tilted her head so that she could see his face.

'I am hoping that you will come back with us. That you will help me raise Jacquot and give him the love that only his sister or mother could provide.'

Alice stopped breathing. Was that all Julien was hoping? His eyes were telling her more than that but was he really not afraid to take an even bigger step into trusting that he could not only give love but *be* loved in return?

'*Je t'aime,*' he whispered. '*Tu as volé mon coeur. Tu as changé mon vie et…je pense que tu es la dernière pièce de mon casse-tête.*'

Oh… Alice's eyes filled with joyous tears. Could there ever be a more beautiful language for words of love? She didn't need a translation.

Or maybe she did.

'What does that mean? What is a *casse-tête*?'

'A puzzle. I said that I think *you* are the last piece of *my* puzzle.'

'Oh…that's exactly what I was thinking about you. I… No… *Je t'aime*, too, Julien. I always will. For ever.'

'*Pour toujours,*' Julien confirmed. And then he kissed her, so tenderly that the tears in Alice's eyes escaped to dampen both their faces. Or had Julien shed some of his own?

The smell of the heating turkey and gravy wafted into the room at that point. Alice's stomach growled loudly and Julien tipped back his head as he laughed.

'I am home,' he declared. 'And it is time to feed my woman.'

He stood up, lifting Alice to her feet, but instead of leading her to the kitchen he wrapped his arms around her again.

'This is only the first of many,' he whispered. 'And I will try to make each one happier than the last. *Joyeux Noël, mon amour.*'

'*Joyeux Noël,*' Alice echoed. And then she stood on tiptoe so that she could kiss Julien again. 'It's a Scottish custom, too,' she murmured. 'The Christmas kiss…'

* * * * *

To raise his little girl up right was more than enough. He didn't need that special woman, after all.

Or so he'd believed until twelve nights ago.

Until Chloe led him into her house and straight to her bed.

Chloe.

She had it all—everything he'd already accepted he wasn't going to find. And no one had ever tasted so good.

Reluctantly, he broke the kiss.

She stared up at him, eyes full of stars. "Come back to my house? Be with me tonight?"

"Damn, Chloe. I was afraid you'd never ask."

* * *

The Bravos of Justice Creek:
Where bold hearts collide under Western skies

THE GOOD GIRL'S SECOND CHANCE

BY
CHRISTINE RIMMER

All rights reserved including the right of reproduction in whole or in part in any form. This edition is published by arrangement with Harlequin Books S.A.

This is a work of fiction. Names, characters, places, locations and incidents are purely fictional and bear no relationship to any real life individuals, living or dead, or to any actual places, business establishments, locations, events or incidents. Any resemblance is entirely coincidental.

This book is sold subject to the condition that it shall not, by way of trade or otherwise, be lent, resold, hired out or otherwise circulated without the prior consent of the publisher in any form of binding or cover other than that in which it is published and without a similar condition including this condition being imposed on the subsequent purchaser.

® and ™ are trademarks owned and used by the trademark owner and/or its licensee. Trademarks marked with ® are registered with the United Kingdom Patent Office and/or the Office for Harmonisation in the Internal Market and in other countries.

Published in Great Britain 2015
by Mills & Boon, an imprint of Harlequin (UK) Limited,
Eton House, 18-24 Paradise Road, Richmond, Surrey, TW9 1SR

© 2015 Christine Rimmer

ISBN: 978-0-263-25174-6

23-1015

Harlequin (UK) Limited's policy is to use papers that are natural, renewable and recyclable products and made from wood grown in sustainable forests. The logging and manufacturing processes conform to the legal environmental regulations of the country of origin.

Printed and bound in Spain
by CPI, Barcelona

Christine Rimmer came to her profession the long way around. She tried everything from acting to teaching to telephone sales. Now she's finally found work that suits her perfectly. She insists she never had a problem keeping a job—she was merely gaining "life experience" for her future as a novelist. Christine lives with her family in Oregon. Visit her at www.christinerimmer.com.

For Kimberly Fletcher, aka Kimalicious, Kimalovely,
Kimhilarious—and more.
You warm my heart and make me smile. I'm so happy
to call you my friend. And this one's for you!

Chapter One

Chloe Winchester woke with a startled cry.

She popped straight up in bed as her heart trip-hammered against her ribs. Splaying a hand to her heaving chest, she sent a frantic, frightened glance around the darkened room.

No threat. None.

Just her shadowed bedroom in the middle of the night, silvery moonlight streaming in the high, narrow window over the curtained sliding glass door.

"Nothing, it's nothing," she whispered aloud between gasps for air. "A nightmare." More specifically, it was *the* nightmare, the one starring her ultrasuccessful, über-controlling, bad-tempered ex-husband, Ted.

Not real, she reminded herself. Not anymore.

Ted Davies was the past. He held no threat for her now.

Chloe smoothed a shaking hand over her hair, pressed her cool fingers to her flushed cheek and took long, deep breaths until her racing heart slowed. Finally, when her pulse had settled to a normal rhythm and the dew of fear-sweat had dried on her skin, she plumped her pillow, settled back under the covers and closed her eyes.

Sleep didn't come.

She tossed and turned for a while, and then tried to make herself lie still as she stared up at the ceiling and willed herself to feel drowsy again.

Not happening.

Finally, with a weary sigh, she shoved back the covers and went to the kitchen. She heated milk and sweetened it with honey. Then she carried her mug to the living area, where she turned a single lamp on low. Gazing out the two stories of windows that faced her back deck, she sipped slowly and tried to clear her mind of everything but the beauty of the Colorado night.

She could see a light on in the big house down the hill from her. Quinn Bravo lived there with his little daughter, Annabelle, and that funny old guy, Manny. They'd moved in a few months before.

Chloe smiled to herself. So. Somebody down there couldn't sleep, either. Maybe Quinn? Could the tough martial arts star suffer from bad dreams, too?

Unlikely. Quinn "the Crusher" Bravo was world-famous for taking down the most unbeatable opponents. No mere nightmare would dare keep him awake. She wished she could be more like him, impervious and strong. He seemed so very self-confident in his quiet, watchful way.

And so different, really, from the boy he'd once been, the one she remembered from when they were children, the wild, angry boy with a chip the size of Denver on his shoulder who was always getting in fights.

Different also from the boy he'd become by high school, still rough-edged, but quieter, with a seething intensity about him. She'd avoided him then, the same as she had when they were children. All the nice girls avoided dangerous and unpredictable Quinn Bravo.

Even if, secretly, he made their hearts beat faster…

Quinn Bravo stood in his living room wearing an old pair of sweats, worn mocs and a Prime Sports and Fitness T-shirt. He stared blankly out the window at the faint gleam of light from the house up the hill. Beyond that house, the almost-full face of the moon hung suspended above the peaks of the Colorado mountains.

He should go back to bed. But he knew he wouldn't sleep. He couldn't stop thinking about what his four-year-old daughter had asked him when he tucked her in that night.

A faint movement beyond the wall of windows up the hill caught his eye. Must be Chloe. She lived there alone. Beautiful, smart Chloe Winchester, who'd gone off to college at Stanford and married some big-shot lawyer as everyone always knew she would. The big shot had carried her off to live the high life down in Southern California.

Quinn didn't know the whole story. He just knew that the marriage hadn't lasted. When he moved back to town several months ago, there was Chloe, minus the rich husband, with no kids, on her own in her old hometown, living in the shadow of the Rockies on the street up the hill from him.

Maybe a little fresh air would clear his head, relax him.

Quinn pulled open the French doors that led onto the back deck. It was a clear July night, almost balmy, the moon very close to full. He stepped outside and quietly shut the doors behind him. Crossing to the deck railing, he folded his arms across his chest, braced his legs wide and stared up at the light in Chloe's house. He indulged himself, allowing his mind to dwell on her a little, to wonder about her, about what might have messed up the smooth trajectory of her life and brought her back to Justice Creek alone.

True, it was none of his business, whatever had happened to bring Chloe back where she'd started. But focusing on what might have gone wrong for a woman he didn't really know took his mind off his little girl and her questions that he had no clue how to answer.

He noted movement again up there on the hill, a glass door sliding open.

And out she came, the one and only Chloe Winchester. Damn, she was gorgeous, even from a hundred yards away. Gorgeous, even in a baggy pink shirt. That long golden hair shone silvery in the moonlight and her fine, bare legs gleamed.

Quinn had no time for chasing women. He had a daughter to raise and a new business to build. But hot damn. Any man with a pulse would want to cut himself off a nice big slice of that.

Chloe went to the railing and rested her hands on it. For a long count of ten, she stared down at him as he looked up at her. She wasn't inviting him up exactly. But he definitely felt the pull.

And how could he help enjoying the moment? Hell. Chloe Winchester giving him the look? Never in a million years would he have guessed that would happen.

And the more they stared at each other, the more certain he became that a hundred yards was too much distance between them. He would much rather look at her up close. Manny was home if Annabelle woke up.

So he went back to the doors, pushed one open and engaged the lock, drawing it shut and hearing the click that meant his daughter was safe inside. When he turned again toward the woman up the hill, she hadn't moved. She remained at the railing, her head tipped slightly down and aimed in his direction, almost certainly watching him.

Fair enough, then.

He descended the back stairs, glancing up when he reached the bottom. She hadn't moved.

So he crossed his small patch of landscaped ground and began ascending the hill between their houses, skirting rocky outcroppings and ponderosa pines, the native grasses whispering beneath the leather soles of his mocs. He took it slow, glancing up at her now and then, expecting any moment that she would turn and retreat inside—at which point he would calmly wheel around and go home where he belonged.

But Chloe stood her ground.

When he reached the base of the stairs leading up to her deck, he paused, giving her a chance to...what?

Run away? Order him off her property?

When she only continued to gaze directly down at him, her eyes steady, her expression composed, he mounted the steps.

And she did move then. She came toward him, meeting him at the top where the steps opened wide. "Quinn," she said.

He nodded. "Chloe."

"Pretty night."

"Yeah, it is."

"How have you been?"

"Doing okay. You?"

A tiny smile flickered at the corner of her lush mouth. "Getting by." With that, she turned and led the way to a pair of cedar armchairs positioned close together in front of her great room windows. She dropped into one of those chairs, a move so graceful it stole his breath, and then gestured with a small, regal sweep of her hand for him to sit beside her.

He sat. And for several minutes, neither of them spoke. They stared up at the clear night sky and the milky smear of the faraway stars. The slight breeze brought her scent to him—like some exotic flower. Jasmine, maybe. And not only that, something...a little bit musky and a whole lot womanly.

Finally, she spoke again. "What keeps *you* awake, Quinn?" Her voice was low for a woman, low and calm and pleasing.

He turned and looked at her. Her eyes were a pale, glowing shade of blue, her face a smooth oval, that tempting mouth so soft and full. She really was a prize, every red-blooded man's fantasy of the perfect woman, a woman who would make a man a beautiful home and provide him with handsome, smart, upwardly mobile children.

And as to her question? He didn't plan to answer her. But then he opened his mouth and the truth fell out. "My daughter asked about her mother for the first time tonight. I'm trying to decide what to tell her."

Chloe hummed, a thoughtful sort of sound. "Her name is Annabelle, right?"

"That's right."

"So I'm assuming Annabelle doesn't know her mother?"

"No, she doesn't. I doubt she ever will."

"Ah." Chloe waited, her head tipped to the side, her eyes alert, giving him a chance to say more. When he remained silent, she suggested, "Tell her only the truth, but tell it carefully. She's how old?"

"Four."

"She wants to know that you love her. She wants to know she's safe and that her mother loves her, too—or would, if she knew her. She wants to know it's not her fault, whatever happened that you and her mother aren't together and her mother isn't in her life." Chloe smiled. God. What he wouldn't give to taste that mouth. "But don't load it on her all at once. Well-meaning parents have a tendency to overexplain. Try to get a sense of what she's ready for and just answer the questions she actually asks."

He faced front again and stared out at the night. She was so tasty to look at, with full breasts, the points of her nipples visible under that pink shirt. She had endless legs, slender arms and that perfect angel's face. He needed to take all that beauty in careful doses. He said, "I thought you didn't have kids."

"I don't. But I like kids." The beautiful voice was weighted with sadness. "Before I moved back home, I did volunteer day care with a San Diego family shelter. I helped out with special-needs children, too. And in college, I took just about every child development class available. I had big plans in college. I was going to be the perfect wife to a very important man— and the mother of at least three healthy, bright, happy children."

Strange. Looking away wasn't working for him. Why deprive himself of the sight of her? He turned his head and faced her once more, something down inside him going tight and hot when he met her eyes. "I remember you always seemed like you knew exactly where you were going."

"Yes, I did. I used to think I knew everything, used to be so sure of how my life would be." A husky chuckle escaped her. The sound rubbed along his nerve endings, stirring up sparks. "And that's what keeps *me* up nights, Quinn. All my big plans that came to dust…"

Somewhere in the distance, a coyote howled. Quinn

considered what, exactly, he ought to say next, if anything. He was still trying to find the right words when she stood.

He let his gaze track upward over those fine legs and her little pink terry-cloth shorts, over the womanly curves under the oversize shirt. The view was amazing. And he needed to thank her for the advice, say good-night and hustle his ass back down the hill.

But then she offered him her delicate, ladylike hand. He eyed it warily, glancing up again to meet those ice-blue eyes. No mistaking what he saw in those eyes: invitation.

It was the middle of the night and he didn't have time for this. He should be home in his own damn bed.

So, was he going to turn such beauty down?

Not. A. Chance.

He took the hand she offered. Her skin was cool and silky. Heat shot up his arm, down through the center of him and straight to his groin. Stifling a groan, he rose to stand with her.

She turned quickly, pulling him along behind her, pushing open the slider, leading him inside, across her two-story great room and down a short hall to her bedroom, which was as beautiful and tasteful as the woman herself, so feminine and orderly—except for the tangled covers on the unmade bed.

She bent and turned on the nightstand lamp, then stood tall to meet his eyes once more. "Somehow I feel...safe with you," she said in that fine alto voice that turned him on as much as her face and her body did. "I've noticed..." Her voice trailed away. She glanced down, swallowed and then, finally, raised her head to meet his gaze again.

He couldn't resist. He lifted a hand, nice and slow so

as not to spook her, and ran the back of his index finger along the silky skin of her throat. She trembled and sucked in a sharp little gasp of breath, but didn't duck away. And he asked, "You've noticed what?"

Her mouth twisted, as though the words were hard to come by. "Since you, uh, came back to town, you seem... I don't know. So calm. Kind of thoughtful. I admire that, I really do."

What could he say to that? Thanks? That seemed kind of lame, so he didn't say anything, just ran the back of his finger down the outside of her arm, enjoying the satiny feel of her skin, loving the way her mouth formed a soft O and her eyes went hazy in response to his touch.

She said, "I've been with one man in my life—my husband, who was supposed to be loving and tender and protective, but turned out to be one rotten, abusive, cheating SOB." She moved slightly away from him again, reaching over to pull open the bedside drawer. "I've been out a few times with nice men, in the year since I came home. I keep thinking I need to take the plunge again, take a chance again and be with someone new. So I bought these." She raised her hand and he saw that she held a strip of condoms. They unrolled from her palm with a snap. "To be prepared, you know?" A soft, rueful smile. "I haven't used a single one. I didn't want to. It never felt right. But tonight, with you... Quinn, I..." Her fine voice gone breathless, she said, "Back in high school, sometimes, I used to think about what it might be like, to be with you..."

Those words hit him right where he lived. "I used to think about you, too, Chloe."

Her amazing face glowed up at him. "You did?"

"Oh, yeah." Not that she ever would have gone out with him if he asked her. She'd had her plans for her life and they didn't include a wannabe cage fighter who could barely read. Plus, her snotty parents would've disowned her if she started in with one of Willow Mooney's boys, the ones they called the *bastard Bravos* because his mother hadn't married his father, Frank Bravo, until after Frank's rich first wife, Sondra, died.

Uh-uh. No way Linda Winchester would have let her precious only daughter get near him, one of Willow's boys—and the "slow" one, at that. And Chloe was always a good girl who did what her mama expected of her.

Chloe scanned his face, her expression suddenly anxious. "I have this feeling that somehow I should explain myself, give you a better reason to stay with me tonight..."

"Uh-uh." He stepped even closer—close enough that her body touched his. Her soft breasts brushed his chest, and the dizzying scent of her swam around him. Slowly, carefully, he lifted his hand and speared his fingers into that glorious mane of yellow hair. Like a curtain of silk, that hair. He loved the feel of it so much that he balled his fist and wrapped the thick strands around his wrist, pulling her even closer, right up against him, nice and tight.

"Oh!" she said on a shaky breath, baby blue eyes saucer-wide staring up into his.

All that softness and beauty, his for the night. He bent enough to suck in a deep breath through his nose. God, the scent of her. She smelled of everything womanly, everything most wanted—everything he'd never thought to hold, not even for a single night. He buried his face against her long, silky throat. "You don't need to explain anything, angel." He nuzzled her neck and then scraped his teeth across her tender skin. She gasped. He muttered, "Not a damn thing."

"I'm not an angel."

"Yeah, you are."

"Just for tonight, yeah?" She wrapped those slim arms around him, clutching him to her, tipping her head back, offering him more, offering him everything. "Just this one time…"

"However you want it."

"Just kiss me. Just…hold me. Just make me forget."

And like that, he...

Chapter Two

Quinn took her by the shoulders and gently set her at arm's length. She swayed a little on her bare feet, gazing up at him, breathless, eyes starry with need.

He said, "First, I want to see you."

A soft gasp. "Okay."

"All of you."

"Okay."

He took her big pink shirt by the hem. "Raise your arms."

She obeyed without hesitation. He lifted the shirt up over her head, past the pink-painted tips of her fingers and tossed it away. Her hair settled, so shiny and thick, spilling past her shoulders, down her back, over her breasts. She let her arms fall back to her sides and gazed up at him expectantly.

Impossible. Chloe Winchester, naked to the waist, standing right in front of him.

He cupped one fine, full breast in his hand and flicked

the pretty nipple. His breath clogged in his throat, and the ache in his groin intensified. "You're so damn beautiful, Chloe."

"I…" She didn't seem to know what to say next. Which was fine. He was getting one night with her. And it wasn't going to be about what either of them might have to say.

He leaned close again, because he couldn't stop himself. He stuck out his tongue and licked her temple. She moaned. He blew on the place he'd just moistened, guiding her hair out of the way and whispering into the perfect pink shell of her ear "Take off those little shorts."

She whipped them down and off in an instant, so fast that he couldn't help smiling. And then she stood tall again, completely naked in front of him, an answering smile trembling its way across her mouth. "Quinn?"

"Shh. Let me look."

She widened her eyes—and then she shut them. And then she just stood there, eyes closed tight, and let him gaze his fill.

Touching followed. How could he help reaching for her? She was smooth and round and firm and soft. And she was standing right in front of him, Chloe Winchester, who had starred in more than one of his wild and impossible sexual fantasies when he was growing up.

He pulled her close again, wrapped his arms around the slim, yet curvy shape of her and pressed his lips into her hair. "Beautiful."

She lifted her face and gazed up at him. "You, too, please." He must have looked confused, because she added, "I want to see you, too."

He chuckled and stepped back. "Yes, ma'am." It took about ten seconds. He kicked off the mocs, reached back over his shoulders and pulled his shirt up and off. He eased the sweats over his erection and pushed them down, dropping them to the floor and stepping free of them.

"Oh," she said. "Oh, Quinn…" She reached out and ran her palm over his belly and then over the series of tats that covered his left arm. And then she touched the one for Annabelle, the angel's wings and the green vines, the trumpet flowers and his little girl's name, written right where it should be written, over his heart. "I never thought…you and me. Like this…?"

"Hey. Me, neither."

"Life can be so awful."

"Yeah."

"But then there are surprising, magical moments—like this one, huh?"

He nodded. "Yeah." He turned and shoved the tangled sheets and blankets out of the way. And then he took her by the waist, lifted her and set her on the bed. "Lie down."

She obeyed, stretching out on her side with a sigh. He went down to the mattress with her. He kissed her, tasting her mouth for the first time, finding it as sweet as the rest of her. Her tongue came out to play and for a while, they just lay there, on their sides, kissing and kissing, as if nothing else mattered in the whole damn world, nothing but his mouth and her mouth, the scrape of white teeth, the tangle of tongues.

One night they had together. He wanted to stretch every second just short of the breaking point, enjoy every touch, every sigh, every soft, tempting curve. He wanted to share her breath and the tender, urgent beat of her heart.

After he kissed her mouth, he kissed her everywhere else, too, taking forever about it, getting carried away, using his teeth as well as his tongue. He knew he left marks, marks he soothed with softer, gentler kisses. She never once objected when he used his teeth.

Far from it. She gasped and cried out her pleasure, clutching him close, telling him "Yes" and "More" and "Again, Quinn. Oh, again…"

He gave her more. More strokes, more kisses, trailing his mouth down the center of her, biting a little, trying not to be too rough, opening her, dipping his tongue in. He pushed her legs wide and settled between them for a long time.

She came twice then, as he played her with his mouth and his hands. She had his name on her lips, over and over. He loved that most of all: Chloe Winchester, calling his name as she came.

After that second time, when she was boneless and open for him, he rose to his knees between her spread thighs. Ripping the first condom off the strip, he took off the wrapper and rolled it down over his length, easing it into place nice and tight. She stared up at him, dazed and flushed and softly smiling.

"Quinn." She reached for him. "Please…"

And he went down to her, taking most of his weight on his arms. She slipped her hand between them, closing those slim fingers around him. He was the one groaning then, the one calling *her* name.

She guided him in. He sank into her slowly, carefully, little by little, stretching her and the moment, making it last. She felt so good—better than anything he'd ever known, soft and welcoming, and a little bit tight.

He varied the rhythm, watching her face, matching his strokes to her pleasured moans, her hungry cries. Somehow he stayed with her, until she went over for the third time. After that, there was no holding back. He was rough and fast, and she clung to him, nice and tight, all the way to the peak and over the edge.

She cradled him close then, stroking his shoulders and his arms, whispering "So good. Just right," laughing a little. "Who knew, really? Whoever would have thought…?"

"Beautiful," he said. "Never would have guessed."

They must have dozed for a while.

He woke to find her sleeping peacefully, one arm across his chest. He'd been hoping that maybe they would have time to play some more.

But it was later than he'd thought. The clock by the bed said 5:05 in the morning. The first glow of daylight would be bleeding the night from the sky all too soon. The houses in their neighborhood were spaced far apart, built to conform to the shape of the land, with plenty of big trees between them. He might make it down the hill in broad daylight with no one the wiser.

But why take that chance? It was nobody's business, this one unforgettable night they'd shared.

With care, he eased out from under her arm. She sighed and rolled to her back, but didn't wake. He slid from the bed. Before settling the covers over her, he stole another long glance at her and got struck by a last hot bolt of pure lust at the sight of the faint marks he'd left on her perfect breasts, her pretty belly.

They would fade soon, those marks. He tried not to wish…

Uh-uh. Never mind. One night. That was the deal.

He pulled on his clothes and went out the way he'd come in, noting that she hadn't rearmed the alarm on the wall by the slider when she led him inside.

Good. That meant he didn't have to wake her to go. He locked the slider and then went out through the front door, which he could also lock behind him, thus securing her inside.

He ran around the side of the house and then on down the hill.

At home, he got the spare key from its hiding place under the stairs and let himself in. The house was just as he'd left it. Silent and dark.

He stepped inside and shut the doors with barely a sound—and found Manny, his former trainer and long-time business partner, sitting in one of the big chairs by the moss rock fireplace. The old fighter switched on the lamp beside him. He wore a knowing grin on that road-map of a face. "Hey, Crush. Where you been?"

Quinn locked the doors. "Since when are you my mother?"

Manny rumbled out a low laugh. "You and that gorgeous uptown blonde up the hill? I never had a clue."

"I don't know what you're talkin' about." Quinn headed for the stairs.

Manny watched him go. "She's a fine one. I find I am lookin' at you with new respect."

"Night, Manny."

"Got news for you, Crush. It's tomorrow already."

Quinn just kept walking. Manny's knowing cackle followed him up the stairs.

Chloe was sound asleep when her alarm went off at seven.

She woke with a smile, feeling thoroughly rested and a little bit sore. If it weren't for that soreness and the small, already-fading red marks and bruises on her breasts and stomach, she almost might have been able to tell herself that the night before was all a dream.

Not that she wanted to deny what had happened. It had been glorious. She'd loved every minute of it.

As she sat up and stretched, yawning with gusto, she couldn't help wishing she hadn't told Quinn that she only wanted one night. Because he was remarkable. He'd given her hope that love and passion and tenderness weren't all just some fantasy, some bright, naive dream that could never come true.

She would love to spend more time with him.

But she let her arms drop and her shoulders droop with a sigh.

No. They had a deal and she would stick by it. He'd been great and the sex had been mind-blowing. Now she knew for certain that there were better lovers out there than Ted. She would be grateful for that and eventually, maybe, she'd find someone who made her want to take another chance on forever.

She got ready for work and then had breakfast. The house phone rang just as she was heading out the door. Probably her mother. She'd check her messages later and call her back then.

As she was pulling out of the driveway, her cell rang. She slipped the SUV into Park and checked the display. With a sigh, she gave in and answered. "Hi, Mom. Just on my way over to the showroom."

"But it's not even nine yet," Linda Winchester complained. "You have time to stop by the house. Let me fix you some breakfast."

"I've already eaten. And I have to get the shop opened."

"Sweetheart, it's your shop. You're the boss. No need to rush over there at the crack of dawn."

"Come on, Mom. A successful business doesn't run itself." Not that Your Way Interior Design was all that successful. Yet.

"I hardly see you lately. We need to chat."

Chatting with her mother was the *last* thing she needed. They hadn't been getting along all that well since Chloe's divorce. And it had only gotten worse after she returned to Justice Creek. Linda knew what was right for her only child and she never missed an opportunity to lecture Chloe on all she'd done wrong. And somehow, whenever they "chatted," her mother always managed to bring up Ted and the perfect life Chloe had thrown away. "Mom, I'll have to call you later. I need to get to work."

"But, sweetheart, I want to—"

"Call you tonight, Mom."

Her mother was still protesting as Chloe disconnected the call.

She drove to her showroom and unlocked the doors at nine, an hour before most of the businesses on Central Street opened. She had a good location and an attractive shop, with neutral walls and sleek, modern cabinetry and red and yellow accents to give it energy and interest. Her motto was Your Space, Your Way. She had attractive displays, and plenty of them, lots of table space for spreading out samples. And she was trained in every aspect of home design, from blueprints up.

Her website looked great and she stayed active on Facebook, Pinterest, Twitter and Tumblr. She kept a blog where she gave free tips on great ways to spiff up your living space. During the school year, she ran a workshop right there in her showroom for high school students interested in interior design. She contributed her expertise to local churches, helping them spruce up their Sunday school rooms and social halls. And she worked right along with the other shop owners in Justice Creek on various chamber of commerce projects.

Still, it took time to build a business. Chloe had found

a real shark of a divorce lawyer who'd put the screws to Ted and got her a nice lump settlement, which Chloe had asked for. The onetime payout was less than monthly alimony would have been in total, but the last thing she wanted was to be getting regular checks from Ted. With the settlement, she'd been able to cut ties with him completely.

She'd tried to spend her money wisely. She loved her house, which she'd redone herself, and she was proud of her business. But the past couple of months, she had more to worry about than putting Ted behind her and whether or not there might someday be love in her future.

Chloe's nest egg was shrinking. Your Way needed to start paying *its* way.

That day, as it turned out, was better than most. She had steady walk-in traffic. A new couple in town came in and hired her to do all the window treatments in the house they'd just bought. She scheduled three appointments to give estimates: two living room redesigns and a kitchen upgrade. When her assistant, Tai Stockard, a design student home from CU for the summer, came in at one, Chloe sent her to the Library Café for takeout paninis. It was turning into a profitable day and they might as well enjoy a nice lunch.

Chloe went home smiling—until she remembered she owed her mother a call.

"Come on over for dinner," her mother coaxed. "I've got lamb chops and twice-baked potatoes just the way you love them. We're leaving for Maui tomorrow." Chloe's mom and dad would be gone for two weeks, staying at a luxury resort where her mother could enjoy the spa and the lavish meals and her father could play golf. "I want to see you before we go."

Chloe went to dinner at the house where she'd grown

up. It wasn't that bad. Linda managed not to say a single word about Ted. And it was good to see her dad. An orthodontist with a successful practice, Doug Winchester had a dry sense of humor and never tried to tell his only daughter how to live her life.

By nine, Chloe was back at home. She got ready for bed, settled under the covers with the latest bestseller and tried not to let her mind wander to the question of what Quinn Bravo might be doing that night.

Quinn heard the soft whisper of small feet across the tiled floor as he stared out the window at the single light shining from inside Chloe's house. "Go back to bed, Annabanana," he said softly without turning.

"I can't."

"Why not?"

"The monsters are very noisy. And I'm not a banana. You know that, Daddy."

"Yes, you are." He turned and dropped to a crouch. "You're my favorite banana."

Dragging her ancient pink blanket and her one-eyed teddy bear, Annabelle marched right up to him and put one of her little hands on his shoulder. "No, I'm not. I'm a *girl.*"

He leaned closer and whispered, "Ah. Gotta remember that."

"Pick me up, Daddy," she instructed. "Get the flashlight."

He wrapped his arms around her and stood. She giggled and hugged his neck, shoving her musty old teddy bear into the side of his face. He detoured to the kitchen, where he got the flashlight from a drawer. Then he returned to the living room and mounted the stairs.

She didn't object as he carried her up to her room, set

her down on the bed, flicked on the lamp and then pulled the covers up over her and the stuffed bear, smoothing the ancient blanket atop her butterfly-printed bedspread.

"Closet," she said, when he bent to kiss her plump cheek.

He went to the closet, pushed the door open and shone the light around inside. "Nothing in here."

"You have to tell them," she said patiently. "You know that."

He ran the light over her neatly hung-up dresses and the row of little shoes and said in his deepest, gruffest voice, "Monsters, get lost." He rolled the door shut. "That should do it."

But Annabelle didn't agree. "Now under the bed."

So he knelt by the bed and lifted up the frilly bed skirt and shone the light around underneath. "Holiday Barbie's down here. With her dress over her head."

The bed skirt on the other side rustled as small hands lifted it and Annabelle appeared, upside down. "Oops." She snatched up the doll and let the bed skirt drop. "Okay, tell them."

"Monsters, get lost." He gave a long, threatening growl for good measure. On the bed, his daughter laughed, a delighted peal of sound that had him smiling to himself. "So, all right," he said. "They're gone." And then he got up and sat on the bed and tucked her in again, bending close to press a kiss on her cheek and breathe in the little-girl smell of her. Toothpaste and baby shampoo, so familiar. So sweet. "Anything else?" he asked, suddenly worried about how she might answer, recalling Chloe's wise advice of the night before. *She wants to know it's not her fault, whatever happened that you and her mother aren't together and her mother isn't in her life…*

Annabelle shook her head. "That's all."

He felt equal parts guilt and relief. Guilt that he wasn't as good a father as Annabelle deserved. Relief that he wouldn't have to tackle the tough questions tonight, after all. "You know there are really no monsters in your room, right?"

She nodded slowly. "But I like it when you scare them away."

He got up. "Sleep now, princess."

She beamed at him. "Princess is good. Not banana."

"Close your eyes…"

"I want a princess room. All the princesses. Snow White and Cinderella and Mulan and Elsa and Belle and Merida and—"

"Time for sleep. Close your eyes…" He heard Chloe's rich alto again, as though she whispered in his ear. *She wants to know that you love her.* "I love you, princess."

"Love you, Daddy." With a little sigh, Annabelle closed her eyes. He turned off the light and shut the door silently behind him on the way out.

Back downstairs, all was quiet. Manny had gone to Boulder for the night to visit his current lady friend. Quinn took up his vigil at the wall of windows in the living room. Up at Chloe's the light remained on. He could see it glowing through the pale curtains that covered the slider in her bedroom. He pictured her, wearing that big pink shirt, propped up against the pillows in her bed, with her laptop or maybe a good book, which she would read effortlessly, turning the pages fast to find out what would happen next.

And then, well, after last night, he couldn't help picturing her other ways—like, say, naked beneath him, moaning his name in that low, sexy voice that drove him crazy. He told himself it was a good thing that Manny wasn't there to watch over Annabelle if he stepped out.

Because climbing that hill again?

Way too much on his mind.

"Crush, I gotta say it," Manny grumbled. "I'm disappointed in you."

It was Friday night, five nights since the one Quinn had spent with Chloe. Annabelle had been tucked safely in bed, the monsters chased away. Quinn and Manny sat out on the deck having a beer under the clear, starry sky. Quinn took a long, cool swallow and said nothing.

Manny wiggled his white eyebrows. They grew every which way and he never bothered to trim them. "Aren't you gonna ask me why?"

Quinn gave a low chuckle. "We both know you'll tell me anyway."

Manny snorted. "Yes, I will. I've spent over a decade makin' sure you learn what you need to know. No reason to change now."

Quinn only looked at him, waiting.

Manny announced, "Romance is like everything else worth doin' in life. You gotta follow up, put some energy into it, or it goes nowhere."

"I don't know why you're telling *me* this."

"I'll give you a hint. Chloe Winchester. Only a fool would pass up his chance with a woman like that."

"That's given that he *had* a chance in the first place."

"See there? That's defeat talkin'. Quinn the Crusher, he spits in the face of defeat."

"Quinn the Crusher retired, remember?"

"From the Octagon, sure. But not from life. Last time I checked, you still got a pulse."

"Leave it alone, Manny."

Manny did no such thing. "A woman like that, she lets you in her house in the middle of the night, you got a chance. You got more than a chance."

"You need to stop sticking your nose in where it doesn't belong. Somebody's likely to break it."

"Won't be the first time." A raspy cackle. "Or the second or the third." Manny swiped a gnarled, big-knuckled hand back over his buzz cut and then took a pull off the longneck in his other fist. "I will repeat. Momentum is everything."

Quinn got up from his deck chair and headed for the French doors. "Night, Manny."

"Where you going?"

"I'm halfway through *A Tale of Two Cities*." He had it in audio book, and tried to get in a few chapters a night. Little by little, he was working his way through the great books of Western literature.

Manny wasn't impressed with Quinn's highbrow reading. "It's just dandy, you improving your mind and all, but a man needs more than a book to keep him warm at night."

There was no winning an argument with Manny. Quinn knew that from years of experience. "Lock up when you come in." He stepped inside and shut the doors before the old fighter could get going again.

The following Monday, Chloe was selling new carpet to Agnes Oldfield, a pillar of the Justice Creek community and a longtime friend of her mother's, when who should walk in the door but Manny Aldovino? Quinn's little girl was with him, looking like a pint-size princess in an ankle-length dress with a hot pink top, a wide white sash at the waist and a gathered cotton skirt decorated with rickrack in a rainbow of bright colors.

Chloe ignored the fluttering sensation beneath her breastbone that came with being reminded of Quinn, and greeted the newcomers with a cheery "Hi, Manny. Annabelle. Have a look around. I'll be right with you. Crayons and paper in the hutch by the window treatment display, in case Annabelle would like to color. And there's coffee, too." She gestured at the table not far from the door.

"Sounds good," said Manny. He winked at Agnes. "How you doin' there, Agnes?"

"Mr. Aldovino." Agnes gave Manny an icy, dismissive nod. She'd always been a terrible snob and she looked down on anyone she didn't consider of her social standing. Also, Quinn's father's first wife, Sondra, had been Agnes's beloved niece. Agnes thoroughly disapproved of Quinn's mother, Willow, and of all of Willow's children. Now Agnes pointedly turned her back on Manny and said to Chloe, "Please continue, dear."

Agnes's attitude could use adjusting. But Chloe reminded herself that she needed the business and she couldn't afford to offend a customer. She sent Manny an apologetic smile and waited on the old woman, who wanted new carpet for three rooms. She'd already settled on a quality plush in a pretty dove gray. Chloe accepted her deposit and gave her the number to call to arrange a time to have the spaces measured.

In her eighties, Agnes always dressed as though she'd been invited to tea with the Queen of England. She adjusted the giant, jeweled lizard brooch on her pink silk Chanel suit and said, "Thank you, my dear."

"Have a great day, Agnes."

The old lady sailed out the door.

"Wound a little tight, that one," Manny remarked drily once Agnes was gone.

With a sigh and a shrug, Chloe joined the old man

and the little girl at one of the worktables. "Now. What can I do for you?"

Annabelle glanced up from coloring an enormous, smiling yellow sun. Chloe saw Quinn in the shape of his daughter's eyes and the directness of her gaze. Really, the little girl was downright enchanting, with that heart-shaped face and those chipmunk cheeks. Chloe felt a bittersweet tug at her heartstrings. Annabelle reminded her of the children she should have had.

But after that first time Ted punched her, having kids had never felt right. And Ted hadn't really cared about children anyway. He wanted his wife focused on him.

"I want a princess room," the little girl announced. Chloe gladly put away her grim thoughts of Ted to focus on the sprite in the darling dress. "Manny says you can make me one."

"Yes, I can."

"I want *all* the princesses. Belle and Merida and—" Manny chuckled and tapped the little girl on the arm. She glanced up at him. "But, Manny—"

"I know, I know. You want all the princesses and you're gonna get 'em, but what did we talk about?"

Annabelle huffed. "To wait my turn and not be rude."

The old man beamed. "That's right."

Annabelle leaned close to him, batted those big eyes and whispered, "But I want my princess room."

"It's yours. Promise. But the grown-ups have to talk now."

"Okay." Annabelle bent to her smiling sun again.

Manny spoke to Chloe then. "Quinn's pretty busy getting the business off the ground." His gym, Prime Sports and Fitness, was just down the street from Chloe's showroom, at the intersection of West Central and Marmot Drive. "You know Quinn, don't you?"

"Of course. We…went to school together."

"Right. So Quinn takes care of the business. I look after Annabelle and run the house. You ever seen the inside of our house?"

Chloe blinked away a mental image of Quinn, up on his knees between her legs. Quinn, gloriously naked, his beautiful blue-green eyes burning down at her. "Erm, your house? No, I haven't been inside."

"It's a good house, big rooms, great light, four thousand square feet. But built in the eighties, and looks like it. Too much ceramic tile and ugly carpet."

"So it needs a little loving care?" she asked, trying to sound cool and professional and fearing the old man could see right inside her head to the X-rated images of Annabelle's dad.

"What it needs is a boatload of cash and a good decorator. Starting on the ground floor and moving on up."

"You want to redo every room?" That would be good for her. Very good. Not only for the money, but for Your Way's reputation. She could put up a whole new website area, if Quinn and Manny agreed, showing the before and after of at least the main rooms. Their housing development was an upscale one. However, like Quinn's house, most of the homes were more than twenty years old. Doing a full-on interior redesign always got the neighbors' attention, got them thinking that their houses could stand a little sprucing up, too. She could end up with a lot of new business from the job Manny described. She asked, "What about the bathrooms and the kitchen?"

"Like I said, all of it. Every room."

She couldn't help wondering if Quinn was behind this? "What will you need from me? I'll be happy to show you examples of my work—my portfolio? We can take a look at the website so you'll have a better feel of what I can do. As for references, I—"

"Naw. I already looked at the website and I liked what I saw."

Was she blushing? Manny had a gruff way about him, but he also knew how to turn on the charm. She really liked him. She liked his way with Annabelle, liked that teasing twinkle in his watery eyes. "Well, thank you."

"I got a good feeling about you, Chloe. A real good feeling." The old guy smiled, deepening the network of wrinkles on his craggy face. She really did wonder exactly how much he knew about her and Quinn and what had happened between them eight nights ago. He went on. "I'm thinking you should come over to the house. I'll show you around, show you what I want done and then you can come up with some drawings and blueprints and all that. We can start right away, as soon as you're ready to go..."

"Do you have an architect or any contractors you want to use?"

"Bravo Construction, if they give you a decent bid on the job—and if you're okay with them. You'll be running this, so you gotta be happy with the people you're working with."

Chloe nodded. "I know them, of course." Quinn's older brother, Garrett, ran the company, from what Chloe had heard. And his youngest sister, Nell, worked there, too. Garrett had been three years or so ahead of Chloe in school, so she didn't remember all that much about him. And Nell was four years younger than Chloe. Still, Chloe vaguely remembered her. Gorgeous, and something of a wild child, wasn't she? Never one to back down from a fight. She told Manny brightly, "They have a great reputation. I'll ask them for a bid, absolutely."

Manny winked at her. "Might as well try and keep it in the family."

Chloe got the message. Manny did want her to use the Bravos. "Sounds good to me." She made a mental note to go with them if at all possible.

Half an hour later, when Manny and Annabelle left, Chloe had an appointment at Quinn's house for two in the afternoon the next day.

She was thrilled.

But then again, come on. It was too much of a coincidence. She suspected rough-edged old Manny of matchmaking, because it just didn't seem like something Quinn would engineer. Quinn Bravo was more direct than that. If he wanted to see her again, he would just say so.

Wouldn't he?

She had to admit she couldn't be sure. Maybe Quinn hesitated to ask her out now, after she'd made such a point of that one night being the *only* night the two of them would ever share.

Maybe he knew nothing about Manny's plans to tear their house apart and redo it, top to bottom.

Maybe, come to think of it, Quinn had no desire at all to ask her out. What if he ended up hating the idea that his daughter's caregiver planned to hire the woman up the hill, with whom he'd had a one-night stand? What if he wanted nothing to do with her now? If she took the job, she would be in and out of his house for weeks.

That would be awful, if it turned out that Quinn really didn't want her around. Here she was, gloating over this plum job that had magically fallen in her lap, when Quinn might know nothing about it—and not be the least bit happy when he found out.

By the time Tai arrived at one, Chloe had made up her mind.

Before she went to Quinn's house tomorrow and consulted with Manny on the changes he wanted made, she needed to know for sure what Quinn really thought of her being there.

And the only way to know for sure was to ask the man himself.

Chapter Three

Chloe sent Tai to get takeout again. They shared lunch. And then she left Tai in charge and walked the two blocks to Prime Sports and Fitness, her heart hammering at her ribs all the way.

Quinn's gym filled a three-story brick building directly across the street from the popular Irish-style pub, McKellan's. Chloe hesitated outside on the sidewalk, ordering her pulse to slow down a little, noting the good location and the clean, modern lines of the building itself. There were lots of windows and various athletic activities visible from the street. In one room, some kind of martial arts class was in progress. Another room took up most of the second floor and held rows of cardio equipment, with people in exercise gear working out on stationary bikes, treadmills and elliptical trainers.

She stood there staring up for a couple of minutes at least. Until she finally had to accept that her nervousness hadn't faded at all. In fact, it was worse. So she smoothed the front of her narrow white pants, tugged on the hem of the light, short blazer she wore over a featherweight black tank, squared her shoulders and went in.

The gorgeous, hardbody brunette at the front desk said that Quinn was just finishing up leading a boxing conditioning class. Chloe could wait in his office. It shouldn't be long.

So Chloe sat in his office, where the walls were lined with pictures of Quinn in his fighting days and more than one big, shiny trophy stood on display. She had become absolutely certain that she'd made a horrible mistake in coming here and was just about to rise and bolt from the building, when the door swung open and there he was, looking sweaty and spectacular in gray boxing shorts and a muscle-hugging T.

"Hello, Chloe." Quinn thought he'd never seen anyone so smooth and beautiful, in those perfect white pants and pointy little shoes, not a single golden hair out of place.

"Quinn." She sounded breathless. He liked that. And she bounced to her feet. "I... How are you?" She held out her hand.

"Good. Real good." He stepped forward and took it, already regretting he hadn't run to the locker room and grabbed a quick shower after class. Her slim fingers were cool and dry in his sweaty paw.

But she didn't seem to mind. She held on and he held on and they stood and stared at each other. She looked a little stunned, but in a good way. And he had no doubt his expression mirrored hers.

Finally, she said in a breathless rush, "I need... Well, there's something I really have to discuss with you."

"Sure." He made himself release her hand and went

back to shut the door as she returned to the chair. "Something to drink? Juice? Tea?" When she shook her head, he slid in behind his desk and gestured for her to sit back down. "Okay. What's going on?"

"I, uh, had a visit from Manny and Annabelle today, at my design showroom. Manny offered me a really good project, redoing all the rooms in your house." She paused to swallow and smooth her already perfect hair. "I agreed to meet him at your house tomorrow in the afternoon to go over the changes he wants. If he still wants to hire me, I'll work out the numbers and put together a contract."

This was all news to Quinn. But not bad news. He asked cautiously, "And this is a problem somehow?"

"Well, after Manny and Annabelle left, I started wondering if you even knew that he was planning to hire me. I thought I should, you know, check with you, make certain you're on board with Manny's plan…" Her voice trailed off.

He watched her try not to fidget. And the longer he sat there looking at her, the more he came to grips with the fact that the one night he'd had with her wasn't enough. Luckily for him, her signal came through loud and clear: she felt the same way.

No, he had no time for romance.

But for a woman like Chloe, he might just have to make time.

Should he be pissed off at Manny for taking the situation into his battered old hands? Probably. Manny had no business butting in.

But Quinn had just spent a week keeping himself from climbing the hill to get to her. Manny's bold move had brought her right to him. Pissed off? Hardly. Downright grateful was more like it.

Not that he'd ever admit that to Manny.

A small, embarrassed sound escaped her. "Oh, God. You *didn't* know, did you?"

"Doesn't matter. Manny's in charge of the house and we agreed when we bought the place that it would need major upgrades. It's his call who he hires to make that happen."

"So you're okay with it—with me, working in your house?"

He was more than just okay with it. "Sounds like a good idea to me—I mean, if you're willing."

She gave him one of those glowing smiles that could light up the blackest night. "Well, then. Yes. I'm willing, definitely." She got up. "So, then, I guess I should be…"

He couldn't let her go. Not yet. He pushed back his chair. "Now that you're here, how 'bout I show you around?"

"The gym, you mean?"

"That's right."

"Yes. Yes, I would like that."

"Well, okay, then. This way…"

Chloe followed Quinn past the reception area, into a series of wood-floored classrooms with mirrored walls and different kinds of equipment stacked in the corners. In one, a fitness ball class was in progress. In another, the participants were paired up for intense stretching. They went upstairs to the second floor and the giant cardio room as well as a room with all kinds of weight machines and one with boxing equipment and two rings.

He explained that Prime Fitness tried to offer something for everyone. "We have martial arts for all ages, boxing, kickboxing, general fitness and yoga classes…"

She listened and nodded, just glad to be walking along

beside him, glad that he seemed to want to keep her there longer, to be drawing the moments out before she left.

On the top floor there was a beginning women's self-defense class in progress. They watched through the observation window as a big guy in a padded suit tried to take down a woman about Chloe's size. The woman shouted and fought him off violently, kicking and slugging at him, spinning away and sprinting off as soon as she got the guy to let go of her.

Watching that made Chloe's mouth go dry and her palms feel clammy. It made her think of Ted and how she ought to be better prepared if anyone ever hit her or threatened her again.

"What do you think?" Quinn asked.

She turned to him, met those wonderful, watchful eyes. "I think I might want to take a class like this."

There was a bench a few feet away. He backed up and sat down. She left the viewing window and sat beside him.

He said, "This class is wrapping up. A new one will start next week, and there's an evening class, too. Starts in two weeks. It's an eight-week course, one two-hour class per week."

"I'll be fighting off guys in padded suits for eight weeks?"

He shook his head. "No. Initially there are sessions on staying out of violent confrontations in the first place."

"How?"

He chuckled. "What? You want an outline of the course?"

"Can you give me one?"

"You're serious?"

"I am, yes."

He watched her for a long moment. And then he shrugged. "Well, all right. The class starts with a section on the nature of predators. Basically there are two types. Resource and process. Resource predators want your stuff. Process predators are in it for the power and the thrill. They want to mess you over. They actually enjoy committing crimes. The class shows you how to identify what kind of scumbag you're faced with and how to deal with him. Next comes a study of avoidance, because the best option is always steering clear of any situation where you could get hurt. After avoidance, there's a section on deescalating conflict. If you can't escape trouble before it happens, the second-best option is to diffuse it. And finally you'll learn how to fight off an attack."

"Wow," she said, and wondered if any guy ever looked as good in shorts and a T-shirt as Quinn did. And he smelled so good, too. Clean. Just sweaty enough to be exciting…

He grunted. "See? More information than you needed or wanted."

She shook her head. "That was exactly what I wanted to know. And how do *you* know all that? Do you teach this kind of class yourself?"

"No. But I've been through every class that we offer here. I run the place. It's my job to know what I'm selling. I want to franchise this operation. This location will be the model for Prime Sports and Fitness gyms all over the country."

"You dream big."

"Hey. Balls to the wall. It's the only way to go."

She made a decision. "I'm taking the next evening class."

"Am I a salesman, or what?" He got up. "Come on." He put his big hand at the small of her back. Such a light touch to wreak such total havoc through every quivering cell in her body. "We'll sign you up."

At the front desk, Quinn tried to comp her the class. She shook her head and whipped out her checkbook. Once she'd paid for the course, he walked her out the door.

He caught her arm as the door eased shut behind them. "So, Chloe…"

She was achingly aware of him, so close, his big, warm fingers wrapped lightly around her upper arm. He walked her forward several feet along the sidewalk and then pulled her gently around to face him.

"Yeah?" she asked low, her voice barely a whisper.

He stepped in closer and spoke for her ears alone. "The other night…?"

Her breath tangled in her throat. "Yeah?"

"You said just for that night, just that once. But you're here and I'm looking in those fine blue eyes and I'm wondering, did you really mean that?"

Her stupid throat had clutched up tight. She swallowed convulsively, and then shook her head hard.

His brow rumpled in a frown, but the hint of a smile seemed to tug on his mouth. "I'm still not sure what you're telling me here."

And somehow she found her voice again. "Sorry…"

"Nothing to be sorry for. You just say it right out loud, whatever your answer is. I can take it, I promise you."

She cleared her throat to get her going. "Ahem. That night, I needed to find a way to give myself permission to do something I wanted to do but had never done before. That night, I needed to think of it as just that one time and never again. But since then…"

"Yeah?"

"Oh, Quinn. I wish I hadn't said what I said. Because I've been thinking about you a lot. And it's really good to see you again."

Those fine eyes were gleaming. "Yeah?"

And she was eagerly nodding, her head bouncing up and down like a bobblehead doll's.

"So, then..." He started walking backward toward the doors.

She resisted the urge to reach out and stop him—and also the one that demanded she follow him. Instead, she held her ground and asked hopefully, "So, then, what?"

He stopped at the doors. "How 'bout Friday night? You and me. Dinner."

"Dinner..." How could one simple word hold so much promise?

"Yeah." He was definitely smiling now. "You know, like people do."

"I would like that." She knew she wore a giant, silly grin. And somehow she had gone on tiptoe. Her body felt lighter than air.

"Pick you up at seven?"

She settled back onto her heels and nodded. "Seven is great."

A trim, fortyish woman in workout clothes approached the doors. Quinn opened one and ushered her in. Then, with a final nod in Chloe's direction, he went in, too.

That lighter-than-air feeling? It stayed with her. Her feet barely touched the ground the whole way back to the showroom.

Strange how everything could change for the better in the course of one afternoon.

All at once, the world, so cruel to her in recent years, was a good and hopeful place again. Suddenly everything looked brighter.

Yeah, okay. It was just a date. But it was a date with a man who thrilled her—and made her feel safe and protected and cherished and capable, all at the same time.

* * *

That night, Chloe made chocolate chip cookies. Once they'd cooled, she packed them up into two bright decorator tins. She took them to the showroom the next morning. One she offered at the coffee table.

The other she carried with her when she went to meet with Manny at Quinn's house after lunch.

"Cookies!" Annabelle nodded her approval. "I *like* cookies." She sent Manny a regretful glance. "Manny's cookies are not very good."

Manny told Chloe, "Never was a baker—or that much of a cook, when you come right down to it. I enjoy cooking, though. Too bad nobody appreciates my efforts." He wiggled his bushy eyebrows at Annabelle. "And what do you say when someone brings you really good cookies?"

"Thank you, Chloe."

"You're welcome."

She turned those sweet brown eyes on Manny again. "Can I have one now?"

"That could be arranged." Manny led them to the kitchen, which had appliances that had been state-of-the-art back in the late eighties, a fruit-patterned wallpaper border up near the ceiling and acres of white ceramic tile. Annabelle made short work of two cookies and a glass of milk, after which she wanted to take Chloe up to her room.

Chloe looked to Manny. The old guy shrugged. "Don't keep her up there all day," he said to the little girl.

"Manny, I want *all* the princesses, but it won't take *that* long." She reached right up and grabbed Chloe's hand, at which point Chloe's heart pretty much melted. "Okay, Chloe. Let's go."

After half an hour with Quinn's daughter, Chloe knew exactly which princesses Annabelle wanted represented in her new room, as well as her favorite colors. They went back downstairs, and Chloe spent a couple of hours with Manny, going through the house, bottom to top, talking hard and soft surfaces, color choices, style preferences and the benefits of knocking out a wall or two. Chloe jotted notes and took pictures of existing furniture and fixtures that would be included in the new design.

Before she left at four-thirty, she promised to crunch the numbers. The contract would be ready for his and Quinn's approval early next week.

"Give me a call," said Manny. "We can decide then whether to meet here or at your showroom."

"That'll work."

Annabelle urged her to "Come back and see me soon, Chloe. And bring cookies."

Chloe promised that she would. She drove to the showroom, let Tai go home and got to work on the contract, planning out the estimated costs, room by room. At six, she closed up and headed for her house, a big, fat smile on her face and a thousand ideas for the redesign swirling in her brain.

She parked in her detached garage and was halfway along the short breezeway to the front door when she caught sight of the gorgeous bouquet of orchids and roses waiting in a clear, square vase on the porch. It must be from Quinn. The arrangement was so simple and lovely and the gesture so thoughtful, she let out a happy cry just at the sight of it.

Okay, it was a little silly to be so giddy at his thoughtfulness. But she hadn't had flowers in so long. Ted used to buy them for her, and since the divorce, well, she had no desire to buy them for herself. To her, a gorgeous bouquet of flowers just reminded her of Ted and all the ways she'd messed up her life. But if Quinn gave her flowers, she could start to see a beautiful arrangement in a whole new light.

She disarmed her alarm and unlocked the door—and then scooped up the vase and carried it in.

Dropping her purse on the entry bench, she took the vase straight to the kitchen peninsula, where she set it carefully down. The card had a red amaryllis on the front and the single word, Bloom. Bloom was the shop that belonged to Quinn's sister, Jody.

Whipping the little card off its plastic holder, she flipped it open and read *Beautiful flowers always remind me of you. I hate that it went so wrong for us. I miss you. Ted*

Chapter Four

"No!" Chloe shouted right out loud, not even caring that she sounded like some crazy person, yelling at thin air. "No, you do not get to do that. You do not." She tore the note in half and then in half again and she dropped it on the floor and stomped on it for good measure. They were *divorced*, for God's sake. He had a new wife. And all she wanted from him for now and forever was never to see or hear from him again.

Her heart racing with a sick kind of fury that he'd dared to encroach on her new life where he had no business being, Chloe whipped the beautiful flowers from the vase. Dripping water across the counter and onto the floor, too, she dropped them in the trash compactor, shoved it shut and turned the motor on. The compactor rumbled. She felt way too much satisfaction as the machine crushed the bright blooms to a pulp.

Once the flowers were toast, she poured the water

from the vase into the sink, whipped the compactor open again and dropped the vase on top of the mashed flowers. She ran the motor a second time, grinning like a madwoman when she heard that loud, scary pop that meant the vase was nothing but shards of broken glass. After that, she picked up the little bits of card, every one, threw them in with the shattered vase and the pulped flowers, took the plastic bag out of the compactor, lugged it out to the trash bin and threw it in.

Good riddance to bad trash.

She spent a while stewing, considering calling Ted and giving him a large piece of her mind.

But no. She wanted nothing to do with him and she certainly didn't want to make contact with him again. That might just encourage him.

She wondered if the flowers and the creepy note could be considered the act of a stalker.

But then she reminded herself that Ted and his bride, Larissa, lived more than a thousand miles away in San Diego. It was one thing for Ted to have his assistant send her flowers just to freak her out, but something else again for him to show up on her doorstep in person.

Wasn't going to happen. He was just being a jerk, an activity at which he excelled.

God. She had married him. How could she have been such an utter, complete fool?

Back in the house, she changed into jeans and a tank top. Then she took her time cooking an excellent dinner of fresh broiled trout with lemon butter, green beans and slivered almonds and her favorite salad of field greens, blueberries, Gorgonzola cheese and toasted walnuts, with a balsamic vinaigrette.

When it was ready, she set the table with her best dishes, lit a candle, poured herself a glass of really nice sauvignon blanc and sat down. She ate slowly, savoring every delicious bite.

A little later, she took a long scented bath and put on a comfy sleep shirt and shorts. Even after the bath, she was still buzzing with anger at the loser she'd once had the bad judgment to marry. Streaming a movie or reading a book was not going to settle her down. She needed a serious distraction.

So she went to the cozy room on the lower floor that she used as a home office and lost herself in the plans for Quinn's house. Within a few minutes of sitting down at her desk, the only thing on her mind was the rooms taking shape in her imagination—and on her sketch pad. And the numbers coming together for each room, for the project as a whole. She worked for hours and hardly noticed the time passing.

When she finally went back upstairs to the main floor, it was almost midnight. Time for bed.

But she didn't go to bed. It was cool out that evening. So she put on a big sweater over her sleep shirt, pulled on a pair of fluffy pink booties and went out onto her deck. It was something she had not done after dark since the night Quinn spent in her bed.

But she was doing it tonight.

She padded to the deck railing and stared down at Quinn's house.

Was she actually expecting him to be watching, waiting for the moment when she wandered out under the stars?

Not really. It just felt…reassuring somehow. To gaze down at his house, to know that she would see him again, would share dinner with him on Friday night.

When the French doors opened and he emerged, she let out a laugh of pure delight and waved to signal him up.

He didn't even hesitate, just went on down the steps at the side of his deck and forged up the hill. She went to meet him at the top of her stairs, feeling breathless and wonderful.

Tonight, he wore ripped old jeans, a white T-shirt that seemed to glow in the dark and the same moccasins he'd been wearing that other night. He said, "Love those furry boots." When she laughed, he added, "I was getting worried you might never come outside."

"And I was absolutely certain there was no way you might be glancing up to see if I was looking down for you." She held out her hand. He took it. His skin was warm, his palm callous. Just his touch made her body sing. "Come sit with me?"

He looked at her as though she were the only other person in the world. "Whatever you want, Chloe."

She tugged him over to the two chairs they'd sat in that other night and pulled him down beside her.

Silence.

But it was a good silence. They just sat there, staring out at the clear night and the distant mountains. A slight wind came up, rustling the nearby pines. And an owl hooted off in the shadows somewhere between his house and hers.

Finally, she said, "I met with Manny. I think it went well."

"He says so, too."

"And I'm in love with your daughter."

He chuckled, a rough and tempting sound. "She has that effect on people. Manny's tough, but Annabelle still manages to wrap him around her little finger. Truth is she rules the house. We just try to keep up with her."

She looked over at him. "Has she asked you about her mother again?"

"Not yet." He met her eyes through the shadows. "I

know, I know. Wait until she asks. And then don't load her up with more information than she's ready for."

"That's the way." She thought of the flowers she'd crushed in the compactor—and then pushed them out of her mind. Why ruin a lovely moment by bringing Ted into it?

Instead, she asked him how he had met Manny. He explained that the old ex-fighter had been his first professional trainer. "I met him at the first gym I walked into after leaving home. Downtown Gym, it was called, in Albuquerque. Manny ran the place and worked with the fighters who trained there. We got along. When I moved on, he went with me. I had a lot of trainers. And over time, Manny became more like my manager, I guess you could say. And kind of a cross between a best friend and a dad." He shot her a warning look. "But don't tell him I said that."

She grinned. "Why not?"

"He already thinks he knows what's best for me. If he ever heard I said I thought of him as a father, he'd never shut up with the advice and instructions."

She softly advised, "But I'll bet it would mean the world to him to know how you really feel."

"He knows. Hearing it out loud would only make him more impossible to live with." Quinn faked a dangerous scowl. "So keep your mouth shut."

She laughed and held up both hands. "I swear I'll never say a word."

"Good."

"So, how did he end up back here in Justice Creek with you and Annabelle?"

"I don't think either of us really considered a different option. He moved in with me when Annabelle was a baby, to help out."

When Annabelle was a baby...

So the little girl had been with her dad from the first? What had happened to the mother, the one Quinn said Annabelle would most likely never meet?

So many questions.

But Chloe had such a good feeling about the man beside her. She trusted him to tell her everything in his own good time.

He said, "When I decided to retire from the Octagon last year, Manny was already taking care of Annabelle full-time." Chloe knew what the Octagon was: the eight-sided ring in which Ultimate Fighting Championship mixed-martial-arts fighters competed. During the rough years when she was still married to Ted, she'd watched more than one of Quinn's televised UFC fights. It had lifted her spirits to see how far the wild, angry boy from her hometown had come. He continued, "I asked Manny to stick with me when I moved back home. He agreed right off, said he supposed it was about time he settled down. Annabelle's a handful, but so far he's managing."

"From what I've seen, he's great with her. He's patient, encourages her to express herself and make some of her own decisions—but he stays in charge, too."

"Yeah. He's a champ with her, all right..." Quinn's voice kind of trailed off and there was another silence, one somehow not as comfortable as the first.

She glanced over at him again and found him watching her. "Whatever it is, you might as well just say it."

"I got a question, but I don't want to freak you out."

An unpleasant shiver traveled down the backs of her arms and she thought of Ted again. Because if her freaking out could be involved, it probably had to do with Ted.

Then again, how would Quinn know that? She'd mentioned her ex once, on the night that Quinn came to her bed. What she'd told him had been far from flattering to Ted, but she'd said nothing about how thinking of him made her want to crush flowers and break expensive vases.

"Ask me," she said. "I can take it." The words came out sounding so confident. She was proud of them.

"All right, then. Does your mama know you're going out to dinner with me?"

Her mother. Of course. "No."

"It's Justice Creek, Chloe."

"Meaning she *will* know?"

"I'd say the odds are better than fifty-fifty, wouldn't you?"

Chloe kept her gaze steady on his. It was no hardship. Looking at him made her think of hot sex. And safety. And that combination really worked for her. "That girl— the mama's girl I was in high school?"

"Yeah?"

She slanted him a teasing glance. "You're not even going to argue that I was never a mama's girl?"

"Hey. You called it, not me."

And she made a low, rueful noise in her throat. "Yes, I did. And I was. But I'm not anymore. I tried living my life my mother's way. It didn't work for me. I'm all grown up now and my mother doesn't get to tell me what to do or whom to spend my time with."

One side of his beautiful mouth curved up then. It was a smirk, heavy on the irony, more like the old, dangerous, edgy Quinn from back in high school than the one she'd been getting to know lately. "*Whom*. Always so ladylike."

"Don't tease me. I'm serious."

His smirk vanished. "So you're admitting that your mother's not gonna like it, you and me spending time together?"

"What I'm telling you is that she doesn't have a say, so it doesn't matter whether she likes it or not."

He reached out his hand between their chairs. She put hers in it, and he lifted it to that wonderful mouth of his. Hot shivers cascaded down her arm and straight to the core of her, just at the feel of his soft lips against her skin. Then he rubbed his chin where his lips had been, teasing her with the rough brush of beard stubble, reminding her of their one night together, making her long to jump up and drag him inside.

But she didn't.

A moment later, he let go of her hand. He started talking again—about his plans for Prime Sports. She told him how much she appreciated the chance to rework the interiors at his house and then she shared with him some of the ideas she and Manny had discussed for upgrading the kitchen and opening up the living-room space.

A couple of hours passed as they sat there talking quietly under the waning moon. She even told him a little about her failed marriage—no, not about the flowers, and not about the times Ted had struck her. This thing with Quinn was so new and sweet and heady. Sharing ugly stories about her ex would definitely dim the romantic glow. Instead, she tried to explain how disappointed she was in the way things had turned out.

"It hurts so much," she confessed, "when something that should have been so right somehow goes all wrong. And I feel... I don't know, *less*, I guess. Shamed, that I didn't make better choices."

He regarded her for several seconds in that steady way he had. "You said the other night that the guy was abusive..."

She held his gaze as she shook her head.

He frowned. "I'll need more than a head shake to get what you're trying to tell me."

She let out a hard sigh. "Oh, Quinn. It's a beautiful night. And you're here beside me. It's good, you and me, talking like this."

"Yeah, it is."

"I probably shouldn't even have brought up my divorce."

"Yeah, you should. Whatever you want to tell me, that's what I want to hear."

"That's just it. I really don't want to go into any of that old garbage right now."

He gave her another of those long, thoughtful looks. And then, "All right."

And just like that, he let it go.

How amazing. He let it go. She'd grown up with a mother who never let anything go. And Ted? He would hound a person to hell and back to find out something he wanted to know.

But not Quinn. She said she didn't want to talk about it—and he just let it go. He said, "Whatever that story is, whatever happened in the past, you're going to be fine."

She made a low, rueful sound. "You're sure about that, huh?"

And he nodded. "You're brave and beautiful, Chloe— and not only on the outside. You're beautiful in your heart, where it matters. I admire the hell out of you."

Tears burned in her eyes at such praise. She blinked them away and whispered a soft, sincere "Thank you…"

By then, she really wanted to take him inside and spend a few more thrilling hours in his arms. But she felt somehow shyer now than that other night—shy and tentative.

And other than kissing her hand that one time, he'd made no move on her.

It was two in the morning when he said good-night.

She stood at the railing watching him jog down the hill to his house, and felt disappointed in herself that she'd let him go without so much as a single shared kiss.

But then, he *had* asked her out. She would see him again on Friday night…

Friday evening, Quinn arrived five minutes early. "Better grab a scarf," he warned.

She ran and got one, then followed him out across the breezeway and around the garage to the side parking space, where a gorgeous old convertible Buick coupe waited—top down, of course. With sidewalls so white they were blinding even in the shade.

"Wow." She couldn't resist gliding her palm over the glossy maroon paint. "It looks brand-new." The bright chrome gleamed in the fading early-evening light. It had round vents on the front fenders and an enormous, toothy grille.

"It's one of Carter's rebuilds. A '49 Buick Roadmaster." Carter, Quinn's oldest brother, designed and built custom cars. "I saw it at his shop a couple of weeks ago. Don't know what came over me, but I wanted it. So I bought it." He opened the door for her. She slid in onto the snow-white, tuck-and-roll bench seat. "Had him put seat belts in it, along with a decent sound system and power windows." He was leaning on the open door, bending close to her, his gray suit jacket already off and slung over his shoulder, hanging by a finger.

She got a hint of his aftershave, which was manly and fresh. He looked so good, in a white shirt and gray slacks, with a dark blue tie. She thought about kissing him, and turned away to run her hand over the leather seat in an effort to distract herself from a sudden, vivid memory of how pliant and hot his lips felt pressed to hers. "It's gorgeous," she said, altogether too breathlessly.

"Yeah." The single word seemed to dance along her nerve endings. She looked back up at him, and he grinned at her. And she just knew that *he* knew what she'd been thinking. "You look beautiful," he said, his gaze taking in her little black dress and her double strand of pearls that her dad had given her when she graduated from high school. "So smooth."

"Um, what?"

"You, Chloe. You're smooth."

"That's good, I hope?"

"That is excellent. Buckle up now." He shut the door as she tied her scarf over her hair.

He took her to the Sylvan Inn, which was a few miles southeast of town nestled in among the pines. The inn had a quiet atmosphere and great food.

"We used to come here when I was little," she said, once they were settled with their tall goblets of ice water, hot bread and giant menus in the traditional Sylvan Inn blue leather cover with the fancy gold lettering on the front. "For special occasions. My dad loves their hammer steaks. So do I, as a matter of fact."

"Good memories, then?"

"Very good." She glanced up at him—and spotted a familiar face across the dining room. Chloe smiled. The tall, thin blonde smiled right back. She gave Chloe a jaunty wave and disappeared behind a potted plant.

"What's up?" Quinn asked.

Chloe brushed a hand over the crisp white cuff of Quinn's shirt. "Don't look now, but we've been spotted by Monique Hightower. Did you know she works here?" They'd gone to school with Monique. The woman never met a secret she wouldn't share with the whole town.

"Uh-oh." He pretended to look worried. "Like I said the other night, it's Justice Creek. You go out with me, everyone in town is bound to know."

Now she brushed the back of his hand, which was warm and tan and dusted lightly with brown hair. It felt so good to touch him. She had to watch herself or she'd be all over the poor guy. "I hope you don't mind that the gossip mill will be churning."

"Me?" He gave a low chuckle. "I think I can deal with it."

"Such a brave man…"

They shared one of those looks. Long. Intimate. Wonderful. Finally, he said, "Read your menu, Chloe."

She closed the blue folder. "I did."

"You know what you want?"

"Oh, yes, I do." She said it slowly, with a lazy smile.

He warned low, "Keep looking at me like that and we won't make it through the appetizer."

But they did. They had it all. Appetizers, a nice bottle of cabernet, salad, hammer steaks with cheesy potatoes and a decadent chocolate dessert. And they took their sweet time about it.

Monique dropped by their table around nine, just after they'd been served their coffee and dessert. "Chloe. Quinn. What a surprise."

Quinn asked, "So, how's life treating you, Monique?"

"I'm getting by." Monique tossed her topknot of curly blond hair and stuck her hands in the pockets of her black service apron. "When did you two start spending time together?"

Chloe sipped her coffee. "This is our first date. I'm having a fabulous time."

Quinn said, "Chloe always had a thing for me, since way back in high school."

Monique blinked three times in rapid succession. "Really?"

Chloe stifled a silly giggle and said with great seriousness. "I finally got up the nerve to tell him." *And to show him, as a matter of fact.* "And then he asked me out. The rest could be history. I mean, if I play my cards right." She lowered her voice to a whisper. "But, Monique..."

Monique leaned a little closer. "What?"

"Don't say a word to anyone."

"Oh. Never. I would never tell a soul..." Translation: she couldn't wait to tell the world. Monique asked about Prime Sports, and Quinn gave her a card good for a free visit and one class of her choice. And then she turned to Chloe again, her dark eyes sharply gleaming. "I was so surprised when you moved back to town. I mean, we all knew you were headed for great things. No one ever would have guessed you'd end up running back home to Justice Creek. I'm just so *sorry* that things didn't work out for you."

Six months ago, Chloe would have been shamed and infuriated by Monique's barbed words and pretended concern. Or at the very least, embarrassed. At the moment, though, all she felt was amused. "Thanks, Monique. You're all heart."

Monique sighed heavily. Across the room, the manager who'd greeted them when they arrived had his eye on her. "Well, good to see you two. Gotta go." She scuttled off.

Chloe took a bite of her delicious dessert. "Everything we told her will be all over town. Twenty-four hours—thirty-six, max."

Quinn leaned closer and spoke low. "Maybe I shouldn't have said that you had a thing for me in high school."

She met his eyes directly and she couldn't keep from

grinning. "Are you kidding? I loved it. Not to mention it was the truth. If Monique Hightower's going to be spreading rumors about us, they might as well be true."

After their slow, wonderful meal, they returned to Chloe's house.

Quinn eased the gorgeous old car into the space beside the garage and turned off the engine. "Are you up for a walk around the block?"

"Sure." It was a nice night. "A walk would be great. We'll work off some of that amazing dessert."

He followed her inside and waited while she changed into flats. Then off they went, down the front steps and out to the street, where they strolled beneath the silver crescent of the moon.

Their development, Haltersham Heights, had no sidewalks. The houses were set back from the street, among the trees. Quinn stopped at a lot three doors down and across the street from Chloe's. It had a For Sale sign at the curb with a big SOLD plate stuck on it. The large contemporary log and natural stone house could be seen, windows gleaming, through the trees.

"The sold sign went up a few weeks ago," she said. "About time. This one's been on the market for months."

"I know. I bought it. Got a great price, too."

She laughed—and then she realized he wasn't kidding. "Wait a minute. You're serious?"

"I am." He put his hand over her fingers, where they curled around his arm. She'd barely had time to enjoy the flare of pleasure at how good his touch felt, when he said, "I bought it before I knew you would be fixing up my house. But it should work out great. We're closing on this one Monday, so we can move in here next week. We'll stay here while you renovate the other one—and not to get ahead of myself or anything, but once we move back to our house, you can start on this one. It's the same story as the other one. Solid construction, but it's begging to be brought into the twenty-first century. When you're finished, I'll sell it."

She only stared.

"Chloe, your mouth's hanging open."

"And why wouldn't it be? You're too much."

"Too much of what, exactly?"

"Well, let's see. Quinn Bravo, world-champion cage fighter, fitness empire builder, real estate mogul…"

"That all sounds pretty good to me."

"You must have made a fortune as a fighter, huh?"

"I did all right. The payout for winning a championship fight is a hefty one. And I landed some big-time endorsements, too."

"I think I'm speechless, Quinn."

He gave her his high school bad-boy smirk. "You'll get over it. And the truth is, Prime Sports will never make much money unless my franchise plan pays off. The housing market's rebounding nicely, though. I *can* make money in real estate."

She admitted softly, "Start-ups aren't easy, and I say that from experience. If you hire me for both of your houses, it will make a big difference for me. I really do need the business."

"So you've got it. Everybody wins."

She made a low, disbelieving sound. "As simple as that?"

His eyebrows drew together. "Why not?"

"I don't know. I wouldn't want to take advantage of you just because you, um, like me…"

He framed her face in his big, calloused hands. "Look at me."

"Oh, I am." She stared straight up into those soft aquamarine eyes and never wanted to look away. "I really am."

"Are you telling me you can't do the job?"

She stiffened and answered with heat, "Of course I can do the job."

He chuckled then. "See? We got no problem here."

Standing there in the darkness of her quiet street with his warm, rough hands cradling her cheeks, she decided he was right. "No, I guess we don't."

He lowered his head, until his sexy, plump lips were a hairbreadth from hers. He had lips like a girl's, but the rest of him was all man. "I got a request, though."

She longed for his kiss. Her heart was beating slow and deep. Sparks flared across her skin. And low in her belly, she seemed to be melting. "Oh, God. Anything."

"Work with my brother's company, Bravo Construction?"

She made herself focus on what he'd just asked of her—and it wasn't easy, with those lips of his so close.

Use his brother's company...

She'd left that possibility open-ended when she talked to Manny. But really, why not? Bravo Construction had a great reputation. She felt confident she could develop a solid working relationship with them. It could be good for everyone. "All right."

His warm breath touched her lips. The guy was driving her crazy. "I already talked to my sister Nell—just paving the way. Nell says she'll fit the project in the schedule and they can start work a week from Monday."

"That's quick."

"Yeah. And I like to keep it in the family if I can."

"I get that." She tried really hard not to sound as breathless as she felt. "No problem. Bravo Construction it is."

"Good, then."

"Quinn…"

"Hmm?" A teasing light shone in his eyes. She realized he knew exactly what he was doing to her.

And *she* knew that she couldn't take it anymore. She only had to lift herself up a fraction higher to get what she wanted. So she did. And it worked.

At last, he was kissing her.

"Chloe…" Quinn whispered her name right into her pretty mouth.

And then he let go of her arms—in order to pull her up nice and close. She tasted so good. Hot and wet.

And all of her, every graceful, sweetly scented inch of her, was so, so smooth.

Worth the endless, twelve-day wait since the last time he'd had his mouth on hers.

He lifted his head an inch. She let out a tiny moan, as though she couldn't bear not to have their mouths fused together. He slanted his head the other way and drank that moan right off her sweet, sweet lips.

Those slender arms glided up his chest and then her soft hands were stroking his collar, caressing his neck, her slim fingers threading up into the close-trimmed hair at the nape of his neck. He scraped his tongue along the smooth edges of her teeth, pushing deeper, into all that wet sweetness.

Coffee. Wine. Chocolate.

Chloe.

There had been women in his life, maybe too many. Especially when he was first making his name in the Octagon. Women liked fighters. And they particularly liked fighters who won. For a while there he'd gotten carried away with all the attention. Beautiful women everywhere he turned, his for the taking.

But even an endless chain of gorgeous women got old after a while. He started to see that to most of them, he was just a cheap thrill. And he wanted to be more than that to someone.

He found he wanted heart in a woman. He wanted someone he could talk to. He wanted real, gut-deep integrity. He wanted truth. He wanted a powerful connection.

Oh, and yeah. Brains and a sense of humor, too.

It wasn't that there weren't women out there with all that. It was just that most of them had no interest in a guy who still couldn't read past about fourth-grade level, a guy who got bloodied and battered for a living. Plus, when he was fighting, it ate up his life. He didn't have time to go looking for the one for him.

And then along came Annabelle. Her life, her happiness, her chance to grow up and take on the world— suddenly that was what mattered to him. To raise his little girl up right was more than enough. He didn't need that special woman, after all.

Or so he'd believed until twelve nights ago.

Until Chloe led him into her house and straight to her bed.

Chloe.

She had it all—everything he'd already accepted he wasn't going to find. And no one had ever tasted so good.

Reluctantly, he broke the kiss.

She stared up at him, eyes full of stars. "Come back to my house? Be with me tonight?"

"Damn, Chloe. I was afraid you'd never ask."

Her belly all aflutter with anticipation, her pulse a rushing sound in her ears and her cheeks feeling way hotter than they should, Chloe ushered Quinn in her front door and then turned to engage the lock and reset the alarm. "You can hang your jacket there." She gestured at the coatrack. He hung up his jacket, and she grabbed his hand. "This way…"

But he held back, tugging her close, into the hard, hot circle of his arms. He kissed her, a slow one that had her knees going weak and a meltdown happening in her core.

However, when he lifted his head that time, his eyes were way too serious.

She frowned, suddenly struck with concern for whatever might be bothering him. "What is it? What's wrong?"

He pulled her close again. And he whispered in her ear, "I want to take all your clothes off and see you naked. I want to kiss every inch of you."

She sighed. "We are definitely on the same page about that."

"But…"

She pushed him away enough that she could see his eyes. "Oh, no. There *is* something. What?"

"Don't look so worried." With his big thumb, he smoothed the scrunched place between her eyebrows. "It's nothing bad. I just have some things I want to say first."

Would she rather be kissing him? Absolutely. But then again, whatever he wanted to say, she wanted to hear. "So…coffee or something?"

"Sure."

She led him into the kitchen and whipped him up a quick cup, pouring cream in a little pitcher because she'd watched him at dinner and knew he took cream.

"Aren't you having any?" he asked.

Her tummy was all fluttery, what with wondering what kind of thing he just *had* to say to her. Coffee would only make it worse. "Maybe later. How about the living area? It's more comfortable there."

"Good enough." He poured in the cream, picked up his cup and followed her to the sofa.

They sat down together, and he set his cup on the coffee table. She folded her hands tightly in her lap. He'd said it was nothing awful, but he seemed so intense suddenly...

Was there going to be drama? Oh, she hoped not. She'd had enough drama to last her a lifetime, and then some.

He said, "There are things about me I want you to know."

Uh-oh. She gulped down the giant lump in her throat and gave him a nod to continue.

"First, about Annabelle's mother."

Chloe realized she'd been holding her breath. She let it out slowly. Annabelle's mother. Actually, she really wanted to know about Annabelle's mother...

"Her name is Sandrine Cox. She's an actress and model. We went out a few times. She got pregnant. She came to me, told me she was fairly certain it was my baby and she felt I had a right to know."

Chloe studied his wonderful face. He seemed... relaxed when he talked about his little girl's mother. Relaxed and accepting. "You believed her."

"Yeah. Sandrine was always straight ahead about things. I believed that *she* believed the baby was mine. Then later, right after Annabelle was born, a paternity test proved Sandrine was right. Annabelle's mine. And I knew from the moment Sandrine told me she was pregnant that I wanted the baby. Sandrine didn't. She didn't want to be a mom. She liked her single life and she had a lot of ambition, a heavy focus on her career. I made her an offer. I would pay her a large lump sum to have the baby and then she would sign over all rights to me."

"And that's what happened?"

He nodded. "She kept her end of the bargain. I kept mine."

"You haven't heard from her since Annabelle was born?"

"No. I doubt I ever will."

"But with something as important as a child, Quinn, you never know. Someday Annabelle's mother might regret her choice, change her mind."

"Anything's possible."

"And if she did come to you, if she wanted to meet Annabelle?"

"Can't say for certain. If she was as honest and up-front as before, we would work something out so that she could know Annabelle and Annabelle could know her."

Chloe liked his answer. It could be difficult for him to make room for his daughter's mother in their lives. But it was the right thing. "That sounds good. For Annabelle, most of all. It's very likely, as she grows to adulthood, that she's going to want to know about her birth mother and meet her, if possible."

"Maybe. But it's like you told me that first night. I'm not going to borrow trouble. I'll answer Annabelle's questions and pay attention to the signals she gives me. And then take it from there." He loosened his tie. "I didn't want you to wonder anymore about how I ended up with sole custody of my little girl and no mother in sight."

Tenderness washed through her—for him, for the kind of man he was. A good man. Honest. True-hearted. A man who would do what was right even if it wasn't the best or easiest thing for him, personally.

She reached out and brushed his hand. "Let me..."

He sat so still, so watchful, as she undid the tie completely. It made a soft, slithering sound as she slipped it from around his neck. She laid it carefully over the arm of the sofa. Then she turned to him again and unbuttoned the top two buttons of his snowy dress shirt, smoothing the collar open, revealing the powerful column of his neck and the sharp black point of one of those intricate tattoos that covered his shoulder and twined halfway down his arm.

"Better?" she asked.

They shared a smile as he nodded. He said, "There's more."

She took his right hand and turned it over, revealing his cuff buttons. One by one, she undid them. "Tell me."

"I'm dyslexic," he said, his voice rougher than usual, freighted with something wary, something wounded. "You know what dyslexia is?"

"I think I do. I think I remember reading that it's when a person has difficulty in learning to read or interpret words, letters and other symbols?"

"That's pretty close to the generally accepted definition."

She took his left hand and unbuttoned that cuff, too.

He spoke again. "Most people think dyslexia is what you just said. A learning disorder, period. It's more. It's a challenge, a tough one. But it's a gift, too." She sat with his hand in her lap, the buttons undone, drinking in every word, as he explained, "You remember how I was as a kid. Trouble. Always getting in fights. Everyone thought I was stupid because I couldn't get the hang of reading. I hated school, hated being the slow kid. I acted out constantly. Only later did I figure out that my problem was I couldn't learn the way most kids learn. A traditional school environment did nothing for me. I don't get phonics, don't get learning things in rote sequence. It completely overloads me. So I would lash out."

She did remember that troubled boy so well. "You always seemed so angry."

"You bet I was. By the time I was eleven, my mother was at the end of her rope with me. As a last-ditch effort to find something I could do well, she enrolled me in a karate class—and everything changed for me. For once, I got something, really *got* it. Yeah, I have to work my ass off to try and get the meaning out of a line of letters across a page. But I'd always been damn good at fighting. The way my brain is wired makes me more capable than most people of visualizing the moves of my opponents in advance. I see the whole picture, I guess you could say. And that makes me more willing to follow my instincts. So I was good at karate, and finally being good at something was damn motivating. It got me going, gave me hope. I was driven to excel." He took her hand then and wove his fingers with hers.

It felt so good, her hand in his. She held on tight. "Answer me a question…"

"Name it."

"You seemed nervous about telling me this. Were you?"

He squeezed her fingers. "Yeah, I was."

"But I can't see why you would be, not after the way your life's worked out."

"There's more. And you need to hear it."

She *needed* to hear it? She almost asked him why, but then decided that the whys could wait. "All right…"

"Dyslexia is often genetic."

She frowned. "So you're telling me that Annabelle is dyslexic?"

"No. So far, Annabelle shows none of the signs. Already, she can recognize her alphabet and sound out simple words. But you should know that any child of mine could possibly be dyslexic."

She should know? It was an odd way to phrase it.

And he still had more to say. "I plan to be proactive. If a kid of mine showed signs of dyslexia, I would be on it, arranging for early testing, providing alternative learning systems and support, working with the school so everyone's on the same page about what needs to be done. If one of my kids was dyslexic, I would see to it that he didn't have to go through the crap I went through. I would make sure any kid of mine never had to feel stupid and incompetent and lag way behind the learning curve." He tipped his head then and asked with wry good humor, "You still with me, Chloe?"

"Absolutely. Yes. And I'm so sorry, Quinn. That you felt stupid and incompetent when you were little. No child should have to feel that way."

"I got past it."

"That doesn't make it right." At his chuckle, she chided, "It's nothing to joke about, Quinn."

He shrugged. "Tell me something."

She had that odd feeling again; there was more going on here than she was picking up. "Of course."

He let go of her hand, reached for his coffee—and said just what she'd been thinking. "Do you have any clue why I'm laying all this on you?"

She watched him take a sip. "Whatever your reasons, I have to say it's really nice to have a guy just sit right down and talk to me about the toughest things. It's rare."

"Right." He set the cup down again and rolled one of his unbuttoned cuffs to the elbow. "It's what women love. A guy who won't shut up…"

"I don't know about 'women.' But I know what *I* like.

And you telling me about what matters to you, about what made you who you are? I do like that. A lot."

"Well, all right." He rolled the other cuff. She watched him, admiring the hard shape of his arms, thick with muscle, roped with tendons, dusted with light brown hair, nicked here and there with small white ridges of scar tissue. He went on, "But I do have a reason for loading you up with way more info than you asked for."

"And I keep trying to make you see that you don't *need* a reason."

He slanted her a teasing look. "Got that."

A low laugh escaped her. "Well, okay, then. I get it. You're trying to tell me the reason—so go ahead. I'm ready for it."

"You sure?"

She groaned and executed a major eye roll. "Will you *please* stop teasing me?"

Now he looked at her so steadily, a look that made her warm all over, especially down in the center of her. "All right." And then, just like that, he said, "I want to marry you, Chloe."

Chapter Five

Quinn wasn't finished. "I want to build a life with you, have kids with you. Like I said, I'm a guy who follows my intuition, a guy who has trouble sounding out a word—but also a guy who gets the big picture. And once I know what I want, I go for it. I want you, Chloe, for my wife. I want you for my little girl, too, because I know you'll be the mother Annabelle needs."

Chloe just stared at him. Words? They'd completely deserted her.

He put up a hand. "It's okay. You don't have to say anything now. All you have to do is take your time. Think it over. And you should know the kids aren't a deal breaker for me. I want more. But if you don't, I can live with that. Annabelle will be enough."

"I, um…" She had no idea what to say next.

That didn't seem to bother him. He simply waited.

And she found that she couldn't sit still. She got up,

eased from behind the coffee table and then kept going to the sliding door, the one she'd slipped out that first night, when he came up the hill and she took him to her bed.

He didn't try to stop her. He didn't say a word, only sat there, patiently waiting for her to process all he'd just said.

She appreciated his silence and stillness now, appreciated it every bit as much as she did all that he'd told her moments before. She flipped on the deck lights and stared out at the two empty cedar chairs.

Was this really happening? Just like that, out of nowhere, he wanted to marry her?

But then again, no. Not out of nowhere, not really. He was such a focused sort of man. Of course, he would decide what he wanted and lay it all out for her so honestly and directly.

She fiddled with the pearls her dad had given her years ago, when she thought she knew everything and saw so clearly how her life would go.

What about love? Quinn hadn't mentioned love.

Should that bother her?

Well, it didn't. She'd had enough declarations of love from her rotten-hearted ex-husband to last her into the next century. And where had all that love talk gotten her but wounded, divorced and bitterly disappointed?

This, what Quinn offered, was better.

It wasn't a fantasy, not perfect. But it was honest. It felt real.

Quinn spoke then. "One more thing. About Manny..." He waited for her to look at him, and then for acknowledgement that she'd heard what he said. When she gulped and nodded, he went on. "Manny's part of the family. So you would not only be getting me and Annabelle. There's Manny, too. He can be a pain in the ass, I know. But he's not going anywhere. If you said yes, you would need to deal with him, work with him."

She felt a soft smile tremble across her mouth. "I would never for a second expect it to be any other way."

He didn't smile. But his eyes were so bright. "Well, all right, then."

The part about Manny had been so easy to answer. But the rest of it… She really didn't know what to say. She stared out the sliding door again.

He asked into the heavy silence, "Want me to go?"

Turning from her study of the empty deck chairs, she faced him once more. "No way. I want you to stay."

He stood. "Will you think about it, consider my offer?"

"I will."

He came for her then. She waited, her whole body humming with sweet anticipation as he approached.

And when he was close enough that the heat he generated seemed to reach out and touch her, she canted her chin higher and gazed straight into those beautiful eyes. "You are like no one I've ever known."

"That's good, I hope?"

"Oh, yes. It's very good."

"Angel." He lifted a big hand and brushed a finger down the curve of her cheek, stirring up goose bumps, making her sigh. And then he lowered that wonderful mouth of his and brushed those lips, so gently, back and forth across her own.

She smiled into his kiss, brought her hands up between them and went to work undoing the rest of the buttons down the front of his shirt. It didn't take long. She spread the shirt wide and pressed her palms to his broad chest, to that beautiful tattoo with his little girl's name in the middle of it. His skin was hot, wonderfully so. Sandy hair formed a tempting T across.

And down.

Best of all, she could count the strong beats of his big heart. She whispered against those velvety lips of his, "I should have made a move on you back in high school."

He chuckled, the low rumble sending a thrill shivering straight to the core of her. "That wasn't your style— and I wasn't your type."

"Oh, but Quinn. You *were* my type. What a fool I was then. I took what I thought was the safe way—and it wasn't safe in the least. It turned out all wrong."

"Hey." His voice was heaven, the perfect blend of rough and tender. He kissed the tip of her nose. "No regrets, huh?"

"But I do have regrets." She slid her hands up over his thick, hard shoulders, and clasped them around his neck. "And I can't just wish them away."

He shrugged out of his shirt and let it fall. Then he bent his head lower, smoothed her hair aside and pressed his hot mouth to the crook of her neck. "Forget 'em, then." His breath so hot across her skin, branding her, burning her. "For now, at least?"

She threaded her eager fingers up into his hair. "Help me with that?"

"Happy to." He breathed in through his nose. "You smell so good…" And then he scraped his teeth where his lips had been.

She shivered and moaned as he kissed his way back up over the curve of her jaw to claim her lips again. She opened for him. Heat speared through her as his tongue swept her mouth.

He lifted her hair off her neck with one hand. With the other, he took down the long zipper at the back of her dress and guided the dress off her shoulders. It dropped to the floor. She broke the lovely kiss in order to step out of it. He bent, picked it up and tossed it on the nearest chair.

Unbuttoning and unzipping, flinging articles of clothing toward the chair as soon as they had them off, they undressed each other.

Finally, when the only thing left was her pearls, he ordered gruffly, "Turn around."

She showed him her back. He unhooked the diamond clasp and took the necklace away. She faced him again in time to watch him reach over and lay the double strand on the nearby side table.

That was it. They were naked. Completely naked. And it seemed such a very long way to the bedroom.

Good thing she'd planned ahead.

He asked roughly, "What are you smiling about?"

And she pulled open the little drawer in the side table and took out the condom she'd tucked in there. Just in case.

"God. Chloe." He hauled her close, licked her ear and whispered in it, "You think of everything."

She whispered back, "A design teacher I had once told me that what I lack in imagination, I make up for in efficiency and good planning. I was really insulted at the time."

He took her earlobe between his teeth and tugged on it, biting down just a little harder than he needed to.

It felt so good it made her moan.

He whispered, "Put it on me."

She pulled back a little, far enough to meet his eyes. They were the color of some tropical sea right then, so deep, going down and down to deeper blue. Focused so completely on her. "Right now?"

For that she got a slow, deliberate nod from him.

She started to tear the top off the pouch.

"On second thought…" He caught her hand. "Wait…" And he pulled her close and kissed her some more. She gave herself up to that, to the taste of his mouth and the heat of his breath, to the feel of him, fully erect against her belly, making her burn for him.

Making her moan. She eased her free hand between them and wrapped her fingers around him, stroking. Oh, he felt so good—his powerful body pressed close, his mouth covering hers, the long, hard length of him held tight in her grip.

He kissed her endlessly, kissed her and caressed her, his fingers tracing magical patterns over her skin, teasing her breasts, first cradling them so gently, then catching the nipples, rolling them, so that she moaned some more. He seemed to really like it when she moaned.

He made a wonderful growling sound low in his throat. "Yeah," he said. "Like that?"

She couldn't say "Yes" fast enough. So she said it again, moving her hand up and down the thick length of him. "Yes…" And again, "Oh, yes, Quinn. Like that…"

And then his hand went lower, all the way to the feminine heart of her.

She cried out as he stroked her, opening her. She felt her own wetness, her readiness for him. She didn't want to wait a second longer. She couldn't wait…

"I…" She got that word out, and then couldn't for the life of her remember what she'd meant to say next.

"Yeah?" He was kissing his way along the line of her jaw, biting a little, licking some, too. Below, his fingers kept up their clever, thrilling play on her wet, secret flesh.

Oh, she was lost in the best way, totally gone. She kept her left hand wrapped around him, holding on for dear life. In her right, she still clutched the unused condom. She kind of waved it at him. "I…" Just that word. Nothing more. It was the only word she seemed to have at her disposal at the moment.

And apparently it was enough. He took the condom from her. She opened her eyes and stared up at him, dazed. Transported.

He lifted the small pouch, caught the corner between his teeth and tore the top off, all the while staring directly into her eyes, his other hand continuing to do amazing things to her below.

"Here," she whispered, holding out her free hand. He gave it back. She let go of him to use both hands, removing the wrapper and dropping it on the little table next to her pearls. And then she rolled the protection down over him. He moaned. And she granted him a small, triumphant smile. "There."

He reached for her, clasping her waist. She gasped in surprise. His right hand was slick and wet. It was *her* wetness, her desire. She was shocked at herself, at her own complete abandon.

Shocked. Amazed.

And gratified.

It was the same as that other night. Only better. He took her, claimed her, carried her right out of herself. He just swept her away—at the same time as he made her feel that she'd somehow come home, that nothing and no one would ever hurt her again.

And then he was lifting her. He did it so effortlessly, as though she weighed nothing. She grabbed for him, hungry for the feel of him, for her flesh pressed to his flesh, hot and tight and hard. She wrapped her arms and legs around him.

He whispered her name.

"Quinn," she whispered in return. "Oh, yes." She sank her teeth into his neck and when he growled at her, a dark, hot laugh escaped her. He bent to nuzzle her and she turned her face to his and claimed his mouth.

The kiss went deeper, wetter, hotter. And he was moving, with her all twined around him like a vine. He went to the short section of bare wall beside the entry closet, just walked her right up to it.

And then he lifted her, positioning her just so...

She felt him there, nudging her, right where she wanted him. And she pressed down.

He made the deepest, hottest, hungriest sound then, as she lowered herself onto him. He was wonderfully thick and large. Still, her body took him easily, gliding down around him until he filled her all the way.

They froze. She let her head fall back and her eyes drift shut. He had her perfectly braced, with the wall to give them stability. He canted his upper body slightly away from her, while below, he held her so close, just right, big hands cradling her open thighs. She clutched his shoulders, fingers gripping tight, her legs locked securely behind his waist.

She was...gone, lost in wonder, swept up in the connection, her breathing harsh and hungry, just like his.

"Chloe..."

And she opened her eyes and looked at him. His bluegreen gaze was right there, waiting for her. He gripped her thighs tighter, pushing them wider, pressing his lower body closer, sliding into her that fraction deeper.

That did it. She felt the gathering, the build—and the lovely, hot sensation, as though all of her was blooming.

She asked, "Quinn?" For permission? Acknowledgment?

She had no idea which.

But he seemed to understand, even if she didn't. "Yeah,"

he answered, one corner of that soft, bad boy's mouth of his curling upward. "Go for it, angel."

And she did. She let go, let it happen, let it roll out from her in a hot, endless wave. Pleasure cascaded from the core of her, sizzling along every nerve, hitting the tips of her toes and the top of her head, spilling all through her in a flood of light and glory. He stayed with her, pressing up into her hard and tight, as the fire flamed so bright and then slowly faded down to a lovely, glowing ember.

And right then, when she thought it was over, when she was more than ready to ease her shaking legs to the floor, he started to move again.

She groaned in sexual overload and shoved fitfully at his rocklike shoulders. But he didn't release her.

And, well, could she blame him? After all, it *was* his turn. He'd swept her right off her feet and straight to paradise. The least she could do was stick with him now.

With a sigh of surrender, she stopped pushing him away and held on instead, bracing to ride it out.

But then, out of nowhere, all at once, it became more than just sticking with it for his sake. So much more.

In a split second, she was catching fire again.

"Oh… Oh, my!" She yanked him tight against her.

He let out a laugh, deep and knowing. Full of heat and joy.

She moaned his name as she pressed her open mouth to his, her body moving in time with his, picking up speed, finding the hard, insistent rhythm he set—and matching it, giving it back to him.

Time whirled away. The edge of the world was waiting for her. Waiting for both of them. She spun toward it, dizzy with the thrill of it. She hovered on the brink—and went over.

And he was right there with her, hitting the peak a moment after she did, pulsing hard and hot within her.

And then following her down.

Chapter Six

It was three-fifteen on Saturday morning when he left her.

Chloe put on a robe and walked him out to his beautiful old car. She kissed him goodbye—a long, slow, lovely kiss.

When he would have let her go, she grabbed him back and kissed him some more.

He laughed when he finally lifted his head. "Hey. I'm only going around the block."

"I know." She sighed, wrapped her arms around his waist, and beamed up at him. "But I want to make sure you don't forget me."

"No chance of that." He took a curl of her hair and wrapped it around his hand. "We got a special thing going, you and me."

"Oh, yes, we do."

He touched her chin with his thumb, brushed one last kiss across her upturned lips. "Get some rest."

She promised she would and reluctantly stepped back so he could open the car door and slide in behind the wheel. Then she waited, her arms wrapped around herself against the predawn chill, as he backed from the driveway and drove off down the street.

As soon as his taillights disappeared, she missed him. She wanted to run inside, grab the phone and call him back.

Which was totally silly. He'd asked her to marry him. And she was redecorating his house—*both* of his houses, as a matter of fact.

One way or another, she would be seeing him very soon.

She saw him the next day. He called and invited her out for ice cream with him and Annabelle. Chloe spent two lovely hours with father and daughter. Annabelle enchanted her. It might be too soon to talk about falling in love with Quinn. But she had no problem admitting she was head over heels for his little girl.

And then, that night, Quinn came up the hill to join her. He stayed for two hours. They talked about Annabelle and about Chloe's plans for his houses— and then they made love. He left at a little past midnight.

Same thing on Sunday night.

Monday at nine in the morning, Quinn closed on the house across the street from Chloe. Then, at eleven, he brought Manny and Annabelle to Chloe's showroom to see the plans and sign the contract for the redesign of the house down the hill. Chloe had cookies on offer at the coffee table, which Annabelle spotted immediately. Manny said she could have one.

Annabelle chose a cookie, thanked Chloe sweetly—

and asked if she knew how to make a fairy princess dress. "I want one, Chloe. Will you *please* make me one?"

Before Chloe could reply that she absolutely could and would, Quinn said, "Anniefannie, you are pushing it."

"Daddy!" The little girl tipped her cute nose high in a perfect imitation of disdain. "I'm not a fannie."

"But will you stop pushing it?"

Annabelle dimpled adorably. "But Chloe can make a *room*. I know she can make me a fairy princess dress." She turned pleading eyes on Chloe, who longed only to give her whatever she wanted. "Pleeeaaase, Chloe."

Manny spoke up then. He said one word. "Annabelle." After which he pushed back his chair and held out his hand.

Annabelle's lower lip started quivering. "Oh, no. Not the *car*. I don't want to sit in the *car*. Pleeaaassse, Manny."

Manny let out a heavy sigh. "Are you gonna stop pestering Chloe and sit quietly at the table while we finish our business here?"

Annabelle announced loudly, "Yes, I am!"

Manny mimed locking his lips with a key.

Annabelle straightened her small shoulders and folded her hands on the table, all the while pressing her lips together and pointedly glancing from one adult to the next.

Finally, Manny nodded. "All right. We'll give it a try."

Annabelle nodded wildly but kept her little mouth tightly shut.

"Eat your cookie," Quinn said in his gentlest voice.

Annabelle made short work of the treat. And then Manny gave her a cup of crayons and some paper. She was a perfect little angel, happily coloring away as the grown-ups finished their meeting.

That afternoon, Chloe visited Bravo Construction, which consisted of three trailers and a warehouse on the southwest edge of town. She met with Nell Bravo, who was in her late twenties and stunningly beautiful, with long auburn hair and a vivid half-sleeve tattoo down her shapely left arm. The baby of the Bravo family, Nell had always been outspoken and tough-minded. Everyone knew you didn't mess with Nell.

Chloe had the plans with her for Quinn's redesign. She spent two hours in Nell's office trailer, going over everything in detail, coming to agreement on the budget and the schedule.

Nell would personally run the job. Tomorrow, Chloe would get busy ordering cabinets and appliances, counters and flooring. Nell would put in for the permits they would need. Demo would begin first thing next Monday morning. If all went as planned—which it rarely did—the project would take nine to ten weeks.

At four o'clock, when they had everything pretty well hammered out, Chloe got up to leave.

And Nell hoisted her heavy black biker boots up onto her battered desk. "Before you head out, we need to talk. Hey, Ruby?"

The plump, motherly looking clerk at the desk near the door glanced around. "What do you need?"

"Take fifteen?"

"Sure." Ruby got up from her laptop and left the trailer.

Chloe had a sinking feeling in her stomach.

Nell proved the feeling right as soon as the door closed behind the clerk. "So, I hear you've had a thing for Quinn ever since high school. Is that true?"

Chloe dropped back into her chair. "Monique Hightower's been talking."

"Did you think she wouldn't?"

Chloe suppressed a sigh. "No. I knew she would." It had all seemed so amusing Friday night. But looking in

Nell's narrowed eyes right now, she didn't think it was funny at all.

Quinn's sister demanded, "Answer my first question."

Chloe drew herself up. "Yeah. I had certain…fantasies about Quinn way back when. Is that somehow a crime?"

"He's not just a piece of tasty meat. He's a good man."

Tasty meat? Chloe took care to keep her voice even. "I know he's a good man, Nell."

"You slumming?"

Chloe didn't let her gaze waver. "I absolutely am not—and why would you think that? Quinn's a brilliant man with a whole lot going for him. The word *slumming* just doesn't apply."

"Oh, come on, Chloe. Your mother was practically best friends with my father's first wife. No way Linda Winchester's going to approve of you seeing one of the bastard Bravos—especially not the 'stupid' one who barely managed to finish high school."

Chloe felt the angry color flooding upward on her cheeks. When would people stop assuming that her mother made her choices for her? "Nell." She made a show of clucking her tongue. "Where do I even start with you? Not fair. Not to Quinn. And not to me. He's far from stupid and he's done just fine for himself. We both know that. As for me, yes, it's true. I *used* to let my mother have way too much influence over me. But that was then. Right this minute, I'm thirty-one, divorced, fully self-supporting and on my own. My mother has zero say about whom I go out with."

Nell's lush mouth twisted. "Does your mother know that?"

Busted. "I'll say it again. *I* decide whom I spend time with."

Nell dropped her heavy boots to the floor, braced both

elbows on the desk and folded her hands between them. "Am I pissing you off, Chloe?"

The perennial good girl in Chloe pushed for denial, for smoothing things over after neatly sweeping them under the carpet. But no. The truth was better. "Yes, Nell. You are pissing me off."

"Good." Nell tipped her head to the side. The overhead fluorescents made her fabulous hair shimmer like a red waterfall. "Don't you hurt him, or you'll be answering to me."

Chloe sat tall. "I don't know for sure what's going to happen. But Quinn's an amazing man who means a lot to me. The last thing I would ever want to do is hurt him."

Nell's swivel chair squeaked as she flopped back in it and folded her arms across her spectacular breasts. She stared at Chloe, unblinking, for a grim count of ten. Then: "Look. I like your plans for the house. You know your job. I like the way you carry yourself. And I hardly knew you, back in the day. You were four years ahead of me in school. I only knew your reputation as the perfect one, the one headed for a good marriage to a rich husband, two-point-two children, a soccer-mom-and-country-club life—and some chichi career that you could fit in between social engagements."

"Something like interior design, you mean?"

"Hey. If the glass slipper fits…"

"As it turned out, it didn't. Not by a long shot. And that was then, Nell. I'm not that girl anymore."

Another long, measuring stare from Nell. Finally, she shrugged. "You know, I think I believe you." She got up and held down her hand. Chloe did want peace with Quinn's sister—with all of his family. After a moment's hesitation, she took Nell's offered hand and rose. Nell said, "Looking forward to working with you."

"I'm sure it will be interesting."

"Right. And listen. When you tell Quinn about this little talk we had—"

Chloe didn't even let her finish. "Why would I tell him? The way I see it, what just happened is between you and me."

Nell arched an auburn eyebrow. "Fair enough." And then she grumbled, "I'm really starting to like you. How 'bout that?"

"I'm glad. I'm going to do my best not to disappoint you—though you did go a little overboard just now."

Always a fighter, Nell stuck out her chin. "You think so?"

"Yes, I do. Then again, it's nice to know how much you love your brother and that you have his back."

That evening, Chloe spent a pleasant hour with a sketch pad, drawing a series of small figures that looked a lot like Annabelle. The figures all wore different versions of a magical, multilayered, brightly colored fairy princess costume, complete with wings—because what's a fairy princess costume unless there are wings?

A little later, when Quinn showed up, she took him downstairs to her home office and showed him the drawings.

"She would love it," he admitted with some reluctance. And then he shook his head. "You know she wants a puppy, too? There's no end to what Annabelle wants."

Chloe laughed. "The puppy's your problem."

"So far, we're holding the line on that."

"I just want to make this costume for her."

He took the sketch pad from her, dropped it to her desk, then wrapped his arms around her and kissed the end of her nose. "You're a pushover."

She grinned up at him. "I promise to get myself under

control soon when it comes to dealing with her. But I want to do this for her. I want her to have her dream room and I want her to have her fairy princess dress."

He chuckled. "You're giving me the big eyes. You're as bad as she is."

She traced the crew neck of his Prime Sports T-shirt with her index finger and then she pressed her lips against the hot skin of his powerful neck. "I would need to take her measurements, and probably let her see the sketches, to make sure I've got it right, got it just as she imagines it. So she would have to know ahead of time that she was getting what she wanted..."

"Yep. The big eyes," he muttered gruffly. "I know what you're doing." He kissed her then, a lovely, deep, slow one, after which she sighed and gazed up at him hopefully. Finally, he grumbled, "Wait a week or two before you bring it up to her. At least she won't think all she has to do is bat her eyes and beg a little and everything she wants will just drop in her lap."

"I'll check with Manny, too, to make sure he's okay with it. And if he gives the go-ahead, I'll wait two weeks to show her the drawings. How's that?" she asked, batting her eyes for all she was worth.

He gave in. "Fine."

"Thanks." She sighed and turned in his embrace so she could lean back against him.

He put his arms around her waist, and she felt his warm lips in her hair. "How'd your meeting with Nell go?"

Chloe thought of his little sister's biker boots hitting the desk, of the hot, protective gleam in Nell's emerald-green eyes. "Great. I like her. I think we'll work well together."

"She can be a hard ass. Don't let her intimidate you."

Chloe smiled to herself. "Not a chance."

And then she caught his hand and led him back up-stairs to her bedroom, where they made slow, delicious love.

He put his clothes back on at a little after midnight. She hated to see him go and she told him so. And then she kind of waited for him to point out that, if they were married, he wouldn't have to go.

But then he just kissed her again and said he'd see her tomorrow.

She put on her robe and walked him to the sliding door in the great room. Once he was gone, she stood looking out at the stars, thinking about saying yes to him.

Wanting to.

Because she wanted *him*. She *liked* him—and she liked his daughter and Manny, too. He wanted a wife and a mother for Annabelle. And all her life, she'd longed to be an excellent wife to a good and decent man, to be a loving mother. The idea of having Annabelle as her own made her heart feel too big for her chest. And the part about having Quinn's babies?

That hollowed her out and made her burn.

But speaking of burning…she'd been burned before, and badly. And it hadn't even been three weeks since that first night Quinn came up the hill and joined her in her bed.

How could she be sure of him in such a short time? With her track record, how could she be sure of anyone?

The stars outside were silent. They had no answers for her.

Tuesday flew by. She had several customers at the showroom. And she had shopping to do, an endless list of goodies that would be needed for Quinn's remodel.

When Chloe got home that evening, she saw a moving van at the house across the street. She went on over. Manny was there, directing the movers. He greeted her with a grin and a hug and said that Quinn was down at the other house feeding Annabelle her dinner on the last night they would spend at home until after the remodeling.

Chloe explained about the fairy princess dress.

Manny said, "She's gonna love that."

"So it's okay with you? You don't think I'm a complete pushover?"

"I think we got a little girl who loves her princesses. And you want to help her with that. Sounds about right to me."

She thanked him and then glanced around, admiring the soaring stone fireplace and the thick log walls. "Give me a tour?"

"Getting ideas for this one already?"

She nodded. "I'm happy that I'll have a chance to get to know this house ahead of time, get familiar with it, you know? I'll have an opportunity to mull over what changes will work best for it. Redoing a log home presents a special set of challenges."

Manny seemed to be studying her. "You're all right, Chloe."

"I'm glad you think so, Manny. I'm growing quite fond of you, as well."

"Quinn pop the question yet?"

Chloe fell back a step. "He told you he was going to?"

"Hell, no. He told me zip. But we been together more than a decade. I got a good idea what's going on with him, whether he lays it out for me or not." The two burly moving guys came in with the dining-room table. Manny said, "Through there, boys." And on they went. Manny lowered his voice for Chloe alone and said, "You haven't said yes yet, have you?"

Chloe pretended to ponder. "Hmm. Let me see. Would Quinn really want me to answer that?"

Manny chortled out a rough laugh. "Come on. Let me show you the house..."

The landline was ringing when Chloe got back to her place. It clicked over to her old-school answering machine before she could pick up.

It was her mother. "Sweetheart, we're home. Walked in the door five minutes ago. Maui was heaven, as always. But it's nice to be back and I can't want to see you, find out how you've been doing and tell you all about our trip. Call me the minute you get this. Love you..."

Chloe stood by the phone and considered getting it over with, calling her mother back right away. Years of conditioning had her feeling she really *ought* to call now, that a good daughter could be counted on to keep in contact with the ones she loved.

But as soon as her mother asked her what she'd been up to in the past two weeks, Chloe would be confronted with the question of how much to say.

Ha. As if there was a choice. Monique Hightower was spreading the news about her and Quinn far and wide. One way or another, it wouldn't be long before her mother got an earful. And it would probably be better if her mother heard it from Chloe.

Better being a relative term, knowing her mother.

Chloe picked up the phone.

And then set it back down again.

Her hand was shaking slightly, and that made her mad.

Why should she live in fear of her own mother? She'd faced Nell Bravo right down and told her that Linda Winchester did not run her life. She'd told Quinn the same thing. She needed to live by her own words.

Chloe turned the ringer off on the kitchen and bedroom phones and turned the volume on the message machine all the way down. Then she switched the sound off on her cell, as well. She'd check to see who'd called her at *her* convenience, thank you very much.

And she would get in touch with her mother later, after she'd had a little time to decide exactly what she wanted to say to her.

The evening went by—a goodly portion of it spent joyfully in Quinn's strong arms. After he left, she had trouble falling asleep. She couldn't stop stewing over what to tell her mom.

Somehow, in the morning, she slept through her alarm. That left her rushing to get ready and out the door in time to get the showroom opened by nine.

Her mother called the showroom number at ten. "Sweetheart, there you are!"

Chloe still wasn't ready to deal with her. "Mom. Glad you're home safe. Can't talk now. You know that. I'm at work."

"But how am I supposed to get hold of you if you won't answer your—?"

"Mom, I have another call," she outright lied. "I'll call you this evening, I promise."

"But—"

"Gotta go. I'll call. Promise."

Her mother was still protesting as Chloe hung up the phone. She knew time was running out. She was going to have to stop being such a coward. All day long, in the back of her mind, she rehearsed the things she would say when she called back that night.

I've been seeing Quinn Bravo. I care for him, Mom. Deeply. He's asked me to marry him and I am seriously considering telling him yes.

It all sounded so simple. It was...what people did. They found each other and they fell for each other and realized they didn't want to be apart. So they got married and raised a family.

Why shouldn't she have that—and with the right man this time? With a good man, a strong man. A man who cared about more than money and power and *things*. A man who considered her a whole person, with a heart and mind of her own, not just his most prized possession who looked good on his arm and had great taste and could work a room with the best of them.

Short answer: she absolutely *should* have that. And she *would* have it. With Quinn.

By the time she locked up the showroom and went home, she was all fired up to get it over with. To call her mother and tell her simply and proudly that she and Quinn were together.

But as it turned out, no call was necessary. When she pulled into her driveway, her mother's Mercedes SUV was parked in the side space next to the garage.

Chloe's stomach lurched at the sight, which was so pitiful it made her want to throw her head back and scream. But she didn't scream. She drew in a slow breath and told herself to man up. It was her life and she was going to live it for herself, not her mother. She would tell her mom the simple truth about her and Quinn and that would be that.

But then, as she left the garage by the breezeway door and caught sight of her mother waiting on the front step, it became crystal clear from the tight, furious expression on Linda Winchester's face that she already knew about Quinn.

Chloe's steps faltered. Only for a second, though. She quickly caught herself, straightened her shoulders and kept right on walking. "Mom. I don't remember you mentioning that you would be dropping by."

"Oh, please." Her mother gave her a truly withering glance. "Let me in. I have a few things to say to you and I'm not going to say them on your front step."

Chloe froze with her key raised to unlock the door. "Look, Mother. I don't want to—"

"Open the door. Now, please."

The temptation was so powerful to tell her mother right then and there that this was *her* house and *she* would decide who did or didn't enter it.

But then again, well, Linda Winchester wasn't the only one who had a few things to say. And she wasn't the only one who preferred to have this out in private.

So she unlocked the door. Her mother brushed past her as she disarmed the alarm.

Carefully, quietly, Chloe shut the door. Her mother stood beside the formal dining table, her blond head high, bright spots of color flaming on her cheeks, her lips bloodless with tension.

Chloe almost felt sorry for her. "Look, Mom. Why don't you sit down?"

Linda whipped out the chair at the end of the table and sat in it. She put her hand to her mouth and shut her eyes.

Chloe took the nearest chair. She waited until her mother dropped her hand away from her mouth and opened her eyes again before she said gently, "You're obviously very upset. Please tell me why."

Her mother sucked in a gasp and snapped, "Don't you play coy with me, Chloe."

"I'm not playing coy," Chloe said with a calm that surprised her. "What I'm doing is trying my best not to jump to conclusions."

"All right." With two sharp tugs, Linda straightened the sides of the linen jacket she wore. "Agnes Oldfield dropped by to see me an hour ago. She says it's all over town that you've been seeing Quinn Bravo. She says you went to the Sylvan Inn with him last Friday night, where you told Monique Hightower right to her face that you were…*attracted* to that man ever since high school. Agnes also says that you've been seen having ice cream with him and that child of his. She says that everyone says how…intimate you seem together, that it's obvious something serious is going on between you." Linda pressed her hand flat to her chest, and shook her head fiercely. "I do not believe this. Tell me that none of it is true."

Chloe just stared. God. She'd known this would be bad. But somehow, now that it was actually happening, all she could think was *What are we doing here? How could I have let it get his far? Why didn't I back her down years ago?*

The questions were all too familiar to her. They were the same ones she'd asked herself over and over about her ex-husband.

"Well?" her mother demanded. "What do you have to say for yourself?"

"You know, Mom. I don't think I have to say anything. But I would like to know what happened to *you*? I just don't understand how you got so messed up."

Another indignant gasp. "Excuse me?"

"It's not going to work on me, Mother. Not anymore. All your trumped-up outrage, your sad, small-minded ideas about who's okay and who's not. Your judgments about the right kind of people and the ones who just don't measure up."

"Wait just a minute, now—"

"No. No, I'm not going to wait for you to try and fill my head with more of your small-minded garbage and your snobbish, silly lies."

"Well, I have never—"

"Stop. I mean it. I don't want to hear it, never again. Quinn Bravo is a fine man and I'm not listening to one more word of this ridiculous crap you're dishing out against him. Yes, I am seeing him. And I am *proud* to be seeing him. Also, you should know that I am redoing his house and I'm gratified that he and Manny Aldovino have confidence in my ability to do the job well. In fact, Quinn has asked me to marry him and I am seriously considering saying yes."

"Dear, sweet Lord. Have you lost your mind?"

"No, I have not. I am perfectly sane, saner than I've ever been in my life before. And all that old stuff about Quinn's mother and his father and his father's first wife, all those ancient, ridiculous distinctions between the *real* Bravos and the *bastard* Bravos... Nobody cares about that anymore. Nobody but you—and maybe Monique Hightower and Agnes Oldfield, who both ought to get a life and stay out of mine."

"But you surely can't—"

"Wake up, Mother. Smell the Starbucks. I mean, look at it this way. Haven't you heard? Quinn Bravo's rich now. He's made a big success of his life. You know how much you love a big success."

Linda Winchester paled. "How dare you imply that I care how much money a man makes?"

Chloe knew she had lost it completely when she shouted, "I'm not implying it, I'm saying it straight out!"

Her mother cringed and jerked back in her chair, as though terrified—which Chloe knew very well she was not. "There's no need to shout," Linda said with a wounded sniff. "And I would hardly consider beating other men to a pulp a 'successful' way to make a living. And what about that motherless child of his being raised by that strange old man?"

"Manny is a wonderful person and he's doing a terrific job with Annabelle."

"Oh, please. It doesn't matter how much money he has. Quinn Bravo will never measure up and I raised you to know that."

"Enough." Chloe stood. "What I know, Mother, is that I'm done. I'm finished. I've had enough of your narrow-minded, holier-than-thou, manipulative behavior to last me a lifetime."

Another hot gasp from her mother. "What's happened to you? What's the *matter* with you? You're acting like a crazy person. I brought you up to be better than this."

"Stop. Quit. There's just no point. I want you to leave now. I want you to leave my house and not come back until you've had a serious change in your attitude."

Something happened then. Linda's gaze shifted away. When she looked back at Chloe, she actually seemed worried. Was it possible she'd finally realized she'd gone too far? She said, more softly than before, with a hint of appeasement, "It's only that I don't want you to throw your life away. It's only that you're special. You deserve the best life has to offer. I want that for you. I want *everything* for you."

"I really do want you to go now." Chloe gentled her tone, but didn't waver. "Please."

Linda didn't get up. She only talked faster. "Oh, sweetheart. I know. I understand. You had it all. And you threw it away. But the good news is, if you'll only make a little effort, you and Ted can work through this rough patch and—"

Chloe put up a hand. "Get back with Ted? You can't be serious. I don't believe you, Mother. How many times have I told you I never want to hear his name? How many times have I told you that he hit me and he cheated on me and there is no going back from that? I don't *want* to go back. All I want is never to have to look in his evil, lying face again."

"You're overwrought."

"Oh, you bet I am." She stepped back and pointed at the door. "Please leave my house. Now."

Finally, her mother stood—and kept on talking. "Can't you see? That new wife of his? She's a pale imitation. She can't hold a candle to you. Ted realizes that now. And you know that you're exaggerating about his behavior, making a big drama out of a little marital spat or two."

"Wait." Chloe really, truly could not believe her ears. "What did you say?"

"I said, you're making a big drama of—"

"'He *realizes* that now'? How could you know what Ted Davies realizes?"

"Well, sweetheart, now listen. You really need to settle down, so that we can speak of this reasonably."

"Reasonably?" Chloe echoed in a near whisper. The awful truth had hit her like a boot to the head. Her ears were ringing. "You've been in touch with him, haven't you? You've been *encouraging* him."

Linda got right to work blowing her off. "Well, I... You know I only want what's best for you and I—"

"You've given him my address, haven't you?"

"Oh, don't be foolish. It's not as if you're in hiding."

"So you did give him my address."

Linda just wouldn't give it up and answer the question. She let out a low sound of complete disdain. "Don't make such an issue of it. Anyone could find out where you live with a minimum of effort."

"But Ted didn't have to make *any* effort, right? Because you'll tell him whatever he wants to know." She grabbed her mother's arm. "That does it. You're leaving."

Linda squealed. "What are you doing?" She slapped at Chloe. "Let go of me. You're *hurting* me…" The tears started then.

Chloe ignored them. She pulled her mother to the door, yanked it open and shoved her over the threshold.

Linda sobbed, "How can you do this to me? You're breaking my heart."

Chloe's answer was to firmly shut the door in her face.

Chapter Seven

That night, it took Quinn an extra half hour to chase off all the monsters and get Annabelle settled in bed. He performed his monster-removing duties happily. Partly because he was a total pushover for his little girl. And partly because he knew she needed the extra attention on her first night in her temporary bedroom in the log house across the street from Chloe.

After Annabelle finally went to sleep, he and Manny took beers out to the back deck, where they touched base on the usual household stuff, finances and the move.

They were just wrapping up when his cell chimed. A text. From Chloe. The first, he realized, that he'd ever gotten from her.

That made him smile—initially. And then he had to deal with the words in the little conversation bubble. At least it was only one sentence: Can you come over now?

Unease curled through him. Something in the starkness of the question didn't sit right. Chloe was generally so gracious and well mannered, the kind of woman to offer a drink and ask a man how his day had been before ever getting down to what she needed from him.

Manny asked, "Chloe?"

"Yeah." Texting was not his best event. He debated the option of turning up the sound on his text-to-speech app and voice-texting her back. Or he could just call her. But she was only across the street and he felt an urgency to get to her. He rose.

"Something wrong, Crush?"

Quinn clasped Manny's shoulder. "Probably nothing."

Manny reached up, patted his hand and let him go without a single wiseass remark.

Chloe must have been standing at the door, peering through the peephole, because she whipped it open before Quinn could raise his hand to knock. One look at her too-pale face and shadowed, red-rimmed eyes and Quinn knew his instincts had been right. Something had gone way wrong.

"Quinn." She grabbed for him.

He stepped inside, gathered her close and shoved the door shut with his heel.

"Quinn…" She curled against him, tucking her golden head under his chin, her slim arms clutching tight around him, as though she wanted to crawl right inside skin.

It freaked him out a little to see her so out of control. That only happened when he had her naked in bed. The rest of the time, she was the queen of smooth, hard to ruffle. Something had really spooked her. He stroked her hair and rubbed her back and reassured her with low, soothing words. "I'm here. It's okay now, all right? You just hold on tight…"

She burrowed even closer against him and confessed in a torn whisper, "I never, ever had the guts to stand up to her and now it's come down to this. Oh, I hate myself. I'm such a wuss. It shouldn't have gotten to this, I should have stopped her a long time ago. I—"

"Shh," he soothed. "Shh, now. Take a breath, a long, slow one..."

Obedient as a cowed and frightened child, she took a long, deep one and let it out nice and slow. "Oh, Quinn..." A sob escaped her.

He caught her beautiful face between his hands, tipped it up so he could see her haunted eyes again and took an educated guess. "This is about your mother?"

She hitched in a ragged breath and nodded. "After tonight, she's out of my life. I never want to see her again."

"Whoa," he said gently. "Come on, now, angel. Whatever she did, she *is* your mother."

Chloe pursed up her lips and stuck out her chin. "Don't even remind me."

"I'm only saying, whatever happened with her, give her a little time. She'll come around."

"Oh, you don't know her, Quinn," she insisted. "You don't know her at all." She sounded downright pissed off.

Which wasn't so bad, he decided. He'd take pissed off over brokenhearted and out of control any day of the week. "Hey." He stroked her hair some more, brushed a quick kiss across her sweet, trembling mouth. "You gonna talk to me? *Really* talk to me? Because I need a better idea of what happened before I can do much more than hold you and tell you it'll be okay."

"It was awful. We went at each other. She was like one of those crazed, jealous girlfriends on *The Jerry Springer Show*." Chloe shut her eyes and sucked in another slow, careful breath. "And I wasn't much better."

Now, there was an image. Chloe and Linda Winchester going at it on *The Jerry Springer Show*. "Come on. Make some coffee or something. You can tell me what happened."

A few minutes later, they sat on the sofa. Chloe sipped the hot tea she'd made for herself. "She was waiting on the front step when I got home from work, and she was furious."

It didn't take a genius to figure out why. "Someone told her about you and me."

"That's right. She..." Chloe met his eyes then. "I don't even know how to tell you how awful she was."

"It's okay. You don't have to give me a blow-by-blow. She's never thought much of me or of my family and we knew that from the first."

"I, well, I want you to know that I didn't back down, Quinn. I didn't evade, either. For the first time in my life I stood right up to her. I told her I was seeing you and I intended to *keep* seeing you and that she'd better accept that."

"But she wouldn't accept it."

"No. We yelled at each other. I realized it was going nowhere and I asked her to leave. That was when she let it slip that she's been in touch with my ex-husband." Chloe's gaze slid away. "I hit the ceiling and threw her out." She fell silent, and she still wasn't looking at him.

He waited. When she didn't volunteer any more, he said, "It's probably about now that you should tell me whatever it is you're *not* telling me about your ex-husband."

She did face him then. And she looked stricken. In a small voice, she said, "I don't even know where to begin." He took her mug from her and set it on the low table. Then he hooked an arm around her shoulders and pulled her close to his side. She crumpled against him. "Oh, God..."

He pressed a kiss into her sweet-smelling hair. "It doesn't matter where you start. I'm not going anywhere until you've told me everything I need to know."

She let out a small, sad little sound. "All my life, all I wanted was to be my mother's good little girl. And look where that's gotten me..."

Quinn said nothing. He held her close.

Finally, hesitantly, she told him the story. "I met Ted Davies at Stanford in my sophomore year. He was four years older than me, in law school. And he was everything my mother raised me to want. Handsome and charming, already rich, from a powerful California family, bound for a successful career as a corporate lawyer. I saw him as perfect husband material, and he saw me as exactly the right wife to stand by him as he climbed to the top. We got married in a gorgeous wine country wedding at the end of my senior year and I went to work being his wife, which both of us considered a full-time job. It was all going so well until Ted lost his temper. He'd decided I'd been too friendly to one of the partners at his office Christmas party. We had a fight. We'd been married for a little more than two years. That was the first time he hit me." She tipped her head up and looked at Quinn then.

He knew that look. She was checking to see how he was taking it. He met her eyes and stroked her hair and didn't let her see what was going on inside him. He was a simple man, really, especially when it came to stuff like this. A simple man who wanted to track down that jackass she'd married and beat his face in for him.

Chloe lowered her head again and tucked herself against his chest. "I left him."

"Good."

She glanced up again. He was ready for that. Playing it easy and accepting for all he was worth, he kissed the tip of her elegant nose. With a sigh, she settled again. "Ted...wooed me back. He went into counseling for anger management to prove to me that he was a changed man."

"But he wasn't."

"I'll say this. He didn't hit me again for a long time, though his scary temper was increasingly in evidence as the next four years went by. Three years ago, I found out he was having an affair with a college student, an intern at his firm. I confronted him. When he couldn't convince me that he was totally innocent and that I was only being a small-minded, jealous wife, he lost it. He punched me in the face hard enough to bloody my nose and blacken both eyes. I left him. And after that, I was done. No cajoling or high-powered charm offensive or promises that he'd get more counseling could sway me. I sued for divorce. As it happened, he was still seeing the other woman—and she wanted to be his wife. So I got my divorce and a nice settlement. And Ted got a new, younger wife. And except for how I still feel guilty that I didn't press assault charges against him, that should have been the end of it, right?"

He rubbed a soothing hand up and down her arm. "But it wasn't."

"I tried to keep going in Southern California. But then Ted started coming around again, talking reconciliation, as if I would even let him near me, as if he didn't have a wife waiting at home. I decided I needed to make a new start—or rather, I realized what I really wanted was to come back where I began and try to get it right this time."

He tipped her chin up then and kissed her.

She said shyly, "I do feel like I'm finally getting it right, Quinn. Getting it right with you."

Those fine words dampened his carefully masked fury against the abusive loser she'd married, enough that he kissed her again. And then he asked, "So you're sure that your mother's been in contact with this guy?"

"She wouldn't admit it straight out, but yes. I'm sure she has. She told me how he wants to get back together with me—and my mother's all for that. That was when I finally threw her out. I'm done with her, Quinn. Finished."

Quinn blew out a slow breath. He was no more a fan of Linda Winchester than Linda was of him. And it turned his stomach that the woman would go behind Chloe's back and encourage the man who'd hurt her.

But there had been deep and painful rifts in his own family, especially back in the day when his father refused to choose between Sondra Oldfield Bravo and Quinn's mother. It wasn't all roses now, but it was better. Since returning to Justice Creek, he'd discovered he actually *liked* his half siblings. That couldn't have happened if they'd refused to give each other a chance.

"Still," he said. "There's a bond there, a strong one, between you and your mother."

"It's broken. Broken beyond repair."

"Chloe, she's family. You gotta keep that in mind, you know? I'm not saying just forgive her and act like nothing happened. But try to be open, okay? Give it time and see if she comes around, makes amends."

"I wish I could be as accepting and patient as you are."

Quinn had to stifle a grunt of disbelief when she said that. Yeah, he might be willing to be patient with her mother. But Chloe's ex? He'd like to meet good old Ted in a dark alley some night. Only one of them would come out, and it wouldn't be Davies.

Chloe snuggled in close again. "Can we just…leave the subject of my mother alone for now?"

"Sure. But I got a question."

She must have picked up something not all that accepting in his tone, because she pushed free of his arms and scooted back to the other couch cushion. "What?"

"You heard from this Ted character since you moved back to Justice Creek?"

Chloe cleared her throat. A definite tell. "No. He, um, hasn't called."

Quinn knew then that the guy *had* been in contact with her. He reminded her, "You and me, we got something special. And I know when you're not being straight with me."

She wrapped her arms around herself and pleaded with those pretty blue eyes. "You have to promise me you won't do anything, won't…go after him or anything."

Quinn's pulse leaped. He couldn't keep a promise like that. "You just gotta tell me what he did, Chloe. You know that you do, you know that's how we need to be with each other. We need to tell the truth to each other—and *then* we can decide what to do about it."

She swallowed. Hard. "All right. One time."

"You've heard from him one time?"

"Yes. He sent me flowers. With a short note that said how flowers remind him of me and he was sorry it didn't work out…"

There was more, he was certain. He pushed for it. "And?"

"The note also said that he, um…missed me. I threw everything—the vase, the flowers, that damn note, too—in the trash compactor and ground it all to bits."

"When was that?"

"A week ago. Last Wednesday night."

He wanted to pick up her tea mug from the table and hurl it at the far wall. But he kept it together and said levelly, "That was the night we sat out on your deck and talked for two hours."

She gazed at him warily now. "What are you getting at?"

"I wish you had told me then—or any day or night since then."

"That's not fair and you know it. It's been happening pretty fast with us. Think about it. I just couldn't tell you, didn't even know *how* to tell you—not the night it happened or the next day, or the day after that. I can barely talk about it now."

She had a point. He knew it. And really, he only wanted to neutralize any threat to her. "I don't blame you, angel." He said it softly, without heat. Because it was true. "No way do I blame you."

Her sweet face crumpled. "You mean that?"

"You know I do." He reached for her. She let out a small cry and allowed him to wrap his arms around her again. He held her tight, loving the way she felt, so soft in all the right places. "That's it, then? That's the only move he's made on you since you came back home?"

"Yes. That's it."

"Did you call him and tell him to leave you alone?"

"Uh-uh. You have no idea how many times in the past I told him to leave me alone. That only seemed to encourage him."

"I hear that. So, then, don't engage him." He lifted her hand and pressed his lips to the back of it. "Did you go to the police?"

"And tell them what? That my ex-husband sent me flowers out of the blue and a nice little note?"

"Don't get defensive. I agree that you don't have anything to charge the creep with. I just want to be sure, to know everything that happened, to know exactly where we stand with this piece of crap."

"We?" She pushed away from him again, smoothed the yellow skirt of her pretty summer dress over her knees and then looked him straight in the eye. "Quinn. Ted is in no way your problem. This thing with him is for me to solve. I will not drag you into my mess. I don't want you going after him, or approaching him, or contacting him or getting near him, ever. I need your word on that."

He would give her anything—the world on a gold platter. But not this. "That guy needs to know you're not alone anymore. He needs to know someone's got your back."

"I couldn't care less what *he* needs, Quinn. I'm talking about what *I* need. And that is to know I can tell you my hardest secrets and trust that you won't go racing off to solve all my problems for me in your own way. Because they are *my* problems and I'm the one who gets the final say when it comes to dealing with them. It's about respect, and you know it. You have to respect me and let *me* figure out how to mop up the mess I created. Please."

He really hated that what she said made sense. "You *will* tell me, if he does *anything*, if you hear so much as a word from him again?"

"I will, yes." She folded her hands on her knees. "And you will honor my wishes and let me handle this in my own way?"

He scraped both hands down his face. "You got me up against the ropes here."

"Because you *do* respect me. I know you only want

to protect me and you have no idea how much I love that about you."

Love. It was a big word. And it was also the first time she'd used it in reference to him. Quinn liked the way it sounded coming out of that fine mouth of hers. He liked it a lot.

What he didn't like was not being allowed to teach Ted Davies an important life lesson. Then again, guys like that always managed to get what was coming to them eventually. Quinn fervently hoped he'd have the honor of taking Ted to church when the time came.

"Quinn?" she asked, all breathless and hopeful. "I need your word that you'll leave Ted alone."

Damn it to hell. He gave it up. "All right. For now, for as long as he never tries to get in touch with you again, you got my word."

Chloe was no fool.

She fully understood what it cost Quinn to make her that promise. He'd done a really good job of hiding his anger at Ted. But already, in the short time they'd been together, she'd learned to read him. He wanted to go after Ted, he *needed* to do that, needed to step forward and be her protector.

What woman wouldn't appreciate that in a man?

But he'd done protectiveness one better. He'd agreed to go against what he needed to do and leave Ted alone. Because she'd asked him to. And if she hadn't already been halfway in love with him, well, that he *had* made that promise kind of sealed the deal as far as she was concerned.

"Thank you," she whispered, taking his big hand, turning it over and smoothing his beefy fingers open.

"Thank you..." She bent close and pressed a kiss in the center of his rough, hot palm.

"Let's just hope we've seen the last of him," Quinn muttered gruffly.

She couldn't agree more. And not only because she wanted nothing to do with her ex. Now there was Quinn to worry about. If Ted made another move on her, convincing Quinn to stay out of it was going to be exponentially tougher.

But they'd spent altogether too much of their evening on unhappy subjects. She forced a brighter tone. "First my mother, then Ted. Let's forget about both of them for now, huh?" She reached up and smoothed the thick brown hair off his forehead. "Now I want it to be just you and me, here on the sofa, doing whatever comes naturally."

He studied her face for a moment, his head tipped to the side. And then he kicked off his shoes. She followed suit, sliding off her sandals and pushing them under the coffee table.

"Come here." He took her by the shoulders, turned her and settled her with her head in his lap.

Chloe stared up at him, feeling better already. The hard things had been said. And now it was just her and Quinn, alone for the evening. He traced the curves of her eyebrows with a slow finger and then caught a lock of her hair and wrapped it around his hand the way he liked to do.

She said, "I hope I didn't drag you away from anything important at home..."

He shook his head. "Annabelle's all tucked in bed. Manny and I were just having a beer on the deck."

"Do you still want to marry me?" The words kind of popped out. She'd hardly known she would say them— until she did.

He gave her his bad-boy half smile. "Oh, yeah. But I'm not pushing. You decide what you want and you do it in your own time."

"Even after all the grim stuff I told you tonight? I'm not sure I'm such a good bet, Quinn."

He unwrapped her hair from around his fingers—and then twined it right back again. "You're not your mother and it's not your fault that your ex is a psycho dog. You *are* a good bet, angel. You're a fine woman with a big heart, the best there is."

His generous words warmed her, made a glow down inside her that all the trials of the afternoon and evening couldn't dim.

I think I'm falling in love with you, Quinn.

It sounded so right inside her head. But she wasn't quite ready to say it out loud yet. Talk of love still had some taint for her. It still held ugly echoes of the past.

She shut her eyes and drifted, cradled, safe, with her head in Quinn's lap.

Marriage. To Quinn.

Was she ready for that? They'd been together such a short time and she'd messed up so badly before. How could she be certain?

She opened her eyes.

And he was gazing down at her, steady. Sure. Not having to say anything, just being there with her.

When she looked in his eyes, her doubts about herself and her future and her iffy judgment just melted away. When she looked in Quinn's eyes, she *was* sure.

And come on. She'd dated Ted for a year before she said yes to him. And then it was another year until their lavish wedding. She'd given herself plenty of time to really *know* Ted. She'd done everything right.

And still, it all went wrong. Ted was the man her mother wanted for her.

And Quinn?

It was so simple. Quinn was the one *she* wanted for herself. He was *her* choice, her second chance to get it right. She trusted him. She knew he would be good to her, that she would be good for him—and for Annabelle and Manny, too.

Together, they could make a full, rich life, the life she'd always wanted. The life she'd given up hope that she would ever find.

Until now. Until Quinn.

He unwound her hair again. And she sat up and took his arm and wrapped it across her shoulders. He gathered her closer. She drew her legs up onto the sofa and folded them to the side so she was facing him. Looking right into those wonderful eyes, she said, "Well, I've decided, then. And my decision is…" She stretched up enough to nip his scruffy jaw with her teeth. "Yes."

For once, he actually looked taken completely off guard. "What did you say?"

"I said yes, Quinn. I will marry you. I want it to be a small, simple wedding, just family and close friends. And I want it to be soon."

"Chloe." He took her face between those big hands. "Seriously? You're sure?" He looked so vulnerable right then, as if he couldn't quite believe she really meant it.

She did mean it. "Yes, I am very sure."

"Damn," he whispered prayerfully.

He kissed her, a kiss that curled her bare toes and created that incomparable heavy, hot yearning down in the core of her. And then he scooped her up in those big arms of his and carried her to her bedroom.

Late into the night, he showed her exactly how happy her decision had made him.

Dawn was breaking when he left her. She stood out on her front porch in a robe and slippers, watching him walk across the street to his temporary home, knowing her hair needed combing and her eyes were low and lazy. She was fully aware that she had the look of a woman thoroughly and repeatedly satisfied—and she didn't care in the least who saw her.

She'd made her decision. She was marrying Quinn and finally getting the life she'd always dreamed of.

Aimee Thurlo

Chapter Eight

At the showroom a few hours later, Chloe called Tai and asked her to come in early.

At ten, Quinn picked her up. They drove to Denver, where they had lunch and he bought her a beautiful engagement ring and a platinum wedding ring to match. She bought him a ring, too, a thick platinum band that she couldn't wait to slip on his finger when the big day came. She was back at her showroom by four.

That evening, just as she was letting herself in the front door, the house phone rang. She saw it was her parents' number and let it go to the machine.

A few minutes later, she checked to see what her mother had said. But it turned out it was her dad. He'd left a two-sentence message: "Chloe, this is your dad. Please call me."

She did, right then.

He asked her if she was all right and Chloe told him that she would be fine.

Doug Winchester said, "Your mother's just broken-hearted over what happened last night."

Chloe refused to let him play the guilt card on her. "We don't see eye-to-eye, Mom and me. And I don't think that either of us will be changing our positions anytime soon."

"She loves you. You know that. *I* love you."

"Thanks, Daddy. I love you, too. But sometimes love really can't make everything right. Not with Mom, anyway. With Mom, it's her way or nothing. And I'm through doing things her way. In fact, Quinn's asked me to marry him and I've said yes."

The line went dead silent. Then her father asked cautiously, "Isn't this a little sudden?"

She resisted the urge to say something snappish. "I care for him deeply, Dad. It's what I want."

"You're sure?"

"I am."

Another silence. And then her father had the good grace to say that he hoped she would be happy. "I think I'll wait a few days to tell your mother about your engagement, though."

"Right now, Dad, I don't care if you tell her or not."

"Chloe. You don't mean that."

She didn't argue. What was the point? "I'll call and let you know about the wedding. It's going to be small and simple." Nothing like the three-ring circus in Sonoma when she'd married Ted. "I hope you can come. Quinn wants me to be patient with Mom, so I'm going to give it a little time before I decide whether I'm willing to have her at the wedding."

Another deep silence from her dad. Then, "Let's just see how things go, shall we?"

Chloe agreed that would be wise. They said goodbye.

A few hours later, when Quinn came over, she cried

a little for her fractured family. He held her and told her it would all turn out all right. Somehow, when he said it, she almost believed it.

Friday morning first thing, Nell Bravo dropped by Chloe's showroom. Chloe broke the big news and showed off her gorgeous ring.

Nell said, "So, then. This makes it official. You're gonna be my sister. And that means we'll have to bury the hatchet permanently, you and me."

"You know, you really scare me when you talk about hatchets."

Nell laughed and grabbed Chloe in a hug and waltzed her in and out of the various carpet and flooring displays. Then Quinn's sister confessed, "I already knew. Quinn told me this morning. And I'm here to find out when you're breaking for lunch so I can get a table at the Sylvan Inn for you and me and my sisters."

Chloe met the Bravo sisters at the Sylvan Inn at one. There were four of them. Clara and Elise were the daughters of Franklin Bravo's first wife, Sondra. Jody's and Nell's mother was the notorious Willow Mooney Bravo, who'd been Frank's mistress during most of his marriage to Sondra. The day after Sondra Bravo's funeral, Willow married Frank. He moved her right into the mansion he'd built for Sondra. Frank Bravo's refusal to observe even a minimal period of mourning after Sondra's passing caused no end of shock and outrage in the angry hearts of the judgmental types in town, Chloe's mother first among them.

Tracy Winham, Elise's best friend and business partner, joined them, too. And so did Rory Bravo-Calabretti, a cousin to the Bravo sisters. Rory was an actual princess from a tiny country called Montedoro. But Rory didn't act like a princess. She loved Justice Creek and she was down-to-earth and lots of fun. Recently she'd decided to make her home in America. She lived with her fiancé, Walker McKellan, at Walker's guest ranch not far from town.

As a matter of fact, all the Bravo women were lots of fun. Even more so after a couple of glasses of the champagne Nell had ordered to toast Chloe and Quinn and their future happiness together. Chloe never drank alcohol at lunch. After all, she still had half a day of work ahead and she preferred to be alert and clearheaded on the job.

But today, she drank the champagne—more than she should have. And she had a fabulous time sharing stories about the old days with Quinn's sisters.

"Quinn was always so moody," said Jody, and everyone nodded. "He was mad at everything and just about everybody."

"But even then there was a certain sweetness about him," said Clara, who was Sondra's oldest daughter and considered the family peacemaker.

Back in the day, when the two sides of Frank's family were constantly at odds, Clara was the one who kept trying to get them to make peace and come together. She and Quinn and Chloe were the same age.

"I remember," Clara said, "when we were in Miss Oakleaf's class, first grade. Remember, Chloe?"

"Yes, I do. Miss Oakleaf was so pretty. I wanted to be just like her when I grew up."

"Oh, me, too," Clara agreed.

"She pinned her hair up in a twist and she always looked so elegant. And she wore high heels and pencil skirts." Chloe frowned. "Were they even called pencil skirts back then?"

Clara considered. "Straight skirts, I think. And yeah. Miss Oakleaf was a beauty. Quinn had a big crush on her."

"She was patient with him," Chloe said softly, remembering how he struggled to keep up with the rest of the class.

Clara remembered, too. "He would get mad and act up and she would talk to him so gently."

"And then," said Chloe, "the Hershey's Kisses started appearing on her desk every morning…"

Clara took up the story. "Just a few of them, lined up in their shiny silver foil wrappers, waiting there for Miss Oakleaf on her desk pad at the beginning of every day."

"No one knew who was leaving them," said Chloe.

And Clara said, "Until Freddy Harmon spotted Quinn in the act. Freddy spied on Quinn through the window, didn't he, and saw him sneak in and put three Kisses on Miss Oakleaf's desk?"

"That's right," Chloe replied softly. "Quinn was so humiliated…" She shook her head, aching for the troubled little boy he'd once been.

Jody said, "The way I heard it, he went ballistic."

Clara nodded. "He chased Freddy around the playground till he caught him, and then he beat the crap out of him. For that, Quinn was suspended for two weeks. Looking back on our elementary school years, it seems like he spent more time suspended or in detention than he ever spent in class."

They all laughed. They could afford to laugh about it now that Quinn was a grown man who'd built himself a fine, productive life.

Nell asked, "Remember that time he and Jamie and Dare got into it on the playground?" James and Darius were Clara's and Elise's full brothers, Sondra's sons.

Elise nodded. "It was two against one. Plus, Jamie and Dare were older and bigger. But Quinn just wouldn't give up and go down."

Rory shook her head. "It's so strange, knowing him now, to hear what a troublemaker he used to be."

"By the time he was twelve or so," Clara said, "no one would fight with him. By then, they all knew that he would never quit. If you took on Quinn Bravo, it was going to be long and ugly and there would be way too much blood."

"But look how he turned out," Tracy piped up. "Rich and successful, with a beautiful daughter, about to marry the one and only Chloe Winchester." Tracy raised her glass and everyone followed suit. "To Chloe. You go, girl."

Chloe blushed a little. "Aww."

Nell shook her gorgeous head of auburn hair. "Chloe. Seriously. You and Quinn? Never woulda seen that coming."

Chloe beamed at her future sister-in-law, her heart full of fondness, her brain pleasantly hazy with the champagne and the good family feelings. She really was starting to feel seriously bondy with Nell. Was it only five days ago that they'd squared off in the trailer at Bravo Construction?

"Heads up, my sisters," Elise whispered out of the side of her mouth. "Don't look now, but here comes trouble."

Trouble in the tall, thin form of Monique Hightower. Wearing jeans, a silk top and giant sunglasses, Monique had just breezed in the door. She said something to the hostess and then spotted the Bravo women at the round table in the center of the dining room. Slowly, she eased the big sunglasses up to rest on her head. And then she smiled.

And then she came striding on over. "Hey, Clara, Elise, everyone. Looks like a party…"

Nell said, "It is. We are celebrating."

About then, Monique zeroed in on Chloe. "Chloe. Well. How's every little thing?"

Chloe raised her champagne glass—with her left hand, so that her engagement diamond caught the light and sparkled. "Remember how I told you if I played my cards right, I might have a chance with Quinn?"

Somebody snickered. Chloe thought it was Elise, but it could have been Tracy.

Monique's eyes got wider. "Wow. That's, uh…" For once, she actually seemed at a loss for words. Chloe savored the moment.

Then Nell instructed, "Pull yourself together, Monique. Quinn and Chloe are getting married. You need to wish my future sister-in-law a life of love and happiness."

Monique sent Nell a quelling glance that had zero effect on Quinn's baby sister. Nell just rolled her eyes and drank more champagne as Monique trotted out another big, fake smile and a too-perky "Best wishes, Chloe. Quinn's a lucky man."

"Thank you, Monique."

Clara, ever the peacemaker, offered, "Monique, why don't you join us for a glass of champagne?"

Everyone went dead quiet then. They'd been having such a great time and Monique would have them trying to remember to watch what they said, because anything Monique heard was fair game for her gossip mill.

Then Monique sighed. "Wish I could. But I got called in early. I need to change and get to work."

"That's too bad." Somehow Nell kept a straight face when she said it.

By then, Monique had recovered her equilibrium.

"Chloe. That ring is spectacular. And truly, I'm so happy for you."

"Monique. What can I say? Thank you again. That's so nice to hear." And strangely enough, it kind of was. Chloe had the definite warm fuzzies at the moment. She was crazy about the Bravo women, crazy about Quinn. Crazy about *everyone*. She was even crazy about Monique, who couldn't keep a confidence if her life depended on it.

Champagne at lunchtime? She should try it more often.

Nobody said a word until Monique disappeared into the kitchen. And then Nell tapped her water glass with her spoon. "So. Engagement party. We need to throw one."

Chloe started to protest that they didn't have to.

But then again, that could be fun, right?

How much fun had she had in her life, really?

Not enough. She'd always been mama's good girl, a busy little bee, working so hard to do everything right, to get straight As and get into a great college and find the perfect husband to make a perfect life.

There'd been no time for fun, not when she was so laser-focused on chasing the life her mother wanted for her.

And after her marriage to Ted? Well, it only went downhill from there. Hard to have fun when your life that looked so perfect on the outside was empty at the core, when you lived with a man you couldn't trust not to hurt you.

But now she had Quinn and anything seemed possible. All the good things: passion and tenderness and lots of laughter. And sisters to call her own.

And, for the first time, champagne at lunch.

Chloe let Quinn's sisters plan the party. She smiled and nodded and giggled a lot.

Nell leaned close to her. "Better cut back on the bubbly, baby."

And Chloe giggled some more. But she took Nell's advice and started drinking ice water. By three-thirty, when they left the restaurant, she was almost sober.

They filed out to the parking lot. There were hugs and cheek kisses. Chloe thanked them all profusely.

Nell tapped her shoulder. "You still look a little high. Ride with me. You can get your car later."

So just to be on the safe side, she let Nell take her back to the showroom. When Nell pulled in at the curb, Chloe leaned across the seats and hugged her good and hard. "I'm so glad you're going to be my sister. I never had a sister before."

Nell hugged her back. "Well, now you've got four—five, including Tracy, who always gets insulted if we don't include her."

That evening, Manny went to Boulder to visit his girlfriend. Quinn and Annabelle picked Chloe up at the showroom and took her back to the restaurant to get her car.

Then she joined them at the log house. They had pizza. And after Annabelle was all ready for bed, they watched *Frozen*, which Annabelle seemed to know by heart.

She kept popping in with "Look out!" or "Watch this!" just before something surprising would happen.

Quinn finally had to pause the movie and remind her that it was no fun to watch a movie when little girls were shouting.

Annabelle was sweetly contrite. She turned to Chloe.

"I'm sorry, Chloe. I'm not s'posed to do that. But I get so 'cited!"

Chloe said, "Well, maybe if you don't do it again, your dad will let us watch the rest."

Annabelle turned those big brown eyes on Quinn. "Daddy, I promise I will be quiet."

She managed to get through the rest of the movie without a single exclamation. And by the end, she had edged up close to Chloe on the sofa and rested her head against Chloe's arm. Chloe treasured that small, perfect moment: the first time Annabelle had leaned on her.

It took a while to get the little girl to bed for the night. Quinn spent twenty minutes or so tucking her in. Then, half an hour later, she came out carrying a ratty blanket and an ancient-looking one-eyed teddy bear and demanded that he chase the monsters away. Quinn scooped her up in his arms, blanket, bear and all. He sent Chloe a sheepish look before heading upstairs to Annabelle's bedroom.

"I think she'll stay in bed now," he said when he returned a few minutes later. He confessed that he enjoyed chasing monsters. "It's more of a game with us than anything."

"Don't even think you need to explain," Chloe reassured him. "It looked like you were both having fun and she didn't seem scared in the least."

"Manny says I'm a sucker for Annabelle's monster act."

Chloe chuckled. "Sometimes being a sucker is a good thing."

"I'm going to tell Manny you said that."

They sat on the sofa in the living room in front of the unlit fireplace, with the lights on low. He reached over and ran a finger along the curve of her cheek.

She shivered a little in pleasure, remembering that first night, when he'd come up the hill to her. His daughter had been on his mind that night. "Did she ever have more questions for you about her mom?"

He idly smoothed a curl of her hair back over her shoulder. "Not yet. Just about every night, I think she's going to bring it up. But then she doesn't."

"Give her time."

"I just hope when she does that I don't blow it."

"No way can you blow it, Quinn. You love her and she loves you. She feels safe and protected. And you give her space, you really do. She's allowed to be a little girl, to let her imagination run a little wild…" Chloe felt kind of wistful suddenly.

And Quinn picked up on that. "Hey…" He touched her mouth, traced the bow of her upper lip. "Why the sad face?"

"I don't know. I had a great time with your sisters today at lunch. And it kind of got me thinking that I never had much fun growing up."

"Too busy trying to please your mom?"

"That's right." She made the edges of her mouth turn up. "But I think I'll look on the bright side. Your sisters will be my sisters. Did I tell you they're throwing us an engagement party? Probably at McKellan's, in the party room upstairs." The popular pub was owned by Ryan McKellan, lifetime best friend of Clara Bravo. Ryan's brother, Walker, was engaged to the family princess, Rory.

"And when is this big event?"

"Tentatively, Saturday night two weeks from tomorrow. Clara said she'd get with Ryan and call me this weekend to firm up the date, location and time."

He hooked an arm around her and drew her close

against his side. His warm lips brushed her hair. "Did you know that Clara and Dalton are getting married in three weeks?"

"I did, yes." Clara had a baby daughter, Kiera Anne, with Dalton Ames, president of Ames Bank and Trust. From what Chloe had heard, Clara had taken her time saying yes to her baby's father. But anyone who saw them together could see how much in love they were.

Quinn added, "It'll be a small wedding, Clara said. Food and drinks at her house afterward."

"I heard. Nell said she thought Clara had too much on her plate. So, as soon as Clara sets up our engagement party with Ryan, Nell's taking over to pull the party together."

"You should know we're going to Clara's wedding." He gave her shoulder a squeeze. "You, me, Manny and Annabelle."

"I would love to." She snuggled in, rubbing her cheek against the soft knit fabric of his shirt.

He traced the line of her jaw with his thumb, and then tipped up her chin so she looked in his eyes. "Hey."

"What?"

"The other night, when you said yes?"

"Um?" Oh, those beautiful eyes of his. She could just fall down inside them and never come out.

"You said you wanted it small—and soon. So…" He lowered his wonderful bad-boy lips and brushed a hint of a kiss across her upturned mouth. "What do you say we set the date?"

Set the date. Her heart contracted. Worse, she was suddenly thinking of her mother, and of Ted. Problems. Unresolved problems. *Her* problems that she'd yet to deal with effectively…

But then again, how resolved were things ever going to

get with those two? She might never speak to her mother again. And Ted? The best that could happen with him would be nothing. Ever. For the rest of her life.

So it wasn't about resolving anything; it wasn't about closure...

"Chloe?" Quinn looked at her so tenderly, reminding her suddenly of the little boy who never fit in at school and used to sneak inside before class to leave chocolate candy Kisses for the teacher who'd been kind to him. "So when you said soon, you didn't mean *that* soon?" He asked the question gently.

She let out the breath she hadn't realized she'd been holding. "I'm thinking if we could at least wait until after the engagement party to start planning the wedding?"

His chuckled, the sound low and lovely. "I just don't get it. Why are you dragging your feet? We've been engaged for two whole days now."

She echoed his teasing tone. "People will start thinking we have trouble making commitments."

But then his expression turned serious. "Is it all going too fast for you?"

"I didn't say that." She hated the edge of defensiveness in her tone.

"Hey. I mean it. We can have a long engagement if you want it that way. It's okay with me."

"But I don't *want* a long engagement." It came out as a whine. Dear God, what was the matter with her? Her emotions were bouncing all over the place. She made it worse by grumbling, "And I meant it about a small, simple wedding, too. I really did."

"Easy." He bent close, nipped a kiss against her throat.

"Sorry," she murmured, honestly contrite, not really understanding herself at that moment.

He nuzzled her cheek. "We got no problem here."

Oh, yes, we do. I'm the problem. My mother's a hopeless bitch and I married a psychopath-in-training.

Why would a great guy like Quinn, with everything going for him now, with a good life he'd worked so hard to earn, want to marry someone with her history and track record, anyway?

People always used to treat her like some kind of prize. She was no prize. Not anymore, anyway. In her case, the bloom was seriously off the rose. Perfect Chloe Winchester? What a joke.

And wait a minute.

Really, she needed to snap out of it.

Where had all these grim thoughts come from?

It was dangerous to start running herself down. Half the battle for sanity and a good life was in keeping her spirits up, fostering a positive attitude.

She'd worked hard to face the tough challenges life had thrown in her path. She'd survived the disaster of her own choice, her own making: her marriage to Ted. She'd fought and fought hard to get free, to make a new life. To hold her head up and move on.

And she'd honestly begun to believe that she'd done it, that she'd put the past behind her.

Until Ted sent her flowers and made her fear deep in her soul that she hadn't seen the last of him, after all. Until her mother showed up on her doorstep spouting such ugliness and rage, revealing such an unforgiveable betrayal, that she'd had no choice but to sever ties with her.

Maybe it wasn't the wedding she was putting off. Maybe she'd had no right to tell Quinn that she'd marry him in the first place.

Maybe she needed to face the fact that he deserved better than her.

"Chloe?"

"Um?"

"We got no problem at all," he said again, more softly, but more firmly, too.

She met his eyes. They were so steady. So knowing and wise. She asked in a tiny, weak, disgusting little voice, "We don't?"

"Uh-uh. We got each other, Chloe. We got it all."

And somehow, when he looked at her like that, when he spoke with such affection and total confidence, she believed him.

She absolutely believed him.

I love you, Quinn. She thought the words and knew that they were true.

If only she felt she had the right to say them out loud.

Chapter Nine

Clara called Saturday afternoon. The engagement party was on for two weeks from that day. Nell called an hour later to go over the guest list.

Monday, the demo began at Quinn's house.

Chloe let Tai run things at the showroom. She put on old jeans and one of Quinn's Prime Sports and Fitness T-shirts and helped Nell and her crew of burly guys bust out some walls. The one between the kitchen and dining area had to go down. And the one between a bonus room and Manny's room needed knocking out, to give him a larger private area. Same thing with the master suite. They were combining it with the smaller bedroom next door. With all the extra space, they would enlarge the master bath and walk-in closet, too.

The men went upstairs. Nell and Chloe took the kitchen. Chloe got right to work attacking that wall. After just one blow, Nell teased her that she was dangerous with a sledgehammer.

Chloe raised the hammer again and sent it crashing through the Sheetrock, making a nice, big raggedy hole that showed light on the other side. "There's something about a demo that makes the whole world seem brighter."

"Whack it down, baby!" Nell made her own big hole.

Upstairs, they heard other hammers demolishing other walls.

"Music to my ears," said Chloe, and gave that wall another serious blow. It was very therapeutic, she decided, to get to beat a wall down.

Since Friday, when she'd realized she wasn't ready to set a wedding date and didn't feel worthy to tell Quinn she loved him, she'd been feeling a little down.

But wielding the hammer helped, made her feel useful and powerful, as though she was getting stuff done. Just what the doctor ordered, without a doubt.

That evening she attended her first Self-Defense for Women class. She got some great tips on how to spot predators and avoid situations where she might be attacked. She almost raised her hand and asked what you did when someone you trusted hauled off and hit you.

But really, she didn't need to ask.

She already knew the answer: you left and you never went back. You started again and rebuilt your life.

And she *was* rebuilding, she reminded herself. Rebuilding in her hometown with a great guy and his sweet little girl. With more family than she'd ever had before, including cool, smart old Manny and a bunch of new sisters, Nell best of all.

A week later, she presented her fairy princess ideas to Annabelle, whose eyes lit up so bright you would have thought Chloe had offered her the moon. "Chloe! I need to hug you." And she reached out and threw her arms around Chloe's legs.

Laughing, Chloe grabbed her up. Annabelle wrapped her legs around Chloe's waist and Chloe spun in a circle, both of them giggling.

When Chloe finally let her go, Annabelle chose the design in lilac, hot pink and purple. The next day, Chloe visited her favorite fabric store and came out with plenty of satin, velvet, bridal tulle, organza, organdy and purple brocade. After the fabric store, she stopped in at the craft store, where she bought special paint and twelve-gauge wire to frame the wings. After lunch, in the studio behind her showroom, she started to work on the costume, taking a break before Tai went home to drive over to Quinn's house down the hill from hers, where the electrician was busy rerouting some of the wiring and Nell's crew was almost finished ripping out the old floors.

She went home that evening feeling good about the remodeling, about Annabelle's fairy princess dress, about pretty much everything. With so much to do and her soon-to-be new family around her, the dark mood brought on by Ted's unwanted flowers and her mother's betrayal had faded. Life seemed bright and full of promise once again.

That Saturday was the engagement party at McKellan's. Quinn hired a babysitter for Annabelle so that Manny could come with them to celebrate. Manny brought his girlfriend, Doris Remy, who was in her midseventies, a widow with fifteen grandchildren and five great-grandsons. Doris had an infectious laugh and loved to dance. She'd once been a Rockette at Radio City Music Hall and she remained slim and spry. McKellan's upstairs party room had a small dance floor, and the Bravos had hired a DJ. Manny and Doris spent most of the evening out on that little square of floor.

Quinn and Chloe danced, too. Chloe also danced with his brothers and with charming Ryan McKellan, who told her she looked happier than he'd ever seen her before. Ryan, like Clara and Quinn, had been in the same grade as Chloe back in school.

Ryan, whom they all called Rye, said, "You always seemed so serious and distant back then."

And she agreed. "Because I was. I had places to go and things to do. Enjoying myself was never on the agenda."

"All that's changed now, though, huh?" Rye asked.

They danced past Quinn, who stood at the upstairs bar with his brother Carter and Clara's fiancé, Dalton Ames. Quinn glanced over as they passed, almost as though he could feel her eyes on him. They shared a smile and a nod and a lovely, sparkly feeling shimmered through her.

And Rye said, "No need to answer. You look at Quinn and your face says it all."

Because I love him, she thought. But she didn't say it. That wouldn't be right, to tell Rye McKellan that she loved Quinn when she'd yet to tell the man himself.

At a little after midnight, with the party in full swing, Quinn's mother, Willow Mooney Bravo, arrived. Chloe, Quinn, Nell and some guy named Ned were sitting at a table not far from the stairs when Willow appeared, looking more beautiful than ever in a white silk blouse with a prim little collar and a black satin skirt, her short blond hair softly curling around her luminous face.

She came straight for their table.

Nell rose. "Mom." Nell and her mother exchanged air kisses. "Big surprise. I thought you were in Miami."

Since her husband's death, Willow traveled a lot. "And miss the party? Never."

Quinn got up and hugged her. She smiled at him so fondly, laying her hand against his cheek, staring up into his eyes. "Congratulations, honey."

"Thanks, Mom."

Chloe rose.

Before she could say a word, Quinn's mom said, "Chloe. So good to see you. You must call me Willow." She took Chloe's hand and laced their fingers together, as though the two of them were BFFs. "Tell you what. Let's steal a few minutes alone and catch up a little."

Catch up? How could she catch up with someone she hardly knew? In her lifetime prior to that moment, she'd exchanged maybe three or four words total with Quinn's mom.

"Mom," Quinn said cautiously. "Are you up to something?"

Willow let out a bright trill of laughter. "What in the world could I be up to?"

Nell made a snorting sound. "Anything's possible. Be nice."

"Of course. I'm *always* nice."

Even Chloe was reasonably certain that was a lie, but she wanted to get off to a good start with Willow. "I'd love to, er, catch up."

"Great." Willow gestured at a hallway across the room. "There's a balcony in back. Let's try that."

Willow led her through the crowd, pausing only for the occasional wave of greeting in the direction of someone she knew.

Accessed through double glass doors, the balcony spanned the back of McKellan's. It had a view of the pub's full parking lot below and the dark humps of the Front Range in the distance.

Willow pulled Chloe to an empty corner. Only then did she release Chloe's hand. She didn't waste time getting right to the point. "So, how are things with your mother?"

Chloe went for honesty. It seemed the only course. "My mother and I aren't speaking. That may be permanent."

Willow gave an elegant shrug. She'd been born in a double-wide southeast of town, but somehow everything she did was elegant. "I can't say I'm sorry. Your mother doesn't speak to me, either, never has. And I like it that way." Chloe had no idea what to say to that, so she said nothing. Willow asked, "Are you saying you and your mother aren't speaking because you're with Quinn?"

"That's part of it, yes. But there are other problems, bigger issues." Chloe shook her head. "And really, that's all I'm going to say about my mother."

Willow rested her slim hands on the railing and stared off toward the mountains. "Quinn has...a tender soul."

"Yes. It's one of the many things I love about him— and Nell's already warned me not to hurt him, so you don't have to go there."

"I didn't think he would ever get married." Willow glanced at Chloe then. "And never to someone like you."

Chloe felt annoyance rising and pointedly did not ask, *What do you mean, someone like me?* Instead, she offered pleasantly, "I think we'll be happy together. We're already happy."

Willow looked toward the mountains again and remarked in a weary tone, "You are a cool one."

"I..." Really, what was she supposed to say to this woman? "What, exactly, do you want from me, Willow?"

Quinn's mother continued her extended study of the distant peaks. "You know, I'm not sure. Except that you never struck me as a person who knew her own mind."

Ouch. That hit a little too close to home. How bad was this conversation going to get? As Chloe asked herself that question, Willow made it worse. "And you were born and raised to marry up, now, weren't you? I just wonder, is Quinn 'up' enough for you? Do you think you're better than he is?"

"Absolutely not." Chloe's voice was hard and final, just as she'd intended it to be.

"You say that as though you mean it."

"I do mean it."

"Wonderful. Then all I need to be sure of is that you can stand up to Linda. You need to be honest with yourself about that. Because if you can't, there will be trouble ahead. Quinn's had enough trouble, enough struggle in his life."

Before Chloe could decide how best to respond to that, Quinn spoke from behind her. "She's doing fine bracing Linda, Mom—not that it's any of your business in the first place."

Quinn to the rescue. Chloe could have hugged him. She turned and slipped her arm through his, finding great comfort in the hard strength of his forearm under her hand, in the solid warmth of him so close to her side.

He slanted her a look both rueful and tender. "How you doing?"

"Just fine. Now."

Willow sighed. "Quinn, you need to stop sneaking up on people."

"I'm in plain sight. You're the one who was looking the other way."

"And it *is* my business," Willow insisted. "You're marrying Linda Winchester's daughter, and Linda and I do not get along. I'm sorry about that, but it's a fact. Chloe needs to be aware of the problem."

"I'm aware," Chloe said. "Painfully so. And I've made it crystal clear to my mother that I run my own life and make my own decisions."

Quinn asked Willow, "Happy now?"

"I only want *you* to be happy."

He put his big hand over Chloe's, a touch of reassurance and support. Really, how did she get so lucky to finally find a man like him? "And I am happy, Mom. Very happy—now, come on. Let's go back inside. It's our party and we want to enjoy it." He offered his mother his other arm.

Willow took it and went in with them. Quinn got her a glass of white wine and she made the rounds, hugging her children, saying hello to various acquaintances. Within half an hour, she was leaving.

"Back to Miami, no doubt," said Nell as Willow slipped away down the stairs. "Or maybe Paris. Or New York. Since Dad died, she never stays here at home for long. I think she's lonely in that big house all by herself."

"She does seem lonely," Chloe agreed. Some of the things Willow had said to her still stung. But the woman *was* alone, and not in a good way. "She seems sad, too."

"Dad was her life. For decades, she battled Sondra to get him for her own. She was always kicking him out in big, dramatic scenes, telling him not to come back until he planned to stay. He would go home to Sondra. But he'd always come around again. And Mom would always take him back, even though he was still wearing his wedding band. Finally, when Sondra died, Mom got what she wanted most of all. For a while, Dad was hers and hers alone. And then he died, too. Now that he's gone, she hardly knows what to do with herself."

"She should sell that house," said Quinn. "It's too big and it's full of stuff that belonged to Sondra."

Nell made a scoffing sound. "Which is why she'll never sell it. In the end, she won out over Sondra. She got Sondra's house and a whole bunch of Sondra's treasures—including her husband." Nell hooked an arm around Chloe and dipped her bright head to rest on Chloe's shoulder. It was a sisterly gesture that warmed Chloe's heart. Nell whispered, "I hope she didn't give you too much crap."

Chloe whispered back, "Look who's talking about giving me crap."

Nell laughed and let her go.

Quinn grumbled, "What are you two whispering about?"

Chloe leaned the other way and kissed him. "Nothing that concerns you."

The following Saturday was Clara and Dalton's wedding.

Quinn sat in the second-row pew with Chloe on one side and Annabelle on the other as Clara and Dalton exchanged their vows. Whenever Quinn glanced at Chloe, she gave him one of those glowing smiles of hers. Annabelle, in a little pink dress with a wide satin bow at the waist and a bell-like skirt, sat up straight with her plump hands folded in her lap, a perfect little lady. Chloe had taken her to Boulder to choose the dress and then made her the cute beaded headband with the big pink silk flower for her hair.

Life was good, Quinn thought. He and Chloe were together every chance they got. Every night last week, they'd shared dinner, the four of them, like the family they were becoming. Chloe did a lot of the cooking, which made everyone happy. Manny had a boatload of great qualities, including a love of cooking. Too bad his cooking sucked.

Yeah. Life was good. Didn't get any better. Though he did feel a twinge of envy as Dalton Ames, his eyes only for Clara, announced proudly, *I do.*

Quinn wanted that, what Dalton and Clara had. He'd never thought it would happen for him. And now that it *had* happened, now that he had Chloe, he wanted it settled, wanted to seal the deal.

Okay, yeah. It had happened pretty fast with them. Some would say too fast.

But he didn't see it that way. They'd known each other since kindergarten. And besides, the way he looked at it, a thing either worked or it didn't. And what he and Chloe had together worked just fine. He wanted her at his side at the end of the workday—and in his bed every night.

She'd said yes. The decision was made. Why not take that walk down the aisle?

Chloe needed time, though. And he knew he had to give her that, had to keep a rein on his growing impatience to set the date and make her his bride, to blend their lives together in the fullest way, be husband and wife for the whole world to see.

Three and a half weeks had passed since the night she kicked her mother out of her house, the night she'd said she wanted to wait to set the date until after their engagement party—but then turned right around and insisted that she still wanted to get married soon.

Well, the engagement party had been and gone. She hadn't said word one since then about when they could stand up in front of a judge.

If she didn't bring it up soon, he would do it. And he had a strange intuition that it wouldn't go well.

Beside him, Chloe shifted slightly. Her fingers brushed

the back of his hand. Heat and longing shivered across his skin. He caught her hand and laced their fingers together, turning his gaze to her.

God, she was beautiful. She stared straight ahead at the altar, where Dalton Ames had just been told he could kiss his bride. A soft smile curved her mouth, a smile Quinn knew was just for him.

When she smiled like that, his worries vanished. What they had was so damn good. And it would only get better. He just had to choose the right moment to remind her that if she wanted the wedding to be soon, they needed to set the damn date.

The next day, Sunday, Chloe gave Annabelle her fairy princess costume, complete with featherweight, glittery lavender wings. Annabelle clapped her hands and jumped up and down with glee. Then she put on the costume and danced around the house, waving the matching wand in the air, tapping the chairs and tables, the sofa and the lampshades. Manny asked her, what, exactly, she was doing.

"Magic," she said, and whirled on to the kitchen.

"I think she's sprinkling fairy dust," Chloe explained. "You know, like Tinker Bell in *Peter Pan*?"

Manny, who was on his way out the door to spend the afternoon in Boulder with Doris, caught the fairy princess as she was dancing by and scooped her up into his arms. "Give me a hug and I'm outta here."

Annabelle tapped him lightly on the head with her wand. "There, Manny. Magic for you. Here's some for Granny Doris, too." She tapped him again. And then she wrapped her arms around his neck and squeezed good and tight.

"How 'bout some sugar?" He pointed at his grizzled cheek.

She planted a big smacker on him. "Now put me down. I'm very busy."

He let her go and she danced off up the stairs, spreading fairy dust as she went.

After Manny left, Chloe packed a picnic for the three of them. Annabelle begged to wear her fairy costume and neither Quinn nor Chloe could see why she shouldn't. Her rubber rain boots had purple flowers on them, and Annabelle decided they were perfect for a fairy princess, so she wore them with the dress. Chloe helped her remove the wings for the ride in the car.

They drove out to the national forest and parked a mile or so from a spot Chloe knew that had picnic tables. Annabelle put her wings back on—and off they went. As they strolled beneath the tall trees, Quinn and Chloe held hands, and Annabelle danced along beside them in her rubber boots and fairy princess dress, waving her magic wand, spreading fairy dust far and wide.

It was a great day. By eight that evening, when Chloe had kissed Annabelle good-night and gone back across the street to her house, Quinn was thinking that this was the night to bring up the wedding date. Manny should be home by ten to look after Annabelle. And Chloe would be expecting Quinn at her place. He would bring up the wedding first thing, before he took off all her clothes and buried himself in her softness.

So yeah, he was maybe a little preoccupied when he tucked Annabelle into bed. She chattered away about her fairy princess dress and how she planned to wear it in her princess bedroom as soon as Chloe finished "dec'rating" down the hill at the other house.

"I will be a fairy princess in my princess room, Daddy."

He smiled and nodded, tucking the covers in around

her and her teddy bear, thinking how she was bound to get princess overload soon and also half rehearsing how best to coax Chloe into settling on a wedding date.

"Daddy?"

"What, Annie-mo-manny?"

"Daddy." She caught his face between her little hands. "I'm not Manny. Look at me. Stop being silly."

He opened his mouth to tease her some more—and something in those big brown eyes stopped him. "Okay."

"I need to ask you…"

"Yeah? What?"

"Well, Daddy. Do you think my mommy would like my fairy princess dress?" She gazed up at him, so sweet and hopeful, her shining brown hair spread across her butterfly-printed pillow.

"I, uh…" His voice had a cracked sound to it and the spit seemed to have dried right up in his mouth. He swallowed hard to get the damn saliva going again and managed, "I think your mommy would love it."

"Can she come to see me, please? I need to show her my fairy princess dress and my wings and my magic wand."

His mind went dead blank, the way it used to do way back in elementary school when he would open a schoolbook and stare down at the incomprehensible chains of letters jittering across the page.

Yeah. Just like being a kid again, his brain refusing to function, his heart like a damn wrecking ball, swinging hard, battering the cage of his chest.

He wanted to leap up and run downstairs and across the street, to drag Chloe back over here, have her handle this. Please God, he really didn't want to blow it.

Annabelle continued to gaze up at him, trusting, serious—and waiting for his answer.

Suddenly he could almost hear Chloe's voice in his mind. *Answer her question as simply as possible.* "No, baby. Your mommy can't come."

"Why?"

His throat locked up tight. But he didn't give up. He squeezed the words right through the tightness. "Because when you were born, she gave you to me. She trusted me to love you and take care of you."

"And then she went away?"

"Yeah. Then she went away."

"Why?"

He realized he hated that question. "She…had a lot of things to do."

"What things?"

"Baby, I don't really know. I only know that she gave you to me to take care of and I am so glad that she did."

"She won't come back, ever?"

"No, I don't think she will. And that's why you have Manny and me, because we love you so much."

"And you like to take care of me?"

"Oh, yeah. We love to take care of you."

Annabelle fingered her old blanket. She had her scruffy teddy bear in a headlock. "Does Chloe like to take care of me?"

He tried a smile, though it probably looked more like a grimace, he was so freaked that he might be royally screwing this up. "Yes, she does."

"Well, then, Daddy. I think it's very good that we have Chloe now."

It damn well was good. And having his first real talk with his daughter about her missing mother had slammed it forcefully home to him: he wasn't the only one who would suffer if this thing with Chloe went south.

Not that it would. They were solid, him and Chloe…

"Daddy?"

"Yeah, baby."

"I love you, Daddy."

His heart seemed to blow up like a hot air balloon, filling his chest, rising into his throat so he had to gulp hard before he could answer her. "And I love you. So much."

She gave him her most beautiful, glowing smile— and hit him up. "So…can I have a puppy, then? Please?"

For once, he felt only relief that she was working him. Because if she was working him, that meant she was okay. It meant that the talk about her mother had gone pretty well. He leaned closer, until their noses touched. And then he whispered, "Nice try."

Damned if she didn't bat her eyelashes at him. "Puhleeeaasse, Daddy?"

He was seriously tempted to just tell her no. But he and Manny were still considering the puppy issue. If he told her no and changed his mind later, she'd only become more adorably impossible, more certain that the word *no* only meant *Keep pushing and the grown-ups will give in.*

She kept after him. "Please, Daddy. A puppy would be so good. Or maybe a little bitty kitten."

He finally spoke up. "Do you want me to say no?"

"Daddy." The big eyes reproached him now. "You know what I want. I want you to say yes, and then I can have a puppy."

"Well, I'm not going to say yes. I'm going to say goodnight. Or no. You get to choose."

"But—"

He put his finger to her lips. "Choose."

"Daddy," she scolded, as though *he* was trying to put one over on *her.* And then she blew out a big sigh that smelled of Bubble Mint toothpaste. "You can say good-night."

He kissed her forehead and gave the covers one more good tuck nice and tight around her and the old bear. "Good night, baby."

She murmured, "Night, Daddy," as he stepped into the hall and shut the door.

At her house, Chloe got to work updating Your Way's website and adding and scheduling posts to the Your Way Facebook page.

It was about time. She'd been seriously neglecting Your Way's online presence. Given a choice between posting decorating tips and picnicking with Quinn and fairy princess Annabelle... Well, what kind of choice was that?

Quinn and Annabelle won, hands down.

Once she had the website spruced up a bit with new content, as well as seven new posts written and scheduled to pop up on the Facebook page daily for the next week, she got to work plowing through email for both email accounts, the one for the website and the one she used for Facebook.

She did the website mail first. There were twenty emails left after purging junk and spam. She tackled them by date, oldest first. The fifth one down was no address she recognized, flwrs4yoo@gotmail.com. The subject line read Question for you.

Should that have alerted her?

It didn't. She assumed it was just someone wanting decorating advice or information about her services.

She so didn't pick up the meaning. She had no clue, just blithely pointed the mouse at the thing and started reading.

Did you like the flowers? I've been waiting to hear from you. We had so much, we had it all. I know you remember. Nothing's right anymore. I can't stop thinking about you.
Ted

Chapter Ten

For a moment, Chloe just stared at the monitor, unblinking and unbelieving. Then she shoved back her chair, ran to the downstairs bath and stood there before the mirror, staring at her too-pale stricken face, not quite sure if she might be about to throw up or not.

Finally, when she felt reasonably certain her dinner wasn't coming up, she went upstairs, poured herself a tall glass of water and drank it down. After that, still shaking, feeling hollow and powerless, vibrating with anger, she went back down to her office and tried to decide what to do next.

Twenty minutes later, she'd trashed and retrieved that damn email five times. She'd composed several replies, all along the lines of *I want nothing to do with you. Do not contact me again.*

In the end, she didn't reply. Any response would only encourage him. How many times had she told him to leave her alone? Too many. It did zero good. She considered blocking the address, but decided against that. If he sent more, she wanted to know about it, wanted to know if he was escalating.

She saved the email itself to a folder that she named TD. Then she wrote a brief description of the flowers and the note he'd sent all those weeks ago. She wrote that she'd thrown the flowers, vase and note in the trash and she marked the date that the incident had occurred. She added that information to the folder, as well.

Okay, it wasn't much. Not enough to get the police interested. But if he kept it up, so would she. From now on, she would have a record of every move he made.

By then, at least, she wasn't shaking. Tomorrow night was the third meeting of her self-defense class. She was on this case, taking responsibility to deal with whatever went down. If she had to confront Ted again, she would be better prepared than she'd been in the past.

She scanned the rest of the website emails and then the messages to Your Way's Facebook page and her own personal timeline page. As far as she could tell, he hadn't tried to contact her again. She decided to consider that reassuring.

She thought about Quinn, pictured his beloved face, the heat of him, the strength and goodness. Instantly, the tears were pressing at the back of her throat. She wanted to feel his arms around her, wanted to tell him everything, about the email, about her decision to keep a record of any and every move her ex made on her.

But then she remembered that look in his eyes the night she'd told him about the flowers. She'd barely been able to get his word then that he would stay out of it.

If she told him about the email, would she manage to get his agreement to stay out of it now?

She knew the answer. Because she knew him.

Really, it was only an email. Only one tiny step along a possible road to another ugly confrontation with the awful man she'd had the bad judgment to marry.

Eventually, if Ted kept it up, she would have to tell Quinn, have to somehow convince him again that this was *her* problem to solve in her own way. When that happened, Quinn would not be happy with her that she'd kept the truth from him now.

But Ted hadn't tried again in the past two weeks. She didn't *have* to tell Quinn now. And she wouldn't. It wasn't his problem and she could deal with this herself.

Downstairs after tucking Annabelle in, Quinn had stretched out on the couch and started *The Great Gatsby* on audio book, expecting his daughter to reappear any minute for their nightly exercise in monster removal. She never came. Bouncing around all day in rubber boots and fairy wings must have worn her out.

When Manny got home, Quinn took five minutes to run down his bedtime conversation with Annabelle, just to keep the old man in the loop on the mommy questions and the ongoing puppy issue. Then he said good-night and headed across the street to Chloe's.

They'd traded keys weeks ago, so he let himself in and dealt with the alarm. She'd left a lamp on by the sofa, as she always did. He could hear the low drone of a television, and light glowed from the short hallway that led to the master suite. Then the TV went silent. She must have heard him come in.

A second later, wearing the same big pink shirt she'd worn the first night he came to her, she appeared in the door to the short hall that led to the bedroom. "Hey." Her sweet mouth trembled slightly. And there was something in her eyes, something that looked a lot like fear.

"What's wrong?"

"Nothing," she said too fast. "I just…heard the door, you know? Came to check…"

"Check what?"

She shivered, though the house wasn't cold. "Nothing. Really." She tipped her head toward the bedroom. "Come on." And then she turned and disappeared back the way she'd come.

Something here was very far from right.

He followed her to the bedroom and found her already in the bed, propped against the pillows. She patted the space beside her.

But he hesitated in the doorway as he tried to figure out what the hell was going on with her. "What's happened?"

"Nothing." Breathless. And lying.

He left the doorway. Her eyes were anxious as she watched him come to her.

Instead of going around to what had pretty much become his side of the bed, he went straight for her. She scooted aside a little to make room. He sat on the edge of the mattress.

She stared at him. He watched her satiny throat move as she swallowed. "What?" she asked finally. "Honestly there's…" She faltered and then seemed not to have the heart to go on.

"See?" he said gently. "You don't want to lie to me, not really." He reached out and speared his fingers in her long, shining hair. He wrapped a thick golden hank of the stuff around his hand and pulled her face right up to his. "I know you, angel," he whispered against her satiny lips. "Know you better every day, every hour, every minute we're together. You're getting inside me, like I'm in you. It's getting so that it only takes me one look in your beautiful face, and I know if things aren't right with you. So I'll say it again. Something is wrong and I want you to tell me what it is."

Her glance shifted away. "Would you let go of me, please?"

He did what she asked instantly, unwinding her sweet-smelling hair from around his fist, sliding his fingers free. "Done." He stood.

She gazed up at him, her eyes like a stormy sea. "You're angry."

He shook his head. And then he turned for the door, more afraid with every step that she was going to let him go.

But she was better than that. "Please, Quinn. Don't go."

He stopped in the doorway and faced her again. "*Is* something wrong?"

She had her arms wrapped around herself, her shoulders curved in protectively. For a moment, she mangled her lower lip between her pretty white teeth. And then, at last, she confessed, "Yes." Once the single word escaped her, she yanked her shoulders back and glared at him. "And if I tell you, you have to respect my wishes. You can't go taking matters into your own hands. I need your word on that, Quinn."

Not her mother, then. The douche canoe ex. Had to be. "Just tell me."

Her delicate jaw was set. "Not until you promise."

He could see it so clearly and it would be beautiful. Just him, the ex and maybe a fat length of steel pipe, up close and personal—and hold on a minute. No. Scratch the pipe. Much more satisfying to deliver the message with his bare fists.

"I mean it, Quinn. You have to promise me."

He studied her unforgettable face for several really

long seconds. No doubt about it. She meant what she said. Plus, a man had to respect the wishes of his woman. He made himself release the pleasant fantasy of teaching Ted Davies a lesson in pain he would never forget. "All right. You have my word. Anything I do, you'll agree to it first."

She watched him narrow-eyed. "Is that a trick answer?"

"Come on. You know me. If I give my word, you can count on it."

Her slim shoulders sagged again. She shut her eyes, drew in a slow breath and when she looked at him once more, she held out her hand. "Please come back."

He couldn't get to her fast enough. He took the hand she offered and dropped down beside her. "I'm here. I'm listening."

She let out a small, sad little sound low in her throat.

That got to him, made an ache in him, the deep-down kind. He hated it when she was sad. He slid his other hand along her soft cheek and then wrapped it around the nape of her neck, beneath the heavy fall of her hair. He pulled her close.

She settled against him, feeling like heaven in his arms, smelling of French soap and fancy flowers he didn't even know the names of. He caught her face between his hands and tipped it up to brush a kiss across those lips he never tired of tasting. "It's okay," he promised, stroking a hand down her hair. "It's going to be okay..." Because he would damn well make it so. He kissed her again.

She clung to him for a minute and then pulled back and settled against the pillows. "I was checking the emails for the Your Way website," she began. And she went on to tell him about the message Davies had sent her and the file she'd started on him. When she was done, she added hopefully, "It was only one email and he sent it two weeks ago. I hadn't gotten around to checking the website in a while. Nothing since then. I really don't think it's that big a deal."

He disagreed, though he didn't say so. It *was* a big deal. The dirtbag refused to leave her alone—after all this time, after she'd pulled up stakes and moved home to get away from him. He said, "You need to write back to him."

She was shaking her head before he could finish the sentence. "That never works. You have no idea how many times I've told him I want nothing to do with him ever again."

"But you're keeping a record now, remember? It's been more than a year since you left San Diego. Unless you have a restraining order on him or some formal proof somewhere that he's harassed you in the past…?"

"No," she admitted unhappily. "God. I was such a big coward."

He took her by the shoulders. "Look at me."

"Oh, Quinn…"

"Listen. This is not your fault. You are not to blame here. This guy is a major scumball and *he's* the one who's causing the trouble. Guys like that, they love to make you think it's all somehow your fault. Don't you fall for that garbage. Don't you let him do that to you."

She pressed her lips together and nodded. "You're right. I know you're right."

"Good." He gave her shoulders a last squeeze and let her go. "So you write a two-sentence email. 'Never contact me again. I am blocking this email address.' And you send it to him. You forward his email and your reply to me and then you block him."

She stiffened against the pillows. "Wait a minute. Why am I forwarding it on to you?"

"I'm going to write to Ted and introduce myself."

"Oh, no. No, now, that is a bad idea…"

"Don't give me that look. There's nothing to get freaked out about. There'll be no dirty words and I won't be making any threats. Just a simple, straight-up little note. I'm going to tell him that I'm your fiancé and I know you've blocked him and told him you don't want to hear from him again. Ever. I'll say that I expect him to respect your wishes and if he has questions, he should write back to me, that I'll be happy to deal with anything he has to say." Her eyes were mutinous. He could see her quick brain working, ticking off objections. He went on. "You can read it before I send it—in fact, emails aren't really my strong suit. Takes me forever to write one. So I'll bring my tablet over tomorrow night. I'll dictate the email to you and you can type it in for me, so you'll know exactly what I'm sending. Then that can go in your file, too."

"But…what if he writes back to you?"

"Oh, angel. I hope he does."

"Quinn. I don't like this. The whole point is that I don't want you involved."

"How can I not be involved? We're getting married, remember?" *If I can ever get you to set the damn date.*

"It's not that. It's not about us. It's my old…*stuff*, you know? My big, ugly mess. I should be the one dealing with it."

He reached for her then and pulled her close. She resisted at first, but then she sagged against him with a long sigh. He wrapped his arms good and tight around her and reminded her, "You *are* dealing with it. You can't get away from it. Look at you. It's tearing you up inside. I'm only backup, that's all. I only want this jerk to know that you're not alone, that you got family and we got your back."

She cuddled in closer. "When you say it that way, I almost feel justified in dragging you into this."

He pressed his lips into her hair. "You're not dragging me. I'm a gung-ho volunteer."

She gave a weary little laugh and then grew serious again as she tipped her head back to meet his eyes. "Any communication you get from him, I have to read, Quinn. You don't get to protect me from anything he says. And I want to read it right away. No putting off sharing it with me while you decide on your own what to do next. You bring it to me. We decide together."

A few bad words scrolled through his head. He'd hoped to have a little more leeway. But at least she'd agreed to the basic plan. "All right. He writes back, I bring it to you, we decide together what to do next."

She lifted herself up and kissed him. "Agreed." She breathed the words against his mouth. Her soft breasts pressed into his chest.

He wanted to kiss her some more, to take off that pink shirt, to see if she had anything else on under it and get rid of that, too. But they weren't finished with the subject of Ted. "There's more."

She moaned. "Oh, God. What else?"

"Do you remember what florist those flowers came from?"

"Bloom. Why?"

He'd figured as much. There were only two florists in town. His sister Jody owned Bloom. Jody had a real flair. Tilly's Flowers, at the other end of Central from Bloom, was kind of boring by comparison. "You call Jody tomorrow and you get her to look up the order for the flowers he sent you. Then you ask her not to accept any more orders from Ted."

"What if the order came from some big online company and Jody only filled it?"

He bent close, nibbled on her ear and whispered, "Jody will know how to refuse any more orders from him, believe me."

"So, then, if he does it again, he'll just use Tilly's."

"And then you'll block him from Tilly's. After that, he'd have to get them delivered from Boulder. All I'm saying is, why make it easy for him? Not to mention, Jody can send you a copy of the original order and of the note that came with the flowers, meaning you'll have proof that he sent them."

"Hmm. Well, proof would be good…"

He studied her worried face. "You're still not on board with this. Why?"

She reached up and pressed her soft hand to his cheek. "I'm ashamed to admit it…"

"You got nothing—*nothing*—to be ashamed of."

"Yes, I do. In the end, I'm my mother's daughter through and through. I don't want to call Jody because I'm worried about what your sister's going to think of me." He probably shouldn't have grinned at that, but he did. And she shoved at his shoulder. "Don't you laugh at me."

"I'm not laughing, and you're worried about nothing. I can tell you what my sister's gonna think."

"Oh, really?" She kind of looked a little like her mother right then, one eyebrow raised, all superior and cool—not that he was fool enough to tell her that. "Now you read minds?"

He shrugged. "Jody will think that you're engaged to me and you don't want flowers from other guys."

She blinked. "Oh. Well. That's a good point. She probably will think that. *I* would think that."

"Damn straight." He bent close and nuzzled her throat. God, she always smelled so good.

She wrapped her hand around the back of his head, threading her soft fingers into his hair. "Come to bed now," she whispered.

He kissed her once, hard and fast. "We're not done here."

She groaned. "I can tell by the look in your eyes. I'm not going to like whatever it is you're going to say next."

"Probably not. You need to call your mother. We need to have a talk with her."

"Quinn! How can you say that? I'm not speaking to my mother."

"Yeah, you are. At least long enough to get what we can out of her. You said she's been in touch with Davies."

"Which is why I don't want to talk to her. She betrayed me."

"Chloe. Think about it. We need to know exactly what she's told him—and what *he's* said to *her*."

"That's assuming she'll answer a single question we ask her."

"We need to try."

"No. Really, I don't want anything to do with her. Everything else will be plenty, *more* than plenty."

He ran a finger down the side of her throat. Smooth as satin, every inch of her skin—and he needed to keep on task here. He explained, "So far, Ted's the aggressor. Always has been. So far, the way it's always been, *he* chases *you*. You see that, right? You see that has to change."

"But I don't want to chase him or *aggress* on him. I just want to be finished with him, to have him completely out of my life."

"Yeah, well, Chloe, sometimes the only way to get rid of a problem is to make yourself ready to stand up against it. So if the time ever comes when you have to go toe-to-toe, you're in the light."

"What does that mean, the light?"

"It means that whatever you can learn about your opponent, you learn. You don't hide from the facts. You don't lie to yourself. You don't go brushing things under carpets and worrying about what other people are gonna think. You admit your own weaknesses and work to get stronger. You never deny his strengths or refuse to admit how far he might go. You bring everything out in the open. Into the light."

She dipped her head close and rested against his shoulder. In a small voice, she asked, "My mother? Really?"

He tipped up her chin to him. "You can call her in the morning."

"Ugh."

"You watch. It's going to be fine."

"Keep telling me that."

He gathered the fabric of her big shirt in his two fists. "Right now I got other things on my mind. Lift up your arms."

Grateful that they were finally through discussing what to do about Ted, Chloe lifted her arms. Quinn took her pink shirt up and away.

"Come here." She tried to reach for him again.

"Wait." He got up, but only to pull back the covers. "What's this?" His eyes had that gleam in them. And the look on his face sent heat surging through her.

"Tap pants."

"Pretty." He bent close and ran a slow finger along the lace band that crossed her stomach just below her navel. Goose bumps chased themselves across her skin, and longing pounded in her veins with every hungry beat of her heart. He eased the tap pants down and tossed them over his shoulder.

By the time he rose to his height and yanked his T-shirt over his head, she'd all but forgotten about her mother, about Ted, about the unpleasant things she needed to do in the morning to bring the situation "into the light," as he called it.

For now, for the rest of the night, there was only Quinn. Only this beauty they had between them, only the feel of his hands on her yearning flesh, the deep rumble of his voice filling her head. Only her need to be with him, held by him, filled so full of him that there was only her love for him and the hope and joy he brought her, day by day.

Naked, he came down to her. She wrapped her arms around him, breathing in the clean, male scent of him, loving the feel of him under her hands. He rolled them until he was on his side of the bed, on his back, with her on top. With a gasp and a short burst of laughter at the suddenness of the move, she gazed down at him. Such a beautiful man, inside and out.

"What?" he asked, gathering her hair and lifting it, wrapping it around his arm the way he loved to do. "You don't want to be on top?"

Any way he wanted it was fine with her. "I'll be on top." She bent and pressed her mouth to his. "On top is perfect." Even better because they didn't have to fumble for condoms anymore, not since the talk they'd had a couple of weeks before. She'd been on the pill for months, long before the first time he came up the hill to her. As for safety, well, there'd been no one for her since her divorce. For him, it had been over a year. And since that slipup that became Annabelle, he'd never gone without protection.

More kisses, deep and wet and never-ending. He unwound her hair and smoothed it back over her shoulder. It only fell forward again, curling between them, tangling around them.

He caressed her with long, lovely strokes. She rose up to her knees above him as he touched her, his big hands moving down her body, cupping her breasts, rolling her nipples between his thumbs and forefingers. When he found the heart of her, she cried out. He answered with a low groan of satisfaction as he dipped inside and, oh, she was so wet and so ready.

She couldn't wait any longer. She reached down and wrapped her eager fingers around the thick, hard length of him. The sound that escaped him then was like a groan of pain.

But it wasn't pain. It was pure pleasure. She guided him into her and sank slowly down, taking him deep and then deeper still. He surged up, meeting her, filling her all the way, until she let her head drop back and gave herself up to him.

The only word in her mouth was his name, the only thought in her head was of him, of the two of them, together, with nothing between them but heat and wonder and the slow, thick pulse of their shared pleasure, their mutual desire.

He came first, his big hands at either side of her waist, holding her down, tight to him, hard. She felt him pulsing and that sent her over, too.

In the end, she collapsed on top of him. He wrapped her up close in those muscled, inked arms of his. And he brushed kisses against her cheek. He breathed them into her tangled hair, laid them in a sweet, hot line along the curve of her shoulder.

A little while later, before they went to sleep, he told her about his bedtime conversation with Annabelle.

When he finished, his sea-green eyes full of fatherly doubt, he asked, "You think I did okay?"

"You did beautifully. Just right."

He grunted. "But I'm not out of the woods on the subject of Annabelle's mom yet, am I?"

"Truth?" she asked.

"Yeah."

"The good news is you've told Annabelle what she needs to hear for now. She probably won't bring it up again for months, maybe years."

"But she *will* bring it up again. That's what you're tellin' me, right?"

"Almost certainly, yes."

"Crap."

"Lighten up, Quinn. It's human nature to want to understand where we came from."

"Yeah. Okay. I know you're right."

"I *am* right—about this, anyway. And you really are a good dad."

"Yeah?"

"Absolutely. You love her. She knows it. She's a happy little girl. That's what matters. The rest, you'll work out as you go along." She turned to glance at the bedside clock. After midnight. "Let's get some sleep." She sat up and turned to reach for the switch.

He touched her shoulder. "Chloe…" His voice was hesitant now. Careful.

She dropped her arm and focused on him. "Now what?" She said it teasingly, with a silly eye roll and a breathy laugh.

But he wasn't laughing. Far from it. He stared at her, a burning kind of look, his eyes gone dark as night. "I want to set the date. I want us to be married. And soon, like you said when you told me yes. I want you living in my house. Or we can buy another house that you like better. Anything you want. It doesn't matter where we live. It matters that we belong to each other and that the whole world knows that we do."

[faint mirrored text from facing page, illegible]

Chapter Eleven

"I..." Chloe had nothing.

It was getting to be a habit with her. Quinn brought up setting the date, and instantly her mind was a muddy swirl of all the stuff she hadn't worked through yet, of Ted and her mother, all the leftover threads of her old, screwed-up life that kept popping back up to remind her of her mistakes, her questionable choices, her longtime fear of facing hard truths.

Quinn's gaze burned right through her. And then he echoed her. "'I...'? One little word. That's it? That's all you got?"

It wasn't all. Not by a long shot. There was so much. Starting with *I love you.* She desperately needed to tell him that. But she just didn't feel she had the right yet. She wanted to be good for him, someone who made his life better, not someone who dragged him down. "There's so much going on."

His full mouth became a hard line. He wasn't falling for her excuses. "Lame, Chloe. You're better than this."

"But that's just the thing…"

"What's the thing?"

What if I'm not better? What if I'm not all you think I am, Quinn?

What if she never really got beyond the stupid choices she'd made in the past? What if he married her and ended up wishing he hadn't?

She had all these horrible doubts about herself. But *he* didn't doubt her. He believed in her, so completely. In a way that no one else ever had.

Somehow she needed to prove herself, needed to be certain that she wouldn't end up letting him down. But how to do that? She didn't have a clue.

"Nothin', huh?" His voice betrayed his disappointment, but his expression had softened. "Go ahead. Turn off the light." He said the words so gently, giving in for now, letting her off the hook once again.

She knew she should do better, say something meaningful and true. But what? He was right. Right now she had nothing more to offer him on this subject, and they both knew it.

So she switched off the lamp—and then didn't have the nerve to cuddle back against him. Instead, she rolled onto her side, facing away from him. Wrapping the covers close again, she clung miserably to her edge of the bed.

His wonderful voice came out of the dark, all rough and low and grumbly. "Come here." He reached out and hauled her back against him.

Shamelessly, she snuggled in tight. She felt his warm breath stir her hair. Safe in his strong arms, she closed her eyes.

* * *

When she woke in the morning, Quinn had already left. She turned off her alarm before it could start chiming and lay back on her pillow and pictured him across the street, sharing breakfast with Annabelle and Manny. She wished she were there with them.

And she *could* be there, living in his house with him, never again having to wake up and slide her hand across the sheet to the cool, empty space on his side of the bed. Even if she wasn't ready to say "I do" yet, he would agree to her moving in if she asked him.

But somehow that didn't feel right, either. When she moved in, it really should be forever, for everyone's sake. And she wasn't ready for forever.

Chloe showered and dressed for work. Before she ate breakfast, she called her mother. No way could she eat anything with that call ahead of her.

Her mother answered on the second ring. "Chloe? This *is* a surprise." Linda's tone was etched in acid.

Chloe ignored the sudden knot in her stomach and got right to the point. "Will you come here, to my house, tomorrow night at seven? I have a few things I'd like to clear up with you."

"What things?"

"We'll talk about them when you get here."

"I don't like your tone, Chloe. I don't like any of this. I don't understand what's *happened* to you. Your father told me that you're engaged to Quinn Bravo—not that he *had* to tell me. Everyone in town knows. Everyone is talking." She started firing off angry questions, not even bothering to pause for Chloe to answer. "Have you lost your mind? What's the matter with you? This insanity is not like you. Are you going through some kind of life crisis?" She stopped for a breath at last.

And Chloe spoke up before she could get rolling again. "Seven tomorrow night. Yes or no?"

A long, nerve-racking silence and then, more softly, almost hopefully: "Yes. All right. I'll be there."

"Good. I'll see you then." Chloe hung up.

She had two cups of coffee and some toast and then went to work. Tai came in at ten that day. It was her first day as a full-time Your Way employee. She'd decided to go to a few online classes for at least a semester and then reevaluate whether to return to CU or not. It was a stretch budgetwise for Chloe, but Tai was willing to take minimum wage for a while, and her presence would free Chloe up to spend more time designing and working with clients. As soon as Tai arrived, Chloe let her handle the showroom and went to the small office room in back to call Bloom.

"Chloe!" Jody Bravo seemed happy to hear from her. "Hey. What can I do for you?"

"I..." Great. She was at it again. Doling out one-word sentences consisting of *I*.

"Chloe? You there? Everything all right?"

She started to lie, to chirp out a cheerful *Oh, yes. Everything's fine*.

But then she thought of all the years she'd told people things were fine when they were anything but. She thought of Quinn last night, telling her she needed to be "in the light."

"Chloe...?"

"Oh, Jody. I'm sorry. This is difficult for me."

"It's okay." Jody really seemed to mean it. "Honestly. Whatever it is, whatever I can do, I'm happy to help."

Chloe forged on. "A month ago you got an order for me. You sent me a beautiful arrangement. Orchids and roses in a gorgeous square vase?"

"Okay, yeah. I remember that. Do you recall the date?"

It was burned in Chloe's brain. She repeated it. Jody said, "Let me look… Got it. Came through FloraDora dot net. From a Ted Davies in San Diego."

"That's it." The truth was right there caught in her throat, pushing to get out. So she let it. "Ted Davies is my ex-husband and I don't want any more flowers from him."

"Whoa. I hear you." Computer keys clicked on the other end of the line. "Okay. That's handled. If I get another order from him, I'll refuse it."

"Thanks. Thanks so much. And one more thing…"

"Just ask."

"Do you have a copy of that order and maybe the text of the card that came with it?"

"I do."

"Could you email that to me?"

"The text of the card, absolutely. I can't send the actual order form. But I can send you a confirmation that I received and filled the order. A confirmation would include the date of the transaction and that Ted Davies in San Diego had the flowers sent to you."

"That would be perfect." Chloe rattled off her personal email address.

Jody said, "Great." More keys clacked. "I've sent what you asked for. And if he tries again, I'll let you know."

"That would really help."

"And, Chloe, just so you know…"

"Please."

"If he starts sending them anonymously from Tilly's or elsewhere, you'll probably get resistance from the florist when you ask for information about who sent them." Jody lowered her voice. "The customer is king and all that…"

"I understand. And I can't tell you how much I appreciate your help."

"Anytime. And, Chloe…?"

"Um?"

"Maybe it's none of my business, but…" Jody hesitated again.

Chloe felt a curl of dread that the conversation was about to veer way out of her comfort zone. But then again, Jody *was* Quinn's sister. And Chloe had already all but said that her ex was a stalker. Comfort zone? Forget about it. Chloe reminded Jody, "We're family, remember?" Or they would be, if Chloe ever agreed to choose a date. "Ask me anything."

"Does Quinn know about this?"

"Yes." It did feel good to be able to reassure his sister that she hadn't kept him in the dark. "Quinn's the one who suggested that I call you."

"Perfect." Jody's relief was clear in her voice. "Exactly what I wanted to hear. You need anything else—anything—you just let me know."

Chloe thanked her again and they said goodbye. She disconnected the call—and the phone rang in her hand.

It was Quinn. "Thought I'd check and see how you're doing."

Just the sound of his voice made her feel better about everything. She reported on her call to her mother and told him that everything was handled with Jody.

"Look at you," he said in that low rumble that turned her insides to mush. "Right on the case."

She chuckled. Okay, it was a slightly manic sound, but a laugh was better than a cry of misery and frustration anytime. "I'm in the light, big guy. Stalker Ted doesn't stand a chance against me."

"Get 'em, killer."

"You'd better be smiling when you call me that."

They talked for a little about mundane things.

She had her self-defense class that night and she was looking forward to more tips on eluding an attacker. Also, for the second half of that evening's class, the guys would finally get into their padded suits. She would have a chance to put some of what she'd learned into practice.

Quinn said that he and Annabelle would miss her at dinner. "Manny's making lasagna," he muttered bleakly.

She teased, "I'm so sorry about that."

Tai appeared in the open doorway to the showroom. A customer wanted an estimate for both a bath and a kitchen remodeling.

Quinn said, "I heard that. See you tonight. I'll be over as soon as I finish with monster removal."

Chloe left her self-defense class that night feeling exhilarated. At first, it was scary, shouting at her "attacker," kicking and flailing, punching and pushing to get out of his clutches, trying to remember the few fighting tricks she'd been taught in earlier classes, like how to behave counter to your natural reaction to jerk away when an attacker grabbed you. Instead, you leaned in, catching him off balance, and then, using that split second when the bad guy wasn't braced, you jerked back and started kicking and screaming for all you were worth.

Bottom line: it didn't pay to be a lady when some scuzzball grabbed you. Once things moved past avoidance and any chance to defuse the situation, a woman needed to be willing to make plenty of noise and fight tooth and nail for all she was worth. She had to accept that she would probably be injured. The battle by then was to survive.

When she got home, she took a long shower and put on cropped jeans and a silk tank top and fixed a light dinner. By then, it was nine and Quinn would be over sometime in the next hour. She went downstairs and checked email, her pulse ratcheting up a notch at the thought that Ted might have tried to contact her again.

But there was nothing from him. Jody had sent her a copy of the note that had come with the flowers, along with the confirmation she'd promised. Chloe copied all that to her TD file. Then she dealt with the few new emails and messages the website and the Facebook page had received.

Finally, she brought up the message Ted had sent her two weeks ago. She and Quinn had agreed that she would answer with a demand that Ted leave her alone and then block the address. She went ahead and composed her reply. It was only two sentences: Never contact me again. I am blocking this address. She zipped it right off, blacklisted flwrs4yoo@gotmail.com and updated the information in her TD file.

Not two seconds later, she heard the door open upstairs.

"Angel?" Quinn called.

"Coming!" She ran up to meet him.

"So, how was the lasagna?" she asked when they met in the middle of the stairs.

He had his tablet in one hand. With the other, he reached out, slid his warm fingers around the back of her neck and pulled her up close. "About as expected."

"That's too bad."

"Yeah." He leaned in even closer, rubbed his rough cheek to her soft one. "You shoulda been there to suffer with us."

"So sorry to miss it."

"I'll just bet you are."

She rubbed her nose against his and then kissed him. When he lifted his head, she stared up at him, feeling distinctly starry-eyed. "How 'bout a beer?" she suggested. "We can sit out on the deck and I'll tell you all about how spectacular the master bath tile work at your house is going to be and what I learned in self-defense class this evening."

He held up his tablet. "First, you're writing me an email to Ted, remember?"

She hadn't forgotten. Far from it. "Actually, I've been rethinking that."

He guided a hank of her hair behind her ear and chided, "We got this all worked out. It's only going to take a few minutes."

Dear Lord, he was a wonderful man. "I've done everything you suggested last night. I'm even going to deal with my mother tomorrow. And I want you to be here when she arrives. But this…" She gestured weakly at the tablet.

"What about it?" He didn't sound happy.

Well, neither was she. "I don't like it, Quinn."

"We've been all through this last night and you agreed—"

She cut him off—but gently. "Yes, I did. And since then, I've had time to think it over a little more and I just…"

"You just what?"

"I just don't want you contacting him. You are not getting directly involved in this—not with Ted. Uh-uh. That is not going to happen."

His eyes had darkened and now his jaw was solid as rock. "You better tell me right now. You think you need to protect that guy from me?"

She gaped in hurt surprise. "No. No, of course I don't. This is about you, not him. This is about—"

"So you're protecting *me*? You think I need protecting from a slimeball like that?"

How had this gotten so out of hand so fast? She drew in a slow breath and told her racing heart to settle the heck down. "Please. Can we dial this back? Can we *not* have this argument right here in the middle of the stairs?"

He answered much too quietly, "Sure, Chloe. Where, then?"

"How about if we just don't have this argument at all?"

He was not about to let it go. "*Where*, Chloe?"

Fair enough. She gestured toward the top of the stairs. "The great room, then."

He turned around and marched back up. Reluctantly, she followed.

In the sitting area, he took an easy chair and she took the sofa. They faced off across the coffee table.

He asked, oh so reasonably, "Did you write that sucker an email and tell him to leave you alone?"

"Yes, I did. And then I blocked the address he used."

"Good." He dropped his tablet on the coffee table and leaned toward her, powerful forearms braced on his spread knees. "So, what's the sudden issue with letting him know that you're with me now and I know what he's up to?"

"It's an overreaction."

"The hell it is."

"Flowers, Quinn. He sent flowers once, a month ago. And he emailed me two weeks ago. That's all he's done."

He made a low, angry sound deep in his throat. "All he's done? He hit you, more than once. He cheated on you. And then when you divorced him, he wouldn't leave you alone. It got so bad you moved back home. And now he's started in again."

"I'm talking about recently."

"You're lying to yourself."

"Two times," she repeated. "Two times he's contacted me in more than a year. Flowers and one email. And now I'm keeping a record of every move he makes on me. I've blocked his email address and he won't be sending me flowers from Bloom again. I've told him, in no uncertain terms, to get lost. That's enough for now. That's... appropriate to the situation."

"Appropriate." He said it as if it tasted really bad in his mouth. "Tell you what. Forget it. Let's drop this right now. Have it your way. Let it go."

"Great. All I need is your word that you won't be looking him up online or calling some private investigator to find him. Promise me you won't go off on your own and contact him."

"I'm not agreeing to that."

"Then we're not done here. I mean it, Quinn. You have to stay out of this. Ted is not your problem."

"You keep saying that." He sat back, then forward again. She saw the born fighter in him so clearly right then. Testosterone seemed to come off him in waves. "Ted *is* my problem." He growled the words. "Anything that ties you in knots and keeps you awake nights and drives a wedge between us..." He jerked his thumb toward his broad chest. "My problem."

She folded her arms protectively across her middle, realized she was doing it, and unfolded them again. "Ted is... He can be a real snake, Quinn." Across the low table from her, he shifted again, furious, coiled, ready for action. She went on before he could interrupt. "He's a really good lawyer. Clever. Ruthless. You get in touch with him, you could end up slapped with a restraining order, or even a lawsuit."

Quinn shot to his feet, the move lightning-fast. He was sitting across from her—and all at once, he was looming above her. But when he spoke his voice was careful and even. "You think I give a good damn about his dirty tricks?"

She answered truthfully, "No, I don't. But *I* do. I care

if he makes trouble for you. I will not be the cause of that. I just won't."

"You won't be the cause of anything. Your ex, *he's* the cause. And I'm responsible for my own actions. It's not on you if I communicate with Ted. So whatever he tries on me, fine. He can bring it."

Where to even start? "Will you please just...sit down?"

He surprised her by doing what she asked, dropping back into the chair and leaning forward on his spread knees again. "I told you last night that I'm not going to be anything but polite and respectful to that piece of crap."

"You're missing the point. I'll say it again. This is *my* problem and you don't get to solve it. I don't want you to solve it. That wouldn't be right."

"Yeah, it *is* right. You're with me and I stand up for what's mine."

"No, Quinn."

"Wait." His eyes burned into hers. "Now you're telling me you're not mine?"

So strange. Such fury in him right now—and yet she wasn't in the least afraid of him. She knew he would never hurt her, never lay a finger on her in anger, that all he wanted was to protect her.

But in this particular situation, she couldn't let him do that.

"Are you mine or not?" he demanded again.

And she gave him a slow, very definite nod. "I am yours, Quinn. Yes. Absolutely."

Heat flared in his eyes and he said, low and evenly, "Give me that email address."

"No."

"Damn it, Chloe."

"Don't swear at me. Listen. I don't feel I have to protect you from Ted and I certainly don't feel I have to protect him from anything. I am with you and only you. You're the one for me. I want your help. I want your strength and your support and I'm grateful for your advice. What I don't want is you standing up *for* me. The whole point here is that I have to learn how to stand up for myself."

He seemed unable to stay in the chair then. Shooting upright again, he glared down at her. "I don't like it. That guy needs to know you got backup, that you're not alone and the man you're with now will fight for you."

"It's my choice, Quinn. Tell me that you will respect my choice. Please."

"Angel, you ask too much."

"Please."

He turned from her, went to the wall of windows and stood staring out, feet apart, hands linked behind him. She resisted the powerful need to plead with him some more. Finally, he said, "I don't like it."

"I get that. It's painfully clear."

He faced her again. "Do I still have your word that you'll tell me if he sends you more flowers or tries in any way to get in touch with you again?"

"Yes."

"Then all right. I won't contact him. Until he makes some other jackass move, I'll stand down."

Chapter Twelve

After Quinn agreed not to contact Ted, the night went on pretty much as usual. They sat out on the deck under the clear night sky. They made beautiful, passionate love.

But it wasn't the same, not really. Except for their love-making, which was as intense and ardent as ever, something was missing. There was a certain edge between them. A certain distance.

Chloe hated that distance. But what could she do? No way would she give him her blessing to get into it with Ted.

The next evening, he came over at six-thirty. In the half hour before her mother's arrival, Chloe reminded him that she was running this little talk. He was there to lend support.

He didn't even argue. "I get that. No problem."

His immediate acceptance of her terms surprised her a little after how hard he'd fought her on the issue of his contacting Ted.

And he knew it, too.

He said wryly, "No worries. I don't want to give your mom a bad time. She's going to be my mother-in-law, remember? Eventually I'm hoping she and I can get along together."

"Have you *met* my mother?"

He chuckled then, an easy sound. She dared to hope that maybe they were getting past their disagreement of the night before.

The doorbell rang right at seven.

Chloe opened the door. Her mother stood there in tan trousers, a cream-colored silk blouse and the triple strand of Mikimoto pearls Chloe's dad had bought her for their thirtieth anniversary four years ago.

"Chloe," Linda said with a cool nod.

"Mom." She stepped back. "Come in."

Linda spotted Quinn as she crossed the threshold. She put her hand to her pearls and arched an eyebrow at Chloe. "I didn't realize *he* would be here."

Quinn moved closer. He didn't seem the least offended by her mother's snotty tone. "Good to see you, Mrs. Winchester."

Her mother blinked at his outstretched hand as though she feared it would bite. But then she gave in and took it. "Hello, Quinn."

Quinn might not be upset by Linda's attitude, but Chloe had to resist the urge to boot her mother right back out the door. "Tell him to call you Linda, Mother."

Her mother sent her a barbed look—then caught herself and said in a tight voice, "Yes. Please call me Linda."

"Will do."

Chloe gestured toward the sitting area, and they filed over there. Chloe and Quinn took the couch. Linda perched on one of the chairs.

"I thought maybe you would bring Dad with you," Chloe said.

Linda carefully placed her folded hands on her pressed-together knees. "He wanted to come. But I was under the impression it would be just the two of us, just… between us." She sent a disapproving glance in Quinn's direction and then swung her reproachful gaze right back to Chloe. "So I insisted that I would come alone." She cleared her throat, an officious little sound. "That's a beautiful ring. I hope…you'll be very happy." The words seemed to stick in her throat. Still, they were a definite improvement over the awful things she'd said about Quinn a few weeks ago and yesterday on the phone.

"Thank you, Linda," said Quinn.

Chloe put in, "Give Dad my love, will you?"

A grudging nod. And apparently, Linda had decided she'd had quite enough of making polite noises. "Now, what's this about?"

"It's about Ted, Mother."

Linda stiffened. "What more can possibly be said about Ted?"

"Well, Mom. In the past month, Ted has sent me flowers and then contacted me by email. I want nothing to do with him and I have told him that repeatedly. I've told *you* that often. But I got the impression from what you said at the first of the month that you and Ted have been in touch."

Her mother sniffed. "Oh. I see. Now it's my fault if Ted sent you flowers."

Quinn shifted beside Chloe. She reached over and touched his arm, reminding him of the agreement they'd made half an hour before—that he was there for support.

She said, "I'm going to ask you a direct question, Mom. I want a simple yes-or-no answer."

Linda wore her I-am-gravely-wounded face. "What is this, an interrogation?"

"Have you been in contact with Ted since I moved back to town? Yes or no?"

"I don't see what—"

Quinn spoke up then, his voice coaxing and gentle, "We just want your help, Linda. I realize that you know already, but I think it can't hurt to say again that Ted Davies wasn't a good husband to Chloe. He punched her more than once and he betrayed her with another woman."

"Well, I... Ahem. Yes, I'm aware. Chloe has told me all that."

Chloe took the lead again. She tried really hard to keep the antagonism out of her voice. "So, have you been in touch with him since I moved back to Justice Creek?"

"I don't..." Linda patted her hair, straightened her shoulders. And then, finally, she confessed, "He called me."

"How many times?"

"Once."

"When was that?"

"The middle of July. A week before we left for Maui. He was, well, you know how kind and flattering he's always been toward me. He just said he was thinking of me and hoping I was all right. At first, when he started talking, I reminded myself I needed to tell him that I didn't approve of the way he had treated you and I was going to say goodbye now and I didn't want him to contact me again. But then he just kept on talking and telling me how horrible he felt about how it had gone with the two of you. He said you were the best thing that had ever happened to him and he missed you every hour of every day. He said that things weren't going well with him and that new wife of his, that he deeply regretted letting you go. He just…seemed so sincere." She let out a small sound of honest distress and brought both her hands up. Pressing her fingers to her mouth, she looked at Chloe through pleading eyes.

Chloe made herself speak gently. "Ted is very good at seeming sincere."

Linda drew in a steadying breath and put her hands in her lap again. "Yes. Yes, he is. Before he hung up, he asked me not to tell you that he had called. He said that he…didn't want to cause any trouble."

Not cause any trouble? Ted? Now, that was a good one. "What did you tell him about me, Mother?"

"Nothing. I promise you. He did all the talking. At the end, he said he would like to send you a little card or something, just to say he was thinking of you. He asked for your address. But I told him I wasn't at liberty to give him any of your personal information. And he said of course, that was all right. He completely understood. He said if he decided to reach out to you, he would get your address some other way. He said it wouldn't be a problem. He seemed…very confident about that."

"I'll bet."

Linda's face crumpled, all her earlier bravado cracking to nothing, falling away. She cried, "All right. I just have to say this. I just have to tell you that I *have* been thinking, I truly have, since that horrible evening four weeks ago when you and I fought so bitterly about this. I need you to know that I… Chloe, oh, Chloe… I *know* I was wrong. I was wrong to listen to him at all, wrong not to tell him immediately to leave us alone and then hang up the phone, wrong not to tell you right away that he'd called me. He…well, he charmed me. He fed my ego. And I fell for his lies. But I did *not* tell him anything about you. I gave him no information. I swear it. I didn't!"

Quinn reached over and brushed the back of Chloe's hand. She glanced at him. His eyes spoke of forgiveness.

But Chloe wasn't to the point of forgiving her mother—not yet anyway. She said, "All right, Mom. I believe you. And the truth is if he's determined to reach me, I'm not that hard to find."

"That's what I *told* you, remember, four weeks ago, right before you…threw me out?"

"I remember. Did Ted say anything else?"

"Not that I can think of. Really, that was it. That was all. I haven't heard a word from him before or since."

"Did you tell Dad about that call?"

Linda shook her head. "Not until last night."

A little wave of relief washed through Chloe that her dad hadn't known, hadn't kept that secret from her, too.

Her mother went on. "After you called to say you wanted to speak with me tonight, I just got so upset about everything. I stewed over what you would say to me, knowing that I really did need to admit to you that Ted had called me, to tell you what he said. I just…well, I started crying and I couldn't stop. Your father was so worried. He had no idea what was the matter with me. I realized I couldn't keep the truth from him a minute longer. So I ended up telling him everything, beginning with the call from Ted and ending with exactly what happened when you and I fought four weeks ago."

"So he knows the whole story now?"

Her mother bobbed her head and fingered her pearls. "Your father's not very happy with me at the moment. I know I can't blame him for that. I only want you to know, Chloe, that I have been thinking about what I've done.

Not only thinking about how I've kept a secret of the fact that Ted called me. More than that. So much more. I've been thinking of the past, too."

"Mother, I—"

But Linda wouldn't quit. "No. Please. Don't stop me. I need to say this. I need you to know that I see now, I do. So many ways that I have been wrong. I've been thinking how very proud I was at your beautiful wine-country wedding. How sure I was that you had everything then— and that *I* deserved a lot of credit for how well you'd done, how I had worked so hard to make you the kind of woman you are, an accomplished woman who marries just the right man. I've done a lot of bragging, about you and your 'great' life down in San Diego."

"Mother, I just don't..." Her objections trailed off as Quinn's big hand covered hers. She drew strength from that simple touch, strength enough to let her mother continue. "Never mind. Go on."

"Thank you," Linda said. "Because there are so many ways I know that I've failed you. That first time you left Ted, when you came home to us and said you weren't happy with him? You said you were finished with him, you never wanted to go back. And what did I do? I pushed you to try again, to work it out, even though you told me he'd hit you, even though you said that sometimes he frightened you. I was so very proud of the fine life I thought you had, the life I had insisted you make for your-self—so proud, that I refused to see your desperate un-happiness. If I had listened to what you were telling me then, you might never have gone back to him. He wouldn't have hit you again. But you did go back. And he did hit you. And he betrayed you, too. And I see that I have to face all that now. I have to admit that it happened, to own my part in it. I have not been the mother that you deserve. But I want you to know, at least, that I do finally see how wrong I've been. I hope that someday you will find it in yourself to forgive me. I love you so much, Chloe Janine. You're the bright, shining star of my heart. I hate having to count all the ways I've let you down, all the—"

Chloe couldn't take any more. "Please stop."

Her mother shut her mouth and stared at her, stricken.

Chloe stood. "I would like you to leave now. I need a little time, you know? To process all this."

Linda gazed up at her, eyes brimming, mouth trembling, looking suddenly every one of her fifty-nine years. "Yes. Of course." She got up. "I understand. I'll just..." She waved her hand, a weak little gesture, as though she couldn't recall what she'd started to say. And then she turned to go.

Chloe followed her and pulled open the door.

Linda said in a small voice, "Please believe me. I am so sorry. And I hope that someday you'll give me another chance."

Chloe only nodded. She knew that if she said another word, she would lose it.

Quinn was right there, at her side. He said, "Linda, do you need me to drive you home?"

A single tear tracked down her cheek. She refused to wipe it away and she kept her chin high. "Thank you, Quinn. But I'll manage."

And then she went out into the fading light. Chloe stood in the open door and watched her walk along the breezeway to her car. As soon as she disappeared around the far corner of the garage, Chloe shut the door.

So gently, Quinn took her by the shoulders and turned her to face him. She didn't want to look at him. He always saw too damn much. But he put a finger under her chin and made her meet his waiting eyes.

That did it. With a hard sob, she threw herself against him.

His big arms closed around her. "Hey, now. Hey..."

Chloe held on tight to him and surrendered to her tears. She didn't even know for certain why she was crying.

Maybe it was the shock of seeing her mother like that—so broken and sad. Or maybe it was relief that for the first time in her memory, her mother had actually admitted that she'd been wrong.

Chapter Thirteen

Two weeks passed. They were good weeks, overall.

Monday through Saturday, Chloe's days were filled with work. When she got home, she went to the log house and had dinner with Quinn and family. At night, Quinn came to her. And most mornings by the time she woke up, he was gone.

He didn't mention setting a wedding date again. But she knew it was on *his* mind. It was on *her* mind, too. She wanted to move forward with their lives together. But she couldn't, not yet. Not until...

She wasn't sure what. She just felt she was waiting. It was like that old saying about the other shoe dropping. She wasn't really sure what the first shoe had been, but it had already fallen. And now she was just waiting for the other one to drop.

On the first Monday in September, Jody called her at Your Way to tell her she'd just refused a second order from Ted. Chloe felt no surprise. None. In her mind, she pictured one of those classic Christian Louboutin black patent pumps, the dagger-heeled ones with the signature red-lacquered soles. She pictured that beautiful shoe dangling from an unknown hand.

Not dropped. Not yet.

But soon, yes. Very soon.

Jody said she would email her the proof that Bloom had refused an order from Ted at Chloe's request. "But aside from that, I just wanted to give you a heads-up," she said.

"You're the best," Chloe said. "Quinn has such amazing sisters."

"Call me. Remember. If I can do anything…"

"You know I will."

Chloe had her self-defense class that evening. Her trainer in his padded suit didn't stand a chance. She went absolutely postal on the guy, screaming and kicking, punching and gouging. The instructor had to shout at her to stop fighting and run. Later, he reminded the class that the point of the exercise was to incapacitate the attacker long enough to get away, not to keep pounding on him once he'd let you go.

She went home that evening and put another entry in her TD file. She didn't tell Quinn about Jody's call. He knew there was something bothering her, but she insisted it was nothing. And she wasn't nearly as upset as she'd been the night she found the email from Ted. Quinn let it go, but he was watchful and edgy the rest of the night.

Yes, she knew she should tell him. She'd *promised* to tell him if Ted tried to get in touch in any way. And she would tell him. She wasn't actually keeping anything from him, she reasoned—not for long, anyway. Ted would find another way to get the flowers to her. And it would be soon. And she would tell Quinn about

Jody's call and the latest bouquet then. Two birds with one stone, you might say.

As long as Jody didn't let it slip to Quinn about refusing Ted's order before Ted sent more flowers, Chloe figured it would work out all right—not that there was anything right about any of this.

And actually, Chloe dreaded telling Quinn more than she did the inevitable appearance of the next floral masterpiece. Every time she told him about some move Ted had made on her, he got harder to convince that this was her problem to solve.

She truly did fear that the time would come when she wouldn't be able to hold Quinn back. He would go after Ted, do physical damage to Ted. And then what? If Quinn ended up in jail because of her...

Well, she just didn't know how she would bear that.

So, for the time being, she was breaking her promise to him, lying about Ted by omission. The issue of Ted was a wedge between them, a wedge that created an emotional gap, a gap that widened incrementally as the days passed and the problem remained unresolved. Her love for Quinn got stronger and stronger as time went by. And she knew the bond Quinn felt with her was equally as powerful.

But sometimes love and a soul-deep connection just weren't enough, not when he needed to protect her and she wouldn't let him do that. Not when he wanted to marry her and she kept putting him off.

She didn't have to wait long for that second bouquet of flowers.

It arrived the next day, Tuesday.

Like the other arrangement two months before, the flowers were waiting on her doorstep. She found them at a little after eight in the evening, when she came home from dinner across the street. She hadn't expected to be that upset when they came—after all, she knew they would be coming. But the sight hit her hard nonetheless.

Her blood roaring in her ears and her knees gone to jelly, she sank to the front step next to the cobalt-blue vase filled with bloodred roses. The little card in the plastic holder had Tilly's logo on it. But she could have guessed that without the card. The vase wasn't anywhere near as nice as the one from Bloom that she'd smashed in the compactor. And roses were always beautiful. But the whole presentation just came off as ordinary.

"Ordinary," she heard herself mutter under her breath. "No offense to Tilly's, but you're slipping a little, aren't you, Ted?" And then she laughed.

It was a slightly manic-sounding laugh, not altogether a sane laugh. But somehow, it helped. The laugh made her pulse slow, soothed the roaring of her blood in her ears and strengthened the odd weakness in her knees. She was able to grab the blue vase and rise to her feet.

Inside, she put the vase on the counter and read the card. *You're not marrying that guy. You know you're not. My darling, we need to talk.*

Ted

"Look on the bright side," she said to Quinn when he arrived an hour later and saw the roses in their blue vase right there on the counter where she had left them.

"Bright side?" He looked at her as though she'd said something in a language he didn't understand.

"Ted signed his name. I called Tilly's and they've agreed not to send me any more flowers from him. So next time he'll have to pay to have them sent from Boulder."

Quinn took a long time reading the card. Finally, he

said flatly, "There is no bright side. We both know that. Something's got to be done about this guy."

This was not going well. She'd known that it wouldn't. She really, really wished she hadn't told him. But lies didn't work; keeping the truth from him was no way to carry on a relationship.

She made herself tell him the rest, "Also, you should know that Jody called me yesterday to tell me he tried to send flowers through her."

His eyes flashed dark fire. "And last night when I asked you what was wrong, you lied and said there was nothing."

"I…" There she went with the one-word responses again. She made herself give him a few whole sentences by way of explanation. "I knew he would go through Tilly's next and that I was going to have to tell you soon. I didn't see any reason we had to fight twice over this. So I decided to tell you about both the call from Jody and the flowers, when they came, together."

His expression was set as a slab of granite. "You lied."

She threw up both hands. "Fine. All right. I lied. And I'm sorry."

"Are we in this together?" he demanded.

"Of course. Where are you leading me with that question?"

"I'm leading to the fact that 'together' means when something happens, you tell me *now*. And by now I mean, if Jody calls you with information, you call me as soon as you get off the phone with her. You don't store up the bad news to deliver in batches."

She really hated that he was right. "Yes. I get that. I won't do that again."

"And who says we're fighting?"

She felt so…tired suddenly. Just tired to her bones. "Look at you. You're furious at me."

"No. Not with you, angel. Never with you." He held up the little white card in his big, rough, wonderful hand. "This. Him. I need to deal with him."

"No. No, you do not need to deal with Ted. And you will *not* deal with Ted."

He shook the card at her. "He knows about me, knows you're with me." His voice was the low, focused rumble of some powerful predator, crouched and gathering to strike.

"Quinn, come on. That we're engaged wouldn't be all that difficult to find out."

"Not the point, Chloe. This card says I'm in this now. This card says—"

"That card says nothing of the kind. You know it doesn't." She dared to approach him. He watched her come with a stillness so total it raised the goose bumps on her skin. The need to take action seemed to radiate right out of his pores. When she stood in front of him, she said, "Put down the card."

"Chloe." Wary. Vigilant. And so very unwilling.

"Put down the card and put your arms around me."

He didn't. Not for several seconds. But then, finally, with a low oath, he dropped the card to the counter and hauled her close.

She wrapped her arms around him, too, as tight as she could. His big heart pounded, hard and insistent, under her ear. She lifted her head and looked up into his eyes. "If you play his game, you weaken us. You know you do."

He scanned her face, as though seeking the right point of entry. "I got demands. I need you to agree to them."

"This doesn't sound good."

"Hear me out."

She sighed. "Of course."

"Tomorrow, we take what little we've got in that file of yours and we go to the police station. They're gonna tell us that no crime has been committed and there's nothing they can do."

She got that. "But they'll write it up and then if he does make trouble, there's at least a record that we complained."

Quinn nodded. "And I don't like to think of you alone here. You move in with me."

She stepped back from the shelter of his arms. "Not yet. Uh-uh. Look, I really don't think he's that dangerous."

"The guy's a whack job, Chloe. You don't know what he's gonna do next."

She took a slow, calming breath. "As I was saying, if he did try anything, I'm not having that happen in the house where Annabelle lives."

"Annabelle." Quinn said his daughter's name thoughtfully.

"You know I'm right, Quinn. We don't want her traumatized by any of this. We just need to go on as we are for a little longer. That note says 'We have to talk.' I get the feeling he means soon." She was actually starting to hope that it *would* be soon, whatever it was. She wanted that other shoe to finally drop. "I'll be extra careful, I promise. I've got Mace and I know how to use it. Plus, you should see me in self-defense class. I'm outta control, I'm so bloodthirsty."

He grabbed her close again. "Don't make jokes about it."

"Sorry. Not funny, I know. The stress is kind of getting to me."

* * *

Chloe had Tai open the showroom for her the next morning, and Quinn took her to the Justice Creek Town Hall. They talked to Riley Grimes, a patrol officer who had been two years behind them at Justice Creek High. Riley went through Chloe's TD file and said he'd write a brief report of their visit for possible future reference. He suggested that they might try for an order of protection, known in some states as a restraining order. But that would be iffy, as Chloe had reported no incidents of abuse during her marriage and the evidence she'd gathered so far didn't indicate she was in any immediate danger.

Quinn was all for calling his half brother James, the lawyer in the family, and seeing if James thought they had a chance of getting a protection order.

Chloe vetoed that for now. "You heard what Riley said. Ted hasn't come near me. He hasn't broken into my house or even shown up in Justice Creek to have that 'talk' he mentioned. He hasn't threatened me in any way."

"Every move he makes is a threat. He's stalking you, Chloe. Aren't you clear on that yet?"

They were standing on the town hall steps. Chloe reached out and took his big, hard arm. "Can we talk about this in private, please—tonight, when we're alone?"

"Sure." He muttered the word out of the side of his mouth. "Whatever you say."

He drove her back to her house to get her car. When she headed up the front walk rather than straight to the garage, he got out and followed her.

"What now?" She stopped to face him on the front step.

He had that look. Grim. Uncompromising. "I thought you were going to the showroom."

"I will. In a little while. I've got some samples I brought home last night I want to take back with me. And then I'm stopping at your house down the hill to touch base with Nell on the remodeling."

"Lock the door behind you when you go in, and reset the alarm while you're in there—on second thought, I'll just wait here until you're ready to get in your car."

"Quinn." She reached out and put her hand against his bleak-looking face. Tenderness flooded her. Oh, she did love him. And one of these days, she really needed to gather the courage to tell him so. "Please stop worrying and go to work. You can't watch over me every hour of every day."

His eyes had a strange gleam to them, bright and dark, both at once. "I don't like this."

She tried for humor. "I think you might have mentioned that once or twice already."

The corners of his mouth failed to twitch even the slightest bit. "I know more than one good man in personal security—"

"No. I mean it. Don't you even start talking bodyguards. You're overreacting. I do not need a bodyguard."

He hooked a big arm around her and hauled her up close against him. As always, she reveled in the heat, the sheer power of him. "You watch yourself. Promise me. Stay aware."

"I will."

He swooped down and kissed her hard and quick. "We're talking more about this tonight."

A resigned sigh escaped her. "Yes, I'm quite clear on that."

He kissed her once more, as swift and sweetly punishing as the time before, and then, finally, he let her go and returned to his car. She waited until he started up the engine and backed from the space beside the garage before letting herself in the house. After locking herself in and rearming the alarm, she ran downstairs to collect her samples and hurried right back up.

The blinking red light on the answering machine caught her attention as she was about to go out the door. She almost left it for later. But it could be something important.

Turned out it was a hang-up call. A swift ripple of unease slithered down her spine, followed by a burst of anger. *Thank you so much, Ted. Now even a hang-up call freaks me out.*

She considered trying *69. But what for? Whoever was on the other end, she didn't want to talk to them.

Enough. She made herself a promise to banish her jerk of an ex-husband from her mind for the rest of the day.

And she kept that promise.

Until she got home from dinner at Quinn's and found two more hang-up calls on her phone. When she went ahead and tried to call back, she learned that both calls were from blocked numbers. That thoroughly creeped her out. Though she had no proof of who had made the calls, she added them to her TD file and tried not to stew over them.

Then Quinn showed up.

Of course, he knew right away that something had happened. "What?" he said when he was barely in the door. "Just tell me."

So she told him about the hang up calls.

His expression grew even bleaker. "You put it in the file?"

"I did, yes. I noted the date and the times that the calls came in and that whoever made them did it from a blocked number. In case it somehow turns out to matter in some way."

"We need to talk about you trying for that order of protection."

She went over, dropped to the sofa and put her head in her hands. "Can we just...not? Please?" She looked up. He was standing over her, eyes stormy with equal parts anger and concern. She got up. "He's running our lives, Quinn. We can't let him do that."

He clasped her shoulders in his big hands and pressed his forehead to hers. "I've been thinking."

"Thinking about...?" She tipped her face back enough to look at him—and then she lifted enough to touch his lips with hers.

He made that low, lovely growling sound in his throat and settled his mouth more firmly on hers. They shared a slow, delicious kiss. He gathered her in. She slid her hands up over his chest and linked them behind his neck.

"Now, that's what I'm talking about," she said softly, when he finally lifted his head.

"Vegas." He bent and kissed the word onto her upturned mouth. And then, soft as a breath, back and forth, he brushed his lips against hers and whispered, "This weekend. We'll fly to Vegas and get married."

"Married?" She jerked back so that their lips no longer touched. "Quinn, we've talked about that."

He scowled. "I know that tone of voice. Here come all the damn objections."

"I meant what I said before. I just need a little more time, that's all."

"Uh-uh. You need to be my wife and live with me and Annabelle and Manny. I don't want you living alone here. Not anymore."

"I'm perfectly safe. You're here half the time and a

lot of the time I'm at your house. And what about Anna-belle? I don't want to put her in danger, I really don't."

"So you do admit you're in danger."

Sometimes the man was too quick by half. "No, no, of course I'm not in danger."

"Listen to yourself, angel. You're 'perfectly safe,' but you're afraid that if you move in with us, you'll put my little girl in danger. You're all over the map about this."

"No, that's not so. I really don't think anything is going to happen. But if something did, I couldn't stand it if Annabelle ended up in the middle of it."

He took her by the shoulders—carefully, but firmly, too. "A few minutes ago, you said that we couldn't let that guy run our lives."

"And I meant it!"

"Then stop."

She searched his face, not following. "Stop...?"

"You're letting him keep you from living your life. You're putting everything on hold for him."

"No."

"Yeah, Chloe. Yeah, you are. How long you gonna do that to yourself, huh? How long you gonna do that to *us*?"

She stared up at him, her heart like a stone, so heavy in her chest. She knew he was right.

And yet she just couldn't do it. Not now. She could not say her love out loud. And she couldn't agree to get married. Not right now. Not until she'd somehow dealt with the problem that was Ted.

Quinn didn't know what to do about Chloe.

She tied his hands at every turn. She wouldn't let him make a move on her ex. She wouldn't marry him and live with him in his house where he could better protect her. She wouldn't let him hire someone to watch over her. She wouldn't let his half brother James check into slapping good old Ted with an order of protection.

She had dark circles under her ice-blue eyes and much of the time she seemed distant and distracted. He only had her full attention when he took her to bed.

Something had to give.

And it had damn well better give soon. She seemed so fragile to him lately and he feared some kind of... breakage. He feared the destruction of what they had together—no, worse. He feared the ruin of her tender heart, her strength, her spirit.

That night, he held her as she slept and wondered what the hell to do.

When Chloe woke in the morning, Quinn was still there. Already dressed in the jeans and knit shirt he'd worn the night before, he sat in the bedside chair, just looking at her.

She pushed up on an elbow and raked her sleep-tangled hair back off her forehead. "Shouldn't you be having breakfast with Annabelle?"

He rose. "I'm going now. I was just waiting for you to wake up."

She saw the shadows in his eyes and felt remorse drag at her—for giving him nothing but trouble lately, for being a source of constant concern. "I'm perfectly safe here. All the locks are sturdy and the alarm system is state-of-the-art. And I promise to keep the system armed when you're not here and to stay alert whenever I'm outside on my own."

He bent close, brushed a kiss on her forehead and said mildly, "I just wanted to wait until you were awake."

She started to accuse him of lying. He'd stayed to watch over her and they both knew that.

But she came to her senses before she could light into

him. He only wanted to take care of her. Had she sunk to snapping at him for trying to keep her safe?

She ended up asking sheepishly, "Give Annabelle a kiss for me?"

He promised that he would and then he was gone.

Wearily, she got up and went about the beginnings of another day.

At a little after eight, as she was eating breakfast, the phone rang. She let out a cry at the sound and splashed hot coffee across the back of her hand. Wanting to slap her own face for being such a nervous twit, she mopped up the spill with a paper napkin and picked up the phone.

It was only Tai calling in sick. "It's just a cold," she said. "I'm thinking if I take it easy today, I'll be ready to go again by tomorrow." Chloe told her to get plenty of rest and drink lots of liquids, and Tai laughed and said, "Yes, Dr. Winchester. I'll take good care of myself."

Chloe left the house at eight-thirty, arming the alarm and locking things up tight. She kept her eyes open and her head up as she crossed the breezeway to the garage. She was careful in the garage, standing in the open door-way to the breezeway, pushing the button on the wall that sent the main door rattling up and then having a quick look around the space before shutting and relocking the breezeway door behind her. Locking herself in the car, she backed from the garage and then sat there until the door was all the way down, just to be certain Ted didn't dart in there when she wasn't looking, to lie in wait for her later.

At Your Way, she exercised the same watchfulness, scanning the little lot behind the building for any lurk-ers before she got out of the car. And then getting out quickly, locking the doors and hustling toward the back entrance, her right hand in a fist and her keys poking out between her fingers, a makeshift weapon ready to gouge a few nasty holes in anybody foolish enough to jump her.

She didn't fiddle or linger, but quickly unlocked the back door, disarmed the alarm and locked the door behind her. Then she went through the rooms—the office, the restroom, the studio in back and the showroom in front.

Ted was not waiting there. Everything was right where she'd left it the evening before.

And did she feel foolish and overcautious and strangely let down?

Yes, a little bit. But she'd kept her word to Quinn, kept her head up and all her senses on alert, just as they'd taught her in self-defense class, all the way from her front door to the showroom.

Truthfully being vigilant was nerve-racking. And her nerves lately had been racked quite enough, thank you.

She spruced up the showroom and got the coffee going. At nine, she unlocked the front door and turned the sign around. Then she went behind the register counter and called Nell over at Bravo Construction to say she was stuck at the store until closing time but would stop by the remodeling site on the way home.

Nell was her usual bold, funny self. One of the new guys on the crew had asked her to dinner. "Big muscles," Nell said, "gorgeous ink. Too bad the brain is practically nonexistent. I like a big brain. It matters to me."

"So he's only a piece of tasty meat and you're not going out with him?"

"Tasty meat." Nell groaned. "I said that, didn't I, when I was busting your chops about Quinn?"

"You most definitely did."

Call-ump. Call-ump. Chloe recognized the sound of

Nell's boots landing on her scarred desktop. Nell said, "So you think I'm objectifying this guy?"

"Well, maybe just a little."

"You know, he *is* really sweet. Is it his fault he's no Einstein? Dumb guys need love, too. And he's so pretty to look at."

Chloe thought of Quinn, who was not only wonderful to look at with a heart of pure gold, he was brilliant, as well. She felt an ache down inside her, just thinking of him. Because she loved him so, because she kept pushing him away when she knew she ought to be grabbing him closer, holding on tight, promising never, ever, to let him go.

She reminded Nell, "People used to think Quinn was slow, remember? And you *can* be pretty intimidating."

"Me? You're kidding."

"You're a force to be reckoned with, Nellie."

"Keep talkin'. I'm startin' to like where this is going."

"Did you ever stop to think that maybe the guy is shy?"

"Oh, and I freak him out because I'm so awesome?"

"Nell, you are a giant bowl of awesome—with extra whipped cream and cherries on top. So yeah, it's more than possible he's intimidated by you."

"A giant bowl of awesome. I like the sound of that a lot. And so you're saying I should give this guy a chance?"

"Yeah. I think you should. He might turn out to be smarter than you think."

Nell said she'd give it more thought. And then, out of nowhere, she asked, "Baby, are you okay?"

Chloe's throat instantly clutched and tears burned behind her eyes. "Ahem." She turned around and faced the hallway to the back door. Swiping at her eyes, she spoke more softly. "Fine. I'm fine."

"Stop lyin' to me, Chloe. It's so not working."

Chloe gulped down a fresh spurt of tears. "Really, I don't even know where to start..."

"Is it Quinn? If he's causing you grief—"

Chloe let out a laugh that caught on a sob. "Wait a minute. Aren't you the one who asked me if I was slumming with your brother and promised to hurt me if I wasn't good to him?"

"That was before I knew you. I was wrong, all wrong. You and Quinn are a great match, a true love match. And I love you both."

Chloe's throat clutched all over again. "Oh, Nellie. Thank you."

"No need for thanks. We're family."

"And that makes me so glad."

"But the problem is...?"

"Well, I can say this much. Quinn is *not* the problem. He's the best thing that ever happened to me and I love him so much and somehow I don't know how to tell him so. Things are scary right now and—"

"Scary, how?"

"Long story. I'll only say that sometimes I think I'm just too damaged, you know? I think that there's really something very wrong with me and I'm afraid that's never going to change."

"Not a damn thing is wrong with you. And we need some sister time."

Chloe started to object. But then she realized she *did* want some sister time with Nell. "You know, that sounds really good."

"Instead of the remodel, let's meet at McKellan's. Best cosmos in Colorado." The entry chime sounded. Chloe swiped at her cheeks again and tried to compose herself before turning to greet her first customer of the day.

Nell said, "Five-fifteen. Be there. Call Quinn and tell him that there will be drinking and he might have to pick us up later."

"I will. See you. McKellan's. Five-fifteen." Chloe sniffed and smoothed her hair. Then she turned around and carefully set the receiver in its cradle.

When she finally glanced up with a bright smile for whoever had come in, Ted was standing not twenty feet away in front of the showroom door.

Chapter Fourteen

Chloe's heart beat a sick rhythm under her ribs and her throat felt like some invisible hand was squeezing it tight.

She'd done it to herself. It was all her own fault. She'd let down her guard. She'd turned around and forgotten all about how she needed to keep her head up and her eyes front.

She'd let her concentration slip to cry on Nellie's shoulder—and her nightmare had found her.

Somehow he'd not only slipped in the door when she was talking to Nell, but he'd whipped the open sign around, too. It was just a regular glass door with a knob lock you could turn from the inside.

She had zero doubt he'd locked it, as well.

Her nightmare had not only found her, he'd locked himself in her showroom with her.

Beautifully turned out as always in a perfectly tailored designer suit and a Seven Fold Robert Talbott tie, not a single dark blond hair out of place, he gave her a slow, charming smile. And then he said in that smooth, cool voice that had slowly turned all her dreams into nightmares, "Hello, Chloe."

Her purse was under the counter. She needed to reach in there and pull out the Mace. Carefully, trying not to move the upper part of her body and give herself away, she felt for the purse, found it...

Oh, God, she'd zipped it shut. He would know if she tried to get it open now.

Run! She needed to get the hell out of there. She started to whirl for the back door.

Ted said, so very mildly, "Please don't do that."

And her mind went to mush as her legs started shaking. She was rooted to the spot.

It was pitiful, really. Such a sad case, she was. He had trained her so well over all those awful, endless years with him. He only had to look at her, only had to speak to her in that smooth, mild voice of his and she couldn't fall all over herself fast enough to do whatever he demanded of her.

She had dared, in the past year, to believe herself free of him—well, except for the nightmares. She had *made* herself free of him. She'd divorced him and moved on, found Quinn. *Her* Quinn, so fine and true, everything she'd always wanted—only better. Only *more...*

She shut her eyes. No. She couldn't think of Quinn now. She needed to focus, needed to remember her self-defense training, to start acting like the independent, self-possessed, self-directed woman she actually was.

And yet, somehow, she stood there, just *stood* there, and did nothing as Ted came for her.

With his fine Italian shoes light and quick on the showroom's wood floor, he walked right up to the counter, stepped around it, and wrapped his perfectly manicured hand around her upper arm. "You're beautiful, my darling, as always. But you look tired."

The faint smell of the signature cologne he always had specially made just for him came to her. She knew she would gag on that smell. But she swallowed, hard, and glanced down at his fingers encircling her arm. "Where's your wedding ring, Ted?"

He actually chuckled. "Larissa and I are through."

"I'm so sorry to hear that."

"No, you're not. You knew all along she wouldn't last. A diversion, that's all she was supposed to be. I work very hard, and you know that I do, to make a fine life for us. I deserve a diversion now and then. But then you left me and I tried to distract myself, tried to convince myself that any beautiful, reasonably intelligent woman would do. I thought I could forget you. I was wrong. You are mine, and you are perfect for me and I'm ready now to give you another chance."

She simply could not let that pass. "But I'm not yours."

"Yes, you are."

"We're divorced, Ted, in case you've forgotten. And the last thing I want is another chance with you."

His eyes shifted, away—and then back. Other than that, he pretended he hadn't heard her. "Let's sit down, shall we?"

"I don't want to sit down with you. Let go of my arm, Ted. Leave. Now. Please."

Again, he ignored her. "This way." He started walking, pulling her with him, into the hallway that led to the back door, pausing at the open arch on the left. "This will do." He led her into her studio and over to her worktable, where he pulled out a chair and pushed her down in it. Then he grabbed another chair a few feet away and yanked it over next her. He sat down, too. And then he said, "I love you, my darling. And I've come to take you home. I know that I hurt you and I swear to you that I will never do that again." He reached out. She steeled herself not to cringe away as he traced the line of her hair along her cheek and down her neck.

Chloe's skin crawled. She swallowed bile again and stared at her worktable, taking a strange kind of comfort from the tools she used every day: the stacks of thick fabric sample books, the color wheels, the sketch tablets, the loose swatches of fabric, the scissors, drafting compass, tape measure, shape templates, colored pencils and fine-point pens...

Ted kept on talking. "I called you three times yesterday. You never picked up. And then I thought, well, that's all right. It's better that we talk face-to-face anyway. Better that we cut to the chase and you can just come home with me. And it *is* better. It's wonderful to see you, my darling. And now I just want you to look at me. I want you to tell me the truth, that you've missed me and you're so glad to see me. I want to work this out with you—and yes, I know. My temper has been a problem. But I'll return to counseling. Everyone needs a little extra help getting things right now and then."

She tried again. "Ted. I'm in love with my fiancé and I don't want anything to do with you."

"You don't mean that."

"Yes, Ted, I do."

"Look at me." He grabbed her chin in a punishing grip and yanked her head around to face him.

"That's going to leave a bruise." She glared at him.

"Darling, I'm so sorry."

"I don't believe you." She realized she was getting

less numb and more angry. Angry was good. At least her knees weren't shaking anymore.

"You know, Chloe. You really shouldn't bait me. If you would only treat me with the love and respect I deserve, our lives would go so smoothly, everything just so, moving along without a hitch."

She shot to her feet.

But before she could dodge around him and make for the door, he grabbed her hand. "Sit *down*." And he yanked her back into the chair so hard that her teeth clacked together. "What's this?" He still had her hand. Her left hand.

"It's my engagement ring. Remember? I'm engaged." She tried to pull away.

He held on. His face was getting that look, his eyes distant, his skin flushing mottled red. "Take it off."

"You'll have to let go for me to do that."

But he didn't let go. "Already, you are out of hand. You are pushing me too far. You know that you are."

"Let go of me, Ted."

"Don't you ever try to tell me what to do."

"Let me go," she said softly. And then she said it again, a little louder, "Let me go." And then she couldn't *stop* saying it, louder and louder, "Let me go, let me go, let me go, let me go…"

And right then, as she repeated that same phrase like a mantra, for the seventh time, he drew back his fist and he punched her in the jaw.

Chloe saw stars as blood filled her mouth. It hurt— and more than just the fist to the face. She'd bitten her own tongue, bitten it good and hard.

Everything got very clear then. Crystal clear.

She needed to defend herself and she needed to do it now.

Chloe let out a scream. It was a wild cry, feral. Furious. Ted stared at her, bug-eyed in surprise. His perfect darling Chloe would never let out such an animal sound—a tasteful little whimper, maybe. But a full-out, full-throated scream of rage? No way.

However, she was no longer his perfect Chloe. She belonged to herself now—to herself, and to Quinn. She needed to end all of Ted's false assumptions and she needed to end them forever and always.

So she reached over, grabbed one of the heavy sample books in both hands, drew it back and whacked that sucker right across the side of his big, fat head. His chair scraped the floor as the sample book connected. He let out a grunt of surprise.

And that was all he got a chance to do.

Because she went kind of crazy. She lifted that sample book and she hit him again. His chair went over and he was on the floor. She jumped on top of him and hit him some more.

By then he was making these ridiculous little whining sounds, his arms drawn up in front of his face. He was calling her name, "Chloe, stop! Chloe, don't!" as she flailed at him with the sample book.

From out in the showroom came pounding and shouts, followed by the sound of glass shattering. And then, wonder of wonders, Quinn's voice: "Chloe!"

"Back here!" She climbed off Ted and stood, panting, above him, still holding the sample book threateningly over her head, as Quinn came flying into the room.

"Angel, my God..."

About then, she noticed there was blood all down the front of her white silk shirt. She explained mildly, her tongue already swelling in her mouth, "He hit me and I bit my tongue."

On the floor, Ted was curled in the fetal position. "Help me," he groaned. "Get that crazy bitch away from me!"

Quinn said, "This must be Ted." Chloe dropped the sample book on the table, pressed her suddenly quivering lips together and nodded. He asked, "How bad are you hurt?"

"I'm okay, really. It lookth worth than it ith."

Ted rolled and started to get up.

Quinn said flatly, "Stay on the floor, Ted."

With a moan, Ted went over on his side and curled up in a ball. He whined, "You people are insane."

"Just shut up and don't move."

Surprisingly, Ted took Quinn's advice.

Chloe zipped past Ted and got to Quinn. He hooked his big arm around her, pressed his warm lips to her forehead and whispered, "I think he's got your message now. You did good, angel. Real good."

She snuggled in close to him. "How did you know to come here?"

"Nell called me. Told me you'd been cryin' on the phone and I'd better get the hell over here and not leave until all your doubts were dealt with and all your tears were dried."

"I love Nell."

"Yeah, well, for once I guess I won't be pissed at her for sticking her nose in." He kissed her forehead again. "You're okay, you're sure?"

"I am. I really am."

"Good, then. Go call 911. Use the phone in the showroom."

It occurred to Chloe that it might not be such a great idea to leave Ted alone with Quinn. "Pleathe don't hit Ted," she whispered. "He'th not worth it."

"I'm not going to hit him. I'm only going to do what I've always wanted to do and that is to have a little talk with him."

"Quinn, I really don't think—"

"Angel."

"What?"

"Go on. Make that call."

What Quinn said to Ted, only Ted ever knew.

Whatever it was, when Chloe reentered the back studio room after calling the police station, Ted was sitting in the chair again. He had nicks and scratches all over his face, and his right eye was swiftly turning a deep magenta. His tie was askew, his fine suit wrinkled and his hair a mess. He told her quietly that he'd been way out of line and he was very sorry and he would not be bothering her anymore.

She believed him. Now that he knew she would fight him, he wouldn't get near her again. She really was tempted to leave it at that. Pressing charges could be messy. He'd probably string the process out forever. Who knew what tricks he might try?

But she kind of wondered if he'd ever hit Larissa. And if, for the third time, she just let it go, would he only find another woman to bully and hurt?

So when Riley Grimes showed up, she told him and his partner exactly what had happened. By then, she had a doozey of a bruise swelling at her jaw. The blood down the front of her made its own statement about what Ted had done to her. Her tongue thick and slow and very painful, she told them exactly what had happened and said that yes, she did intend to press charges. So Riley and the other officer took Ted away in handcuffs. They'd called an ambulance for her. Quinn had smashed the glass in the front door, so he got hold of his brother Carter to come over and secure the showroom entrance. Then he went with Chloe in the ambulance to the hospital southeast of town.

At Justice Creek General, they took pictures of her injuries and an X-ray of her jaw. Nothing was broken. Her tongue was a mess. They advised saltwater rinses, ice packs and aloe vera gel. The good news? The bleeding had stopped on its own. The doctor said that if she still had pain in a week, she should see her family practitioner.

Quinn hovered close, and Chloe loved that he did. She knew she was going to be fine now. Yes, her face ached, her tongue throbbed and she was talking with a lisp. But all of that was temporary. Down inside, in her heart and soul, she'd never felt better.

She'd never felt so free.

Quinn couldn't wait to get her home to Annabelle and Manny, though he did kind of worry that she might give him grief about it, might demand that he take her to her house.

But no. She just smiled with that beautiful, battered face of hers and said, "Yeth. Take me home to Annabelle and Manny. Thath where I want to be."

At home, Quinn told Manny what had happened. Manny settled Chloe on the sofa with a mountain of pillows at her back and a light blanket over her knees. He brought her an ice pack and a saltwater rinse for her poor, aching tongue.

When Annabelle came bouncing down the stairs, they told her that Chloe had been hurt and she needed them to take care of her. Annabelle demanded to be allowed to kiss the boo-boo on Chloe's jaw and make it all better. She insisted that Chloe have her one-eyed teddy bear. "Hug him real hard, Chloe. Then you will feel much better."

Quinn called Nell to let her know what had gone down. Nell turned right around and called everybody. Within half an hour, family members started arriving. By late afternoon, Chloe had had visits from all of Quinn's sisters and three of his brothers.

Nell even called Chloe's parents. Linda and Doug Winchester rushed right over. Chloe took it well, Quinn thought. She let her dad hug her and then her mom, too. Linda cried. She pulled Quinn aside and said she needed to tell him personally how very wrong she'd been. She hoped, she said, that someday, somehow, she would find a way to make things right with her daughter and with him.

He gave her a hug and told her there was nothing to make right. "We're family now, Linda. Everything's going to be just fine."

That caused Linda to cry even harder.

Then Doug clapped him on the back. "I know I don't have to say it. But I'm a father and that means I'll say it anyway. Take good care of my little girl. She hasn't had it easy."

"I will, sir," Quinn promised. "You can count on me."

Then Doug took Linda home.

Chloe made a list of what she needed from her house. Quinn went over there and gathered everything up.

And that night, for the first time, he had her in his bed where he'd always wanted her. He brought her aspirin for the pain and he wrapped himself around her and he held her all night long.

Chloe never went back to the house across the street. Slowly, she and Quinn and Manny moved everything she needed to the log house.

Within a week, her tongue was fully functional again. On a Thursday night late, she and Quinn sat out under the stars and said the things they'd never managed to say before.

She told him what was in her heart. "I love you, Quinn. So, so much."

And he said, "I love you, angel. I've been wanting to tell you forever. But somehow the time never seemed right."

"I think maybe you sensed that I wasn't ready yet. To say it. To hear it. But I'm ready *now*."

"Yeah," he said gruffly. "I see that. I feel that. I love you, Chloe Winchester." He stared deep in her eyes.

She gazed back at him and knew she'd gotten it exactly right the second time around. "I went all wrong there, for so many years."

"No."

"Yes. I went wrong, took the wrong path. But I'm back where I belong now. I think deep down I always knew you were the one for me, from way back when we were little, from when you used to put those Hershey's Kisses on Miss Oakleaf's desk."

He groaned. "You remember that? Nobody remembers that."

"Well, yeah. We all kind of do." She got up from her deck chair—but only so that she could sit on his lap. Wrapping her arms around his neck, she whispered in his ear, "It was so sweet and so romantic, you leaving chocolate for Miss Oakleaf. Everybody said so."

"You think so, huh?"

"I do, yes."

"I love you, Chloe." He nuzzled her hair. "I love you. Now that I'm finally saying it, I just can't say it enough."

"Good. Because I love you, too."

"Vegas?" he asked, his mouth so warm and soft against her cheek.

She turned her head—just enough so that their lips could meet. They shared a long, sweet kiss. And then she answered him, "Vegas. Definitely. Name the day."

Five weeks later, they moved back to the fully renovated house down the hill. Annabelle put on her fairy princess costume and danced around her new princess bedroom, scattering fairy dust as she went. That same day, Manny presented her with a tiny, long-haired, big-eared Chihuahua puppy, which she promptly named Mouse.

And a week after that, Quinn and Chloe were married in the wedding chapel at High Sierra Resort and Casino in Las Vegas on the Sunset Strip. Annabelle was the flower girl. Manny stood up as best man. Quinn's sisters and Tracy Winham and Rory Bravo-Calabretti were all bridesmaids, with Nell the maid of honor.

Doug Winchester proudly gave his only daughter away for the second time. "This is the one that counts," he whispered to Chloe as he walked her down the aisle to Quinn. Linda Winchester cried all through the ceremony—tears of joy, she said.

For Chloe, it was the happiest day of her life.

So far.

* * * * *

Don't miss CARTER BRAVO'S CHRISTMAS BRIDE,
the next installment in Christine Rimmer's
THE BRAVOS OF JUSTICE CREEK *series,*
coming in December 2015

MILLS & BOON®

Christmas Collection!

Unwind with a festive romance this Christmas with our breathtakingly passionate heroes. Order all books today and receive a free gift!

FREE GIFT!

Order yours at
**www.millsandboon.co.uk
/christmas2015**

1015_MB515

MILLS & BOON®

Buy A Regency Collection today and receive FOUR BOOKS FREE!

4 BOOKS FREE!

Transport yourself to the seductive world of Regency with this magnificent twelve-book collection.
Indulge in scandal and gossip with these 2-in-1 romances from top Historical authors

Order your complete collection today at
www.millsandboon.co.uk/regencycollection

915_ST19

MILLS & BOON®
The Italians Collection!

2 BOOKS FREE!

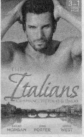

Irresistibly Hot Italians

You'll soon be dreaming of Italy with this scorching six-book collection. Each book is filled with three seductive stories full of sexy Italian men! Plus, if you order the collection today, you'll receive two books free!

This offer is just too good to miss!

Order your complete collection today at
www.millsandboon.co.uk/italians

0815_ST17

MILLS & BOON®

Why shop at millsandboon.co.uk?

Each year, thousands of romance readers find their perfect read at millsandboon.co.uk. That's because we're passionate about bringing you the very best romantic fiction. Here are some of the advantages of shopping at www.millsandboon.co.uk:

* **Get new books first**—you'll be able to buy your favourite books one month before they hit the shops

* **Get exclusive discounts**—you'll also be able to buy our specially created monthly collections, with up to 50% off the RRP

* **Find your favourite authors**—latest news, interviews and new releases for all your favourite authors and series on our website, plus ideas for what to try next

* **Join in**—once you've bought your favourite books, don't forget to register with us to rate, review and join in the discussions

Visit **www.millsandboon.co.uk**
for all this and more today!

MILLS & BOON®

Cherish™

EXPERIENCE THE ULTIMATE RUSH OF FALLING IN LOVE

A sneak peek at next month's titles...

In stores from 16th October 2015:

- **Housekeeper Under the Mistletoe** – Cara Colter *and* **Coming Home for Christmas** – Marie Ferrarella
- **His Lost-and-Found Bride** – Scarlet Wilson *and* **The Maverick's Holiday Masquerade** – Caro Carson

In stores from 6th November 2015:

- **His Texas Christmas Bride** – Nancy Robards Thompson *and* **Gift-Wrapped in Her Wedding Dress** – Kandy Shepherd
- **The Prince's Christmas Vow** – Jennifer Faye *and* **A Husband for the Holidays** – Ami Weaver

---

Available at WHSmith, Tesco, Asda, Eason, Amazon and Apple

Just can't wait?
Buy our books online a month before they hit the shops!
visit www.millsandboon.co.uk

These books are also available in eBook format!

B